OATHS
OF LIFE AND
DEATH

Cover Design by Lesia T.

Map by Thiago Liuth

ISBN 979-8-9895166-0-5 (paperback)

ISBN 979-8-9895166-1-2 (ebook)

www.lcyruswhelchel.com

Many thanks to the ladies of Hololive Myth: Ninomae Ina'nis, Takanashi Kiara, Gawr Gura, Calliope Mori, and Watson Amelia.

You taught me the importance of chasing your dreams. Without your inspiration, this book would have remained a drop in the vast sea of my imagination.

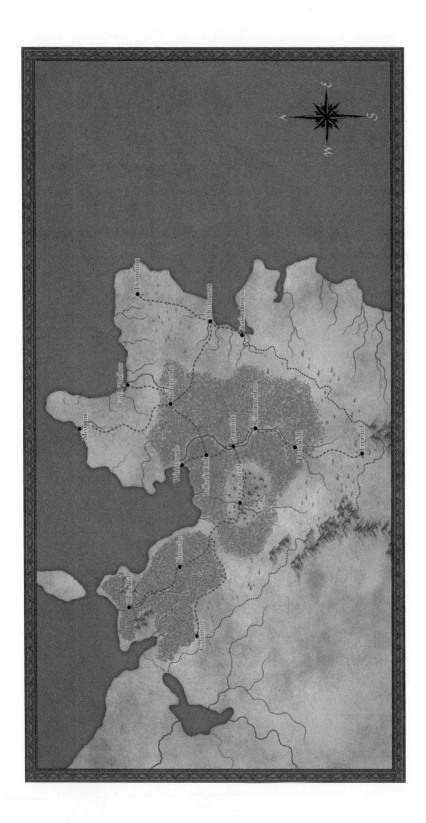

CHAPTER I

D espite standing in a pristine mansion, the scent of death filled the air.

Vizent Doulterre had seen many strange and disturbing things in his long life, the last 15 of which he spent serving the Livorian Royal Navy. This room, however, was beyond anything he ever encountered. His eyes shifted back and forth, even as his body stood rigid in a neatly pressed uniform. He found nothing overtly suspicious. The entire space looked like any noble's study should. Why, then, did an aura of decay permeate the room like a suffocating miasma?

Sparse decorations lay scattered throughout the room. Behind a heavy wooden desk, the back wall was lined with bookshelves containing hundreds of organized tomes. The carpet was thick, made of ox hair if his guess was right, with flowing symbols woven across the surface. The symbols reminded him of a language he once saw but couldn't remember the name of, from the times before Centric took over as Alezon's primary trading language. The desk itself was the sole messy object in the room, with piles of parchment and baubles leaving little space. Inkwells and feather quills sat near the smallest piles, possibly documents under review.

Vizent's lips curved upward as he gazed at the quills. The feathers were much too long for any normal bird. Without a doubt, they were Aerivolk feathers. The rank stench of blood, however, was everywhere. The only light came from an oil lamp on the desk, leaving shadows to cover the room's outer rim. The brass stars signifying his general's rank glimmered every so often in the flame's glow. He needed to get used to being called a general rather than admiral.

The crinkle of parchment and scratch of a quill drew Vizent's eyes to the man sitting behind the desk. While he kept a hood up concealing the upper half of his face, the old soldier could still make out two distinct features: a faint red mark circling half of the man's neck and a neatly trimmed beard. His deep black cloak's shoulder was embroidered with purple filigree. The crest of the local forger's guild was emblazoned on the breast in the same violet shade. The lamplight flickered and exposed a pair of tinted spectacles resting on the man's nose, which Vizent found intriguing.

Are his eyes sensitive to light? he wondered. It would certainly explain the lack of lighting.

The man's hands were calloused and scarred. Backbreaking labor was common enough in the forges and storage houses that littered the Corlati Federation, and Vizent knew of the man's position as master of the largest iron forge and weapons company in the realm. In Vizent's opinion, it made the scars more impressive. It suggested he rose to his current position through merit rather than connections. Vizent's musings stalled when the man set his quill down, steepling his fingers. Though unable to see his face, Vizent detected a strange aura around him.

"I must admit, General Doulterre, I'm curious about your purpose here. I don't often entertain visitors from Livoria. Considering the present difficulties, I feel it's in my best interest to know your goals," the man said slowly, his voice smoother than silk yet carrying a harsh tone mixed with amusement.

Vizent blinked. If he didn't already know the man's identity, his voice alone would have made the general believe he was speaking to a senator or nobleman rather than a craftsman. "Master Razarr, I shouldn't be surprised you know of the troubles facing my country. Livoria's fracturing is the biggest crisis our continent has seen in over seventy years. The Livorian Liberation Army is in dire need of equipment for the upcoming war. We received glowing recommendations of your reputation as a weapons dealer and-" Vizent's impassioned speech was interrupted when Razarr slammed a fist on the desk, jabbing a gnarled finger towards the officer.

"Do *not* take me for a fool, General," he snapped. "I know your army is ill-equipped and lacking in discipline, despite your impressive numbers. It's unfortunate since your primary sources of manpower are volunteers, conscripts, and those brave enough to desert the Royalist Navy. Your equipment consists of anything looted from storehouses in towns under your control. This, of course, assumes my scouts are correct, which they are.

"For it to be worth expending the effort to supply you, I want to know what you plan to do against the Royalists. Going into battle without a plan is certain to bring defeat, and I have no desire to aid a losing side. My businesses would be crippled otherwise," Razarr drawled, rapping a pointed nail against the wood.

Vizent gathered his satchel from the floor. "Sir, I was authorized to discuss our initial objectives for your review. The man who referred us mentioned your experience with military dossiers. However, if you require clarification, don't hesitate to ask. Here is a copy for your perusal." He pulled a small ream of parchment and held it forward. Razarr took the stack and silently read.

Several minutes passed by with no sound from either man. Vizent gave a silent prayer this would work. Without equipment, any hope they had of winning the war would be lost.

Finally, Razarr laid the parchment down, matching the general's eyes. Vizent caught a brief glimpse of the man's sharp gaze beneath the spectacles. "This is rather ambitious. At first glance, it looks like a fool's errand. I'm most curious about your path of attack. I agree an early offensive will offer the best chance for victory, but why take such a long route to the capital's eastern side? Would it not be easier to march through the forest and strike Whistlevale from the west or south?"

Vizent chortled, leaning back to stare at the hanging tapestries. "Sir, I'm not sure what you know of Livoria's inner conflicts, but no strategist with an army of novices would be stupid enough to attack the capital by way of the Videring Forest. Especially novices that follow our more 'traditional' beliefs. Do you know why?"

"I have a theory. However, I'd like you to humor me and assume I'm an ignorant buffoon."

Vizent grimaced. His former colleagues liked to think him reckless, but not even he was crazy enough to think of calling Razarr an ignorant buffoon to his face. He held up two fingers. "First, the main road through the Videring passes close to Duskmarsh. As you mentioned, my men are nowhere near disciplined enough. They wouldn't be able to restrain themselves from attacking it. You know our side's stance on those beasts and the target would be too tempting." Vizent's lips thinned. His hand tightened into a fist thinking about Duskmarsh. In his opinion, the entire swamp-based city and its inhabitants needed to be wiped off the map.

Razarr nodded. "And the other reason...?"

The general's fist clenched. "I refuse to put my men too close to Havenfall before they are ready. Even taking the merchant roads north of Duskmarsh would keep us within a few days trek of that village, and the risk is too great." Vizent could see a sliver of a smirk beneath Razarr's hood and held back a shudder. This man knew more than expected, but Vizent was suspicious of *how* he obtained his information.

Razarr tapped a finger on the desk in a rhythmic pattern. "You provide sound, logical reasons to avoid the Videring. Despite its small size, Havenfall would be a difficult opponent, and there is no doubt they would strike without orders if they suspected the Grand Duchess was in danger. But you already know this. Do you have plans in case they move against you early?"

Vizent let out a sigh of relief. Razarr asking for details was a good sign. He already had his own ideas to handle Havenfall, though he would keep those in reserve. Dealing with the Hunter village was his personal mission. "We have several plans in place, organized within the dossier. Our goal is that, with a surprise strike from the east, Whistlevale will fall before Havenfall ever becomes a nuisance. If you are willing to equip our army and help put down the Royalists, I'm certain my superiors within the

Conclave would be willing to provide opportunities to expand your forge operations within Livoria."

Vizent felt his offer gave adequate incentive for Razarr to reach a deal. No merchant worth their salt would pass up an easy chance to improve their profits, with Livoria's lower taxes and renowned craftsmen making an enticing motivator. The deal would let Razarr rake in higher profits after establishing operations.

Razarr's fingers continued tapping, the steady sound filling the silence. A thin smile stretched across Razarr's face. He leaned back with a heavy sigh.

"I have one final question: Do you have officers capable of molding your soldiers into a respectable army?" A deep chuckle escaped his lips as he gave Vizent a sly smile. "After all, having hordes of men does no good if they don't know which end of the sword to hold."

Vizent gave his first true grin since the meeting started. "A valid point, sir. Several of our officers served as training instructors with the Navy and were among the best. The men will be ready to fight."

"If this is true, then I believe we have a deal, General. I shall supply your forces with armor and weapons, at a price agreeable to both of us. In return, your government will assist in setting up forges and shops within Livoria once peace has settled. As a symbol of our partnership, I may also be able to procure...extra help."

Vizent perked up. He was curious, yet also hesitant to accept anything without knowing details. His father's lessons on contracts sifted through his mind. He'd heard rumors Razarr was not a man you wished to be indebted to. Being caught unawares now would be a disaster.

"What kind of assistance do you mean, sir? My contacts didn't say you bartered in materials outside of weapons and armor," he asked. Razarr flashed another knowing smirk.

"I don't. However, what I *do* have is the ear of certain individuals within the Federation. They share your cause's beliefs and might be persuaded to supply men to fight alongside you and assist in training. Acting under the guise of sellsword companies, of course."

Vizent blinked. This was beyond anything he could have imagined. "Sir, that would be an excellent boon. Knowing the Federation supports our cause and is willing to fight alongside us. That would certainly inspire our men for the fight ahead." Razarr's smirk grew, something the soldier noticed at once. "I do have one question," he continued.

"Yes?"

"What do you hope for, in exchange for this assistance? I assume you aren't making this offer out of the goodness of your heart." The question sent Razarr into braying laughter, setting Vizent on edge. To see so much expressiveness on the man's face was disconcerting.

"Very shrewd, General. Indeed, I'm not doing this for free. However, I expect the price I ask is one you'll be glad to pay."

Vizent blinked in confusion. "And what is your price?"

Razarr's grin exposed a flash of pointed ivory teeth. "Simple. I want you to deliver any Norzen you capture to me. I'm conducting a unique project requiring the use of those damned cats. The young adults will be most useful for my experiments. Any spare Aerivolk you get your claws on would also be appreciated. As you can see, I have an extensive collection that requires constant replenishing," he explained, gesturing to the container of quills.

This time it was Vizent who erupted into a deep belly laugh. A wide grin split his face in two. Of the five faumen tribes, his rage against the Norzen burned brightest. In the deepest corners of his mind, he knew he was making a dangerous gamble, but the offer was too good to pass up. "Master Razarr, if that's your price for this boon, then you and I shall get along wonderfully. Any excuse to rid Livoria of those disgusting creatures is welcome. I agree to your terms on behalf of the Conclave."

Razarr nodded and waved a hand, inviting the soldier to sit. The two men spent a considerable time hammering out the details of their new partnership for Vizent to take back to his superiors.

Razarr's smirk never left as he watched Doulterre leave after hours of negotiations. It was amazing what people would do for their own agendas. He saw a lot of his younger self in the general, though the man's prejudices were obvious. He was not blind to the way Doulterre looked at his Aerivolk quills before the talks began. Or his reactions to Duskmarsh. Razarr frowned as he thought about the Norzen city. Still, he felt it would be beneficial to put an effort into their cause. It coincided so well with his own plans.

The thud of approaching footsteps outside gave him pause. The servants knew better than to disturb him this late. The door opened enough for a young woman to poke her head in. Her eyes were downcast, and her expression indifferent.

"Master, I apologize for disturbing you. Mr. Dilmear demanded I come, however. Did you request to be informed when the capital's envoys arrived?" asked the woman, her body stiff. Razarr frowned, turning to the window. He wasn't expecting the envoys for another few days.

He waved a dismissive hand and instructed her to arrange food and beds for them, as he wouldn't have time to begin their discussion until morning.

"Oh, and Mirabell?"

The girl flinched. "Yes, sir?"

"Inform Dilmear if he ever sends someone to disturb me this late again, I will take it out of *his* hide, rather than his messenger's."

Mirabell's shoulders slumped forward. "It shall be done, Master. Have a pleasant night."

"You as well. I have no need for your assistance tonight, so finish your tasks and get to bed. We have much to accomplish going forward." Razarr ignored Mirabell's audible sigh as she left to carry out her orders.

Razarr let out a groan and set his glasses on the desk, massaging the bridge of his nose. Dilmear was a competent steward, yet cowardice often drove him to push others in front of Razarr's ire. The forge master couldn't afford to give him an idea he was protected from such foolish mistakes.

At least Mirabell had uses beyond her maid duties. In Razarr's mind, that made her less expendable than Dilmear.

Suddenly, the shadows in the corner shifted.

Razarr gave an irritated sigh and felt his eyes twitch towards the hunched form lurking in the darkness. "I was wondering where you scuttled off to. I assume your assignment is done?"

Silence was all he received. The form tilted its head in a deft nod. As Razarr's eyes returned to the documents he and the general signed, a thought popped into his head. It was a risk, for certain, but he didn't reach his current position without taking a few of those. He rose to his feet and strode to a map of Alezon splayed on the wall.

"I have a job for you. According to that fool Doulterre, the Liberation Army will begin their attack here," he said. Using a riding whip, he tapped a specific point. "I want you to head there first and stir up some chaos before their arrival. I don't care how many you kill in the process, but ensure the results are messy, if you please."

A low-pitched cackling trill echoed through the study, almost like laughter, until the form slinked across the room. Razarr focused his gaze at the map, refusing to watch the figure push open the window and leap over the balcony. With only a gust of wind, they were gone.

Razarr felt a sense of relief wash over him. He had waited many years for this. With an inroad back into Livoria, he would make sure the job was done right. He thought back to his conversation with Doulterre, his lips curving upwards.

"Disgusting creatures, indeed. Well, it's been, what, 22 years since my last foray into Livoria. Berelmir willing, this visit will be more fruitful than the last." He already failed once before. He would not do so again.

This time, he would fulfill his family's oath or die trying. Both those insufferable brats would be dead, and he would be one step closer to bringing all of Alezon under the guidance of the True Savior.

Chapter II

Kai nursed his mead with a contemplative scowl as his companions chattered. He was quite certain he didn't like Mistport.

It wasn't the smell that irritated him. The aroma of the nearby fish market seemed ingrained into the air itself and was more than pleasant. Mixed with the market's harvest stands and bakeries littering the nearby streets, full of fresh fruits and sweet rolls, it created a delectable fragrance that could make a stone drool. Both his tails curled in excitement at the scent.

There was nothing wrong with the locals, either. Most of them, anyway. Despite being several moons into this damned war, the people of this quiet northern port remained cheerful and amicable. Friendlier than he was used to, in any case. In fact, this was the first time in a while for him to enter a town and not be harassed on arrival. Scratching an itch in the thick mane of ebony fur on his upper chest, he glanced around and noticed some heated glares pointed at him from patrons around *The Sunken Anchor*, the meadhouse they stopped at for a quick meal.

No, Kai's troubles revolved around the weather. The widespread, thin fog giving Mistport its name made the air wetter than normal and visibility a pain. The dampness clung to his fur, weighing it down. The morning dew also left droplets of water in his ears, perched atop his head like a cat's. He twitched them a few times to shake the water off. He refused to shake his head like a common house cat; he had at least *some* dignity.

His hesitance about this job didn't help either. The squad was given little information regarding their task, which rattled Kai's nerves. His gaze shifted towards the trees swaying in the breeze outside. If only he could have such a carefree existence. Trees didn't have to worry about such things, did they?

His attention was drawn back to the table when a plate dropped in front of him. The smell of steaming food brought a tilted smile to his lips. A massive filet of peppered trout covered half the plate, accompanied by a mixture of rice, spiced vegetables, and a thick butter-covered sweet roll. Three more thuds echoed as his companions received their meals. Reaching into his pouch, Kai flipped a silver coin to the tavern maid. The older woman smiled and pocketed it, flashing Kai a discreet wink as she bustled back to the kitchen.

"Damn it, Kai, what are you doing? I wanted to tip her!" the man to Kai's left muttered, his body unsteady and bloodshot eyes burning with envy.

Kai chuckled, taking a bite from the roll. "There's no rule saying you still can't, Marko. Besides, I doubt flirting with her would do you any good," he shot back with a content look on his face. He would have to ask the cook for this roll recipe. They tasted almost as good as his Da's back home.

"You tipped her a silver, too! You're making the rest of us look bad, Travaldi. Seems pricey to toss twenty marks on a tip for four meals. That coin would pay for half of everything we ordered, including ale and mead," Marko answered with a slight hiccup. "And how do you know it wouldn't help to flirt with her?" The flush on his cheeks and four steins surrounding him stood as a testament to his inebriated state.

The stocky, bald man with a round face across from Kai rolled his eyes and smacked Marko behind the head, provoking a yelp. In a snarky tone, he asked Marko how he was already wasted and trying to flirt with a woman who was not only older than him but wearing a wedding ribbon to boot.

Marko groaned, slamming his forehead on the table with a resounding thud. "Aww spit, are you serious, Calvino? Why are the cute ones always taken?"

"Marko, we all know you'll bounce back by the time you sleep this binge off. You'll flirt with anything that has breasts. I'm honestly surprised you haven't tried seducing one of old Rafi's cows back home," the fourth man answered in an imperious tone. His cobalt eyes glimmered with mischief while shooting a smug grin at Kai, who struggled to contain his laughter. Marko's hopeless ardor was a topic of hilarity among the younger Hunters back home. His two older sisters were infamous for their taunts when they caught him wooing visiting ladies.

Calvino had no such control and snorted, sprinkling mead onto the table. "By the winds, Faust, why did you put that picture in my head? Now I'm losing my appetite," he groaned.

"Cal, the day you lose your appetite will be when you die, and I half expect your corpse to *still* be shoveling food into its mouth while your wife gives the eulogy," replied Kai, sending the others into gales of laughter.

"Well with you around, Sir Gravebane, I expect that day to be a long time coming," Cal shot back with a wide smile. Kai bit back a groan and shifted his gaze around the meadhouse, wondering if anyone heard the older Hunter. His hand instinctively reached for the left breast pocket of his russet brown vest and pushed the contents deeper. He hated having *that* name bandied about. One never knew who might recognize it.

The tavern maid returned with pitchers of mead and ale. "You boys are a lively bunch. Tell me, what's a squad of Hunters doing out here in the sticks? You're a bit far from Havenfall," she said, refilling the steins and gathering up the pile forming around Marko. The confusion was understandable. Havenfall was clear on the other side of the duchy.

"I assume you've heard about the recent deaths in town and the surrounding area?" Cal asked her. She nodded with her eyes downcast. "Our team was working a job nearby, so we were ordered to investigate. Whatever is responsible, our duty is to take it down."

The woman's eyes flashed with excitement, clapping her hands together and cheering. "Is that what you boys are here for? Praise Luopari! The constables are too terrified to find out who or what it is. If you four need anything, just let Miss Ione know. I'll do what I can to help." Cal smiled and raised his stein to the woman, along with several men at the surrounding tables, all of them murmuring 'Hail Luopari.' Kai wasn't surprised to hear so many repeating the mantra. Luopari, as the patron of faith and life, was a popular Wind Saint often invoked during life-or-death crises.

Marko perked up. "Miss, not Missus?" he asked. Ione shook her head, heaving a sigh and fiddling with the blue ribbon around her wrist.

"Not anymore, I'm afraid. My husband disappeared eight years ago. They never found his body. I guess you can say I'm still in mourning and I doubt I'll ever remarry," she said. "I will admit I'm curious about one thing."

All four glanced at the woman. The other three turned to Kai when they noticed her eyes lingering on him.

"It ain't often you see a Norzen in these parts, and I've never heard of one in the Hunters. Aren't you worried about...the war?" she asked.

Kai flinched when several patrons glared at him. Norzen were not well regarded among the faumen tribes. Even in Livoria, where the Grand Duchess was vocal about tribal equality, Norzen had trouble acquiring respectable jobs outside certain cities and often turned to banditry or smuggling to feed their families. It was obvious the feline faumen were barely tolerated, and the growing war didn't help. But then, none of the five tribes were having an easy time.

It was still better than living somewhere like Corlati, where human supremacy was preached as gospel and most faumen were considered property to be bought, traded, and abused as their owners saw fit. At least in Livoria, a Norzen could live outside of chains and cages.

"To be fair, ma'am, Kai doesn't know many other Norzen," Marko said, his face gaining a bit of color back. "He was raised by humans in Havenfall, and I've known him since we were sprouts. He can take care of himself."

Ione shrugged and gripped Kai's shoulder, giving him a warm smile. "Well, I won't be making a fuss. You boys are here to help, and that makes you good in my books. Besides, anyone willing to tip an old gal a whole silver can't be all bad." The three men grinned when Kai's face burned brighter than the oil lamps hanging from the ceiling. Marko lowered his head and made a show of weeping into his hands, to the others' amusement.

"I told you you're making the rest of us look bad, Kai!"

The nearby tables joined in laughing at Marko's expense. Ione blushed, swatting the drunken Hunter with a rag. "Hush, you! He may be Norzen, but it seems Mr. Kai could teach you some charm," she said, her lips tilted into a bemused smirk.

Kai chuckled and reached for his vest. Numerous stone vials with painted markings dangled from hooks stitched under the garment's gray fur trim. He plucked one filled with red flakes from its hook, a red dot on its side. The other three choked and pushed their chairs back. They watched in horror as Kai opened the vial and sprinkled the contents onto his meal.

"By the winds, Travaldi, put that away before you kill us!" Faust growled out. Ione coughed and held a rag over her face.

"What is that?" she gasped. "Smells like someone made a spice out of fire."

Kai shrugged. "You aren't far off. Dried cappara pepper is one of the most potent spices in Alezon. Importing it from the Rodekan Empire can be expensive, so it's rare here. I've heard some use it as beast repellant because it causes contact burns on skin." Ione looked at him agog.

"And you're going to *eat* it?"

He admitted a pinch of cappara gives the food the nice kick he likes.

Marko scoffed. "Kai, only you would think that stuff gives a 'nice kick.' I've seen wirochs kick softer than that." Kai cast a wry smile at the other man and speared the trout with his fork, taking a small bite with a look of bliss. The group was stunned when he didn't reach for his stein.

Ione turned and winced. Kai peered behind her to see the cook sending a harsh glare from the kitchen. She told the men she needed to get back to work.

While Ione walked away, the group ate in silence. Once finished with their meals, they huddled over the table. Calvino pulled a scroll from his pack and spread it out, revealing a map of Mistport and its surrounding area.

"What do we know about the situation?" he asked.

Marko leaned over the table with a hiccup, gesturing to several black dots scattered around the map that denoted the location and number of victims of each attack.

Kai tallied the dots in his mind. "That makes 26 people killed in the last moon. The last attack was two days ago. Is there anything odd in the timing? The war just started, after all."

Faust tapped one of the fields. "No. The reports from Whistlevale said the attacks started in the outer farms here some days after the Libbies began skirmishing with the Navy. It makes me wonder if they sent someone to cause trouble. The question is, why send them here? Mistport is a bit isolated if they want to attack the capital. They've been braying about it enough."

Marko shook his head. "Not if the goal is to draw attention away from the capital," he replied, emitting a small hiccup that prompted snickers from the other men. "And this assumes the Libbies are even responsible. Do the victims have anything in common?"

"Other than the fact that all of them are dead? No. The strange thing is some bodies appear to be torn open while others were crushed. From the constable reports, most of the human victims were among the crushed while all of the faumen victims were torn apart. Whatever caused this doesn't care who it kills, though. Old or young. Rich or poor. Man, woman, or child. Human or faumen. All have been killed at some point, with nothing tying them together," Kai answered, both tails twitching.

Cal dug his fingers into his temple. "The way most of the victims were killed suggests some kind of beast. Not even a Norzen thieving band would be this vicious. No offense," he explained, shooting Kai an apologetic glance.

The taller Hunter waved it off. "None taken. I'd be willing to wager it's a beast. If it's not, we're dealing with a sick individual. There were rumors of similar attacks near the Federation border a few moons back, but the bodies were cleaner. Less blood."

The four shared a grim look. None wanted to think of the possibility of a person being responsible, no matter how remote. Regardless, without witness reports, they were running blind.

Kai stretched back, gazing at the oil lamps. A sea breeze came in through the windows and caused them to sway like a pendulum. The movement soothed his mind. It reminded him of laying on the riverbank back home, watching the trees move in the same manner.

With a sigh, he pushed himself upright again. Now wasn't the time to reminisce. If they didn't figure this out, more would die. An agitated humming sounded from Kai's chest, drawing the others' attention.

"You okay, boss?" Faust asked.

Kai shot the man a grimace and leaned over the map, regarding it with an edge in his eyes. Finally, he pointed to a single dot near the southern gate, where the river led deeper into the grasslands. "This was the most recent attack, yes?"

The others nodded.

"That's where we'll start searching. Someone had to see or hear something." Any further comments were halted by the door of the meadhouse swinging open with a bang.

A young sienna-skinned woman in scholar's robes strode in with aplomb, hazel eyes skimming over the crowd beneath a pair of boxy spectacles. A cobalt overcoat billowed with each confident step. Her curled black hair fell over her left shoulder like a shawl, tied into a side ponytail with a silver silk ribbon. With elegant features and a rigid posture, she presented the striking appearance of a city noble.

The engraved emblem clasped over her breastbone piqued Kai's interest. What was someone from the Citadel doing way out here? The symbol looked familiar, though he was unsure of its significance. He never bothered memorizing the Citadel's divisional emblems.

The woman's eyes settled on Kai. He noted a hint of panic before she slipped into a harsh glower that made the hunter raise an eyebrow. Whoever she was, she held no love for his tribe. None of the other faumen in the meadhouse received the same withering look.

Ione came out to investigate and began wiping down an empty table near the Hunters once she noticed the woman. "Good to see you again, Miss Dineri! The usual?" she asked.

The woman nodded. "Thank you, Ione. If you do not mind, I shall sit over there," she replied with a curt tilt of her head, gesturing to an empty table near the opposite corner.

The distinct lilt of her voice carried an elegance Kai recognized from the noble houses of east Livoria. He dealt with enough nobles to know the regional accents. Kai noticed the table she chose was the one farthest away from the Hunters without leaving the meadhouse.

"Sure, I suppose. Is something wrong with this one?"

The woman turned her eyes away with a scoff. "Not with the table itself. I just prefer to not be seated near the riff raff."

Ione looked at the nearby tables and locked eyes with Kai, who shook his head. The tavern maid's face burned scarlet. Without a word, she led the woman to the table and shouted orders to another girl. Kai gave Ione a soft smile when she turned back with a sorrowful look.

Marko took a deep draw of mead. "Looks like you got yourself an admirer, Kai." The Norzen leveled a blank stare at the giggling Marko, then glanced at the other two.

"Is he really that drunk or did you two slip him something from my satchel's 'special pocket' when I wasn't looking?"

The reaction was immediate as Marko spat his mead out mid-gulp, drenching Cal and Faust. Kai leaned back to avoid the spray. The two older Hunters shrieked and lurched away too fast, toppling over with a crash.

Kai covered his mouth and bit his tongue hard enough to draw blood. The other patrons howled with laughter while Ione came rushing to the table. She quickly helped the two back to their feet.

"What in blazes happened? Are you boys alright?" she asked, fretting over the fallen Hunters. Faust used the chair to haul himself up and waggled his pinky at Kai.

"Dirty trick, Travaldi. Did your sister put you up to that?"

Kai snickered and nodded, all the while clutching his stomach. "Sorry guys, you know Serafina would tie my tails in a knot if I didn't get you at least once."

Faust took the offered rag from Ione, wiping the mead from his face. "I should have known. Thank you, Miss Ione. We apologize for the commotion."

Ione shook her head and picked up the scattered and upturned plates. "Not to worry. You gave me a shock, is all. And I'm sorry about Miss Dineri. I never would have expected her to react like that," she said. Her downcast eyes and silent tears prompted Kai to offer her a handkerchief.

"Don't stress over it. I've been called much worse. Finyt, I'm pretty sure the four of us are called worse by the other Hunters."

"Oh come on, Kai, Miss Ione's a devotee of Luopari," Marko berated while flailing his arms around. "Are you really gonna invoke the name of paradise itself in vain in her presence?"

Kai rolled his eyes, knowing that Marko was grasping at flies with that comment to put himself in Ione's good graces. Finyt was supposed to be a land of paradise where the faithful went after passing on. Invoking its name was certainly preferable to the alternative.

Ignoring the drunken Hunter's rambling, he pointed a discreet finger at the newcomer. "Who is she anyway?" he asked.

Ione peered at the woman before leaning next to the Norzen's ear. "Her name is Lucretia Dineri," she said. "She's an Archivist from Runegard who arrived almost a moon ago, just before the attacks started. Rumor says the local magistrates needed help repairing some historical tomes after a flood and Lucretia was chosen to oversee the work."

Kai nodded and gave Lucretia an inquisitive glance. An Archivist? That would explain why the emblem looked so familiar. As the Citadel's field scholars, they were the most visible and vocal staff of Livoria's most prestigious learning institution.

"Again, sorry for the ruckus. I'm certain your boss wants us to make tracks after that show, so we'll leave. Many thanks for your hospitality, Miss Ione," Cal said. Following the bald man's lead, the four reached for their pockets and a pile of copper coins found its way into the woman's hands. Tears streamed down her face as she gave each Hunter a warm hug.

"Aww, you boys are going to make me cry. You be careful."

"Don't worry ma'am. We'll be fine. I'll even buy the house a round when we get back with our quarry on a pole," Marko gloated, puffing his chest out.

Marko's words made Kai's fur crawl. Even as drunk as he was, he should know better. Boasting before a hunt was terrible luck. Calvino and Faust both sent him a sour look. Kai found himself hoping this whole mess didn't pitch a ditch, as his Da said.

When the four Hunters left *The Sunken Anchor* for the edge of Mistport, they weren't sure what to expect. They heard from locals the southern section of town, on the other side of the market square, was in bad shape. What they found near the city wall was a series of alleys and walkways that would barely qualify as a habitable slum in larger cities. The houses appeared built in a hurry from planks of rotted wood and held together by twine, bricks, and a hardened mash of algae and mud. It was a startling contrast from the square stone structures of the main plaza and port street.

A musty odor of mold, fish, dust, and animal leavings fouled the air. Kai didn't have a Soltauri's nose, but his sense of smell was still stronger than a human's. The stench forced him to tie a scarf over his mouth and nose to avoid losing his lunch.

The three humans didn't enjoy the dank air any better. All wore scarves over their faces as well. The fog was thicker, making their advance a slog. A feeble Aerivolk man with white feathers and a tattered cloak gave a weak greeting as they passed. Kai tilted his head towards a group of children chasing each other through the alleys, their feet splashing in murky water from numerous puddles. Water that, to their disgust, at least one older man was scooping into his mouth by the handful.

"Do we truly want to start our search here? This smell might kill us before whatever we're hunting does," Marko hacked out. The putrid smell seemed to have sobered the man up in a hurry, though he still looked ready to vomit all over the place.

Kai agreed the smell was horrendous, but he reminded the other Hunter of the recent attack. Finding a lead would be easier if they investigated before the trail got cold.

The group tightened their scarves and passed the crowd of children. Many scrutinized them with baleful looks. As the Hunters passed, the children shuffled aside and pointed at Kai while huddled together.

One was heard whispering, "My dad always says to stay away from Norzen. He tells us they do all sorts of awful things. I think he called them 'abobimations,' or something like that. Dad likes to use big words." Kai resisted an urge to snicker. The things he heard about his tribe got stranger in every town he visited. Instead of responding, Kai ignored the comments, held his head high, and kept walking.

After a short walk, the group reached a small building with a cracked sign advertising a tanning shop. Cal and Faust went inside to interview the shopkeeper while Kai and Marko slipped into the side alley where the attack occurred. Marko scowled at the bloody stains covering the walls and cobblestones. Obviously, the constables decided the area wasn't worth cleaning more than needed. Only the remains of the body were removed; the blood remained.

"This is creepy. What kind of beast could do this, and why?" Marko asked, kneeling to inspect the street for tracks or marks.

Kai scratched his mane. "I don't know of anything native to Livoria that *would* do this. We both know a daggertooth lion could pull it off, but they eat their kill. Few of the bodies were consumed. It's like the one responsible is doing it for fun," he said.

Their conversation was cut short as Cal and Faust led the tanner into the alley. The old man's work apron was dirty and glistening with oil. His thinning hair lay hidden beneath a dusty cap and thick arm-length gloves covered his hands. Cal sidled next to Kai and shook his head at the blood stains. "See anything out of place?" he asked.

"A few liters of blood soaked into the street," Kai quipped. Cal glared at him.

"Nothing I can see. To be fair, it's hard to see anything in this soup," Marko answered while rising and patting the dust from his trousers.

The tanner shivered and made a gesture with his hand, drawing a circle in the air before touching first his forehead, then the center of his chest. A common prayer of protection in the Windbringer church. "You youngsters better leave well enough alone. If not, Grimghast will do you in just like it did old Rufus," he said. The Hunters turned to face the man in unison.

"Who?" Marko asked, a look of befuddlement on his face.

Cal snorted and met the tanner's stare. "Grimghast is an old folk tale meant to spook children. As you can see, what did this is something real. Did you see anything, old man?"

The man shook his head, gazing at the stains with a forlorn look, his eyes clouded. "I didn't have to. I heard well enough. We all did. It was horrible. Rufus, I ain't ever heard anyone scream like that. Once we heard his body ripped apart, the screaming stopped. We didn't poke our heads out 'til we heard Grimghast slipping away. All we saw was a big shadow climbing the wall and heading for the grasslands. Damned thing left Rufus in pieces all over the alley I'd say it's using the longgrass or groves for cover."

The four Hunters looked at each other in confusion. Kai gazed up the town wall. "What is Grimghast? I don't recall hearing of it before."

Faust slapped Kai on the back. "It's just what Cal said: An old fairy tale about a monster wandering the land, snatching up naughty children. My parents told me and my brother the story when we were sprouts. They say it looks like a giant wolf or bear that wears the bones of its victims, depending on where you hear the story from." Kai and Marko wrinkled their noses.

"Sounds pleasant," Kai said with a heavy drawl. "I say we head to the grasslands and look around. If we're lucky, we'll find some tracks, hunt this thing down, and finish up. I'd like to get home before winter sets in."

"Don't forget, Kai, we're stopping at *The Sunken Anchor* before we leave. I need to buy the house a round," Marko shot back, earning a groan from the others.

Faust berated the other Hunter for wanting another chance to flirt with Ione, sparking a heated argument. Cal ignored them and turned back to the tanner. He asked if the man had seen anything else. Even the smallest detail could be vital. It was a lesson Kai knew from experience.

The man sat with a contemplative look and took his cap off, running a gloved hand through his hair. "Well, I don't know if it's important, but me and some of the fellas saw a strange Soltauri in the slums these past few days."

This drew Kai's attention. "A Soltauri? What was strange about him?" The tall, goat-like faumen were common in the north. For a local to mark one as strange was worth another look.

The man's eye twitched. "Nobody's ever seen him around. We know most of the regulars that come into town off the farms between here and Faith Hollow. He wasn't wearing farming clothes, either. His clothes were strange. Looked like one of the Feddy priests you see in the capital. His horns stood out too, thick and curved back like a mountain goat's."

Kai and Cal shared a look. "Well, thank you for your time. We'll be on our way, and we're sorry for what happened. With any luck, we'll bring this thing down and everyone can sleep in peace," Cal said. The Hunter adjusted his pack while swatting Faust and Marko on the head, ordering them to prepare.

"You fellas need more than luck if you wanna kill Grimghast. I feel bad for what happened to Rufus, but you oughta take this old man's advice: You'd be safer heading home, lest you end up just as dead."

The four Hunters thanked the old shopkeeper once more. They marched at a brisk pace to the southern gate down the road. Upon arrival, the town guards wished them luck.

Kai gave a final look at the town before the gates swung shut. Something about this job sent shivers down his tails. Whenever that happened, he learned to keep his head on a swivel to keep it on his shoulders. Patting himself, he did a swift inventory of his vials and satchel. He cursed at the number of empty bottles he found. A restock was needed when they returned.

Assuming they made it back in one piece, that is.

CHAPTER III

Kai remembered a silence this deep only once in his life, and his left arm throbbed as memories of that day floated through his mind. He scanned the area with a narrowed gaze, searching for the slightest movement. Livoria's northern grasslands were an expansive maze. Pathways needed to be hacked into the longgrass to make travel easier. These makeshift roads were maintained by the surrounding hamlets. There were still plenty of hiding spots, though, making this part of the duchy a bandit haven.

It was also a sprawling home to many animals. From tiny crickets and beetles infesting the grass, to vibrant birds perched in the sparse groves, to giant nobletusk bison grazing on the riverbanks. The variety of sounds these animals produced would normally fill the air with a soothing melody. It was a common game for Hunters to compose songs from the sounds. But today was different.

There wasn't a single sound to be heard.

The quartet trudged along with weapons drawn, eyes darting everywhere. Calvino and Marko carried simple longswords with bucklers strapped to their off hands. Faust stood at the vanguard, opting for a war axe with a wide blade and leather-wrapped handle. For defense, he preferred a leather undershirt covered by an iron breastplate. Kai's primary weapon, a flanged mace, remained tucked into his belt. Instead, he covered the squad's rear with a crossbow, a bolt nestled snugly in place.

"I don't like this," Kai muttered, eyes roaming for the slightest twitch of movement. Instead, there was nothing. Not a bird chirped. The rodents and insects were nowhere to be seen. Even the bison vanished without a trace. His throat went dry as memories barraged his mind. The echoing thuds from that day felt real enough to bring a dull, painful ache to his temple.

Cal looked back and gave the younger hunter a concerned glance. "What's up, kid? I don't think I've seen you this spooked before."

Kai twisted his body to check behind them. His ears were in constant motion, swiveling back and forth. His tails stayed low to the ground, lashing in random directions. His grip on the crossbow tightened enough that Cal worried he might crack the stock.

"There's something out here that shouldn't be, I can feel it in my tails," he replied. Faust chuckled, giving his axe a few swings. The three humans stood tall and relaxed, a stark comparison to Kai's tense crouch.

"Kid, paranoia doesn't suit you," Cal said. "I agree something probably scared the animals off, but you're taking it too far. Now relax and let's split up to cover more ground and find this beastie."

The edge of Kai's mouth twitched, and he sent Cal a baffled expression. "Split up? I know you're the squad leader, Cal, but listen. That's a bad idea."

"Kai, you're scaring me. What do you think is going on?" Marko asked. He turned to Kai and felt his own weapon hand twitch at the Norzen's nervousness. He snapped for Kai to point his crossbow away before he shot someone.

Faust's breath hitched as he stopped, holding his fist up to signal a halt. He pointed to a spot ahead and motioned to something in the grass.

The hunters crept forward, Faust kneeling to examine a line of large footprints. Each was half a yard in circumference, with deep impressions at the palm and toes.

"What in the name of Tapimor?" Faust murmured, invoking the Saint of the forests. "These look kinda like bear tracks, but there aren't any breeds this large in Livoria. What do you think, Cal?"

Cal knelt next to Faust and pressed his fingers into the soft dirt. He agreed he'd never seen anything this big before. Measuring the placement of the footprints, he estimated the beast to be between four and five yards long. Marko stumbled back.

"That's impossible, Cal! Bears don't get that big! Even a flatland grizzly only measures two yards from nose to tail at most. Where did it even come from?"

Kai gave Marko a grave look. "Remember our Trial, six years ago?"

Marko's face turned ashen, like a corpse pulled from the river. "Aww spit, that's what has you spooked, isn't it?" he groaned. "Nothing else would make you so jumpy. But there's no way one of those could be here!"

Kai pointed to the massive footprints. "It may not be the same, but it's just as bad. The whole damned forest was quiet as a grave that day. Tell me, what do you three hear?"

The humans shared a look and examined the surrounding grasses. Now that it was pointed out to them, the silence was as deafening as it was ominous.

"T-there's nothing. I don't hear a damned thing besides the river and the wind," Faust said, his eyes bulging.

"He's right. It's like all the animals packed a carriage and fled," Cal remarked.

Without warning, a guttural roar exploded from the nearby groves. The sound rattled the men to their teeth. Kai was certain everyone back in Mistport heard it.

Marko tittered. "Well lads, there's at least one beastie left."

Cal cuffed the younger hunter behind the head and reminded him they needed to treat the situation with caution. Their job was to deal with this, no matter what.

Kai circled the group and scanned the grove with narrowed eyes, searching for movement. Sweat trickled into his mane, but he ignored the itch. He focused on the spaces between the trees. A flash of movement caught his attention. A figure darted between the trees, but the distance made identifying them hard. They weren't tall or long enough to be responsible for the footprints. Kai wished he had an Aerivolk's eyes. Of the five tribes, the feathered faumen had the best eyesight, able to spot a worm in the grass at a hundred yards.

He pointed his crossbow towards the figure. Cal slapped the Norzen on the back. "I see them, Kai. Good eyes."

Kai grumbled that it wasn't good enough. He cautioned everyone they still didn't know what their true target was.

"Don't fret, boss. We'll take it down easy enough. What's your plan, Cal?" Faust asked. He got off his knees but stayed in a low crouch.

Cal motioned to Kai and pointed to the right; the same direction the figure was moving. "Travaldi, track that one and find out who they are. We don't know if they're friend or foe, and you're the only one here skilled enough to go in there alone. The three of us will go left and find this bear, or whatever it is. That shouldn't be too hard, considering its size."

Kai nodded. He slipped a hand into his pack and retrieved several blue vials. He handed one to each Hunter. "Understood. Watch your backs, though. Take these energy tonics as a precaution. They'll strengthen you enough to keep up with this thing. I'd rather not spend all night stitching you lot back together after we're done. I hear you all whine enough as is."

Marko uncorked the bottle, downing its contents. "Thanks, Kai. I know we don't say it enough, but I'm grateful you're here. You could have easily told the Elder you wanted to stay home to run the dispensary. Instead, you're here in the thick of it. With the Libbies arming up, that says a lot. Word says most of the Norzen bands outside Duskmarsh went underground."

Cal clapped a broad hand on Kai's shoulder, almost toppling him over. "Marko's right. A good apothecary is damned hard to find, and it's a huge risk coming here during a war," he said. Kai's face flushed, swatting the older hunter's hand away.

"I couldn't sit back and do nothing. I became an apothecary to save people, not sit in a dispensary all day. There are over twenty people dead here, so this is where I'm needed. Stella and Serafina can handle things back home."

Cal pointed again to the right. "We know, kid. Now get over there and do your job. We'll get you once we bag our beastie. And try not to sit on any thorn bushes in there." The other two sniggered at Kai's indignant glare.

"By the winds, it was one time, Cal!"

Kai's words fell on deaf ears as the three took off at a trot, cackling. Muttering to himself, Kai lifted the crossbow against his shoulder and lumbered into the woods. Alone.

"I swear to Tapimor he's going to regret that tonight. Damned bush," Kai grumbled under his breath, stepping over a thick root. He kept his head on a swivel, searching in an arc for any sign of the figure. Their skill at hiding was impressive, however, and that worried him. Evading a Hunter wasn't simple. As a Norzen with sensitive hearing, dodging Kai was even tougher. Other than the odd snapped branch, Kai found no clues suggesting his target's location.

He wiped a layer of sweat from his brow and twisted his ears again. Until he finished, the others would be tracking whatever made that roar themselves. He trusted their skills, but the potential danger meant having every hand available would make taking it down easier.

"Where did you go, you bastard?" Kai whispered. He took an uneasy step to the side, backing up against a nearby tree. He growled some choice words he knew would have his mother shoving a soap cake in his mouth if she knew.

The thought of his mother made him smile. Even though they hadn't given birth to him, the Travaldi family raised him as their own. Raising a Norzen child wasn't easy for humans. They still made it work and treated Kai like everyone else. His father taught him everything about hunting, though he often used those skills to sneak into the woods. Mother taught him to cook and fend for himself no matter where he was. Even without a bond of blood, they were there for him when no one else was. He never would have reached adulthood if they hadn't found him on the banks of the Great Ardei River that day.

The snap of a twig to his right shattered the quiet like a flintlock. Kai's body jerked towards the sound, swinging his crossbow up. The sound of his teeth grinding filled his skull. His blood pulsed through him like a roaring river. Nothing moved. Not even a leaf fluttered. Kai frowned, lowering the crossbow. Maybe Cal was right. He was so twitchy he was hearing things that weren't there.

Until his ears picked up a faint sound from behind that brought a sudden, heavy chill to his heart. The whistle of a blade slicing through the air.

Without thinking, Kai dove forward and rolled as a loud crash rang through the woods. He twisted into a kneel on the other side of the tree. A massive axe sat embedded in the wood, cleaving halfway through the trunk in one stroke. A large, broad hand clutched the shaft, with the figure from earlier moving into his vision, though the shadows blocked Kai from making out any distinguishing features. The person's hulking frame looked close enough, however. He brought the crossbow up without hesitation and pulled the trigger. A sharp twang signaled the bolt streaking towards its target, who lurched sideways with a curse. Kai swore when the bolt passed, just missing the figure's shoulder.

No time to reload, Kai thought as he tucked the crossbow into its loop on his pack while backing away. *I'll have to hold him off the hard way.*

He pulled the mace from his belt. The weapon's heavy flanges couldn't penetrate plate armor. However, they could still dent metal and shatter bones through an iron breastplate with a strong enough swing. Kai shivered when a deep chuckle reverberated from the figure. "You are either very brave or very stupid to send an arrow at me, little Norzen," the man rumbled, his deep baritone voice carrying a touch of mirth. Kai glared, watching as a bulky Soltauri stepped into the light.

Standing at least half a yard taller than Kai, the man held the typical burly build of his tribe. He wore a Cadist monk's cowl in deep brown which did nothing to conceal a pair of thick, curved horns extending from his curly black hair. Bulging muscles stretched the cotton robe covering his torso to its limit. A braided cord with a loop tied into it wrapped around his waist, likely meant for the twin-headed axe he swung.

Kai held his ground. He was quick and agile in a fight but risking a kick from the man's hooves was suicide. Even a small Soltauri could break through iron-braced doors with no trouble, and this one was bulkier than any he'd faced before.

"You truly intend to fight with that flimsy weapon? You have nerve. I'll give you a burial befitting a true warrior after I kill you," he said, freeing his axe with a flick of the wrist. The Soltauri's eyes flashed like burning amber.

Kai took a deep breath and settled for a blank stare. He wouldn't give this bastard the satisfaction of seeing his nervousness. "I don't intend to die here. I am curious as to why a Cadist monk is out here, though. You folks tend to stay close to your temples, and the closest one is in Whistlevale."

"You are a fool if you believe me an ordinary monk. My name is Duarte, and I've come here from Corlati by order of my master," the Soltauri responded, eyes brimming with barely restrained rage.

Kai tilted his head. "Master? So, you're the lapdog of some Feddy senator, or whatever they call the nobles over there." He remembered hearing that retaining a fully trained Cadist monk was something only the powerful in Corlati could afford; then again, it was possible the man was a slave. Most faumen in the Federation were.

Duarte's face burned scarlet. "How dare you! My axe will drink Norzen blood today," he bellowed. Duarte rushed forward with murder in his gaze.

Kai gripped the mace and waited. As Duarte closed in, Kai dug the toes of his back foot into the ground and kicked upward. A mix of dirt, grass, and pebbles were flung into the monk's face. The move forced Duarte to look away mid-charge and left an opening as Kai lunged sideways. He ducked beneath the axe and sent a backhanded strike into Duarte's lower ribs. The flanges bit deep, judging from the pained groan coming from the taller faumen. Kai hopped backwards and braced himself.

"Crafty little wretch. I'll enjoy killing you. This is more fun than those pathetic humans from the past moon," huffed Duarte while clutching a hand to his bleeding ribs. Kai blanched and stepped back in horror.

"Wait. You're the one who's been murdering those innocent people?" he shouted.

Kai's grip around the mace tightened. His mouth hardened into a fierce scowl as thoughts of the reports flashed through his mind. Each report was quite detailed on the damage done to the bodies, and six of the human victims were children. He skulked around the tree Duarte struck, noting the broken trunk. The splintered wood cracked and shifted in the gusts.

Duarte faced Kai and lifted the axe onto his shoulder. "They were humans, you fool. Humans by their nature lack innocence. Considering your heritage, you should know that better than other faumen."

Kai chuckled, which left Duarte blinking in confusion. "You'll have to forgive me if I find that to be a load of *bulskein*," he replied, using one of the few words of High Norzen he learned from an old traveler. "I never grew up around other Norzen, and I've seen places where faumen can be just as cruel. You've proven yourself a perfect example. Cruel is cruel, no matter the reasoning. Your actions may make sense to you, but that doesn't make it right in the eyes of the Saints. Some actions are just horrific, regardless of who performs them."

"You have much to learn, boy. Pity you won't live long enough to gain that experience."

Duarte brought the axe close, gripping with both hands. Kai stepped back and prepared a swing. The moment Duarte stepped forward; a deafening roar echoed through the grove. Both men clutched their ears in pain and fell to the ground.

"Great merciful Cadell! What in hoarfrost was *that*?" exclaimed Duarte.

Kai frowned, facing where the sound had come from. "I don't know. We thought that was the one responsible for all the humans and faumen murdered over the last moon," he replied.

Duarte turned a puzzled glare towards Kai and admitted to not touching a single faumen since his arrival.

"Wait...but if you didn't kill the faumen, who did?" A gut-wrenching scream rent the air. One Kai recognized. His eyes widened.

"Cal!"

Kai turned and ran towards the sound. He heard the crunch of broken twigs from behind. Throwing himself behind the tree, he flinched when a breeze from Duarte's axe passed over.

The weapon tore another gash into the tree as Duarte slid to a stop. The tree buckled as cracks spread over its trunk. "You're going nowhere! We aren't done yet."

"Well I'm done with you. Have a pleasant day, Duarte. Winds willing, we'll never meet again," Kai snapped back, a grim smirk sliding over his face. He gripped the mace with both hands and struck the tree above the gashes caused by Duarte's axe. The blow toppled the tree, splintering apart as it fell towards the monk.

Duarte swore, diving aside. The tree hit the ground with a deafening boom, branches snapping off mid-fall and burying the Soltauri beneath them. Kai gave a barking laugh and hurtled over the bushes before Duarte could get back up.

He leapt into the trees, using the trunks to launch himself from one to the next. All the while, he heard Duarte's furious bellows behind him.

Kai took a deep gulp of air with each jump, emitting ragged breaths as dark thoughts assaulted his mind. Luckily, it would take Duarte time to catch up. Only a few minutes had passed, but to Kai it was an eternity. Cal's scream echoed in his mind. He needed to find the man, and fast.

Landing on a low branch, Kai stopped to catch his breath and swiveled his ears, listening for anything.

You idiots better still be alive, he thought. A heaving gasp broke the silence nearby, one Kai heard many times in his Hunter career: the sound of a creature taking its last breaths. He dropped to the ground like a leaf and crept forward. The wheezing grew louder and heavier as he approached a clump of bushes near the base of a wide tree. He pushed the foliage aside and choked back a sob. Even knowing what to expect couldn't prepare him for reality.

Calvino leaned against the tree; his Hunter vest ripped to pieces. Strips of brown cloth and fur lay scattered. Blood covered his face and two shallow cuts curved from his chin to behind his left ear, giving him the appearance of a frightening grin on one side. The man's sword was on the ground, broken in half. His right arm showed clear signs of an animal bite, with multiple puncture wounds forming a curved line from shoulder to elbow. The flesh at the front of the arm was shredded, as if a carpenter's saw had been run across it. Raw, swollen blisters formed along the bite marks that pulsed with the slightest movement. The worst was the fountain of blood gushing from Cal's left leg.

At least, where his leg used to be.

Cal's leg was torn off just beneath the hip, leaving a ragged mess of flesh and splintered bone. A pool of blood grew beneath the man's broken form, leaving nearby plants painted crimson and deepening the sinister aura.

"By the winds! Cal, what happened?" Kai whispered, kneeling to inspect his comrade. He saw a glimmer of defiance in the man's eyes that made Kai smirk despite the situation. Even facing Cacovis, the Saint of Death herself, Cal refused to quit.

"Run away, kid. That thing might come back," he croaked. He attempted raising his arm but couldn't muster the strength. Kai could tell that the arm and shoulder were too damaged from the bite to allow much movement. He repeated his question to the injured Hunter.

Cal chuckled, coughing up a bit of blood. "I guess...the old man knew what he was saying," he continued. It was obvious that speaking was painful. His voice was raspy, and he spoke at a snail's pace.

Kai checked the man's wounds with careful intensity. On closer inspection, he saw a translucent lavender fluid mixing with the blood and oozing from Cal's wounds. He plucked several empty bottles from his satchel and filled them with the strange liquid before tucking them into their own satchel pocket. He wasn't sure what it was, but it deserved further investigation.

Cal spewed another splatter of blood, "Kai, you need to find the others, get back to Mistport, and warn everybody."

"I know, Cal, but I need to know what we're dealing with. Where are Faust and Marko?" Kai asked. He tore a strip from Cal's vest and tied it around what was left of his leg, tightening it to staunch the blood flow. He needed the man to live. Without information, making it back to Mistport alive looked like a wish in the winds.

Cal gave a weak shrug. "It ambushed us. No one saw it coming. The others scuttled back in the direction of town. You need to evacuate Mistport."

"I'm not leaving you here, Cal. Not a chance."

Even wounded, the bald man shot Kai a heated glare. "Don't be stupid," he snapped, "I'm as good as dead. This thing has venom in its bite. My eyes are getting hazy, and this arm burns like Nulyma."

Kai wiped away fresh tears. "Damn it, Cal, this wasn't supposed to happen."

With blood dribbling down the side of his mouth, Cal turned away. "Seems you were right too. Even before we got here, you said this whole mess smelled bad, and now look at us."

"*Taen!*" Kai hissed, pounding a fist into the dirt. The outburst drew a groan from Cal.

"Kaigo Travaldi, if your mother heard you swear in High Norzen, she'd scrub your mouth out!" The men shared an uneasy look before snickering.

The rustle of shifting leaves caused both hunters to turn their gaze. Kai scowled, shifting into a stance as Duarte stalked into the open, a triumphant grin on his face.

Just how much time did I waste standing here? Kai wondered.

"I told you our fight wasn't done, boy. Now we finish what—" Duarte growled, before his eyes landed on Cal. The sight of the Hunter's body stunned him into silence. It didn't take long for him to regain his voice, however.

"What in hoarfrost happened to him?"

Kai snorted. "Remember that sound we heard earlier?" he asked. Duarte nodded. "*That* happened. Which reminds me, Cal, you still haven't said what it looks like," he continued, casting a worried glance to the wounded man.

Cal gave a rattling sigh and opened his mouth. Before he could speak, a string of fluid fell from above and splattered against his injured shoulder. The sudden contact made him wince and bite his lip.

The liquid trailed down Cal's arm. As it passed over the wounds his face writhed in pain. Kai gaped when he noticed the fluid's opaque purple color in the narrow sunbeams piercing the treetops. His ears twitched and a shiver went through his tails. Then, he heard it. A low, rumbling growl from above.

Kai peeked at Duarte before glancing up. Something was slinking among the branches, but for some reason, he couldn't see it. He knew something was there, though; the air was shifting around the figure as it slinked among the branches. Whatever it was, it moved with a predator's grace. The rumble grew louder with every moment. The air shimmered in the sunlight before the creature's body seemed to melt into existence before their eyes.

Kai's eyes widened. *Tapimor's hairy ass, that thing can blend into its surroundings like a chameleon!* His entire body went stiff, blood running cold as he took in the terrifying sight.

He knew the creature would be massive, but what he saw was unsettling. Standing on all fours, he guessed it to be five yards long and two tall at the shoulder. While it did have a bear-like appearance, its body was gaunt and emaciated. It rose up, standing on two massive paws which looked out of place on its lanky body.

The beast's hide was covered in thin, matted grey fur. The chest looked sunken and withered with dried blood spattered over the upper ribs. Ivory bone-like plates covered its shoulders, jaw, ribs, and upper legs like armor. Its throbbing muscles were stretched tightly from the edges of the plates to underneath its skin. It looked as though the creature was wearing a skin too small for its muscles and bones.

The head had a short snout, rounded ears, and beady crimson eyes that darted everywhere. Its upper jaw was long and gave it a severe overbite that, in any other situation, Kai would have laughed at. Instead, it left the dagger-like upper canines, covered in blood, exposed. Lines of viscous saliva soaked the beast's muzzle and dripped from its mouth. One wiry arm was wrapped around a tree, its sharp claws buried into the wood keeping it anchored.

Kai held his breath and remained still. Whatever this creature was, it looked like something from his darkest nightmares. All he knew was he did not want to draw its attention. The head moved from side to side, its eyes squinting as it sniffed the air. Every once in a while, its eyes would drift to Cal, only to continue searching for something. Kai suspected its eyesight was weak and relied on smell and hearing to hunt.

So that's what the old tanner was talking about. This must be Grimghast. It must know we're here, and it knows where Cal is because of all the blood, but it can't find us unless we move excessively.

His eyes sought out Duarte again. The Soltauri looked like a stone statue, his face set in wide-eyed shock. The monk's body trembled, sweat glistening in the sparse sun.

Kai turned to Cal, lying prone with Grimghast on the branch above. The older man was giving him a peculiar smile. It almost looked as if he-

The taste of blood took over Kai's senses after biting his own tongue. *No, you idiot. Don't do it.* In the back of his mind, he knew Cal wouldn't listen, even if he shouted the words.

"Down here, you ugly bastard!"

Cal's yell broke Duarte out of his stupor. Grimghast jerked its head towards the Hunter's limp form. With a roar, it dropped from the tree and crashed on top of Cal. The ground quaked from the impact. Kai and Duarte lost their footing, tumbling backwards. Kai rubbed behind his head, feeling a small lump where he'd struck a rock. His eyes fluttered open and saw Cal sneering at Grimghast, its gaping maw hovering over him.

"No," Kaigo whispered. His mind screamed for his body to move, but he felt frozen to the ground. He could only watch as Grimghast lunged. Its jaws snapped Cal up, cutting off his screams before crushing him in a single bite. Even at this distance, Kai could hear bones crunching and see blood splattering the grass below. The beast flung Cal's body aside, splattering against a tree with a sickening plop.

A lone tear slid from Kai's eye and dripped onto his mane. The itchy sensation broke him from his reverie. He eased himself up, watching Duarte do the same. Both men kept an eye on Grimghast, though Kai couldn't muster the will to grab his mace. Seeing Cal's fate, it seemed foolish to attack the monster head on.

An odd whistle broke through the silence; it sounded like a gust of wind blowing through a reed. Grimghast sniffed the air, charging through the trees with Cal's blood dripping from its mouth. Kai wondered why it decided to ignore them. It should've been able to see them at that distance.

Still, I'm not looking a gift wiroch in the beak. I'm still alive, though I wish I could say the same for Cal.

Duarte scoffed and faced Kai after the rumble ebbed away. "I don't know what that beast is, but at least with all that blood it undoubtedly swallowed, its hunger should be-"

"Finish that sentence, Duarte. I dare you, because I swear on the eight Wind Saints, I will rip your fucking throat out if you do," Kai growled, turning a frosty glare on the monk. A vibrating rumble resounded from the Norzen hunter's chest that halted Duarte's advance. He backed away under Kai's hardened gaze and the Soltauri responded with a single nod.

"I-I apologize. For what it's worth, your friend died with a valor any warrior would be proud of."

Kai nodded back. "It appears we finally agree on something," he said.

Duarte hoisted his axe and walked away. "I suppose we shall finish our battle another day. Seeing that creature gives me much to think about. What is your name, Norzen?" he asked.

"Kaigo Travaldi, of Havenfall." Even though they tried to kill each other moments ago, the encounter with Grimghast sapped any desire to fight out of the pair.

Duarte quirked a bushy eyebrow. "Travaldi? It's rare for Norzen to carry a family name the way humans do."

Kai laughed, giving the Soltauri a knowing grin. "Well I *was* raised by humans after I was found abandoned, so it's natural. They could've left me to die on the Great Ardei riverbank but chose to save me instead."

His response prompted a tight smile from Duarte. "I see. You have also given me much to think about, Kaigo. Try not to let that beast kill you before we can cross blades again." Kai's eyes widened. He turned to the fallen trees where Grimghast rampaged during its escape. A quick glance skyward said its path led north. Towards Mistport.

Cal mentioned the others running back towards town after the ambush. Kai felt his throat constrict.

"*Taen!* I need to warn everyone. That monster is heading straight for them!"

Chapter IV

Kai's feet hammered the ground at a lightning pace, his chest heaving as he raced towards Mistport. His anger approached a steady boil the more he contemplated everything that happened. The pressure building in his temple was becoming unbearable. After catching up with Marko and Faust, he weighed the idea of beating them senseless. Hunters were forbidden from abandoning a squad mate under any circumstance, no matter what orders they were given. It was the Hunter Corps' cardinal rule.

Because they fled, their squad leader was dead and the monster responsible was approaching a town ill-equipped to handle it.

Uncorking an energy tonic, Kai downed the fluid. He would have to wait a few hours before taking another. It was common for Hunters and sailors alike to drink too much at once, attempting to push past their limits. The consequences were often messy and stomach-turning. Just thinking of the last case he treated made Kai shudder.

Charging through the grass, Kai noticed an odd smell filling the air the closer he got to Mistport. A deep frown slipped into place. Why did the air smell of blackpowder? He had never heard anything about a festival in the area.

"No, I can't think about that. Damn it, Kai, don't lose focus!" he berated himself. This was not a time for distractions. Not when he needed to—

Kai burst into the open field several hundred yards from the town gate and slid to a stop, almost tripping over himself. A column of smoke rose over the town like an ominous cloud, a shimmering red glow peeking just above the rooftops. Somehow, Mistport caught fire while they were gone.

The apothecary took a tentative step forward, eyes focused on the smoke. "How? We weren't even gone that long," he muttered.

He gnashed his teeth and kept running. Regardless of how or why, he had to help. Finding the others and evacuating the townsfolk were the priority now. But if he happened to run into that monster...

As Kai approached the town, he felt a rush of energy. By the time he reached the gate, his muscles pulsed with every movement. Grey eyes swept the area, noting the guards from earlier missing. In their place was a steady stream of people from every tribe fleeing town. Many hurried past Kai without acknowledging his presence.

Well, I don't have to worry about the evacuation so much, Kai muttered to himself.

Perhaps the guards went to deal with the fire, leaving the gate open for the townsfolk. But why didn't they leave at least one man behind to direct everyone? Instead, the crowds were knocking each other over in a mad scramble down the road.

He shuffled aside and gazed at the wooden wall surrounding the town. Built from tree trunks and tied together with thick ropes, it was a dozen yards tall and served as a blockade against the wild animals roaming the grasslands. If the fire spread too far, the entire structure would collapse.

Then again, Grimghast proved the wall didn't hinder it like it should have, either. Despite its size, it scaled the wall and killed within the town multiple times. The monster was larger than any normal bear and yet nobody laid eyes on it until now. Its concealment ability needed to be dealt with if he wanted to kill it.

Pressing forward, Kai slinked around the throng and entered Mistport. Those who noticed called out, warning him to run. Kai brushed off their concerns and charged through the slums. Glancing around, he noticed the empty streets. The children were gone. Many buildings were boarded up in a rush or abandoned. Bits of food and clothing lay scattered across the cobblestones. Anyone outside was scrambling for the gate.

From the position of the smoke, Kai guessed the fire to be at the port. But before he could investigate, he needed to find Marko and Faust. Now where could they have—

Kai's eyes widened as he thumped his forehead. How could he have forgotten? The *Sunken Anchor*! If he could rely on anything, it was Marko's skirt-chasing. He would make a beeline to the meadhouse to try and rescue Ione. Kai never understood why the man was so obsessed with women; it was his biggest weakness. The Norzen even remembered a time he nearly got himself killed trying to protect a traveling merchant woman from a pride of daggertooth lions by himself. Marko was so busy flirting that he almost got ambushed from behind when Cal saved his ass.

Kai hissed and rapped himself on the head with his mace. He leaned against a wall, inhaled, and focused on his breathing. He forgot how easy it was for his mind to wander under stress. He searched for any signs of movement, but the cobblestone roads remained quiet.

"War has come."

Kai swore. He leapt away from the wall and threw a backhanded swing on his off foot. The awkward strike soared over an Aerivolk man emerging from between the buildings. Where in the blazes did *he* come from? Kai hadn't heard anything until the stranger was behind him.

Kai backed up and felt a rumble in his chest. Upon closer inspection, he saw it was the same infirm Aerivolk the squad greeted earlier.

"By the winds, man! Don't scare someone like that. I could have hurt you," Kai said, clutching his chest. His heart hammered through his mane.

The man gazed up at Kai with a tired smile and a weak chuckle. "My apologies. You looked distressed with everything going on, but it seems I've simply made things worse. Oh, how rude of me! I never introduced myself. My friends call me Locke."

"I'm Kai," the apothecary replied. He took in Locke's gaunt form and winced. Aerivolk often had brilliant plumage, but the silvery white feathers of Locke's head and wings looked dull and frayed. The man's ribs poked from under the skin, barely covered by a tattered tunic. Locke was also short, even for his tribe. The dorsal feathers on his forehead barely reached Kai's chest. "What did you mean by 'war has come'?"

"It means what I said. The Liberators are invading and attacking Mistport as we speak. From what I've heard and seen, they plan to raze the town and everyone within."

Kai growled, moving to sprint for the port. Locke reached out and snatched an arm before he could take one step. Despite his frail appearance, Locke's grip was strong.

"You cannot stop them yourself. You are one man, a Norzen no less, standing against over a thousand enemies with more set to arrive soon. If you rush in, you'll die a fool."

"I'm aware, Locke. I intend to find my squad and escape with the rest of the civilians. I don't wish to fight that army alone," Kai snapped.

Locke released Kai's arm and backed away. "A sensible goal. I'll wish you luck, in that case. I daresay I should leave myself before I'm found out. Rumors say the Liberators are just as horrible to all faumen as the Corlatians, though their hatred for the Norzen runs particularly deep. May the winds of fortune guide you." The Aerivolk gave a worn smile before heading further into the slums.

Kai tugged the hood of his tunic up. He tied his tails in a loose knot, making them look like a common fur belt worn by forest dwellers. If Locke was right about the Liberators, then being found out was the last thing he needed. He held no delusions and knew the army would tear the town apart looking for him.

Hefting his mace over one shoulder, he rushed towards the market district. Families dashed past towards the southern walls, carrying their children and what few provisions they could fit into packs. The stench of blackpowder filled the air as smoke mixed with the area's natural fog, stinging his eyes like tiny needles. Several Soltauri men were fending off a pack of Liberators at the end of the road as what he assumed to be their families escaped. A woman of the fish-like Vesikoi tribe was being dragged away screaming by a pair of soldiers.

The farther he went, Kai could hear the cackles of invading soldiers and desperate cries from the locals. Turning his ears, the wailing chirp of an Aerivolk girl cut through the noise, begging for her parents to wake up. Only the bird-like faumen made a noise like that. She sounded close, maybe less than a dozen yards away. Kai pivoted towards the sound. He didn't have to lay eyes on the family to guess what happened. The girl's parents would never wake.

From the same direction, a cruel, hacking laugh reverberated. He heard the whistle of a blade, followed by a frightened chirp. There was a soft thump, then nothing.

Kai couldn't remember ever feeling a rage this deep before. A scarlet haze settled over his eyes. The girl's cries thundered in his head, and he found himself disagreeing with Locke's words. The Liberation Army wasn't as bad as Corlati towards faumen.

They were worse.

He clutched his mace in a white-knuckled grip and stalked towards the laughter, his body moving on its own. A twinge of fear grew within Kai's mind when he realized that he had no control over his movements. Kai rounded the corner and into a short alley. A tall, bearded man in ramshackle armor stood at the end with a sword in one hand and a lit torch in the other. A dead Aerivolk couple clung to each other against the wall, covered in blood. A tiny figure lay sprawled and burning at the man's feet. A single winged hand was visible through the flickering flames.

"Stupid feather-brained beasts! It's about time we dealt with you bastard faumen!" the man grumbled, swaying in a drunken stupor. He set his sword against the wall and pulled a bottle from a sack at his feet. The man wiped a blood-covered hand over his beard and took a long drink, focused on the small body.

Kai growled and dashed forward while winding up a swing. In the depths of his mind, he knew he couldn't save the girl, but his feet thundered ahead. The fear grew as he fought to wrench back control, to no avail. Lost in the haze, he screamed at his body to listen. When it refused to heed, a wave of futility washed over him before a stray thought crossed his mind.

It was true he couldn't save her, but at least her spirit could have peace.

The soldier turned towards the sound of rattling vials. He froze when his eyes landed on the charging figure. A gauntleted hand reached for his sword but proved too slow. Kai's mace struck the man in the ear, snapping his head sideways. The sharp flanges rent flesh and sent the soldier's body careening into the wall with a sickening clang. Blood pooled under the cracked skull, seeping between the cobblestones.

Kai sucked in a breath, staring at the man's corpse. He stared at the mace like a viper poised to strike. His thoughts felt jumbled and fractured. Even though he regained control of his body, it felt clunky and uneven; like a house with slanted windows and a door on the side opening to a blank wall.

Staring at the soldier's corpse, a sinking feeling settled in his stomach. If anyone knew a Norzen just killed a human, there'd be crowds calling for his head, regardless of his position. He decided to worry about that when he wasn't fighting for his life. Turning to the dead girl, he knelt next to her smoldering body and touched his fingers to the base of his neck.

"May Cacovis guide you on your final journey, little one," he whispered. It was a common prayer to guide the dead to Finyt. Despite being considered a heretic, Cacovis was still guardian of the dead. Without a cleric nearby, Kai felt compelled to offer the prayer himself.

Screams rang out from all around. Kai left the alley, staying close to the buildings as he continued towards the *Sunken Anchor*. Crowds of screaming people ran from the ports. Kai prayed nobody would notice him. The last thing he needed was a Libby soldier asking where he was going.

Kai felt a prickle in the back of his neck. He clutched his vest tighter and glanced around. A pack of Liberators stood near a burning shop, staring in confusion. They looked him up and down before turning away in a huff. Kai blinked, then inspected himself. His vest, pants, and boots were frayed and covered in dirt and blood from his time in the groves.

They think I'm a beggar, Kai realized. This was unexpected, but it was a boon he planned to take advantage of. He slowed his pace and added a limp to his gait, bumping against a wall every few seconds. Those giving him a passing glance would figure him for a blind vagrant.

Sticking to the side roads, he avoided any further close calls. Every scream and cry for help pierced his heart. He wanted to help the people of Mistport. Kai couldn't do anything, however, without the others.

Another shriek pierced the air, bringing Kai to a halt. The voice was familiar. Then, he heard a war cry cut through the growing inferno. One he heard often since his boyhood.

Marko!

Kai ran to a nearby collapsed building, clambering up the rubble. The apothecary peeked over and scowled at the scene below. Marko and Faust were side by side, facing off against ten Liberator soldiers. Ione and Lucretia Dineri, the Archivist from before, were behind them, backed against the burning wreckage of what Kai guessed was once the *Sunken Anchor*. The bodies of the cook and numerous patrons lay scattered amid the street alongside broken tables and shattered plates.

Faust struggled to lift his axe with only his left hand. Kai noticed a pair of arrows stuck in the man's right shoulder. Marko kept his buckler in front, sword held ready for a quick jab if any soldiers moved close enough. While not as injured as Faust, he was still limping while covered in small cuts and bruises. Both women were armed, guarding the Hunters' flanks. Lucretia wielded a short rapier and Ione an iron pan. The soldiers surrounded the group in a half circle and closed ranks around them. Soon, their only escape would be to go over the burning rubble, which wobbled uneasily in the wind.

Kai pulled the crossbow from its loop; he was glad he remembered to load a bolt before entering the city. Broadening his stance, he found a sturdy stone to brace his back foot against. He raised the bow and assessed his potential targets, taking aim. Kai inhaled and focused on a single point. He squeezed the trigger after exhaling and braced his shoulder.

The bolt sliced through the air, striking the man on the far left in the neck. He gurgled and reached up to grab the bolt. A misstep on a piece of debris sent him tumbling backwards. The fall rammed the bolt through his throat, erupting in a spray of blood. The other nine shouted in unison, scattering for cover. Several dashed for the body while all ignored the injured Hunters and two women.

Seeing the Libbies' panic brought a devilish smirk to Kai's face. Had he opted to shoot the soldier straight ahead, he would've been discovered in moments. Instead, he now had time to reload and pick them off while the others escaped. He aimed the weapon down and hooked a foot into the stirrup, cranking the string back. After cocking, he pulled a bolt from the quiver on his satchel and settled it into place. Kai kept down and shuffled to a new spot.

His ears picked up the soldiers arguing over where the attack came from. Behind them, Marko and Faust led the women towards the alleys. Kai peeked around a crumbling chimney and frowned. One of the soldiers was turning back towards the four and alerted his comrades to their escape.

Marko pulled Ione to her feet after tripping over a pile of debris. Kai could hear her labored breathing and saw a pained wince when Marko helped her up. The soldiers raised their weapons and charged them with murder in their eyes.

Kai knew what he was about to do was stupid. Incredibly so. He leapt into the open, yanking his hood back to reveal his ears. Lifting a single leg, he slammed his boot against the base of the cracked chimney. The structure collapsed forward with a deafening crash. The soldiers slid to a halt, craning their heads in confusion at the sudden noise.

"Up here, you clay-brained oat buckets!" Kai shouted.

The soldiers turned around again and gaped. "A Norzen," the tallest soldier shouted. "Grab him, men! We'll split the bounty and eat well for weeks!" The man seemed to be an officer of some sort, judging by the red ribbon adorning his upper arm. The command sparked the remaining soldiers to action. The group dashed towards Kai, pushing and shoving to reach their quarry first.

Kai held his ground, allowing them to scramble up the rubble halfway before bringing his crossbow up.

The officer whistled. "Shields up, you idiots!" he screamed.

A twang resounded before another bolt cut through the air and struck the vanguard soldier between the eyes. The others lifted their shields above their heads while diving to the ground. Meanwhile, their comrade's body rolled to the bottom of the rubble.

The officer pinched his nose. "You can still climb while shielding! Half of you use your flints and give the rest cover. Now grab him!"

Kai brayed with laughter when he saw half the men continuing to climb while the rest fumbled to load their flintlock pistols. "Must be hard finding good help. I've seen goats back home with more brains than all of you put together!"

The officer fumed, pointing his sword at Kai. "You'll regret that, Norzen! There's a bounty of 30 gold marks for each of you mongrels we bring back. The general only demanded you be alive. They don't need you undamaged," he said with a cruel sneer.

"If this is the best you can do, then you'd better find a more profitable trade, like cleaning privies. At least then you'd make a few marks," Kai retorted. He waggled his pinkie at the officer and ducked behind the rubble.

The soldiers' faces flushed red with rage at the rude gesture as they hurled obscenities at Kai. The officer turned back to face the other Hunters and found an empty street. "Damn it all, where'd they go?" he shouted.

Kai hopped among the rubble, advancing towards the alley he had seen the others slip into. He expected a mind-numbing lecture after they made it back home. It would be impossible for Marko and Faust to keep their mouths shut about the reckless stunt he pulled. And once his parents found out...

A faint rattle nearby stopped him short of the corner wall, eyes darting around in search of movement. Everything but the flames stood frozen, though Kai heard the disorganized shouts of the Libbies on the other side of the rubble. Backed against a crumbling wall, he took a tentative step towards the corner and jostled a small pile of debris. He heard a low hiss coming from near his feet groaned. The last thing he needed was a rattlesnake slithering around. He always kept anti-venom on hand but having to stop and use it would leave him vulnerable. He needed to make slow and steady movements, lest he irritate the little bastard.

From nowhere, his senses erupted in blinding pain when an explosion went off in a blinding flash. His ears rang in agony as he held them flat against his head, stumbling around. He squinted, noticing what looked like a pair of fireworks a yard away, their fuses hissing. He cursed, bolting for the corner wall while tucking his head in. The crack and flash that accompanied the explosion stunned him. Unable to see, he tripped over a pile of stones and fell into the rubble face first.

Kai tucked his body inwards and allowed himself to roll. The moment his back hit flat ground, he rolled onto his stomach and brought himself to a painful stop. Keeping his eyes closed, Kai groped for anything stable. He fought the stabbing sensation in his head and kept searching; he needed something solid at his back before he was caught. His fingers bumped into a flat surface, and a quick check revealed what he was looking for. Whether it was a wall or door, Kai didn't know as he leaned against it as fast as his aching body allowed.

An amused chuckle came from the right. "You didn't believe you could escape, did you? I can't decide whether you're uniquely brave or stupid for one of your kind."

Kai eased his eyes open. A gauntlet-covered hand grabbed his hair, wrenching the Norzen's head up. Grey eyes met blue as Kai swallowed the impulse to spit in his captor's face. While tempting, Kai knew he needed to bide his time. That wouldn't stop him from giving the asshole a few verbal punches, though. They did say they needed him alive, after all.

He inspected the newest soldier. The man's face still held some baby fat in the cheeks, but his chiseled jaw, cropped hairstyle, and short beard made him look older. It was hard to tell what his true age was, though the beginnings of wrinkles around the eyes suggested he was older. A pair of gleaming, silver aspen leaf pins on his epaulettes marked him as a lieutenant. Of course, this assumed that the Liberators used the same ranks as the Royalist Navy.

Kai gave a weak chuckle. "Your lackeys' performance doesn't inspire confidence. Besides, those drones of yours attacked my friends," he coughed out.

The man laughed. "Friends? I can't believe a peltneck like you would have *any* friends, especially human ones," he replied. Kai's ears twitched, hearing a stunned gasp nearby. He watched the man examine him before his eyes locked on Kai's vest. "What's this?"

He snagged the chain hanging from the pocket, peering into the pouch with interest. Its contents brought a mocking leer to the officer's face.

"My, my...I couldn't imagine a peltneck risking capture while carrying this, even *if* it's an obvious fake. You do realize you'll be executed for possessing it, right?"

The rattle of armor drew Kai's gaze to the soldiers from before. They surrounded him and the pompous officer.

The soldier with the ribbon on his arm walked up and saluted. "Captain Agosti, shall we secure the Norzen and take him back to camp?"

Captain? Why in Nulyma are they using the ranks of the Corlatian Army with Livorian insignia? Kai wondered.

Agosti released Kai's vest and leveled a withering glare at the man, who flinched and took a step backwards. "You and I will have a discussion at camp tonight, Sergeant, concerning your complete and utter *incompetence*," he snapped. *So that one's the equivalent of a petty officer, then.* "Your men may secure the peltneck, but I'll return him to camp myself. Galen knows you'd let the wretch escape if what I've seen is any indication. This is one peltneck that we cannot lose. He's committed a hanging offense."

The sergeant turned scarlet. "Sir, with all due respect, we found him. We deserve our share of the bounty." The officer turned and pointed to the dead soldiers Kai had downed.

"You think you deserve a reward, when you lost multiple men attempting to capture a single peltneck. Something which you failed!"

"But Captain..."

"Silence!" Agosti snapped. The soldiers lowered their eyes in shame. "As I said, we'll discuss this tonight. Until then, I suggest you keep your head down and your mouth sewn shut. Should you fail in even that simple task, then perhaps a cleansing is in order, at which point I'll shut you up myself. Permanently."

Kai noticed each soldier shivering in terror at Agosti's threat. He decided to stay silent and watch. If they wanted to bicker amongst themselves, he wouldn't complain.

"You aren't taking him anywhere, you Libbie bastards," a weary voice rang out. Agosti and his men spun to find Marko and Faust staring them down, weapons drawn. Kai wanted to tell the two to stay back, but it was too late. Now he prayed to Tapimor they could hold their attention long enough for him to recover.

"Is that so? And how do you plan to stop us? You look more ready to pitch over, rather than fight," Agosti replied with a sneer. He signaled the sergeant with a dismissive wave. "Take your men and find the two women. I shall deal with these two." The sergeant saluted and hurried off with the remaining soldiers. Agosti drew an ornate sword from its scabbard, sliding into a stance.

Faust wiped an arm over his face, spitting a wad of blood to the ground. "Fancy. Can you even use that blade?" he asked.

"Care to find out, maggot? What I don't understand is why you're protecting a peltneck carrying a forged emblem of official title," Agosti shot back. He stepped forward and sent a weak thrust at Faust. The Hunter parried the blow with his axe and backed away.

Kai's tails twitched and thrashed around his waist, a low growl coming from his throat. A soft touch to the shoulder stilled him. His heart pounded as a hand slid down his chest, rummaging through the vials on his vest. He tilted his head just enough to spot a familiar blue ribbon. He uttered a silent prayer of relief. The Saints were looking out for him today.

"Sorry I startled you," Ione said. Her soft voice soothed Kai in more ways than one. He would have felt guilty if anything happened to the kind woman. "Is there anything here that can help?" she asked in a whisper. Kai noticed she was hidden behind the broken wall behind him. A liberal coat of dust covered Ione's face and clothes, allowing her to blend into the debris.

"There's a vial with a red dot on my left side. Slip it into my hand and stay back. Find Miss Dineri and conceal yourselves until we can clear a path," Kai answered. He felt Ione's hand shift and heard a click as a vial was removed. A moment later, the smooth stone settled into his hand. One flick of the thumb popped the cork loose as he rolled his shoulder. Ione gave his arm a comforting pat before scampering away.

Faust and Marko were holding Agosti at bay, but their injuries hampered any ability to counter the officer's viper-like movements. Kai staggered into a crouch, sprinkling the contents of the vial into his open hand before corking and tucking it into a pocket. A sudden glint of light brought his attention to a figure closing in from behind.

"Marko, dodge left!" he shouted.

Agosti spun towards Kai as Marko threw himself into a roll. This caused the sergeant's wide swing to miss, throwing him off balance. Faust turned and threw his weight into his good arm. The Hunter's axe caught the man in the breastplate, sending him soaring until he hit the cobblestones hard. Marko scrambled up and returned to Faust's side.

Agosti snarled and lunged for Kai, thrusting at the Norzen's ribs. "Perhaps I should just save myself the trouble and kill you here and now, heretic!"

Kai sidestepped with a wide grin. "Let's see you turn that trick!" He swung his arm in a wide arc, opening his hand and slapping Agosti across the eyes with the vial's contents.

The cappara flakes' effect was immediate. Agosti stumbled back, screaming the moment the dust touched him. His sword clattered to the ground as he clawed his eyes and nose. He collapsed to the ground, reaching for the canteen on his belt. However, in his haste to uncork it, the canteen slipped from his fingers and landed close enough for Kai to kick it away.

Marko and Faust guffawed at the screaming Agosti. Kai spotted a new group of Liberators approaching. A band of twenty soldiers stared them down with the captain writhing in agony between them. The main road lay at their backs, littered with debris and bodies.

The rattle of shifting rocks drew Kai's attention. Ione and Lucretia emerged from the wrecked building, the scholar clutching her rapier in a defensive stance. Lucretia stood in front of the tavern maid while giving Kai a wide berth and suspicious glance.

One of the soldiers stepped forward. "You'd best surrender. We will soon have the square surrounded. If you turn yourselves in, I promise you won't be harmed on the way to our camp."

Faust thumbed his nose at the soldier. "Perhaps, but what's stopping you from killing us afterwards? I trust you bastards as much as a drunk woodcutter." The burly Hunter bolted down the main road. Kai groaned, ordering him to stop. A rumbling growl echoed through the square, freezing everyone stiff. Lucretia's eyes widened, darting everywhere in a frenzy.

"What in Finyt was that?" she asked.

Kai's breath hitched, his fur standing on end. He ducked low and scanned the area with his ears swiveling in an arc. A glimmer caught his eye and he turned towards Faust. The other Hunter stared back in confusion. Kai tried to give him a reassuring smile, but his lips refused to curve. Then he saw it.

A large shimmering silhouette, standing over Faust. Kai glanced at Marko and saw a look of realization in his eyes. He saw the silhouette too. Kai hissed at Marko telling him to keep quiet. But he didn't notice, too focused on the figure behind his friend.

"Faust! Get out of there!" Marko screamed. All eyes swung to the large Hunter.

Only for Grimghast to phase into existence behind him and lunge down with a deafening roar. Faust screamed in pain as the monster clamped its jaws over his waist, lifting him into the air. A massive paw gripped Faust's upper body. Then with a wrench of the head, it tore the Hunter in two, swallowing the man's waist and legs with a single gulp.

The Liberators scattered in a blind panic. A pair grabbed Agosti by the arms and dragged him away, still scratching his eyes.

Ione choked out a sob and stumbled against Kai, who caught her before she could fall on her rear. Lucretia swore, almost knocking Marko over as she backed away.

The beast threw the rest of Faust's body aside, leaving his upper body among the rubble, eyes staring into the abyss in perpetual terror. Sniffing the air, it hunched down and stalked the outer edge of the square. Kai noticed it was chasing the frenzied Liberators. He glanced at the others and saw Marko, Ione, and Lucretia all staring at him.

"Well, you really are the boss now," Marko hissed. "Got any ideas?"

Kai never wished for an idea so hard in his entire life. Not even his Trial was this terrifying, and his brush with death that day remained vivid in his mind. He pressed a hand against his pocket, taking a deep breath. He didn't have time to overthink. He would have to rely on instinct for now. But then, everyone he knew said he was best at thinking on his feet. They would have to worry about how to kill that thing later.

Right now, they needed to escape it before ending up as its next afternoon snack.

CHAPTER V

The market plaza of Mistport was the fitting image of a warzone. Liberator soldiers scattered like bugs to escape Grimghast's lumbering form. The beast swiped its heavy paws at the men, plucking them from the ground to devour in one or two bites. The shouts from all directions were confusing it. Its head swung back and forth, unable to decide who to chase.

Kai searched for an opening. A gust of wind brushed aside enough smoke to spot a massive hole in the city wall. He tapped Marko on the shoulder and pointed.

"That's our path out. The civilians are already in the process of evacuating, so they should be mostly safe. And with the Libbies so busy avoiding that thing, no one will notice us," Kai explained.

Marko whispered to Ione and Lucretia, gesturing for them to follow. The group rushed for the collapsed buildings between them and the hole. Kai raised his arm, waving for the rest to follow. They weaved through the smoke, covering their mouths to avoid inhaling any fumes. Kai skidded to a stop next to a burning stall. The others stopping just short of colliding with him. Marko smacked the Norzen's shoulder.

"What in Finyt are you doing, Kai? The exit's right there! There's maybe thirty yards between us and survival. Let's move!"

Kai's ears twitched as the wind whistled around them and he glanced back towards the plaza. The Liberators were regrouping, but something looked off. "Wait...? Where'd that damned beast go?" he muttered.

A roar from the side caught them by surprise. Kai twisted and felt a gangly forearm hit his chest. He soared through the air and struck his back on the cobblestones. Ione and Lucretia screamed, the former rushing to Kai. Marko charged, swinging his sword at the beast's thigh.

Grimghast snarled when Marko's blade bit, lunging at the Hunter. Marko stepped back while shouting at the furious creature. With every parry, Marko used the debris as a shield from Grimghast's claws. The beast pursued him into the expanding blaze.

Ione slid next to Kai and tried lifting him up. No matter how much she struggled, however, he didn't budge. "Lucretia, help me, please! He's too heavy," she called to the other woman. Lucretia scowled but rolled up her sleeves before kneeling to help. After some effort, the pair hauled the apothecary to his feet.

Kai staggered around before examining the new pulsing knot on his head. He gave the two women an appreciative smile, though Lucretia responded with a withering glare and flared nostrils. Kai grimaced. Just because he was used to those looks didn't mean he had to like them. "Ma'am, I don't know what your problem is with my tribe, and frankly I don't have time to care. We have bigger things to worry about, like not dying."

"The fact that you are Norzen is bad enough. I have my reasons for hating your kind, so you dying would not bother me in the least. I only helped you as a favor to Ione. Nothing more, nothing less," the woman replied.

The sound of a roar drew their attention back to Grimghast. The Liberators were helping by attacking the beast themselves. Marko was worn and exhausted, his sword hanging limp at his side. He circled around while it was occupied, but the flames were spread enough to separate him from the others.

Kai met Marko's eyes and the wounded Hunter gave a sheepish grin. "Kinda missing that old hog about now, aren't we!?" he shouted over the crackling fire.

"Speak for yourself, Marko!" Kai shouted back. "I still can't eat bacon after that!"

Another bone-rattling roar reverberated through the plaza as Grimghast rushed the Liberators. The soldiers tossed their weapons aside and ran screaming. Marko let loose a braying laugh. "Why was Her Grace so worried about these fools again? Just a bunch of cowards." With the Liberators vanishing into the scorched town, Grimghast turned back and sniffed the air, its ears twitching. After a moment, it set its beady eyes on the cackling Marko.

"Aww, spit," Kai muttered. "Marko, shut up and move!" To Marko's credit, he snapped his mouth shut and scrambled behind a pile of debris. The beast stalked towards Marko's hiding place, saliva dripping from its maw.

Eyes roaming the area, Kai searched for anything to use as a distraction. He spotted a chunk of stone a yard away. Reaching down, he hefted the stone with one hand and twirled, launching it towards where the Liberator soldiers ran. It struck a burning watch tower and brought the entire structure down.

The distraction worked, sending Grimghast lumbering to the broken tower. Kai pointed at the hole and beckoned Marko to follow while helping Ione over the rubble. He extended a hand to help the scholar up as well, only for her to slap the appendage away in a huff.

Marko tried slinking away, but the uneven terrain caused him to stumble multiple times. The further he went, the more sluggish his movements became. Ten yards from the hole, he tripped over a piece of broken wall and collapsed.

Kai followed the women as they scrambled for the open grasslands, his eyes shifting to Grimghast every few seconds. If they could reach the longgrass, they had a chance to evade the eyes of both the Liberators and that beast. Once they were out of danger, he could focus on Marko's wounds.

He turned his gaze back and blanched, seeing the fallen Hunter. "*Taen!*" he hissed. Already, Grimghast was returning to their position. The piles of rubble and erratic smoke were all that shielded them from being spotted.

Marko returned Kai's stare with a lopsided grin. Then, he lifted his hands and began gesturing in a controlled pattern. *"Don't worry about me,"* he mouthed. *"Take the girls and run. I'll just slow you down."*

Kai returned the gestures in kind, all the while shooting the other hunter a piercing stare. *"Don't be stupid,"* he mouthed back. *"I can't do this alone."*

Ione and Lucretia kneeled in the grass, watching the exchange from afar. "What are they doing?" Ione asked with a tilt of her head.

Lucretia shrugged and turned away, grabbing the other woman by her arm. "I am not sure. It appears to be a form of hand signals, though I have never seen such a method before. Now come, we must find somewhere safe."

Growling, Kai pointed at the approaching Grimghast. The beast trudged through the flaming debris, smashing everything in its path. Marko hobbled to his feet. Even at a distance, Kai could see him struggling to stand and favoring his left leg.

Marko stood defiant and faced Kai. Shifting his sword to the left hand, Marko lifted his right arm and saluted the Norzen with a pained expression. The man's limb trembled and fell after scant seconds, dangling at Marko's side.

Kai gave a final pleading look to the other Hunter, who replied with a shake of the head. Shouting out a war cry, Marko limped back into the burning plaza.

Even though he wished to run after Marko, Kai whispered a plea to Tapimor before hurrying into the grass. He needed to find the women and hoped Marko had an escape plan. Kai moved through the thick foliage without a sound. Years of experience gave him soft, yet quick, footwork. Ears twitching, the sounds of battle from Mistport were muffled enough for him to hear their voices ahead. He found them resting on the riverbank two hundred yards from the hole they escaped through.

"We need to—gah!" Kai yelped, twisting his body to avoid Lucretia's rapier. She stepped into another lunge, smirking when the blade nicked Kai's neck before he brushed her aside with his mace.

"Finyt's sake, Lucretia!" Ione cried out, putting herself between them. "You could've killed him!"

Lucretia sheathed the blade with a huff. "What did you think I was trying to do?"

Giving the scholar an uneasy glance, Ione searched the area. "Kai, where's your friend?" she asked. The fear in her eyes felt like a knife in Kai's heart. Suddenly, an anguished scream broke the muddled silence. A gurgling roar followed, sending shivers through the three.

There was no doubt about what happened to Marko.

Kai dropped to his knees and choked back sobs. Tears flowed down his cheeks as his body shuddered. He slammed a fist into the ground, crushing a stone beneath his knuckles. "That damned idiot!" he screamed. "He didn't have to die. None of them did!" Marko's death scream hammered the reality of the situation into his head; all his squad mates were dead. It was as if a giant hole had been torn in the Norzen's chest.

Ione wrapped her arms around the grieving Hunter. "I know it hurts," she whispered. "The pain never truly leaves. But at the very least, we still have our memories of those who've passed on to Finyt. I don't think your friends would want you to lose yourself in grief and get yourself killed."

Pondering Ione's words, Kai knew she was right. There was no doubt any of them would've beaten him around the head for moping. He took a deep breath and exhaled slowly. Opening his eyes, he smiled at the tavern maiden.

"Thank you, Miss Ione. I needed that. I'll have time to grieve once we're out of immediate danger." Kai dusted himself off, tugging his mace from its loop. "Now, we should put as much space between us and that *thing* as we can."

"What even was that creature?" Lucretia asked. "I have seen many animals during my travels, but that looked like something from the pits of Nulyma." Kai and Ione flinched.

While he had never been very pious, Kai grew up with a healthy fear of Nulyma like any Windbringer. It was one thing to be sentenced to a lifetime in a dingy, filth-infested gaol. It was considerably worse to wonder if you would rot in the blank void of Nulyma after you died. There, it was said that you couldn't see, hear, or smell anything. Your only companion in Nulyma was the pain of your sins tearing you apart for the rest of eternity.

"I don't know. I've been a Hunter for six years, and I thought I'd seen most of Livoria's creatures, including several that didn't belong," Kai murmured, gripping his left upper arm. "But that creature was unlike anything I've ever seen or heard of."

Lucretia scoffed. "So even the legendary Hunter Corps does not know what we are dealing with. That is comforting," she said, venom dripping from each syllable.

Kai matched the Archivist's glare. "Right now, our best option is to avoid it. That monster would tear all of us into pieces. Whatever it is, it can blend into its surroundings, like how a chameleon hunts. I'd need a squad of at least seven or eight to take it down. And that's after gathering more information on it. Anything less would be a suicide mission. I swear on my honor, I *will* bring that monster down one day."

The three sat in silence, staring at the river. It was both humbling and terrifying for the Hunter to think about. Kai trained from boyhood to tackle dangerous beasts, so coming across something that forced him to skitter away like a mouse battered his pride.

Hoisting his pack, Kai stood and turned his ears outward. "We should get moving. There's no telling how long that beast will stay occupied, and I'd prefer to get you both somewhere safe as quickly as possible."

"*Safe?*" Lucretia hissed, clutching a small pack to her chest. "Can anywhere be considered safe after all we saw today? Furthermore, I have made my opinions on your tribe clear. I have no desire for your assistance and shall find my own way." With a huff, the woman tramped along the riverbank.

"By yourself? With no map? Besides, say what you want of my people, I'm an apothecary first and foremost. It would go against my oath to let you do this alone after everything that's happened."

Silence. Lucretia skittered to a stop. Though she wasn't facing him, Kai could hear her heavy breaths and grinding teeth as she stood there, contemplating. While there were some villages within a two day walk of Mistport, many would be evacuated before their arrival. Trying to find a large town without a map was a fool's errand at best. And judging from Lucretia's shaking form, Kai and Ione figured she knew it too.

"Very well," she said. Her voice was clipped with a bitter tone. "I have no desire to die out here. As much as it hurts to ask, may I accompany the both of you?" Kai waited until she turned to face him before nodding, a soft tilted smile gracing his features.

"But—" she continued, "only to the nearest large town. I will procure supplies and my own map from there."

Kai shrugged. "That's fair. I have no problem with you coming on one condition: Please don't try to stab me again."

Lucretia crossed her arms under her chest. "I shall resist the temptation," she purred, a giving the Norzen a slanted smirk.

Squealing in joy, Ione embraced the other woman. "Oh, thank Luopari," she said as Lucretia returned the gesture. "This will be much easier if we work together. Now, where can we go from here?"

Pulling his map, Kai unfurled it on the ground. Ione grabbed small stones to weigh down the map's corners while Kai and Lucretia examined it. "Is there anywhere in particular you need to go, Lucretia?" Kai asked.

The Archivist tugged a stubby quill from her blouse and encircled a city. "Yes. I must return to Runegard and report to Highmaster Nerod about the attack."

Ione peered over Lucretia's shoulder. "That looks like a mighty long walk," she piped in. "Can we make it there without supplies?"

"It's possible," Kai answered, "but not ideal. I can handle securing food on the trail. The problem would be water. Going straight to Runegard from here would force us to travel across the grasslands, which are a known bandit haven, with limited river access. In addition, we'd be looking at perhaps ten days of travel, maybe two or three more if we run into trouble. It would be dangerous, especially if the Liberation Army marches in the same direction."

Lucretia's face settled into a withdrawn frown. "You bring up a valid point, Norzen. To make matters worse, I must admit that Ione and I are not accustomed to traveling over terrain on foot the way you are. What path would you suggest?"

"To start with, I have a name," Kai snapped. "I'm not asking you to like me, but I would appreciate a modicum of decency. My name is Kaigo, but Kai will keep things simple." With an exasperated sigh, Lucretia gave a stiff nod.

"Thank you." Lucretia quirked a surprised eyebrow at the hunter. "As for a path, I believe the best option is Faith Hollow. To start with, there are several rivers along the way to refill our canteens and wash. We'll be harder to track if we don't smell. Even better, the trek is at least three days shorter and lets us resupply and rest at a large, fortified city. The path to Faith Hollow is also more out of the way and should allow us to avoid the known bandit hideaways. From there, you can hire a boat. If my memory is correct, Runegard is perhaps another five days by river barge. You could be back home within a moon."

Kai heard her whispered mutterings as she considered his words. He stifled a chuckle at the concentration in her eyes. After a few minutes, she decided.

"I wish I could return home at once. However, your arguments are compelling and logical. Considering the situation, I will defer to your expertise. We make for Faith Hollow."

Ione clapped her hands together with a gleeful laugh. "Excellent! Now, what say we hit the trail? I'd rather be somewhere that ain't here by nightfall."

"Agreed," Kai said. Tucking the map away, he refilled the canteens tied to his pack. After handing each woman a full canteen, the trio plodded along at a sedate pace. For better or worse, they needed to work together to survive.

When they left Mistport, the sun had just reached its zenith, basking the ground in its warmth. Now, as the trio settled in for some rest, the last rays of sunlight peeked over the horizon with the twin moons floated on opposite sides of a star-filled sky. The winds whistled, leading a soothing symphony in the air.

Ione tugged the cloak Kai gave her tight around her shoulders while she helped him finish their dinner: stew made from a large rabbit he was lucky enough to trap. The smell, filled with the aroma of various herbs, made all three salivate in anticipation. Kai scooped a hearty amount into the ladies' bowls, smiling as they sat down and whispering a prayer of thanks to Tapimor before eating. As Saint of the Forests, Tapimor was also invoked by Windbringers to bless the harvest and meals.

Lucretia side-eyed the stew. "I must confess, I have never eaten rabbit. The Citadel's kitchen always uses beef or chicken." Ione gaped at the other woman in stunned awe.

"Truly?! You've never *once* had rabbit?" The scholar shook her head, her cheeks tinted pink as if ashamed to admit it. "Well, I suppose that makes sense. Lots o' folks see rabbit as peasant food since it has to be hunted. Living in the Citadel, I doubt you had much cause for hunting to keep food in yer belly. But it's good, I promise!" Without another word, Ione lifted a spoonful to her mouth and sipped the steaming broth. Her eyes bulged and emitted a throaty groan from her throat. She chewed for a few moments before swallowing. "By the winds, Kai! What did you do to this rabbit?" she exclaimed.

Kai flinched and gave his own stew a suspicious glance. "Is it that bad? I admit I tried a new herbal mix for the seasoning. I can cook the leftover meat a different way if you'd prefer."

"Are you serious?" Ione questioned. Her eyes bore through Kai like an arrow. The hunter debated if he should make a run for it before the tavern maid took a swing at him with her pan. "This is the most delicious stew I've ever tasted! I swear the meat melts in my mouth! And the aroma is strong, but not overpowering. I've met chefs working the noble district back home in Grantide that can only dream of doing this." True to her words, Ione attacked her bowl with a gusto the other two found astonishing.

Lucretia took a hesitant sip. An unexpected squeal erupted from the woman. "My word! Ione is right, this is impressive! Did you have some sort of training?" she asked. The scholar studied Kai with an aura of intrigue, which intimidated him. The woman made him feel like he was being judged by a magistrate for some sort of mischief.

"I assure you; I've had no training, just lots of practice over the years. Hunters need to know how to live off the land. We don't always have the luxury of inns, as you can guess."

Seeing the pair nod, he continued. "Most hunters are taught to prepare their own food. Admittedly, not everyone can make it taste good. I think my apothecary training helps in knowing how to mix herbs to enhance the flavor. Also, my Da is a baker and retired Hunter. I learned a few tricks from his experience."

The sound of skittering rocks and a loud splash split the air, sending the three scrambling. Ione and Lucretia grabbed their weapons and dove for the longgrass. Kai planted himself in front of the women, mace at the ready. Kai's fur stood on end and his ears swiveled back and forth, twitching at the slightest sound. All he heard was the rustling of leaves. Grey eyes swept across the riverbank, searching for movement. But all that moved was the flowing river.

Ione peeked out from the grass and whispered, "What was that?"

Pressing a finger to his lips, Kai clutched the mace tight and slunk to the edge of the water. He stumbled over a large stone and hit the gravel face-first. He scrambled to his feet with teeth clenched. Suddenly, a pained groan echoed from upriver, in the direction of Mistport.

As if something, or someone, was following them.

Kai swore, inching up the riverbank while staying close to the grass. He made sure both Ione and Lucretia were hidden before cresting the small hill they set up camp behind. If they were lucky, it was an injured bison or some other creature following the river behind them. A daggertooth, while uncommon in the north, was still a possibility and more problematic.

The real problem was being found by a Liberator scout. Or, Saints forbid, Grimghast.

Kai's ears perked at the sound of shifting rocks, accompanied by a softer splash, and another groan. Not an animal. Sniffing the air, he recognized the familiar iron tang of blood mixed with sweat. He was close. Judging from the ripples in the water, he guessed them to be inside the reed patch nestled at the water's edge. The reeds whistled in the wind, muffling the movements of whoever lay within.

Taking a calming breath, Kai sidled next to the reeds and pushed them aside. His breath hitched when he saw what lay in the water.

A large, armor-clad man lay on his side, head partially submerged and covered with dried blood. Kai couldn't make out many distinguishing features in the darkness other than his large size. A quick check of the armor revealed no emblems or military insignia. That meant he was either a sellsword or his accoutrements were removed at some point. Cursing, he dropped his mace, grabbing the man's shoulders to pull him back onto the bank.

"Ione! Lucretia!" he called. "There's an injured man here! I need my satchel!"

The two women burst from the grass. "Merciful Galen!" Lucretia gasped, invoking the leader of the Wind Saints. Ione passed the satchel to Kai after he dragged the man onto the bank, laying him back. The tavern maid dropped to her knees in fervent prayer. The apothecary could hear her mumbling a plea to Luopari to save the man's life.

Kai rustled through his tools, cursing when he remembered his spark-stone was in his traveling pack. "We need to remove his armor so I can check for wounds. Please get this off while I get my sparker and start a fire."

"Are you sure you should treat him?" Lucretia asked. She eyed the newcomer, one hand resting on the hilt of her sword. "What if he's a Liberator?"

"We won't know for certain until he wakes, so for now I'll treat him like anyone else," Kai answered. He noticed Lucretia giving him a curious glance as she loosened the man's armor straps. The task was cumbersome in the dark, both women struggling to undo the knots holding it in place. Working together, the pair tugged the heavy breastplate off and rolled it to the side.

The man groaned the moment his armor was removed. Seeing the rise and fall of his chest, it was obvious he was breathing easier. Curling into a ball, he rolled over and struggled to stand. The ladies backed away, but Kai gripped the stranger by the shoulders, helping him to a sitting position. "Easy, now," Kai said. "You're in rough shape. Just rest for a moment and I'll patch you up."

"Patch me up?" he replied in a gruff tone. His voice was hoarse, as if his throat were full of gravel. "You a 'pothy or summit?"

Kai quirked an eyebrow. "If, by that, you mean apothecary, then yes. Just hold still and let me see your wounds." He reached out, only to have his hand batted away with a growl.

"I don't need no damn 'pothy! Leave me be!" the man snarled. Kai held his hands up and stepped back.

"Calm it, sir. Even nicks and scratches can fester if you leave them. I promise I won't hurt you."

"Don't make promises ya can't keep, boy. And don't think I'm blind either. I ain't ever heard of a Norzen 'pothy before. Then again, it's rare to see your folk at all back in Corlati. How do I know you won't poison me or some such rot?"

Kai winced. If the man was Corlatian, then a fight might be inevitable. "I can understand the hesitance, but I prefer to not murder my patients. Bad for business and all that. Also, the name is Kai, not 'boy.' And the two ladies are Ione and Lucretia," he said while pointing to each woman. The Norzen's eyes flickered back and landed on Lucretia. "Tell you what, here's the deal: Let me treat your wounds, free of charge, of course. If at any point you feel threatened, then Lucretia here can stab me in the shoulder on your behalf."

Lucretia grinned. "Do it. For the love of the winds, take the deal."

Ione slapped Kai behind the head hard enough to draw a yelp. "Kai! What kind of a deal is that, you daft fool? And Lucretia, I thought we agreed to work together? We'd never get you home if you stabbed him."

The scholar shrugged and jerked her thumb at Kai, who was rubbing his head with a wince. "Do not blame me when he made the offer in the first place."

"That doesn't mean you should sound so eager about it!"

A deep rumble brought the trio's attention back to the stranger, who was bent at the waist laughing himself into a coughing fit. "You three are interesting, if nothing else! You haven't tried killing me yet, even with my injury, so ya can't be all bad." Kai and the others pressed a finger to their lips. "Oh, sorry 'bout that. Guess you never know who's lurking around. But what the hell, I'll let you work your 'pothy magic, on one condition. You gotta promise not to run."

Well, that was unusual. "An odd request, sir, but very well. Just let me grab my sparker and—"

"Here, you can use mine. And another thing, don't ever call me 'sir.' That's my old man. The name's Morgan. Morgan Cauzet." With that, the man flipped a small stone to Kai, who took it with a bow as Ione grabbed a handful of grass. Soon a fire crackled between the four. Morgan stepped into the light with a toothy grin and arms spread wide.

A soft gasp escaped Ione's lips. Lucretia's face turned ashen. Kai quirked an eyebrow, fully understanding what the man meant.

Broad-shouldered, stocky, and muscular, Morgan cut an imposing figure in a burgundy, thigh-length monk's habit and brown trousers. The Cadist garment reminded Kai of his encounter with Duarte. His sandy blonde hair was tied back in a ponytail with a thick, matted beard on his chin. A falchion hung from his sash and, judging by the blood covering the blade, was recently used.

What shocked Kai most was the array of glittering silver scales on Morgan's exposed hands and neck, with several dusty blue feathers protruding from the waist of his habit. Scales and feathers that weren't connected to any type of armor. "You're mixblood? Sodding Nulyma, I thought you said you were from Corlati!"

Morgan chuckled. "Ay, you'd be right about that. My grandfather on mom's side was Wasini if it weren't obvious enough. We don't have too many troubles with the constables in our stretch of the southern coast. Not enough of 'em to care. Though you can probably guess Grandpap wasn't too keen on the law anyways."

That was an understatement. As bad as Norzen were treated, Kai was grateful they weren't hunted like rabid dogs. From the rumors he'd heard, being a mixblood in Corlati was akin to a death sentence if discovered, for both the mixblood in question *and* their entire family.

"I think it is safe to assume you are not with the Federation Army. For that matter, how does a Wasini mixblood happen?" Lucretia asked. Kai wondered the same thing. The Wasini had snake-like tails for their lower bodies, which likely made having *relations* a bit cumbersome.

Morgan leered while pulling a small bottle of golden-brown liquid from his boot. "How do you think, sweetheart?" Lucretia's cry of, "How rude!" only served to make Morgan snicker, a deep rumble emitting from his chest. "Also, a Wasini and human being together isn't too crazy. The parts fit together perfectly fine if a bit awkward." Lucretia and Ione stared in disbelief.

Kai's nose crinkled from the overpowering scent coming from the bottle. He didn't have to be a scholar to know its contents. "Are you sure you should be drinking in your condition? I still need to examine you, after all."

"Bite me."

Kai waggled his pinkie at Morgan. He knew his mother would box his ears for the rude gesture, but he was growing frustrated with the crude mixblood. "I'd rather not. Finyt knows what you rolled around in before we pulled you from the river."

Without a word, Morgan turned and leveled a blank stare at Kai. Ione and Lucretia remained silent. The apothecary heard the tavern maid clasp her hands together, uttering another prayer to Luopari.

"Wha' did you just say, peltneck?" Morgan muttered.

Kai stood tall, meeting the other man's stare with a flippant smirk. "Did I stutter?"

Probably not the most intelligent response, but Kai was fed up with Morgan's brash attitude after the day's events. If he wanted a fight, he'd get one.

The tension was thicker than fog. For what felt like an eternity, nobody moved or spoke. Kai and Morgan faced each other in stony silence while Ione and Lucretia eyed both men. Finally, Morgan fell to his knees and clapped a hand over his mouth to muffle his raucous laughter.

"You...you got some *stones*, 'pothy!" he choked out. Kai scanned the area for any movement.

"I'm going to assume that was a...compliment, I suppose? But if you would please keep quiet, I'll make sure you don't have any festering wounds."

"Very well. Anyone brave enough to say that to my face must be competent. I can respect that," Morgan said, laying back and resting his hands on his stomach.

Kai leaned over the man, inspecting every nick, scratch, and patch of blood with a critical eye. It had been some time since he last examined a mixblood, but he knew enough about Wasini anatomy to be confident in his assessment. "So, what are you doing way out here?" Kai asked. He had a good idea of the reason but wanted to hear it from the source.

Morgan grinned. "I can see it in your eyes, 'pothy. You already know. I'm a sellsword, a blade for hire. The company I worked for was hired to ship weapons for the Liberation Army after the hullabaloo in your capital. It was supposed to be an easy job. Get in, drop the goods, and leave." As he finished speaking, a heavy aura surrounded Morgan. His slumping form exuded an ambiance of pain.

"Supposed to be?" Ione asked.

So she picked up on it too, Kai thought.

"Aye. Things didn't go well. Right after we finished the delivery, we were ambushed." The trio gasped. Betraying a sellsword band never worked out well. Not only would it make hiring another group difficult, but outside companies and even independent sellswords might consider it reason enough to put a bounty on the traitor.

"The Liberators betrayed you?" Lucretia asked. To their shock, Morgan shook his head.

"That's the thing, they got hit as hard as us. Some sort of...animal, I guess. It came out of nowhere and wiped us out. Ugly bugger, too, let me tell you! I only got away cause one of my buddies shoved me in the river before it got me. I think I hit my head on a rock because I can't remember much after that."

Kai paled. "This animal, it didn't happen to look like a massive bear covered in bony plates, did it?"

"Th-that's exactly what it looked like! You saw it too?"

All Kai could do was nod. "Unfortunately. That damned monster wiped out my whole squad. I'm still having a hard time believing everything that's happened. We still don't know what the damned thing is, either."

Morgan pounded his beard with a meaty fist. "Bloody hoarfrost! If I ever see that thing again, I swear I'll kill it. The Scarlet Spears were my brothers in everything but blood."

To Kai's relief, there were no signs of infection. He wrapped the worst of Morgan's injuries. "Let me tell you, you're a lucky man. Those scales probably saved your ass. The good news is, you'll make a full recovery. However, you did lose a decent amount of blood from those cuts. You might feel woozy for a couple days, so get plenty of rest."

Morgan nodded. "Thanks. So where are you three off to? You're a bit of an odd party. And if you think I'll go running back to the Liberation Army, you already know what those bastards will do to me, so don't worry. I'll even swear Sellsword's Honor on it."

Kai was a surprised at the sudden declaration. He met his fair share of sellswords, having worked with a few in the past. To them, swearing their honor on anything was as close to a blood vow as they would go. He avoided looking at Lucretia, who was doing her best to set the Norzen ablaze with her glare.

"That makes sense. They seem to be taking their philosophy straight out of the Corlatian lawbooks. I suppose you could say this is a temporary truce. We're heading for Faith Hollow to resupply and help Lucretia find a boat to Runegard. After that, I'll have to return to Havenfall to warn the Hunter Corps about that monster."

"Makes sense. Sellswords form truces like that more often than you think. You seem like a swell fella, for a Norzen. And I owe you for patching my wounds. Mind if I tag along? Heck, I won't even charge you, same as you did for me."

Lucretia and Ione shared a furtive glance before pulling Kai into a huddle. "Can we trust him, Kai?" Ione whispered.

"We'll have to. For now," the apothecary answered. "Besides, that monster wiped out his comrades, so we at least have a common foe. Having an experienced sellsword could be handy."

"Again, you bring up good points," Lucretia said. "I suppose we shall trust him for the time being. With luck, he will decide what to do by the time we reach the city."

Nodding to each other, the trio turned to face Morgan. He grinned at Kai's extended hand. "Welcome aboard, Morgan. Come morning, we head southeast for Faith Hollow. We'll decide our paths after we arrive, no matter where the winds take us."

Morgan clasped Kai's hand in a firm grip. "Aye. You got yourself a deal, friend."

Such an interesting word. Friend. Hearing it sent a strange prickling sensation through Kai's mind. At times, he thought the concept of friends was like the wind: something you knew was there but couldn't grasp in your fingers. His squad had been the closest thing he'd known to it, but there was always a social barrier between him and the other three.

Hearing the word directed at him from a relative stranger made Kai wonder if the concept was more tangible than he believed.

CHAPTER VI

Overlooking the ruins of Mistport from a nearby hill, Vizent felt a mix of pride and worry stirring in his chest. The battle was long over, but even now his men were extinguishing the largest fires and securing usable supplies. His eyes stopped on a group digging a massive pit in the sandy shores outside of town. From the pile of corpses, Vizent assumed they were preparing a mass grave to burn the dead. It would keep predators from scouring the area for easy food. One specific predator, if the rumors were true.

The invasion was a rousing success from a military perspective: The small town was destroyed, and its inhabitants scattered to the winds. Vizent ordered a small pursuit force to break from the main army and run down the refugees, preventing them from reaching the capital. The longer Whistlevale went without news of the invasion, the better their chances of landing a decisive strike against the Royalists. He still expected them to find out soon, but every second counted at this stage. When facing a superior force, the element of surprise was vital to victory.

Still, he lost more men than expected. According to his officers, the townsfolk barely put up a fight. Most of the resistance came from the town guard, a few ordinary citizens, and the faumen. Clearly, the beasts were prepared to die fighting. That suited the general just fine. It wasn't any fun when the prey made it easy.

Hearing the thud of armored boots, Vizent observed a young captain approaching. His armor looked dirty and dented. A liberal coating of dust covered his cropped hair, and one of his epaulets was missing. The general saw the man's eyes were blazing red and the skin around them looked raw.

The captain came to a stop and saluted, prompting Vizent to return the gesture.

"Sir, Captain Valdis Agosti reporting!" the captain said, his body rigid. Vizent waved for him to continue. "You'll be happy to hear we've nabbed three peltnecks, sir. We also snagged a dozen Aerivolk and several dozen faumen of the other three tribes. They're being loaded into carts as we speak. With that, the east quadrant is secure, and we've acquired plenty of supplies."

"Excellent work, captain," Vizent replied. "Keep this up, and you'll earn your commander's leaves before long. Were there issues? You look a tad scuffed compared to the other officers."

Agosti ground his teeth. The general noticed the other man's hands clenched tight, as if he wanted nothing more than to punch something. "Your observation skills are impressive, General. We were set upon by some unnatural beast during our attempt to secure one of the peltnecks."

Vizent choked on his canteen. "So, the rumors of a monster in the area were true?"

"Aye, General. A great ugly beast. Looked like a starved bear with multiple bones sticking out. Bloody monster tore my men apart and even slaughtered some Hunters we were fighting." Vizent's eyes widened.

"Wait a tic, there were Hunters? Here?" That did *not* bode well.

"Correct, sir," Agosti continued. "They were protecting a peltneck we almost captured when the beast attacked. From what my men say, both were eaten by it."

Vizent held up a hand and snapped, "What do you mean 'both'? Where were the other two?"

"Other two, sir?' Agosti's confusion was evident in his blank stare.

"Bloody Cacovis, man, are you telling me you didn't know Hunters always travel in squads of four!?" Vizent hated invoking the name of the heretic Saint, but he thought it appropriate in the face of such blatant ignorance.

Agosti's face turned grey. "I only saw the two. Other than the Hunters and my men, the only others there were two women they were protecting and...that peltneck!" Vizent would admit he was impressed with Agosti's ability to switch facial colors from porridge grey to tomato red that fast.

"You keep mentioning this Norzen. What happened? Is it among the three you captured?"

The captain let his head droop. "No, sir. As far as I know, this one escaped. He's the one who did this to me after he slapped my face with some red powder. It burned so much; I thought my face was stuck in a smith's kiln! It's strange, though, how the Hunters were so determined to protect that peltneck. And there is one other thing..."

Vizent cocked an eyebrow. "Oh? Do tell."

Agosti raised his head to meet the general's stare, and Vizent saw a mad gleam in his gaze. It was a look he saw in many soldiers during his career, including himself. It was a look of obsession tinged with fury. It could make soldiers brutally efficient. Or a liability.

"This peltneck had something interesting. I'm certain it was a forgery, but even that would be enough to put him on the executioner's block," Agosti explained. He described the object he had seen.

Vizent's face turned pale, snapping his fingers in rapid succession. "Impossible," he whispered. He began pacing back and forth, muttering under his breath and threading a finger through his beard.

It couldn't be, the general thought as he reached into his pocket and extracted a small, warped piece of metal, rolling it along his knuckles like a coin.

Returning the metal to his pocket, he faced Agosti and breathed deep. "This is useful information. The idea of a Norzen carrying that object bears further investigation. However, it does remind me of rumors I in Whistlevale years ago." Upon seeing the curiosity in Agosti's eyes, Vizent pressed on. "Rumors...of a Branded Norzen."

Agosti stomped the ground several times, grinding his boot into the soft dirt with a snarl. "With all due respect, General, that's preposterous! Who would recommend a peltneck for such a prestigious title! That would essentially make it..."

"An official of the Royalist government. I'm aware of the implications, *Captain*," Vizent spat, hissing the other man's rank with apathy. *It couldn't possibly be the same Norzen. Could it?*

A loud cough came from behind, startling both soldiers to spin in place. A newcomer was able to sneak behind them without a sound. Short, and enshrouded in a blood-red cloak, only the figure's youthful face was visible. They stood in a confident stance belying their stature and exuded a familiar aura that put Vizent on edge. He rattled his mind thinking of why he recognized it.

"May we help you?" the general asked.

The man guffawed; a wide grin spread across his face revealing pointed fangs. His ice-blue eyes were fierce and gave Vizent the feeling he was facing a dangerous predator.

"I would certainly hope so, General," the man replied. His voice was velvety and enunciated. Despite his aura, it was clear the man was educated. Either that or he was slicker than fresh lard. "My name is Obram. I come with a message from my employer. You know him as Master Razaar. He would have sent it by carrier hawk but decided to entrust it to me. After all, I'll be traveling with you for the time being. I've also been tasked with relaying reports of your progress."

Vizent's eyes bulged. Now he recognized the aura! It was just like Razaar's, though not as overwhelming as the forge master.

"I see. I must confess, Obram, I'm amazed you arrived so soon after our victory. How did you manage it?" An amused chuckle rumbled from Obram's chest. He explained he was already on a separate mission nearby when he received the missive directing him to join Vizent's army. The man's ominous laughter sent shivers down Vizent's spine. He didn't like the sound of this.

Agosti put himself between the two, reaching for his sword with an imperious sneer. "Do you take us for fools?! I can tell by the look of you. You're a faumen, aren't you? A dirty beast like the rest of them!"

"Stand down, Captain. Even if he is faumen, he works for the man supplying our weapons. Learn some restraint." Despite his steady tone,

Vizent was sweating arrows. Every primal instinct in his body screamed that angering this faumen would be dangerous.

"I don't bloody care who he works for! I refuse to report to some filthy—" Anything else Agosti wanted to say was cut short when Obram struck, sending a brutal backhand to the officer's cheek. The blow blasted Agosti off his feet, sending him careening down the hill. His armor rattled and clanged until he finally hit flat ground. A pitiful groan escaped Agosti's lips, though Vizent noticed a lack of movement.

Obram's cackle reminded the general of a hyena, and his leer gave Vizent the jitters. "I do love putting fools like that in their place. Now, we aren't going to have any additional problems will we, General?"

"Of course not. Please accept my apologies for my subordinate's behavior. It appears I still have a way to go before the men are disciplined enough for this war. Perhaps a moon or two in the vanguard scouts will cool Agosti's temper before it gets him killed."

"You speak with wisdom, General, but your eyes betray you. A man can talk of peace and restraint and still lie. You see it all the time in my trade. The eyes always speak the truth. I see the hate in yours. A burning desire to spill faumen blood. It makes me curious."

Vizent refused to let the other man know how much the words unnerved him. "I have my reasons for why I think this way. However, experience has taught me the importance of choosing my battles. Even if I detest faumen, you and I are still on the same side, strange as that seems. I'm willing to work with you if it helps us achieve our goal."

Obram smirked. "Excellent! I appreciate the candor, my fair-weather friend. It's best to have these things out in the open. By the way—" Vizent's inquisitive glance was enough to spur the odd faumen on, "Master Razarr requested I inform you of some side projects of his you may find interesting. He is developing new weapons to use in the field."

Now Vizent's interest was piqued. "New weapons?"

"Indeed. One of them is absolutely devastating, from what I've heard. The destructive potential alone is enough to leave a hot-blooded warrior like me in tears. Besides, I have some ideas for tactics that I'm certain you'll find delicious."

The general couldn't hide the bloodthirsty grin from spreading across his face. "Now this is interesting. Tell me *everything*, Obram."

Chapter VII

It was times like this when Kai appreciated the calming power of nature.

The northern grasslands of Livoria were vast. Outside of scattered groves, the land was covered in a sea of longgrass surrounding the main roads. The twittering of birds filled the air with a cacophony of soothing chirps and trills. The deep bellow of a bison added a hint of variety. While different from the sounds of home, Kai still basked in the tranquility of the land. The Norzen felt that, for a moment, he could ignore the tension in his gut. Then again, the tension might be from the painful cramps wracking his stomach.

At least they shouldn't have to worry about bandits. He chose this path specifically because it was far off the normal trading routes. That meant less chances to run into bandits looking to prey on travelers and merchants.

Then a deafening belch sent the birds fluttering away, making Kai question all his decisions over the past five days.

"Ugh! Morgan, that was disgusting!" Lucretia shrieked. Ione and Kai shook their heads as the scholar and sellsword devolved into another argument. Despite her obvious distaste for his tribe, Kai found himself feeling a morbid sense of solidarity with Lucretia regarding the mixblood.

Morgan had thus far proven himself rude and crude. He ate more than a feral hog, had no concept of shame, and a nonchalant attitude regarding everything.

Kai was impressed at Lucretia's restraint, surprised that she hadn't stabbed him by now.

"What's the problem, sweetheart?" Morgan brayed. His booming voice carried across the grasslands, something Kai found impressive, yet foolish.

"You really should quiet down, Morgan. What if the Liberation Army finds us?" Ione pleaded. The tavern maid's clothes showed obvious signs of wear. Small cuts covered her skirt, and the bottom button of her dirndl was missing. Kai promised to mend the items once they reached Faith Hollow, to Ione's visible relief.

Morgan slung an arm over the woman's shoulder and laughed. "Come on, you worry too much! There's not a soul for hours, and we're halfway to Faith Hollow. I swear, not even my pappy was as paranoid as you, and he swore for ages the squirrels were out to kill him." The other three shared a dumbfounded look. Squirrels?

Lucretia rubbed her temples in a circular pattern. "I suppose the old saying is true: Fruit never falls too far from the tree." Kai found it hard to disagree.

"Morgan, I understand things were different with your sellsword comrades," Kai said, "but I have to ensure these young ladies' safety. There's also the fact that I've been ill since this morning. If you add a headache onto the pain I'm already in, I'll let Lucretia skewer you."

Morgan's shrug said it all. "I get it, I get it. Aye, you're a cranky one."

Before Kai could comment, a rustle in the grass ahead piqued his interest. Something was moving towards them. Turning his ears forward, he focused. The other three's arguing faded to an irritating buzz he tuned out. Expanding his pupils, he scanned the area in a wide arc. Adjusting his eyes in the sunlight burned, but he ignored the pain.

Then he saw it. A patch of grass moving erratically. Then another off the left. Wincing from another cramp in his gut, he noticed a third patch moving further back to the right. He muttered a curse and gripped his mace.

"Enough!" Kai hissed, prompting the others to turn. "We have visitors, and I don't think they're here to chat." A grim laugh echoed from a scarred Norzen rising from the grass.

"Got it in one, mate," the newcomer said. Dusky-skinned and tall with a roguish smile, he pulled a dagger from his belt, wiping it on his amber mane. "I didn't think there'd be travelers this far out after that shit with the Libbies up north. Guess it's our lucky day, eh, boys?"

Another two Norzen revealed themselves, brandishing daggers of their own. The left one was shirtless and taller with rust-colored fur, a burn mark on his right shoulder, and a savage look. The shorter one had black and white fur, a patch over the left eye, and was so twitchy Kai wondered how he kept ahold of his knife.

Lucretia frowned, turning her eyes on Kai. "What do they mean 'mate?' Do you know these brutes?!"

The middle Norzen smirked. "We Norzen gotta stick together, don't we? Now, if you don't mind, we'll take the women and your valuables and be on our way. Nobody has to get hurt. Not yet anyway." The men leered at Ione and Lucretia in a way that made the Kai's skin crawl.

And here I thought we'd be able to avoid bandits by going out this way. I guess I should've expected them to make the same move to avoid the Libbies. Rookie mistake, Kai berated himself.

The apothecary hummed, giving the bandits a sideways glance. He bit back a wince at the tightening in his stomach. "Let me think. Alright, I thought about it, and you can all fuck off. I'm no friend of yours."

The middle Norzen stared at Kai with his eyes half open, as if unable to comprehend what he heard. "Excuse me, what did you just say? Who in bloody Nulyma do you think you are?" The man's body trembled, his nostrils flaring as he fingered the dagger in his clutches.

"Let me make it so even a brainless oaf like you can understand. Leave or die. I'm not one to condone killing, but you caught me on a bad day. And he's probably as dangerous than I am," Kai replied, jerking his thumb back at Morgan, who drew his falchion with a grin.

"Hoarfrost, I've been spoiling for a good fight!" Morgan shouted. His clanged the side of his blade against a nearby boulder, his smile threatening to split his face in half.

The bandits brandished their weapons, eager to accept Morgan's challenge. In response, Kai drew his mace and slid into a stance. "Don't be stupid," the rust colored Norzen said, inching himself around the group's flank. "You don't look well, and we ain't afraid of some piddling chimera. Hell, the Libbies might reward us for bringing that creature in."

"If you truly believe that," Ki sighed, "then you're dumber than I imagined."

The smallest bandit piped up, "What did you say, ya damned traitor?!"

"If you waltzed into a Liberator camp with a mixblood, you'd all be tied up and sold to the highest bidder. Those bastards are paying their soldiers 30 golds a head for any captured Norzen. You'd be better off avoiding them until the war ends."

"Listen here, bastard. We ain't leaving without loot!" the leader shouted. He rushed Kai, tucking the dagger close to his body before thrusting it at the hunter's heart.

Kai threw his satchel behind him and sidestepped. He landed a solid punch to the bandit's gut, staggering him. Ione grabbed the satchel and the women ducked behind a boulder. Kai clutched at his chest with a hiss. That gave his opponent the confidence to lunge again.

I can't afford to waste time here, Kai thought, ducking beneath another stab. He found himself cursing his breakfast as it threatened to come back up with another wave of cramping.

He was thrown off-balance when his foot dropped into a rabbit burrow. The bandit pivoted and slammed a boot into Kai's chest. The apothecary tumbled backwards and felt the air knocked from his lungs. The bandit leaped, pinning Kai down. He jerked his head aside, feeling the dagger's blade on his cheek before it dug into the dirt. Kai drove his knee into the bandit's groin, grabbing hold of the man's leather cuirass and throwing him off.

Looking over, he saw the other two bandits engaging Morgan and proving to be more of a challenge than expected. The larger Norzen parried Morgan's blade with a deftness that contradicted his bulk. The smaller one darted in and out, landing sweeping cuts on Morgan's arms and sides when he could. The only reason Morgan remained standing was because the scales beneath his habit prevented the daggers from drawing blood.

He parried a stab from the larger bandit but lost sight of the small one until he was stabbed behind the calf. Before Kai could rush to help, Morgan reached out and caught the small Norzen by the mane. With a devilish smirk, Morgan pivoted on his good leg, swinging the startled bandit like a club into his larger comrade. Both hit the dirt in a pile. His jubilation was short-lived, however, when he dropped to his knees after putting weight on the injured leg.

Ione scrambled through the group's packs with tears in her eyes, muttering a prayer that there was *anything* that could help. She pulled a small bundle from Morgan's pack, gave it a shake, and tossed it aside. The paper fell open on impact, revealing a small cylinder. Lucretia saw the object and picked it up, smirking. "Ione, wait," she whispered, grabbing the other woman's shoulder. "We can use this!"

The tavern maid turned, her eyes widening when she realized what they had found: a small firework. Tearing open the bundle she tossed, the ladies discovered a pile of tiny explosives. "Gracious, what are these doing in Morgan's pack?" Ione queried.

Lucretia shrugged, pulling a sparkstone from her pouch. "We can ask later. These will not cause damage to buildings or heavy armor, but they are certainly more than enough to harm a pack of bandits."

"What should we do with them?"

"Quite simple. Those brutes are too occupied with the men to think about us. I believe shoving these in a hard-to-reach place will distract them enough for them to explode and put them down. I will assist Morgan and you handle Kai. It that acceptable?"

Ione frowned, knowing the real reason Lucretia chose to help Morgan. Deciding to stay silent, she took the offered firework with a single nod.

After a few failed attempts, Ione's firework was lit and the women split up, rushing into the fight.

Kai lay on the ground, knocked on his back again by the bandit leader as the pain in his stomach burned. The apothecary's movements were sluggish, unable to keep up with the bandit's relentless attacks. His vest and tunic were tattered and bloody from numerous cuts.

"Give up," the bandit snarled. "I'd rather not kill a fellow Norzen, but if you keep fighting, I'll slit your damned throat right now!"

Kai felt the pressure on his chest ease as the bandit was thrown off. He eased himself up and saw the bandit spinning in circles with Ione holding onto his back and beating a fist against his head. The woman had taken a running leap onto the bandit's back, knocking him over. Ione grabbed the man's cuirass and tunic with one hand and pulled back, stuffing the lit firework inside. She threw herself off the bandit's back, curling into a roll as she hit the ground.

The Norzen growled, stalking Ione with murder in his eyes. Kai struggled to get back on his feet, watching the tavern maid scramble backwards.

He saw her reaching behind the boulder, where their packs lay. Ione's arm swung around moments later, revealing her pan. She raised it behind her shoulder, ready to swing. The bandit leader stared for scant moments before bursting into laughter.

"Wha-what in bloody Finyt are you going to do with *that*?" he taunted, pointing his dagger at the woman. "You gonna cook me dinner tonight, sweetheart? Sorry, but you need a real weapon if you want to take me on! Oh Nulyma, my side hurts!" The bandit descended into hysterical cackling, tears streaming from his eyes. He was so distracted by Ione's weapon, that he failed to notice Kai retrieving his mace while tucking his ears down. The bandit, bent at the waist and clutching his sides, also missed the firework's prickling sparks.

At least until the firework exploded against his bare back.

The bandit was launched face-first into the dirt, roaring in pain. His two comrades spun towards the blast, taking their eyes off Morgan and the approaching Lucretia.

She tossed a firework with a cut fuse to the sellsword while gesturing to the bandits. Morgan grinned and followed the scholar's lead in sneaking behind the pair. A couple strikes of the sparker, and both fuses hissed. Seconds later, they rolled the fireworks just in front of the bandits' feet.

"Boss, you okay!?" the smaller Norzen called out. "What did those bastards d—" Twin explosions at their feet cut the man off, pitching them both backwards. Lucretia drew her rapier and, hooking her arm around the smaller Norzen's neck, rammed the blade through his heart.

Morgan swept the taller Norzen's feet out from underneath and stomped down with his boot to pin the bandit down. The falchion flashed through the air, decapitating the prone man before he could react.

The bandit leader saw his comrades fall and bellowed. The amber furred Norzen dashed for Ione, aiming his dagger at her chest.

Ione steeled herself meet the bandit head-on, only for Kai to appear from the side, smashing his mace into the man's hip with a heavy crack. There was no doubt; the bone was pulverized. The bandit collapsed in a screaming heap. His attempts to get back up left him crying and grasping his shattered hip. Ione reeled back and put all her weight into a downward swing. A deafening clang resounded as the flat side of the pan hammered the bandit's face into the dirt, rendering him immobile.

Kai inched forward at a snail's pace, holding a hand to his pained stomach. Prodding the bandit with his foot, Kai noticed blood pouring from the head wound. The apothecary chuckled, threading his fingers through his mane. His eyes flickered to Ione, but he couldn't maintain eye contact for more than a few seconds. Finally, Ione rushed forward and threw her arms around the surprised Norzen, weeping into his shoulder.

Kai was unsure how to proceed. He couldn't remember ever being hugged by anyone outside of his family. Gazing at the sobbing Ione, he glanced at Morgan and Lucretia. The former was giving him a sly smirk, while the latter pierced him with a frosty glare. He finally settled for patting the woman's back, her tears soaking into his mane. Whenever water got into his fur, it felt itchy and irritating. For some reason, though, it didn't feel that way now.

"I'm glad you're alright," she whispered.

"Thank you, Ione," Kai replied. Pulling away, he gave the woman a quick check for injuries. "Remind me to never brass you off. With a swing like that, you'd be a natural at paddlepod," he quipped. He was never allowed to play Livoria's national sport much as a child, being excluded by the other kids. But he still enjoyed watching a game on occasion.

Lucretia laughed and agreed with Kai, for once. "Indeed. I daresay even Her Grace's legendary Exarch Knights would hesitate taking a blow like that." Kai quirked an eyebrow.

Ione stood there blinking for some moments before she started giggling as well. "Aw shucks, I pray I'd never find myself fighting an Exarch. They're the best warriors in Her Grace's service for a reason! To be honest, I've never felt that angry about anything in my life. Still, that bastard was trying to *kill* you. I couldn't just sit by and do nothing."

The four travelers mulled over their shared experience. Kai found it odd the bandits were out this far but decided it was a case of being in the right place at the wrong time.

Come to think of it, he thought, *Marko mentioned most of the Norzen thieving bands were laying low to avoid the Libbies.*

Morgan wiped his blade off on the taller Norzen's trousers and sheathed it. "Well, that was a pain in the scales. Where do we go from here?"

"By the way Morgan," said Ione, "why did you have those fireworks in your pack?"

Scratching his beard, Morgan gave a hesitant chuckle. "Believe it or not, some of my buddies put those there. They liked playing with fireworks, but they aren't allowed when we're on a job and the company commander almost caught them with a bunch. They ended up stashing a few in my pack to get them past the commander. Anyways, thanks for saving our butts back there. You girls are damned tough."

Kai paced in a slow circle, tired eyes peering upwards every few moments. Referring to the map, he conferred with Lucretia to verify their position before pointing to the right. "That way. We're not far from the Guaca River. We'll refill our canteens and wash up before crossing underground." His arm shook with every word. It was clear his muscles weren't holding up in his weakened state.

"Underground?" Ione asked, her eyebrows rising as she surveyed the map.

"There's a labyrinth of abandoned mine tunnels running beneath the Guaca," Lucretia explained. "Some were used to transport materials from one side of the river to the other without needing to build a bridge. We can use one of those to cross."

Morgan scratched his head with a half-lidded stare. "Uhm, how will we know which tunnel to take? Won't they all look the same?"

"The transport tunnels are marked and go from one end to the other in a straight line. Ever since the mines were abandoned, travelers and merchants use them as shortcuts."

After securing the map, Kai began marching, slowed by a falter in his steps. Ione reached over and grabbed the apothecary by his mane. Before Kai could respond, he was yanked back with a yelp and forced onto a boulder. Ione's blazing eyes burrowed into his own.

"We're not going anywhere until you're healthy again," Ione seethed. Even without yelling, her voice carried an edge that made it clear arguing wasn't an option.

Kai ignored Morgan's wild gesturing to keep quiet. "But we need to—" An instant later, he was staring down the edge of Ione's pan. The utensil was close enough for Kai to make out the metal's texture and scent.

"What we need is to make sure our guide doesn't drop dead from whatever's made him so sick. Therefore, we're staying right here until you feel better. Now sit! Unless you'd prefer to take a kip the hard way," she finished, tapping Kai on the head.

If the wicked gleam in Lucretia's eyes wasn't enough of a hint, Kai's instincts screamed that Ione wouldn't hesitate to follow through on that threat. So, in blatant self-preservation, he opted to avoid angering the tavern maid any further.

"Yes ma'am."

Chapter VIII

F usette clenched her teeth to prevent the yawn in her throat from escaping. Growing up, she knew the daughter of a noble family who loved saying a particular phrase.

"It's such an honor to lead our nation. It must be so much fun!"

Fusette couldn't remember the girl's name, though her face remained clear as day in her memories. Remembering names was never her strength unless she saw someone on a consistent basis, or they made a significant impression on her. She never forgot anyone's face, though.

As for the girl's declarations, Fusette realized something since her ascension eight years ago: They were utter balderdash, made from either blissful ignorance or optimistic hope. As far as Fusette was concerned, being Grand Duchess of Livoria was most certainly *not* fun!

And the last past several moons beat that fact into her skull more than anything. If she ever remembered which family the girl belonged to, Fusette would have to be restrained from throttling the girl with her own ribbon!

It was times like this she was grateful for the open expanse of the throne room. The ample space kept a steady temperature, a godsend in the balmy Livorian weather. Examining her everyday wear, she appreciated it more. The full body silken robe was breathable but stuck to her body if she was outside for too long. And the cotton cowl covered her entire head except for the face and fringes of her obsidian hair. She found herself wishing she could let her hair flow free instead of keeping it tucked in a cowl all day.

Remain calm, Fusette reminded herself while curling her locks around a thin, dainty finger. *Remember your training. Pride is a ruler's greatest vice.*

Her thoughts were interrupted by the doors bursting open to reveal an older man scampering across the marble floor. The intricate vestment adorning his thin body marked him as a high-ranking cleric in the Order of the Windbringers: The Archbishop, in fact. A scarlet stole lined in cream was draped around his shoulders. Seeing the stole made Fusette's heart swell and brought cherished memories of the man forward. Few men in the church claimed Vadako the Maiden as their patron. As the Wind Saint associated with marriage and the home, she was a popular choice among young women. But she was also the Saint of Generosity, and those who devoted themselves to her were often adamant caretakers of the less fortunate.

While Fusette, as Grand Duchess, was required to follow the teachings of Galen, she felt a distinct kinship with Vadako. One that was missing in her prayers to the Sage.

The bishop's labored breathing shook Fusette from her thoughts as she sauntered forth. "Archbishop Jovanni, whatever is the trouble? You shouldn't be running at your age," she said with a calm, collected voice.

"Oh posh, Your Grace," the old man retorted. "I may be, what is it now, 64? Bah, the days start blending like stew after a while. I still got some pep in these old bones when I need it. I used to run every which way back in my days as a bard." His voice, while heavy, carried a fire that belied his many years.

Fusette giggled. "I see. Now, what's going on? You wouldn't be running for no reason."

"Piddlewick, I almost forgot! An ambassador from Galstein has arrived and is requesting an audience. He says it's regarding the war."

The duchess's breath hitched. An ambassador from Galstein? After the incident that started everything, the thought of a Galstan emissary brought trepidation. How would they react? What would they demand in retribution? Still, it would be rude to keep him waiting. Travel from the

Galstan capital of Rosenholm to Whistlevale was not quick or easy, so for him to arrive so suddenly there must be a reason.

"Very well. Instruct the guards to lead him in. I don't wish to waste any time, Jovanni."

"As you command, Your Grace." Without another word, the spry old man retreated from the room.

This gave Fusette time to think of how to proceed. Given the abrupt request, she thought it best to let the envoy speak first. Once he delivered his message, she could determine the best way to smooth things over. The last thing her people needed was another side rising in the war. Livoria would be doomed having to fight on two fronts.

After a time, a sharp rap echoed. Fusette gave the guards a single nod, prompting them to open the door. Clacking footsteps echoed through the cavernous room as the ambassador made their way forwards. Fusette couldn't help but gape.

All things considered, Fusette was stunned to see Queen Isolde sent an Aerivolk as her envoy. Tall for his tribe, the man wore a well-tailored smoke-grey vest with a deep golden sash wrapped across the body. The sash's color showed he belonged to Galstein's Foreign Ministry. Below the waist, he wore a long silken burgundy kilt. Quite a difference from the traditional woolen garment Livorian Aerivolk wore, but one Fusette attributed to his job. He kept his black-feathered wings crossed in the front, giving the impression of an ebony cloak. A pair of bone horn-rimmed spectacles rested on his nose. As the ambassador approached, he dropped to one knee and bowed, speaking in a sharp, modulated voice.

"Greetings, Your Grace. I am thankful for this chance to speak with you. My name is Hanblum, of the Canton of Envoys. I have been sent to discuss, and perhaps reaffirm, our alliance in the wake of this war.

Fusette fought an urge to exhale in relief. If Hanblum was here to reaffirm the alliance, then there was still hope for them yet.

"This is wonderful news indeed, Sir Hanblum. I confess I was surprised by your sudden arrival. Had we known you were coming; I would've been better prepared."

"Please accept my apologies. Her Majesty opted for swift action, and so we failed to send word ahead of time. There have been rumors that the Liberation Army has invaded eastern Livoria. What information do you have?"

Fusette fiddled with her chartreuse robes, soothed by their softness. "I'm afraid I don't have much information yet. Our scouts report the invasion began at a northern village named Mistport. After ransacking the town, they traveled further east."

Hanblum rose, cocking his head to the side. "East? Such an odd path. We were under the impression they wanted to besiege the capital."

"We believed the same. However, their soldiers are inexperienced and undisciplined. My admirals think they plan to train up their forces before attempting an attack on Whistlevale."

"That makes sense. The Livorian Navy is much more skilled compared to the Liberators' fresh troops." The man's eyes glimmered with clear mischief.

Fusette smirked, waving off the compliment. "Flattery shall get you nowhere, Sir Hanblum. I'm aware our forces are a tad out of practice after so many years of peace. However, there have been other, disturbing reports coming out of Mistport."

"What reports?" Hanblum's question was simple, yet his voice was laced with concern.

"There was some sort of monster involved. Something never seen before. Even worse, the same scouts who told me this confirmed a squad of Hunters was also there."

Hanblum's expression shifted to befuddlement. "Hunters?" the ambassador queried, "there were Hunters that defected to the Liberators?"

Fusette shook her head. "No, thank the Saints. The squad in question was investigating a series of deaths in the area when the invasion occurred. Sadly, the scouts confirmed that three Hunters died in the attack, slaughtered by the aforementioned monster."

"How certain are they? And what was the fate of the last Hunter?"

"Very much so. Bits and pieces of the dead Hunters were strewn about the area, including their shredded identity markers. As for the final one, they either escaped or were devoured. We sent a request to Havenfall to determine which squad was there."

Hanblum nodded, pulling a thin pipe from his pocket. "Terrible news, in any case. Do you mind if I smoke? This has been a harrowing tale and I find that the fumes calm my nerves."

At Fusette's nod, the Aerivolk lit up, taking a quick puff. "Now, I'd like to discuss relations between our nations."

There it is, Fusette thought. The real reason for Hanblum's visit.

"I assure you the people of Livoria are committed more than ever to maintaining peace and goodwill between our realms," Fusette soothed. "The Eastern Alezonian Alliance has been alive for three hundred years, and I would see it continue for three hundred more, if not longer! What happened was horrendous and we are striving ensure any future visits by Queen Isolde's representatives will be safe."

Hanblum adjusted his spectacles and eased the nervous Fusette with a glowing smile. "I believe you, and so does Her Majesty. Gerhardt Falber was a good man, an amazing Minister of Trade, and a close friend. I admit we were stunned when the one implicated in his murder was an Aerivolk—"

"You're not the only one. Pardon my interruption, but I feel there is more to that situation than meets the eye."

"Your Grace, are you saying you believe there was an accomplice, or someone backing the murderer?"

Fusette mulled over her next words, but decided it was better to get her theories in the open. "Either Ambroz had support or, in a worst-case situation, he's innocent of everything and being framed by someone trying to break the Alliance."

Hanblum's eyebrows rose into his hairline. "By the winds, do you believe it possible? The real question, if it were true, is why."

"There are more than a few groups here and across our borders that could benefit from the Alliance fracturing. It doesn't help that the Liberation Army formed immediately following Ambroz's arrest. I knew the anti-faumen faction in Livoria was growing brazen, but I never believed them organized enough to put together a functioning army this fast."

Fusette's mind flashed through several possibilities behind the rise of the Liberation Army, but each was more ridiculous than the last. She knew several guilds, and their masters, which had reasons for wanting the Alliance to fail. But she couldn't imagine them capable of murdering a high-ranking Galstan nobleman without her scouts' knowledge. "Regardless of who is ultimately responsible," she continued, "we must stand strong together going forward. The Liberation Army is disjointed, but they are passionate about their cause, and that alone makes them dangerous."

Hanblum took a deep draw from his pipe. Fusette caught the scent of lavender in the smoke and felt a sense of calm permeate the air. "You are correct, Your Grace. As a predominately faumen nation, Galstein has a vested interest in making sure the Liberation Army doesn't assume control of Livoria. Their political stance on the tribes would make the Alliance impossible. Therefore, we are willing to provide military support to the Livorian Navy."

Relief washed over Fusette like a wave, filling her chest with a hope she hadn't felt since the war started. "That is wonderful news! Thank you—"

"However," Suddenly, that burgeoning hope felt squashed, flattened under a sense of impending unease. "As a gesture of good faith, Her Majesty wants to see your troops accomplish a major military victory against the Liberation Army within the next moon. It has been almost three hundred years since Livoria's last true war, after all. If you can prove your forces capable of fighting the enemy on even ground, then the Holy Queendom of Galstein shall aid you."

Fusette pondered the condition and felt her hope restored. While several senior officers defected, she still had plenty of capable sailors under her command. Plus, there was always the Exarch Knights and the full might of the Hunter Corps.

It might be time to bring them into the fray, she thought. "I will agree to your terms, Sir Hanblum. I appreciate your candor in these matters."

"Excellent! I look forward to hearing the bells of victory. Now, Her Majesty has requested I take up residence here, serving as her representative within Livoria. Once you fulfill your end of the bargain, I shall alert Rosenholm by carrier hawk."

Before Fusette could reply, the door burst open once more. A guard rushed forward, his face caked in sweat and chest heaving. A regal speckled hawk sat upon his shoulder; a furled scroll tied to its leg with a black ribbon. The bird fluttered away the moment it was relieved of its burden. "Many apologies for interrupting, Your Grace! However, this carrier hawk arrived with an urgent message. I was instructed by the Lord Chamberlain to bring it to you at once!"

Taking the offered scroll, Fusette rested a hand on the guard's shoulder. "You have nothing to apologize for. I can see you're tired, but I do one last request. After I review this, I would like you to arrange quarters for Sir Hanblum. He shall be our guest for the near future."

The guard kneeled with a sigh of relief. Fusette opened the parchment and began reading. Most of it contained repetitive information from previous reports. However, there was a series of notes near the bottom she was hoping for.

So, they found the Hunter squad was assigned to Mistport. So, who was it? Oh, now this will be interesting.

Fusette couldn't contain her mirth as she tittered. The two men looked at the duchess with trepidation. "Your Grace, may I ask what you find so amusing?" Hanblum inquired.

"I don't know about amusing, but it could have a visible impact on the war. We've learned the identity of the missing Hunter from Mistport, and it's one of the few names I truly remember, if only because this Hunter is rather extraordinary. If he's still alive, the Liberators have made a dangerous enemy. In fact, I think it's time I made a trip. Guard!"

The armored man stood and snapped a salute. "Fetch Saredi," she commanded. "He will accompany me on this journey." The guard left the room at a brisk march, leaving Fusette and Hanblum alone.

Several emotions crossed the envoy's face. "Saredi? A trip?"

"Saredi Bastion. My Lord Chamberlain, and head of the palace staff. He's also my chief advisor, and makes a fair bodyguard as well. Enough so that I would entrust him with my life."

"Your Grace, where in Finyt do you plan to go during a war? Would it not be better to stay where it's safe?"

"I could, but my duty is to my people. I must do what's necessary to protect Livoria. My instincts say the rivers run swift, and we require more information. We shall depart for Runegard and conscript the help of the Citadel's scholars. While not warriors, they will make fine tacticians. Not to mention, the library there contains certain tomes I wish to consult. One-of-a-kind volumes not housed in the palace archives. With luck, the winds may guide me to our wayward Hunter along the way."

"Milady am I to understand we are leaving?" a voice rang out, low and confident. Fusette turned to face the newcomer, a Vesikoi man in his 30s with slicked back ebony hair and ocean-blue eyes. He wore a pressed charcoal uniform suit with a white ruffled shirt. Like most Vesikoi, the skin at the front of his body was a pale ivory. The back of his neck exposed a darker, muddy green toned.

"That is correct, Saredi," Fusette answered. "We are leaving for Runegard first thing in the morning. I trust you to arrange the necessities."

"It shall be done, Your Grace." Saredi bowed and introduced himself to Hanblum before leaving to carry out his orders.

It was evident that Fusette would not be stopped. Her features burned with an intense willpower, eyes blazing and focused. Hanblum gave a deep bow.

"If this is how you feel, then I shall wish you safe travels," Hanblum demurred, "Do try to avoid anything too dangerous. Livoria needs you now, more than ever."

Fusette clasped her hands together in prayer and returned the bow in kind. "Many thanks, Sir Hanblum. Saints willing, we will return with good news. May the winds of fortune guide you."

"May the Wind Saints protect you from harm, Your Grace."

CHAPTER IX

F ollowing the bandit incident, the party decided to rest for the remainder of the day. Kai told the others his stomach cramps, while gone for
now, were an occasional affliction he coped with for years. In setting up
camp, the work was divided equally, to ensure everyone contributed.

Kai focused on wrapping everyone's wounds and preparing herbs for
tea and poultices. Morgan rigged a fishing pole and hauled in some perch
from a nearby creek. Ione dressed the fish, using a dagger taken from one
of the bandits, and fried them with some of Kai's herbs for flavor. Lastly,
Lucretia set up the tents and gathered firewood from a nearby grove.
During the night, Morgan offered Ione some tips on how to wield her new
dagger. Kai held a small board in his hand, scratching away with a pencil.

By morning, they were refreshed and ready for anything the world could
throw at them.

After another day of travel, the Guaca River was in sight. While not as
big as other rivers cutting through the grasslands, it marked a major point
on the path to Faith Hollow. The grasses along the river were shorter and
smoother compared to those near Mistport.

The groves had given way to scattered fruit orchards, providing shade
from and the occasional bounty of apples. While this made it easier to
see, it also meant they could be spotted.

The party sat at the base of a small hill, basking in the shade of an apple
orchard while Lucretia studied the map. "Well, I have good news," she
said, a rare smile gracing her lips.

"Finally!" Morgan crowed while taking a large bite from an apple. "It's
about bloody time we got some good news. Uh, what kind of good news?"

Lucretia rolled her eyes, not caring about the hurt look on Morgan's face. Gesturing to the map, she pointed out a red mark indicating a transport tunnel. Several similar red marks were dotted along the river. The scholar explained the mark lining up with a sloping path ahead.

Made of trampled grass, the 'path' was like many others they encountered in the grasslands, created from sheer use over the years rather than an active feat of engineering. It reminded Kai of paths he'd seen made by forest-dwelling animals.

"Perfect. Once we cross the river, it's only another three days to Faith Hollow, depending on how much ground we cover," Kai said. He pushed himself up and stretched until a loud pop was heard. "Oh, by Tapimor, that felt good!"

Stifling a giggle, Ione gathered her cooking gear. Grasping her dagger, she shooed away a small squirrel scurrying about the fire.

"That sounded painful, Kai. Did you break anything?" she asked with a mischievous grin.

"Nah. Believe me, if anything snapped, you'd hear about it. No shame in admitting I pitched a fit when I broke a foot back in my rambunctious youth; fell out of a tree and landed crooked."

Lucretia snorted. She poured some water into her hand and splashed it over the back of her neck. Even though it was well into autumn, the heat from the sun was strong. "Are you admitting you were a little hellion?"

Taking a moment to swivel his ears, Kai heard the chattering of birds as he threw his satchel over one shoulder. "I don't know about a hellion, but I had a reputation, to hear the villagers talk. I blame Da. He would goad me into sneaking around the woods behind Ma's back when I wasn't supposed to."

Kai began walking further into the grove. "Oy, you're not cutting out on us, are ya, 'pothy?" Morgan quipped, using a small knife to pick his teeth.

"Nah, just need to use the privy before we move on, and I'm sure you lot don't want to see that."

"Point taken," Morgan conceded. Both men ignored Lucretia's look of disgust. "If you're not back in, let's say ten, I'm dragging you back whether your trousers are up or not."

Ione fell over in hysterics while Lucretia slapped the cackling sellsword on the shoulder. "Must you be so crude!" she shouted. "The last thing I ever wish to see is that man's furry backside!" Lucretia chased Morgan around the camp, beating him on the head and shoulders.

Kai chuckled, marching away from the clamor of his companions. Once the noise dipped to a manageable level, he dropped his satchel against a tree and settled into a mass of bushes several yards away to conduct his business.

The sound of rustling trees grew louder. Kai's ears twitched, turning towards the trees. Hearing a soft chittering, he tuned the noise out, attributing the rustling to squirrels. Tapimor knows he saw enough of the little blighters following them, begging for scraps. Once done, he filled in his hole, set himself to rights, and turned to grab his satchel.

Only to see nothing at the tree's base. The satchel was gone.

Scratching his head, Kai scanned the area for his wayward bag. He couldn't afford to lose that satchel, and not just because it held his medical supplies. Rather than wallow in anger, he wondered if one of the others was pulling a prank. He wouldn't put it past Morgan; the Wasini mixblood seemed the type who would be right at home in the fool's trade.

Kai's ears pivoted to the sides as he focused on identifying each of the noises around him. There was a whistling coming from all sides. *The wind,* he told himself. A squeaking chorus coming from the branches above. *Squirrels.* A variety of chirps, squawks, and musical twitters. *Birds. A lot of birds.* A soft trilling giggle followed by humming rising from the bushes...

Wait, what?

It was unlike any sound Kai ever heard. The laugh was too high pitched to be Ione or Lucretia. He already recognized the timbre of their voices. This was too... musical. The humming had a soothing lilt that could lull one to sleep. It reminded him of the days his mother would hum a tune while they worked the family garden together.

Rather than alert the others and risk letting the stranger escape, Kai rested a hand on his mace while stalking forward. The apothecary moved over the grass like a spirit. The closer he crept, the more pronounced the humming became. In the back of his mind, something about the melody felt calming. Soon, he was close enough to touch the foliage. The surrounding noise was reduced to a mere buzz. Kai raised his arm and stepped forward, ready to swing.

The crack of a twig was his only warning before a pressure tightened around his ankle, yanking his feet out from beneath him. Kai's face hit the grass with a startled yelp. He jerked his leg back on instinct and felt the pressure vanish. Looking back, he noticed a thin rope wrapped around his ankle.

Now Kai was brassed off. How in Finyt did he make such a rookie blunder? He hauled himself up and spun around, hearing movement from the bush.

A flash of yellow filled his vision before something smashed into his chest, sending him flying onto his back.

A pained groan escaped Kai at the unexpected weight, and several sharp pinches digging into his ribs made him pause. His assailant had claws. There was also the sharp point of some sort of blade pressed against his neck to be concerned about. He heard the same soft giggle that captured his attention in the first place.

"Hiya!" an excited, feminine voice rang out with a mountain drawl. "What ya doing all the way out here?"

As much as he wanted to lie there berating himself, Kai knew he was not in a good position. Instead, he decided to open his eyes and see who got the drop on him.

Violet. The first thing Kai saw was a pair of shining violet eyes boring into his soul. They were so close he could see nothing else, not even the pointed nose brushed up against his own. But the eyes carried no malice, only curiosity and an excitement Kai found intriguing. The eyes blinked. He blinked back.

The newcomer leaned up, and Kai got a full view of his assailant: a female Aerivolk, around his own age. That explained the pinching. A quick glance confirmed her talons clutching his sides firmly but not deep enough to draw blood.

A pair of broad wings growing from behind her arms, the most distinct feature of Aerivolk, were raised and quivering. An arrow was gripped in one hand, which explained the pointed object she had on his neck before. Kai wondered if she was frightened. However, the smile splitting her face was too jubilant for the shaking to be anything but excitement. Her feathers were a blinding shade of lemon, deepening to ochre at the tips. Compared to Locke back in Mistport, Kai noticed her feathers possessed a glowing sheen. Her dorsal feathers curved up from the temple like fluffy horns.

Her clothing looked basic and handwoven; a woolen brown shirt and thin skirt, both with frayed fur sewn along the bottom, with a wide sash draped around her bare shoulders. Just over the left breast, poking from underneath her shirt, Kai noticed a large branching scar. A glimmer from her legs drew his attention to a pair of spike-lined greaves strapped to her shins. The apothecary shuddered at the thought of being kicked with those.

Taen! Kai cursed in his mind. *I can't let anyone back home know I got my bell rung by an Aerivolk. Serafina would never stop laughing!* A pleased chirp came from the woman, who was prodding the vials hooked to Kai's vest.

"It's been a while since I last saw a Norzen," she said. "These are herbs, aren't they? What are they for? Did you buy them? Or do you pick them yourself? Are you selling them?" The questions came faster than lightning. Kai was impressed at her ability to rattle them off without catching her breath.

Kai answered the questions one at a time. The moment he mentioned using the herbs in his apothecary work, the woman's eyes shone like lighthouse beacons.

How does she do that? Those eyes can blind someone!

"An apothecary? I ain't ever met a Norzen apothecary before. This is exciting!" Her feathers were quivering more than ever. "Oh, Finyt, I'm so rude!" she exclaimed, striking a palm on her forehead.

Kai looked down, noting her position. *Yeah, knocking someone over and sitting on them* does *seem a touch rude*, he thought.

She stammered out a quick apology for swiping Kai's satchel, admitting she was worried he might be a bandit. "A lady's gotta protect herself nowadays, with the Libbies and bandits running around. I haven't even introduced myself. The name's Maplyne, but everyone calls me Maple. I'm gonna be the most beloved merchant in all Alezon!"

"Uh, I'm Kaigo Travaldi. You can call me Kai."

"Travaldi? That sounds familiar, and it's rare to see a Norzen with a family name. My, you're just full of surprises, ain't ya?" Maple teased, her eyes glinting.

"That's me, the village oddball," Kai grumbled, though something felt strange. He already heard every backhanded comment imaginable. It was a daily occurrence for most Norzen outside Duskmarsh. But for some reason, his gut told him Maple wasn't being malicious about it. She just seemed too damned happy to be that cruel.

A pricking in his side reminded Kai of exactly *where* and *how* Maple was perched. His face flushed scarlet as he propped himself on his elbows. "Uh, Maple? Would you mind letting me up? I need to get back—"

Kai's blood froze when Morgan's voice boomed from nearby. "Oy, Kai! You fall in the hole, you damned fool!?" Before Kai could move, all three of his companions emerged from the trees, stopping cold at the sight. To her credit, Maple regarded the new faces with a chipper smile and a wave.

Ione let out a horrified squeak and covered her eyes, turning away from the pair. Morgan collapsed against a tree, banging his fist against the trunk and crowing with laughter. Lucretia stood still as a statue, one eye twitching. With practiced ease, she drew her rapier and fingered the blade, all the while piercing Kai with a deadly glare.

"You are supposed to be protecting us on this journey," she snapped with an edge in her voice, "and yet here we find you, assaulting an innocent Aerivolk girl!"

Kai raised both palms up, facing out. "I've done nothing of the sort! In my defense, *she* got the drop on *me*!" He hated admitting to being caught by surprise, but embarrassment was preferable to death.

Maple hopped off Kai's chest with a giggle, allowing him to take a needed gulp of air. "It's true," she confessed. "I thought he might be a bandit, so I snatched his satchel to see if he was carrying anything dangerous. I didn't know he was in a traveling party."

To prove her point, she returned to the bush and pulled the missing satchel out. She removed a bundle of appleberries before tossing it to the prone Norzen.

"I was going to eat those," Kai groaned. Maple replied that she couldn't help herself; appleberries were her favorite. Thinking about it, Kai shrugged and told her to enjoy them. She squealed in joy, embracing the Norzen with her wings.

A long-winded sigh came from Lucretia. She sheathed her rapier and gave Kai a pointed stare. "Very well, you have avoided a skewering. For now. Grab your gear. We will set up camp for the evening and cross the river at first light." Without waiting, Lucretia spun around and stomped away. Morgan and Ione followed in her wake, each flashing Kai a smirk.

Maple tilted her head to the side, frowning. "Is she okay?"

"I believe so," Kai responded. "Lucretia doesn't have a high opinion of Norzen, so you can imagine how that's like." For the first time, Kai saw disapproval in Maple's eyes.

"That's silly. I've met many Norzen, and I'll be the first to say most of them are foul mouthed and rude, though I've only met those living outside Duskmarsh, to be honest." Seeing Kai's face fall, she brushed a wing over his cheek. "But you're different. Papa tells me every tribe has both good and bad berries. I reckon my heart says you're one of the good ones." She took a standing leap, plucking a small yellow apple from the tree. Buffing it on her arm, she tossed the fruit to Kai and winked.

His face still crimson, Kai took a bite and returned Maple's smile. "Thank you. Maybe we'll meet again. We're traveling to Faith Hollow."

"Really? I'm heading there too! Would you mind if I joined you?"

Kai shrugged. "I don't mind, and I doubt the others would either. To be honest, I'd wager it's safer to travel in numbers."

Maple squealed in glee, giving Kai another hug. "Thank you! I've been traveling alone for so long; I was losing my mind. It'll be wonderful to have someone to talk with again. By the way..." The mischievous gleam in her eye returned full force as she hooked a finger around the brass chain hanging from his vest pocket. "I spotted this when I knocked you over. At least now I know why your name sounds familiar." The apothecary's hand shot to his chest, both eyes wide.

Giving Kai a coy grin, Maple released the chain and poked him in the chest. "You're an interesting man, Kai Travaldi," Maple proclaimed. "But I think that's a good thing. In my line of work, interesting often means profitable. Tell you what: I won't say anything about that little trinket if you promise to share the story of how you got it one day. Deal?"

Kai decided that all things considered, he got off lightly. He didn't want to imagine the results if Lucretia ever saw the contents of his pocket.

She'd probably skin me alive. Not seeing any other options, Kai nodded.

He watched Maple pull a rucksack from the bushes and saunter away, a spring in her step. Despite the blackmail, Kai couldn't feel bad. Something about the woman's cheerfulness was like an infection, and not the kind he treated with tonics.

Bringing Maple back to the camp was less stressful than Kai thought it would be. Lucretia and Ione took to the young merchant like fish to water. He watched with a smile as Maple showed the other women some of the wares from her pack, including some jewelry and accessories she crafted herself using the small tool kit she kept in a pouch on her hip.

Kai and Morgan sat on their own a fair distance away, working the small fire pit they dug to cook the mixblood's most recent catch for dinner. Twitching an ear towards them, Kai listened in on their conversation.

"So you all were at Mistport when the Libbies attacked?" Maple asked after hearing the two explain their situation. "That had to be terrifying! I can only imagine what happened to all the faumen that lived there. Didn't the newsletters say they were rising up because of what happened in Whistlevale?"

"Correct," Lucretia answered, taking a sip of her tea. "Sadly, not all the newsletters have the story. When Minister Falber was murdered at the treaty celebration, an Aerivolk man named Ambroz was accused of the crime. They found a flintlock nearby with his feathers stuck to it. Afterwards, a group of anti-faumen nobles calling themselves the Conclave declared everything west of the Videring Forest independent from Livoria. The Liberation Army was amassed for the sole purpose of taking over the entire realm by usurping the Grand Duchess and exterminating the faumen."

"When will people understand that violence only breeds more violence?" Ione whispered, clasping her hands together. "I pray the Saints will weather us through this horrible war. I only hope my family is okay."

Lucretia regarded the tavern maid with curiosity. "I remember you once told me your husband went missing. Do you have other family that lived with you at Mistport?"

"No, thank the Saints for that. I grew up in Grantide, actually. My husband and I had a little girl. Her name's Larina. After Athos disappeared, things went from bad to worse for me, and my parents decided to take Larina with them until I could fix the troubles I got myself into. My deepest wish is to return home one day, even if it's just to see my girl one last time."

"How sad," Maple murmured, her dorsal feathers drooping. "How long has it been since you saw them?"

"Seven years. My Larina was four when Athos vanished, so she'd be eleven now."

Hearing that sent a shiver of sadness down Kai's tails. He couldn't imagine the thought of losing his entire family and being alone for that long. It was bad enough he lost his squad in the midst of all this. Thinking of them still stung, and he was sure it would stay that way for a long time coming. He should have fought Cal more on splitting off away from the group. At least then they might have had a fighting chance. Without the senior Hunter there to rein them in, Faust and Marko got reckless once they were back in Mistport, and they paid the ultimate price for it.

"You alright, 'pothy?" Morgan asked. "You look like someone pissed in your soup."

Emitting a low growl from his throat, Kai cast an agitated glare at the sellsword. "Just thinking about my squad. We made some dumb choices back there, and it kinda feels like it was my fault in a way. I knew better than to split up, yet I still let my squad leader send me off and they all ended up dead because of it."

Morgan picked up a small twig, using it to turn the fish over. They built a tiny, raised stove from rocks along the riverbank, stoking a fire beneath the flat stone that served as the cooking surface. "Listen, 'pothy, you can think about what-ifs and all that if you want. But it was your leader's choice to split up because he thought that was the best option available. Sometimes...they get it wrong, and the ones who survive are left to pick up the pieces and try again. I've never been a leader myself, and I don't wanna be. I ain't smart enough for all that. I got my fighting instincts, and that's good enough for me."

Nodding his head, Kai considered the man's words. "You say you're not smart, but that's a rather profound way of looking at it. And it makes sense. I just wish the feelings in my gut would agree with you the way my mind does."

Morgan guffawed. "I just know a few things I picked up along the path I've walked. I'm 41 years old, for Cadell's sake. I ain't no scholar like that Lucretia gal, but I figure I learned a little about the way the world works."

The two men shared a chuckle, and Kai noticed the ladies giving them a sideways glance before going back to their own conversation. Unable to resist, he swiveled his ears towards them and focused.

"So what's the deal with the Norzen?" Maple asked. "He seems...interesting."

An angry snort came from Lucretia, who sent a scowl Kai's way before answering the Aerivolk. "I'm not sure why you're so intrigued. He's a Norzen, and that's all there is to it."

"Oh come off it, Lucretia," Ione hissed. "You've been too hard on him. What's your problem with Norzen, anyway? They can't all be bad."

"I've yet to meet a decent one in my entire life," the scholar retorted. "I have my reasons, but for simplicity's sake, all I'll say is that their tribe has hurt me in ways no one should be hurt." The two women exchanged hardened stares as Maple looked between them with a nervous smile.

Not willing to give in, Ione pointed a dainty finger at Kai, forcing him to look away lest they catch him eavesdropping. "There's one right there. I don't care what your problem is with the tribe as a whole, but I refuse to let you keep insulting *him*. Say what you want, but Kai is a good man, and I consider myself a decent judge of character. If Norzen are really as bad as you think, then why would he put so much effort into protecting us? Even with your attitude, he still works hard to keep you fed and safe."

"With how staunch you are at defending him, I wonder if you're beginning to harbor certain feelings for that man," Lucretia shot back. Kai's eyes widened in shock. He couldn't stop himself from turning his head just enough to see the trio. Maple was gaping at the scholar with blatant disbelief.

To her credit, Ione huffed and shook her head rather than make an excessive fuss. "Perhaps in another lifetime, I could see it happening. As it stands, my heart still belongs to my Athos, even though he's been gone so long. I'll admit Kai is proving to be a good friend, but that's all we'll ever be. I don't think I could ever give my heart to another, no matter how sweet and noble they might be."

Kai was unable to keep the smile from crossing his lips. He felt much the same way. Ione was a lovely woman, but he still wasn't sure what exactly he wanted in a wife. Perhaps he needed to give it more thought. His mother was sure to start in on him soon enough with pleas to settle down and start a family. Glancing back at the trio, he saw Maple releasing a sigh as the other two settled into an uneasy truce on the matter.

"Hear anything good?" Morgan quipped. Kai's gaze swung back to the sellsword, who was leering at him with a smug grin. "You ain't half as slick as you think you are."

"Shut your yap, Morgan," Kai replied. "Besides, it's just ladies' gossip. Nothing you or I'd find interesting."

"Keep telling yourself that. I am curious about something."

"Hmm?"

"I noticed you use a mace as a weapon. Why choose something like that? Wouldn't a sword or a one-handed axe be a better option?"

Emitting a short chuff, Kai pulled the weapon from its loop and set it between them. "It's funny, really. I chose this because it represents my way of thinking."

"Now I'm *really* curious. What do you mean by that?"

Raising the weapon, Kai gestured to its thick flanges. "Like me, a mace is simple and straightforward. As an apothecary, I prefer not to shed blood if I can help it, and that's the only thing swords and axes are good at. A mace, however, can punch through heavy armor and break bones without drawing blood. It's also easier to wield and maintain than a bladed weapon."

"Huh...I never thought of it like that. Well, so long as it works for you, that's all that matters."

Now it was Kai's turn to grin, giving the older man a poke in the ribs with his elbow. "So what's your story? How's a Wasini mixblood from Corlati end up all the way out here?"

"It's nothing crazy. I grew up in a tiny little fishing village called Sandix on the southern coast of Corlati. Winters are pretty chilly there, so Mam and Grandpap tend to hibernate through the cold moons. I guess I got enough human blood in me that it don't bother me much."

"Makes sense," said Kai. "Wasini are cold-blooded, so they're more susceptible to drastic temperature changes. So you don't have to carry the heat packs that fullbloods use?" Kai knew heat packs, leather pouches filled with water and a heated iron ball, were a rarity in Livoria. Wasini usually only used them during the coldest parts of the mild Livorian winters, as they kept a Wasini's body temperature from falling too low to cause unconsciousness.

"Nah. Never needed one as a brat, and I don't need one now."

"Fascinating. Even here in Livoria, we don't see many mixbloods, regardless of tribe. There's still so much we don't know."

"You ain't wrong. Heck, I still learn new things once and a while, and it's my body!"

The sound of laughter rose from behind them, causing the men to turn and face the ladies as they returned to the fire pit.

"I hope you boys didn't burn dinner," Ione warned, waggling her pan at them threateningly. Kai held his hands up and swore the fish was cooking fine.

Morgan brayed with laughter at the uneasy look in Kai's eyes, leading to Lucretia sending another glare his way and gesturing at him with the tin fork in her hand. "Do not test me, Morgan. I will smack you with this."

"That's quite enough from all of you," Ione declared, putting herself between the two. "Let's settle down and have a nice, quiet dinner before getting some rest. We still have a long journey ahead." Kai and the others agreed with her and made small talk the rest of the evening as they enjoyed the brief respite.

As Ione said, they still had a long trek to reach Faith Hollow, and who knew what additional dangers awaited them along the way.

Chapter X

As the sun peeked out over the horizon the next morning, Kai found himself in yet another odd position. Waking up earlier than the others, he sat against the tree the party camped under and pulled a wooden board and some parchment out. Plucking a pencil from his pocket, he looked out towards the nearby river and began sketching. He found painting to be much more relaxing, but he rarely brought any along on his travels due to the unnecessary added weight. The apothecary was so focused on what he was doing, he failed to realize one of their number didn't sleep in a tent as the others did.

He was jolted from his drawing when a familiar musical voice chirped from above, "I never would've taken you for an artist."

Kai emitted a strangled yelp, throwing himself away from the tree and looking up to find Maple perched among the branches, giggling at him. Relief washed over him like a wave. "Oh, thank the Saints. You nearly made my heart stop, Maple."

A thin, smug grin spread over the merchant's face as she hopped down next to him. "Is that so? Is this your way of telling me I'm pretty?" she asked, batting her eyelashes at him in an alluring manner.

Flailing his arms about, Kai was trying to figure out how the conversation took that sudden turn. "No, that's not it at all! Wait, I mean, you *are* pretty, it's just—" Kai's breath stopped short when he thought about what he just said. His mind ground to a complete halt, grasping for any plausible way of salvaging this.

What in Nulyma am I thinking! Kai screamed at himself mentally. *I'll admit she's attractive, but we just met yesterday. And we wouldn't even be allowed to have a relationship like that anyway. She probably thinks I'm a freak for saying that about her.*

To his unmitigated shock, her cheeks burned red as she brushed the bangs from her eyes, giving him a shy glance. "Thanks," she whispered. "That...means a lot, actually." Her smirk shifted into a timid little smile. The sight of it sent a tingling spark down Kai's tails, leaving him unsure of how to respond.

His heart sank into his feet when he heard the unmistakable sound of a sword being drawn behind him. "I am beginning to wonder if you *enjoy* being threatened with bodily harm," Lucretia muttered. Kai gulped and retreated until his back was pressed against the tree. He knew from the woman's simmering look she would relish the idea of using that sword on him, and the apothecary had no desire to be a pincushion!

Lucretia glanced at their newest member, offering to stab Kai in the rear on the Aerivolk's behalf if he was doing anything untoward. Maple talked the scholar out of the idea while Ione, having woken up in time to hear the exchange, berated her. Morgan found the entire scene hilarious and suggested some celebratory ale after they reached Faith Hollow.

Once the evidence of their presence was removed, the party trudged along towards the river. Kai chatted with Morgan as the women questioned Maple further on what it was like being a traveling merchant.

A rare sense of peace settled in his gut, but Kai wondered how long it would last.

Soon they were halfway between the orchard and the tunnels. A chunk of riverbank twenty yards wide was dug up, transformed into an abandoned encampment of shanties from the mine's heyday stretching from a downward slope to the tunnel entrance. Leftover tools like shovels and pickaxes were strewn about the camp, half-buried and rusted. Much of the path had been reclaimed by nature, with low grasses and scattered bushes covering the area.

A gust passed over, carrying a strange scent. "Does anyone else smell something burning?" Kai asked. Lucretia shot him a sideways glance.

"What are you talking about? We filled the fire pit before leaving the orchard."

Morgan sniffed the air and frowned. "No, he's right. There's coal burning nearby. It's a live fire."

"Maybe it's those folks back there," Maple chimed in. Everyone spun and saw Maple pointing at the hill's summit. Kai noticed the moving figures with some focus, but they were so far away he couldn't make out any distinguishing features. He was impressed Maple spotted them so fast.

"What are they wearing?" Kai asked.

"Well, their armor looks worn and rusted. They're also riding wirochs," she said. Hearing that filled Kai with dread. Shoddy armor meant Liberators. The wirochs posed a new problem altogether.

They were a common enough sight on the Alezonian continent. The world's largest birds by height and weight, they had long legs and curved beaks reminiscent of a sickle, coming in a wide variety of colors. Despite their intimidating appearance, wirochs were docile and easily trained. This led to them often being used as riding mounts or to haul carriages.

"The one in front is wearing an officer's rank. Silver leaves," Maple pressed on.

Bloody Cacovis, it better not be who I think it is. Kai pulled a small spyglass from his pack. He made a silent count of five soldiers on the hill. Sure enough, each one sat bareback atop a wiroch. *If there were more, I'd be concerned the whole army found us. They look like ordinary forward scouts.* It didn't take long for Kai to locate the officer. It was easy to pinpoint the one shouting orders at the rest while waving a sword. His face fell. He recognized the officer.

Damn it, it is him.

"I've got good news, bad news, and irritating news," Kai quipped, slamming the scope shut and ordering everyone to keep moving.

"Can we get the bad news first?" Ione asked.

"They're bloody Liberators." Everyone groaned. "The good news is," Kai continued, "they haven't spotted us yet and appear to be forward scouts, rather than the main army. I only count five of them."

Lucretia cursed, scanning the slope. "If we make a break for it, we should be able to reach the tunnel first, but those wirochs will close the gap fast. And I find myself concerned with what you consider irritating news."

With a heavy sigh, Kai tapped the collar of his vest. "The one leading them is the same ass who almost captured me in Mistport." Maple and Morgan shot the Norzen a curious glance.

A soft gasp reached his ears. Kai turned to see Ione staring; her eyes filled with worry. "Is he the one your friends fought with before—" her voice trailed off, hesitant to dredge up bad memories. Kai inclined his head and said nothing. The pain in his heart still felt raw, even after several days. Regardless, they needed to reach the tunnel before they were spotted. He would have time to grieve later.

A sudden clamor arose from the hill. When he looked back, the Liberators were pointing in their direction and spurring their wirochs down the slope. Kai wondered if the Saints were gauging his patience in the most vexing ways possible. He decided a candid assessment of the situation was best.

"Run!"

Everyone broke into a sprint. Kai saw Morgan digging through the pouches attached to his belt. He let out a triumphant laugh, holding up a small grey stone. A sparkstone.

Without slowing down, Morgan scooped a rock from the ground and struck the sparker. When Kai asked him what he was doing, the sellsword veered off towards a dilapidated shack, beckoning the others to follow.

"Wirochs fear fire, don't they? If we tear this apart and burn it, the fire might slow them down!" Morgan instructed while throwing his body against the building. The attack splintered the boards apart, the shack collapsing in a thunderous boom. Kai pulled broken boards from the heap and threw them among the grass. Morgan flipped the sparker to Ione while telling Lucretia and Maple to help Kai spread the wood around.

Ione fanned the sparker over the wreckage in a sweeping arc, scattering sparks over the makeshift kindling until a raging inferno formed. For good measure, Kai and Lucretia took several burning planks and hurled them at the oncoming soldiers. Before long, the blaze became a wall of flames separating them from their pursuers.

The air was thick and heavy from smoke. Gritting his teeth, Kai ignored the stifling heat and prickle of flames licking his skin. He called for everyone to retreat into the tunnel.

Without looking back, the five grabbed what they could and bolted for the open tunnel. Ione tripped in her sprint down the slope, only for Lucretia to haul her back up. Kai allowed the others to run ahead, making sure everyone made it to safety. He prayed to Tapimor the fire would slow the Liberators down long enough for them to fully cross the river, but he knew deep down they wouldn't be that lucky.

Inside, the fire's crackle was muffled by the stone walls. The air remained heavy, but from moisture rather than smoke. Kai breathed deep and loosened his vest, letting the cool, moist air seep into his mane. While it would be itchy later, he needed a swift cool down after being so close to that fire. Water droplets splashed into the abundance of puddles covering the ground.

Kai rapped on the wall with a knuckle, inspecting the thick tree trunks formed into door-like frames. The frames were set between algae-covered stones every ten yards. He donned a pair of gloves, wiping a finger against the stones. He noted the thick sludge sticking to the leather. He brought it to his nose and took a tentative sniff. "Black lime, mixed with loam and ocean sand."

"Aye," Morgan said, sidling up to Kai's side. "Makes for a solid mortar if done by a competent mason. We use something similar back home in Sandix. They must have used it to hold these bracing walls together."

"That makes sense," Ione chimed in. "The riverbed is primarily dirt, mud, and sand. They would have needed frames of stone and wood to keep the mines from collapsing on themselves." Her face burned red when she noticed everyone goggling. "My brother-in-law is a mason," she explained. "And a talkative one at that. I had to pick up at least something from all his prattle."

"I am not sure how long that fire will slow those bastards down," Lucretia commented as they eased their way down the slippery path. "We should move fast. Just be careful not to slip. The floor is nothing but mud."

To Kai's immense relief, the torches once used to illuminate the tunnel were still attached to the walls. It was a simple matter to soak the tips in cooking oil and set them alight.

Morgan inquired why they weren't leaving the torches unlit to make following them harder, but Maple reminded him that only she and Kai could see well in the low light. Plus, the light would help them avoid slipping into any dark crevices that might be hidden in the shadows.

"This place gives me the heebies," Morgan said. "What did they even dig up in here?"

Lucretia shrugged, taking Maple's hand to clamber over a small ledge. The mud gave way to stone the further they advanced. "It is hard to say," she replied as Maple squinted at something in the distance, wandering away. "There are few records detailing the mine's purpose. However, written records were not enforced much in those days. Whether it was from a lack of administration, or some deeper subterfuge is anyone's guess." Lucretia was so focused on her lecture that she failed to realize the others' amazed stares. "There were rumors of a rare ore found here. Some say it was mined for military purposes. Others believed it could be applied in crafting. It is unfortunate the mine went defunct a hundred years ago. Anyone who worked them would be long dead by now, so the true knowledge is likely lost forever."

After a lengthy silence, Lucretia finally turned around a noticed the stunned looks. She flushed crimson. "My apologies. I do tend to chatter without thinking, as much as it annoys me."

Kai shook his head, giving the scholar a warm smile. "Don't be. I'll be the first to admit I'm impressed. The fact you know so much about such an obscure topic is amazing."

Lucretia's face turned an even deeper shade of red as she glowered at Kai. "I...well, you really should not—" she stammered before stopping herself. She took a deep breath and nodded to Kai. "Thank you."

Maple's voice rang out from further down, near a side entrance to the vast underground labyrinth. "Over here, everyone! I found something!" A soft purple glow rose from the area, growing brighter the closer they got. Her talons clicking against the stone floor, Maple rushed back and revealed her find: a cluster of lilac crystals growing from a sandstone slab. Altogether, the cluster was half a yard in diameter and around a hand tall.

"Good job, Feathers. You found a pretty rock," Morgan deadpanned, inviting a bevy of irritated looks. Maple's enthusiasm was unaffected, though, as she turned the crystal in her hands, inspecting every nook and cranny.

"Such a strange crystal! It's way heavier than it looks. I've never seen anything like this, and it's so beautiful! It would make a wonderful accessory if I can find a craftsman to work it," Maple chirped.

Lucretia ran a finger over the trigonal surface, then lightly tapped a sharpened point. As if provoked, a blinding light erupted from the cluster that shocked the party.

No one was more surprised than Maple, who heaved the cluster upwards and shook her hands as if burned. She bit her lip and hissed, clenching her hands. "What the fuck!? It burned me! What in Finyt is that thing?" she cried while blinking back tears.

Pulling his gloves tight, Kai snagged the crystal mid-drop and nearly dropped it himself. The cluster was emitting a scorching heat! "This is disturbing," he said. "Whatever this is, it's dangerous." Kai set the cluster down away from everyone, then opened his satchel. He asked Maple to show him her hands.

The merchant whimpered and uncurled her hands, exposing the glistening red skin. Because of how she cupped the crystal, the burns were concentrated on Maple's palms, with minimal redness on the fingers.

Kai sat her down and poured water over the scarlet skin. "You're lucky. These burns don't look too bad. Nothing worse than you'd find in a kitchen accident," he consoled her. The Norzen dabbed a liberal amount of translucent cream on Maple's hands and massaged it into the skin in a circular motion. He felt her pull away from his ministrations, but his firm hold kept her in place. He tried reassuring her with a smile. "You did good to let go of that right away. Any longer and you could've caused irreparable damage to your hands. I could feel the heat through my gloves, and they're crafted from nobletusk hide."

After applying the cream, Kai wrapped both palms in strips of cloth. He showed her a small bowl of the cream, nestling it into her pack. "This should help with the pain and keep you from blistering. We'll apply more tonight during dinner, but you'll need to use this for at least two or three days and wash your hands after every meal. You'd be shocked at how easy it is for untreated burns to get infected."

Packing his satchel, Kai caught a brief glimpse of Maple's beaming smile. It warmed his heart and reminded him of why he became an apothecary in the first place.

The sound of sudden, fast footfalls and a chorus of shouts echoed from behind them. Mixed among the noise was a loud honking Kai recognized as wirochs. The Liberators bypassed the fire, and judging from the yelling, they weren't pleased.

Lucretia spewed some choice expletives that made even Morgan stare in astonishment. "And my Mam says *I* have a dirty mouth," said the sellsword as they gathered their bearings, clambering down the path.

"I see the exit!" Ione cried out, pointing to an orb of light. It felt farther than it really was. In an unloaded sprint, Kai guessed he could cover the distance in forty seconds on his own. Carrying his kit and making sure everyone else escaped unharmed would triple that time, at least. They needed to move quick.

Maple ran a talon over the algae-covered floor. "We might not be able to make it with them riding those wirochs. Their talons can grip slippery and uneven surfaces like algae. Mine can't."

A pulsating light drew Kai's focus to the cluster. Gazing at the purple crystal, then at the Liberators' glowing torches, the Norzen got an idea. "Maybe this will distract them," he said while running back and scooping up the blisteringly hot crystal.

"Tapimor's hairy ass, this thing is hot!"

Juggling the burning stone between his hands, Kai almost let go when a loud snap came from it, a web of cracks forming along the sides. The cluster shook, giving off a hum that set off every primal instinct in Kai's brain. "*Taen*, find cover!" he roared, winding his arm back and hurling the crystal at the oncoming Liberators. Kai hurried down the path, slipping and falling on his rump. Two pairs of arms grabbed him as Maple and Ione dragged him into a crevice. Scanning the area, Kai spotted Lucretia and Morgan huddling behind a boulder across the tunnel.

The Liberators spurred their wirochs forward, Agosti in the lead. The officer shielded his eyes from the crystal's light flying over his head. He shouted in glee when he spotted Kai and the party. "Hah! I've got you now, peltneck! This time, you won't get away so—"

His ranting was cut short by a sound like shattering glass coming from behind. The five soldiers wheeled around, eyeing the shining lilac light. The crystal hit the ground on its sandstone base, whirling along the floor and emitting cracks and pops. One soldier urged his wiroch to the cluster, ignoring Agosti's shout to stay put. Before anyone could stop him, the man leaned down and poked it with his sword.

The cluster exploded with the force of a thousand firecrackers. Despite holding them down, the blast reverberated in Kai's ears. It felt as though a white-hot iron was being jammed into his skull. The unfortunate soldier who triggered the detonation was vaporized in a flash of searing fire. Agosti and the remaining soldiers were rendered airborne. Stone fragments and crystal shards sliced through the air like tiny arrowheads.

The tunnel floor, unable to withstand the explosion, collapsed in a wave of mud and stone. Agosti could be heard screaming in anger as his soldiers disappeared into the void. The captain himself clung to the edge, dragging himself back onto solid ground.

As quick as the destruction started, everything went still. Only the sound of crumbling rocks echoed in the dark cavern as the sinkhole settled into an eerie calm.

Kai staggered to his feet, choking on the explosion's dusty remnants. Glancing around, he was relieved to see the others getting back up. "Oh, thank the winds!" he sighed while helping Ione to her feet. "Is everyone alright? Any broken bones? Sprains? Aches?"

Morgan's gruff voice came from behind him. "Feels like I had a few too many steins at the meadhouse! I don't think anything's broken, but damned if it's not all sore."

"In other words, you will live. Pity," Lucretia shot back from the far right.

"Alright, you two, pipe down," Maple said from next to Lucretia. "I reckon we ride the tailwinds and get out of here before those Libbies get back up!"

Staring into the black abyss, Kai shivered. "If they're still alive after being buried in there, I'd be impressed."

A loud curse startled them. In unison, they spotted Agosti on the other side. The Liberator stamped his feet, digging his fingers into his scalp.

Spinning to face the party, Agosti shouted, "You peltneck bastard! Just you wait. One of these days, I'm going to skin your hide and make a rug out of it!"

"He's a pleasant chap, isn't he?" Maple trilled, her voice dripping with sarcasm.

"Indeed. We should invite him to tea, next time," replied Kai. The others snickered and left Agosti to his wild ramblings.

A low rumble reverberated through the tunnel, followed by a gurgle that reminded Kai of a boiling soup pot. He peered back into the sinkhole and squinted. His heart sank when he saw something moving.

"We need to leave. Now."

"What's the rush, 'pothy?" Morgan chuckled. "The danger's gone. That bastard is no threat, and the rest of 'em have gotta be fish bait down there."

"It's not the Libbies worrying me. Trust me on this." Kai replied. He shuddered when a hand rested on his shoulder. He turned to see Ione looking at him, eyes full of worry.

"Kai...what is it?"

In response, he pointed at the sinkhole, where a stream of water shot from the hole with the force of a geyser. "I think the collapse of the floor opened up an underground water source. What do you think will happen if it makes like a volcano and spews all that water up here?"

Seeing their widened eyes, he knew they understood.

Maple looped her arm around Kai's. "Well, I'm sold. I *hate* getting my feathers wet, and I'd rather not drown after surviving that explosion. Get moving!" Without another word, she tugged him towards the exit, the other following alongside.

Side by side, the five rushed into the bright sunlight. Kai swallowed a deep breath of air, taking a moment to slow his breathing.

Only a few more days before we reach Faith Hollow.

His mind flitted back to their most recent adventure. Thinking about it, he realized that there'd been no shortage of adventure ever since Mistport. Though he wasn't sure how he felt. He supposed the one good thing about it all was that it kept him from thinking incessantly about his squad.

Kai tapped Maple on the shoulder and muttered, "Mind if I ask you something?"

"What is it?"

With a sly smirk, Kai replied with a straight face, "You still think that crystal would make a nice accessory? I mean, if you do it right, the sales could *explode*!"

The Norzen wasn't surprised in the least when Maple's wing slammed into his face and his legs were swept from under him, dropping him to the ground. The others burst into laughter, not bothering to help the man up.

Calmly opening his eyes, Kai found his vision filled with Maple's mischievous, violet orbs for the second time that day. He shivered at the feel of her breath caressing his ears.

"Cute," she murmured. "Dumb, but cute."

Chapter XI

K ai remembered his last visit to Faith Hollow, three years ago. All that time, and not much had changed. Most travelers still preferred to arrive via the busier southern gate, through which the Galen River flowed. The party opted to enter from the west, as it was quieter and allowed them to avoid too many stares.

Unlike Mistport, a small town of mostly humans, Faith Hollow was the third-largest city in the Duchy and prided itself as the nation's center for faumen trade. And it showed.

The West Ward contained the faumen residential district and market plaza, with stalls and storefronts lining the roads along the river. Everywhere Kai turned, faumen of all five tribes worked and chatted amicably. A Soltauri farmer haggled over the price of melons with an Aerivolk woman flanked by two children. A Vesikoi man scrutinized a Norzen craftsman's glass wares. The throng of merchants and customers created such a din that Kai's ears throbbed. He forced himself to block out the pain by focusing on other things. Glancing sideways, he saw Maple eyeing the plaza with glee. Her entire body shook with the thrill of a child in a toy shop.

The others almost wandered into the mob, but Kai coaxed them back, suggesting they secure rooms at an inn first. Everyone agreed except for Morgan, who whined about needing a drink. Lucretia inquired why they couldn't head down to the South Ward's riverport at once to secure her boat to Runegard.

To everyone's shock it was Ione who snapped a reply. Her voice sounded calm but carried an edge that sent a chill down Kai's tails. "Lucretia Dineri,

I know you want to get home. However, we've been traveling for ten days since Mistport. I'm exhausted. Everyone is exhausted, including yourself. And to be frank, I plan on sleeping in a proper bed for at least *two nights* before we leave, and not even those damned Libbie bastards can stop me. Understood?"

Lucretia nodded, and Kai didn't blame her. Ione was brandishing her pan like a club.

It didn't take long to locate a member of the town guard and ask for directions to the nearest open inn. The Soltauri guard swept his eyes over the party before bursting into laughter. Lucretia growled, demanding an explanation.

"You folks aren't likely to find open beds around here. Not these days," the guard managed to choke out between chortles. "Everywhere is full, thanks to the war. Hordes of faumen coming in, but nobody's leaving."

"Can you think of anywhere that might have at least a place to sleep?" Kai asked. "We mainly need rest and supplies. Some of us are heading for Runegard as soon as possible."

The guard turned in a slow circle, his neck craned high. "Can't say that I do. Besides, getting to Runegard right now will be difficult."

Lucretia frowned. "Why is that?"

"The headman has forbidden boat travel until the Navy secures the river against Liberator attack. He even closed the sluice gates and drained the main canal. I tell ya, that decision made the town's Vesikoi madder than a flock of wet hens. Here's an idea: head east to Temple Square. The garrison stables are on the far side of Stahl Granz. My brother is the stablemaster and might be willing to let you kip in the barn for a few coppers. It ain't much, but better than sleeping on the cobbles like a lot of poor folk are doing."

The five convened and decided to give the man's suggestion a try. The guard was kind enough to provide a city map and write a letter of introduction. He directed them due east, past the market.

Gathering their gear, they thanked the guard and trudged on while studying the map. The central canal bisected the city diagonally into two main sections: West Ward and South Ward. The market road stretched across the entire length of West Ward, connecting it to Temple Square in the ward's eastern side. Four bridges led over the central canal into South Ward, including one directly across the road from the temple entrance.

The market road was wide to accommodate the flow of travelers and heavily guarded. Colorful banners identifying the shops waved and shimmered in the sunlight, while merchants called out to prospective customers. The party noticed crowds of children playing on the roadside, kicking balls and chasing each other. One group upturned a pile of boxes into a makeshift shop of their own, trading pebbles and small crystals for flowers and other items. Kai noticed Maple giggling at the crude shop.

"They seem to be having a good time," she commented.

Suddenly, an uproar broke out. One of the children, a small Aerivolk boy in a ragged brown tunic broke off from the rest, dashing down the road. He was chased by three larger boys. Weaving through the crowds, the boy was able to stay far enough ahead to avoid getting grabbed by his pine-green feathers. Approaching a wall of people blocking the path, he pivoted on a mark and ran for the river edge. His escape seemed a sure thing. The other boys were spinning in circles, trying to spot him.

The boy risked looking back and crashed into Kai, stumbling back with a cry of surprise. Kai knelt and asked the boy if he was hurt.

The little Aerivolk shook his head. "No sir, I'm fi—" he started, his voice faltering when he stared into Kai's pewter eyes. His face turned the shade of oatmeal as he scrambled back. "You-you're a Norzen!" he stammered.

Kai quirked an eyebrow and examined himself, tails whipping about and his mane in full view through his Hunter's vest. "Yes, yes I am," he drawled.

Maple rolled her eyes, patting the boy's head. "Please excuse our apothecary; his bedside manner needs some work," she said with a beaming smile. "Now then, sugar, what's your name?"

The boy's face burned crimson. "Uh, Dannel." His eyes flickered to Kai again, refusing to meet the Norzen's gaze.

The three boys from before ran up, prompting Dannel to crouch behind Maple. The leader, a stocky Vesikoi, reached out to grab Dannel's wings before Kai swatted the hand away.

The boy gave Kai a savage glare. "Stay out of this, peltneck. This is between us and him."

Putting herself between the children, Ione rested a hand on Dannel's shoulder and gave him a reassuring squeeze. "If I were your mother, young man, I'd wash your mouth out. Who taught you that word?" The boy's burned red at the admonishment but stayed quiet. "Now where I come from, three on one isn't a fair shake. What did Dannel do to get you so riled?"

"He took my coppers, the dirty thief!" the Vesikoi shouted, trying to push his way past Ione. She stood firm and held the boy back.

Maple wrapped a protective wing around the younger Aerivolk and asked, "Dannel, is this true? Did you steal from this boy?"

Dannel choked back a sob and wiped his tears. "I-I did, but I had no choice! One of the other kids at the orphanage takes my food every day and throws it in the bin. I'm so hungry," he cried, unable to hold his tears back. He threw himself into Maple's embrace.

The other boy cracked his knuckles. "Who cares if they take your food," he sneered. "That just makes you weak. Give back my coppers, you orphan freak!" he shouted. He ducked around Ione and swung a vicious hook.

The punch didn't make it halfway before Kai stopped it. The boy looked up with a scowl, ready to shout again. Instead, his anger faded, shifting into nervous fear.

A rush of anger coursed through Kai, but he knew he couldn't hit a kid. Instead, he settled for a venomous look that stopped the boy cold. "That attitude will get you in trouble one day. Dannel, return his marks, please. We'll get you some food. My treat."

Terrified, Dannel thrust the coins into the other boy's hands. With a nod, Kai let go of the boy's fist and knelt in front of him. "Now learn this well. Just because someone is an orphan doesn't make them a freak. Not everyone is blessed with loving parents. Imagine how hard it would be if it were you. Having no one to hug you, cook your meals, or say they love you every day; it doesn't sound very fun, right?"

Seeing him nod, Kai waved the three off with a warning as they scampered away. Feeling eyes on his back, Kai turned to see the others gaping. He noticed Lucretia giving him a strange look. If he didn't know any better, he would say it was respect.

But that was impossible. Right?

"Wasn't that a bit harsh, 'pothy?" Morgan asked.

"It had to be said," Kai replied. "Kids can't grow up looking down on the less fortunate. That's how you get adults that think the same way certain nobles do. I'm an orphan myself, so I'm not one to let something like this pass. The world is full of mysteries; in different circumstances, their lives could've easily been reversed. Let's get Dannel something to eat first."

Everyone consented and found a stall nearby offering local dishes. Maple stayed close to Dannel, telling him to pick anything he wanted. Kai wasn't surprised when he chose a large roasted chicken with steamed vegetables. Morgan ribbed that maybe the boy was eating a distant cousin, only for Ione to thwack him in the rear with her pan. Dannel edged closer to Maple, staring at the frowning tavern maid in fear.

Dannel proved to be a bright and curious child, asking why the party was there and where they were going. Once everyone had eaten their fill, Maple gathered their marks and paid the tab. When Kai mentioned that they were heading for the stables near Stahl Granz Temple, Dannel winced.

"Oh no, I live at the temple orphanage. Sister Orelia is going to be so upset with me," the boy said. Lucretia chuffed, poking Dannel's forehead.

"Consider yourself lucky someone cares enough to worry," the scholar explained. "Besides, we cannot simply leave you alone. Our current priority is getting you home safe," With Dannel leading Maple by the arm, the party soon left the market behind.

* * *

In all his visits to Faith Hollow, Kai never saw Stahl Granz Temple. Now he wondered how he missed it. The temple was a beautiful structure, built fifty yards tall with two wings surrounding the main entrance like stony arms. The building's sharp edges contrasted with the flowing curves of its stained-glass windows, each gleaming in a rainbow of colors. Glancing down, Kai noticed they spread the sunlight over the walkway into a spectrum of light.

Dannel pointed forward, explaining the stables lay on the far side of the temple. He tried strolling past the building, but a feminine voice called out from near the left wing, stopping the Aerivolk boy in his tracks.

"Dannel? It *is* you! For Galen's sake, child, where have you been?" the voice asked, exasperated.

The party spun to see a young Vesikoi woman approaching, her shining blue eyes carrying a look of indignation. Her vermillion hair was braided into a ponytail with a yellow ribbon, resting over the shoulder. She carried a cudgel of solid oak almost as tall as she was with a metal cap over its rounded head. Her vestment was cream with intricately designed gold trim and oval holes on the side, revealing four gills on each side. The sleeves were separate from the main vestment, leaving her thin shoulders bare.

Blinking, Kai shook his head and verified that he wasn't imagining things. Sure enough, her skin was mostly bronzed except for a splash of grey surrounding her gills. Not a common look for Vesikoi, whose skin was usually two-toned, being pale in the front but dark in the back.

Kai stepped forward, clapping his hands together at heart level while bowing his head: a standard respectful Windbringer greeting. "We bid you well, Sister. May the winds guide you through all trials." The party each introduced themselves in turn while performing the same greeting. Even Morgan attempted the gesture, though he didn't get it quite right. He put his hands too high and looked like he was offering an apology, which set Lucretia into a fit of snickers.

The woman rested her staff against a nearby fence and offered her own greeting. "May the winds guide you as well, travelers. I am Orelia Basner, priestess superior of the temple orphanage. I do hope Dannel hasn't caused you trouble."

Maple pushed Dannel forward. "He hasn't been any trouble at all. There was a small argument with another child, but we smoothed things over."

The young priestess gave Dannel a searching gaze before her lip shifted into a tiny smirk. "The little rascal got caught stealing again, didn't he?"

Morgan barked with laughter and tapped Dannel on the head. "She's got you figured out, don't she?" Orelia twirled her staff with one hand and struck Morgan on the shin with a loud thwack, her lips set in a thin line. The sellsword hopped on one foot, shouting in pain. Everyone else took a hesitant step back.

Lucretia whispered to Ione, "I like her already." The tavern maid stifled a giggle.

"It's hardly a laughing matter," the priestess said. Turning to Dannel, she continued, "We've talked about this, young man. How do I make you understand? Stealing goes against the—"

"The Eight Virtues," Dannel finished, slouching with a tear in his eye. He told her of the other child stealing his food and ran forward to embrace the woman in a desperate hug. Kai heard him whisper to the young woman that the child taking his food threatened to beat him if he told anyone. He frowned, listening to Dannel beg Orelia not to mention that he snitched.

"You know you can always tell me if anyone gives you trouble. I will be having a talk with everyone about this tonight, and anyone who thinks to hurt you will not enjoy the consequences. I'll talk to the other priestesses into making sure you're fed."

Dannel gave Orelia a dull look. "You think the bishop will allow that? You know he doesn't like us. Or any of the orphans, really."

Ione stepped forward and apologized for interrupting the two. She reminded the party they still needed to secure a place to sleep. Orelia asked Ione what she meant, which led to Maple detailing the guard's explanation about the inns. The priestess asked to see the guard's letter, taking the offered parchment.

Reading the letter, she chuckled. "Good old Fabalio. His heart is certainly in the right place, though he's still new. Regardless, you won't be sleeping in stables tonight."

Everyone stared, brimming with curiosity. "What do you mean?" Maple asked. "Are there open rooms somewhere?"

"I'm afraid he wasn't lying about that. Not much space for new travelers these days. However, you'll stay here with us. It's the least I can do to repay you for watching out for Dannel. We have plenty of open beds in the orphanage. We take up the entire west wing of the temple, so there's more than enough room."

Kai inquired if the bishop would permit them to stay. Orelia grinned and explained that Bishop Adalbard gave her total autonomy over the orphanage, citing that his traditional duties were more important. Thus, if she wanted to allow travelers to use the beds, there was nothing the bishop could do without reneging on their agreement. The five thanked Orelia and followed her towards the orphanage entrance.

Kai saw a group of five faumen children wandering the hall. To his amazement, he noticed a young Norzen girl at the group's rear. He heard a hiss, spotting Dannel hiding behind Maple once more. The other children approached at a run, shoving each other along the way.

"Looks like the runt's back, and he even brought a peltneck with him," said the child in front, a Soltauri boy. "I bet you went out thieving again." Dannel couldn't hide his wince, which the other boy saw with a nasty smirk.

"That's quite enough," the priestess ordered, grabbing the boy's shirt and dragging him away. "First of all, you ever say that word again and you'll get worse than soap in your mouth. Understood?" The boy pushed and pulled, but the priestess's grip was unyielding. "Next, you're judging Dannel for stealing, but I've noticed how *somebody* treats him at mealtimes." The boy's face paled.

"Oh yes, there will be a long discussion tonight for everyone about manners. I have eyes all over this temple. Now return to your rooms. All of you," directed Orelia, giving Dannel a firm look while letting go of the

Soltauri boy's shirt. "And if I hear any fighting, that'll be extra chores for a moon." With mutters of affirmation, the children plodded along, entering a pair of doors halfway down the hall.

"I haven't seen tough love like that since my mother. She used to give me and my sister the business if we ever got into a scuffle," Kai noted. Orelia regarded him with a slanted grin. "If you don't mind me asking, what's the bishop's problem with you? You seem cheerful enough, if a bit firm," he asked as Orelia led them into a room with ten empty beds.

The priestess thanked Kai for the compliment before stopping a pair of maids, requesting clean linens. "The children are a rough bunch, but they're good kids. They just got a bad shake in life. The prevailing theory says he hates that I'm an outsider. I am from Galstein, after all" she said. "Personally, I think he's just bloodist against mixbloods."

"What the spit, you're a mix too?" Morgan exclaimed. "I thought you were fullblood." In response, Orelia confirmed she was half-human on her father's side.

"Well of course you'd have human blood. What else would it be?" Lucretia asked.

Orelia took Morgan's hand and pressed the fingers against her arm. "It's not slick," the sellsword muttered.

"Indeed. Unlike fullblood Vesikoi, my body doesn't need to produce the same mucus they use to cool their bodies on land. It also helps the air is more humid here than back home."

The maids returned with the linen. The party thanked them and went about making their beds. Lucretia grumbled about traveling from Mistport only to arrive at a city with an active ban on outgoing travel. Orelia's ears perked up.

"Did I hear you right? You all came from Mistport; wasn't that town razed by the Liberation Army? And now you're trying to find a boat out of town?"

The party explained the story leading to their arrival in Faith Hollow, including their battles in Mistport and along the way. Orelia sat on an empty bed, tapping her cudgel on the stone floor. Her eyes were unfocused, staring at a single point on the floor. "You've all been through so much. If I may ask, what are your plans going forward?"

After an uncomfortable silence, Kai replied, "I will likely be sending a message to Havenfall by carrier hawk before heading back. To that end, I will be traveling to Runegard as well. It's the next major city going south."

Lucretia snorted. "Are you stalking me, Kai?" she asked.

The apothecary's skin turned a light shade of green at the implication. "Absolutely not," he shot back. "I think I'd rather chew on rusty nails than pursue someone who wants to shove a sword in my rump."

Ione thumped the two behind their heads before speaking her turn. "If I'm honest, I think it best for me to head home to Grantide." Peering at Kai, she continued, "While not as far as Havenfall, it's still on the same path, so if you'll still have me, I'd like to join you." She visibly calmed when both expressed their agreement.

Morgan took a long draw from his ale, ignoring Orelia's question of where he acquired the bottle. "Truth be told, I haven't put much thought into that. What I do know is I owe my life to Kai and the ladies for saving me. I know I didn't give the best first impression, but until my debt is paid, my sword is yours."

Everyone's heads turned to Maple, who found her talons much more interesting in that moment. "I know we haven't traveled together long, but if we're being honest, this is the best I've felt in years. Traveling with y'all, it's almost like having friends again," she sniffled. She wiped away a tear glimmering on her cheek.

No one said anything as Kai sat next to the merchant. Inching an arm up, he wrapped it around her shoulder. "Maple, I can't speak for anyone else, but when I say I already consider you a friend, it's the wind blessed truth." Ione squeezed Maple in her arms, swearing on Luopari's name they would be friends for life.

"Thank you!" Maple cried.

The sound of a clearing throat drew their attention back to Orelia. "If you're all traveling to Runegard, you'll need a boat." Seeing everyone nod, she pressed on, "Yet the restrictions on boat travel make that difficult. The good news is I know someone who can get you there."

In an instant, Lucretia demanded to know what the bad news was.

The priestess gave Lucretia a smug side-eyed glance. "Whether it's good or bad depends on your values, I suppose. The man happens to be a smuggler. A damned good one, too. Also, he's presently out of town and I'm not yet sure when he'll return."

Morgan crowed with mirth. "Well I'll be, the sister swore! What kind of holy woman are you?"

"The kind not afraid to do what's necessary. That might be another reason the bishop doesn't care for me," Orelia commented. Her penchant for sarcasm made it clear she didn't put much stock in the bishop's opinion. It made Kai wonder what the man was like.

Bidding everyone goodnight, Orelia took her leave. The party nestled into their beds for some well-deserved sleep. Kai found himself staring at the ceiling, his mind racing.

They made it to Faith Hollow, but even now the war followed them. He muttered a silent prayer to Ausrina the Wanderer, thanking her for guiding them to Orelia. As the patron of travelers, Ausrina was often invoked during arduous journeys. Widely popular, she trailed only Galen and Luopari in total devotees.

To make things worse, he still thought about his encounter with Grimghast. If allowed to roam unimpeded, the beast had the potential to cause more damage than the Liberators! He knew what he needed to do, but even summoning a full company to bring it down wasn't a sure thing. The beast was clever, fast, and vicious. Then there was its concealment ability. So many variables, and no visible ways to mitigate them.

Pulling the blanket over his head, Kai clenched his fingers tight around his vest pocket. He would message the Hunters Corps commander at first light. It was best to let him make the decision. Regardless of his other duties, Grimghast proved beyond the abilities of a Hunter squad and needed to be addressed. The commander would know how to handle it.

The very next morning, Orelia took him to the postal hawkery to send his report back to Havenfall. In it, he explained what happened and described Grimghast's abilities, as well as outlined his plans to return. Watching the carrier hawk fly away, Kai realized that nobody really knew how the birds knew who to deliver their parcels to; they just did. Still, he was grateful for them.

Over the next two days, Orelia was an invaluable guide. She introduced them to several prominent merchants and craftsmen, helping them re-stock on supplies. And despite her firm hand with the children, the party saw that they adored her. More than once, they witnessed Dannel and Tuvi, the blonde Norzen girl Kai saw upon their arrival, presenting the priestess with flowers and other handmade trinkets. In talking with Tuvi, who was barely tall enough to reach Kai's waist, he discovered she was thirteen years old and dreamed of being a painter one day.

"I'm sure you'd make a fine painter, Tuvi," said Kai. "Perhaps one day I can come back and teach you a few techniques. I dabble in the art myself." Seeing Tuvi's eyes shine at those words filled Kai's chest with warmth. The girl hugged him and tight and refused to let go until he promised to return and teach her everything he knew.

As the sun peeked over the horizon after their second night in town, Kai stretched with a loud yawn. Glancing at the sunlight peeking through the window, Kai decided to head into the market for breakfast ingredients, snatching his money pouch and satchel. He also wanted to see if there were new herbs he could use for tea. A cup of tea sounded delicious.

He wanted to bring Maple along; the woman had a glib tongue and was a master negotiator from what he saw during their visits to the market. However, he couldn't bring himself to wake her. She looked rather cute perched on the wooden frame of her bed, gently snoring with her wings encircling herself like a shroud.

Wait, cute? Kai thought, shaking his head. *Dangerous thoughts, Kai, very dangerous thoughts.*

Grabbing a spare parchment, he wrote a quick note informing the others of his location and placed it on his bed before leaving.

"Going somewhere?" a gruff voice came from behind. Frowning, Kai twisted to face an older human coming out of the main chapel, with weathered skin and a scowl that looked chiseled onto his face. His intricate vestment, triangular mitre cap, and ornate staff identified him as the temple bishop, though Kai was surprised to see the man. According to Orelia, he despised visiting the orphanage.

Undeterred by the rude tone, Kai greeted him formally, "A pleasant morning, Your Excellency. My companions and I are guests of Sister Orelia. You must be Bishop Adalbard. I was on my way to the market to procure ingredients for our breakfast."

"Is that so?" the bishop asked. His eyes were shifty and constantly moving, making Kai wonder what the man was searching for. "If you are the good Sister's guests, then why not eat in the meal hall? Is our food not good enough for a peltneck?"

It was obvious the older man was goading Kai into losing his temper, something the apothecary found amusing. He'd been insulted in worse ways by more intimidating men than some pretentious priest. Besides, Kai felt it too early to put up with insults. He hadn't even had his morning tea yet!

"You know, I've lost track of how many times I've been called that slur lately. Learn something original. Also, this has nothing to do with the quality of your food. I simply felt it more respectful to fend for ourselves rather than take from your struggling congregation."

The reversal worked. The bishop's face flushed as he sputtered at Kai's words. "St-struggling?! What in the Galen's holy name makes you believe our congregation is suffering?" he squawked. Adalbard advanced on Kai until their noses inches apart, yet the move provoked no reaction from the apothecary.

Kai shrugged and admitted hearing that at least one child in the orphanage had inadequate food. Thus, he could only assume they were going hungry because the temple was in dire straits. After all, were the temple prospering, would it not be able to properly care for its charges?

By now the bishop was floundering, waving his staff in a white-knuckled grip. "How dare you!" he shouted. "You have the audacity to besmirch the reputation of our temple after we provide you shelter? You will pay for this insult!" Adalbard raised his staff and aimed a sloppy swing at Kai's head.

The blow was stopped halfway by a rounded cudgel, snapping the end off and sending it skittering down the hallway.

"Your Excellency, I pray you weren't about to strike my guest in full view of the congregation?" Orelia hissed. Kai backed away on instinct. The priestess's eyes were dilated and emitted a cold fury that he only saw in Hunters and veteran sailors. He didn't doubt for a moment that Orelia would use that cudgel if pressed, and she wouldn't be gentle about it.

Finally realizing the priestess's words, the bishop spun to see a crowd of people standing stock still in the chapel doorway. Worshipers arriving for morning service. Their faces were pale with wide, unblinking eyes etched in horror. Turning pale himself, the bishop dropped his staff with a clang. The clatter of footsteps came from behind as the rest of the party barreled into the hall.

Turning to Kai, Orelia knelt and bowed. "Words cannot begin to express how sorry I am for this, Kai. No one should face such vitriol, regardless of their tribe and especially not in a sanctified house of prayer. Please wait for me in the outer square. I will accompany you into town." Kai nodded and led the party to the doors.

That left Orelia with the bishop and a throng of frightened worshipers. "I hope you're proud of yourself," she spat. From the overt venom in her voice, if words could kill, the bishop would have been dead several times over. "Those travelers arrived from Mistport seeking aid and comfort. All of them faced the shroud of Cacovis and survived. Rest assured that certain individuals will be made aware of this."

Against all possibility, the bishop paled even further. "You wouldn't dare! Your family has no standing in the Livorian church. And you are nothing but an illegitimate chimera yourself." Several women fainted at the vehement curse.

"It's true, I wasn't born of my father's legitimate wife," Orelia admitted. Carrying her head high, she thumbed her nose at Adalbard. "Nevertheless, I have been publicly acknowledged as a child of House Basner. Our family's connections to prominent members of the clergy are numerous, including the Holy Matriarch." The older man's face faded to ashen gray in an instant. "I may not hold the same prominence as my brothers, but Father won't stand for this insult towards me. You'd best prepare your defense." The priestess turned on her heel and stomped away. Adalbard stumbled into the chapel, away from the growing whispers of the crowd.

The party stood in the plaza, sharing nervous glances. As Orelia approached, Kai thanked her. Lucretia admitted to being in awe of her verbal lashing. High ranking priests were often considered respected members of the community, regardless of their personal beliefs. Being chastised in public by a member of their congregation was the height of disrespect. For a priestess to do so was unheard of.

Brushing off the compliments, Orelia announced that her contact would be returning tomorrow. When asked how he could leave and enter the port with no consequences, she giggled. "Who says anyone knows when he leaves?" she replied. Kai didn't have an answer for that.

Waving goodbye to the orphans as they swept the pathway leading to the temple entrance, Orelia led everyone to the bridge leading into South Ward's noble district. Morgan asked how the river kept running even with the sluice closed and the central canal dried up. Kai was curious about it himself and was pleased when Orelia decided to explain the canal system's workings as they walked.

Closing the sluice gates diverted the river through an underground tunnel system beneath the city. This kept the river from overflowing and served as a pathway for Vesikoi citizens to reach their underwater homes. Every sluice gate along the river was controlled by a steam engine within a control building in Temple Square. The engine was always maintained by a team of three engineers. The main canal had five alternating branches on each side spread throughout the city, with each branch kept full by a pump system in the underground channels. These were in turn powered by the river while it was diverted. The gates to each branch were connected to the central steam engine.

Ione asked what would happen if the steam engine broke. "That would be a disaster," said Orelia. "That engine is designed to lower the gates gradually. If it stopped running, the gates would drop and release a small tidal wave into the canal as the river rushed to fill in the empty space. Anyone inside would be killed if they weren't Vesikoi."

With the canal empty, a thriving Vesikoi-run market took up residence inside. The market covered a space forty yards wide, with stone steps leading down on both sides. Stalls and carts stretched from one end of the canal to the other.

Just as in Mistport, there was a marked difference between the major sections of town. That difference just wasn't as blatant. Both wards made use of stone in their architecture. However, South Ward was famous for its use of decorative basalt and marble in its buildings compared to the west's preference for granite. The nobles of Faith Hollow flaunted their wealth through ornate metal fences and hand-dug ponds. Kai noted that, while not as luxurious as the noble districts of Whistlevale, the South Ward had an exuberant charm of its own he found more appealing.

When questioned on where they were going, Orelia said she wanted to introduce them to the town guard commander. According to back-alley rumors she'd heard, a battalion of Royalist sailors had arrived in the city to protect it from Liberator attack. She elaborated that the guard commander was a friend of hers and would have more detailed information.

A familiar voice came from a nearby alley, "I'm afraid they won't be enough."

Ears twitching, Kai almost dropped his pack in shock when he peered into the alley. He knew those withered white feathers. "Locke? What in Tapimor's name are you doing here?" The thin Aerivolk waved from his spot against a wall. Noticing the others' questioning looks, Kai explained how he met Locke in Mistport during the attack. He returned his attention to the Aerivolk, asking how he managed to reach Faith Hollow.

"Oh, I arrived this morning," he said. "I was lucky to come across an older couple seeking refuge. They allowed me to ride in their carriage. They took a longer route to avoid the Liberation Army, not that it will do any good. I certainly won't be staying long."

"What do you mean?" Maple asked. Her eyes were bright and curious.

"I like to keep an eye on the trail during my travels. My body may not be in prime condition, but these eyes still work. The Liberators are marching on Faith Hollow as we speak. I would guess their numbers at around six thousand." The party gaped. Six thousand troops?

"I don't think a battalion will be enough," Kai said after an extended silence. A typical Navy battalion numbered around 1,500 sailors, so the odds facing them were grim.

Morgan huffed and clasped his hands together, popping his knuckles. "No, it damn well won't," he grumbled. "They'll be outnumbered at least four to one! Hoarfrost, where'd they even get that many men?"

Pushing to the front, Ione said it didn't matter how they had gathered so many soldiers. What mattered was that they *did* have them and were marching on a city of innocent people. All of whom would be slaughtered if something weren't done.

Lucretia begged the question of what they could do. She reminded them they were ordinary travelers with no real ability to change the situation. And especially not against an army that large.

Locke shrugged his shoulders. "That's a valid point, ma'am. Those soldiers would swallow you like a wave. I suggest you follow my lead and find a carriage to get yourselves out now. My guess is they'll reach the city by tomorrow night. I pray the winds of fortune guide you to safety." The Aerivolk gave a weak wave, walking away towards the southern gate.

With Locke gone, everyone was too stunned to move. What hope did a 1,500-man battalion have against a force that large?

Kai muttered to himself while pacing back and forth. He could think of several ways to save the citizens, but the methods were drastic. Most would cause significant damage to the city.

A soft rattling rang in his ear. He gazed at his vest pocket and sighed. His gut knew what he had to do, but he wasn't sure he wanted to deal with the backlash.

The party was arguing over what to do. Ione believed they should try to help the people of Faith Hollow. However, Lucretia said interfering was too dangerous and liable to get them killed. Maple and Morgan were undecided, as they both wanted to save the innocents, but realistically knew a frontal battle would be suicide.

Kai ran a finger through his mane, biting his lips as he racked his mind trying to come up with a plan that wouldn't leave them all dead.

"Orelia," Kai inquired. "Did that rumor mention where the battalion was headquartered?" The priestess answered that the troops were quartering in the warehouse district near West Ward's seaport. It was the only place with enough room.

"Good. Take us there." Without a word, Orelia marched ahead with Kai leading the party after her. Maple and Ione exchanged nervous glances as they followed Orelia through the streets.

Lucretia thumped the Norzen behind the head. "I think you owe us an explanation. What are you thinking? You cannot expect to fight that many Liberators without a plan. If anything, we should advise them to evacuate the city. They need to open the sluice gates and get everyone out on the river."

Kai skidded to a stop. "The river...that's it. There *is* a way to do this." Everyone quirked their eyebrows in confusion.

Sidling next to Kai, Morgan chimed in. "No offense, my friend, but what makes you think they'll listen to us, or to be blunt, you? Even I can tell Norzen are barely tolerated, and I ain't that smart. They're either gonna laugh at you or arrest you."

Kai knew it was a valid concern, but he had to try. He ran a finger over one of his mace's flanges. The cool metal felt familiar and brought a sense of calm security. "If we're lucky, the battalion commander will listen without forcing my hand."

Orelia stopped and spun to face Kai with an incredulous gape.

"I don't think I heard that right," she said. "Did you just suggest forcing a Royalist officer to listen to you? Have you lost your damned kettle? That *will* get you killed!"

In his heart, Kai couldn't fault her concern. The idea of a Norzen walking up to a navy commander and making demands was, without a doubt, outrageous. Regardless of how much better Norzen were treated in Livoria compared to other nations, many outside this city were killed for less. He remembered seeing a Norzen child once stabbed by a noble for daring to beg for food. His eyes hardened at the memory, seeing Tuvi's face replace the child he saw that day.

Kai met Orelia's gaze. "I've never been good with public attention, or with asserting myself. It sets my nerves on edge. However, I'm still an apothecary and I refuse to let innocent people die on my watch. Especially any of you. Besides, I have both a plan and an advantage that shifts the negotiations in my favor, as much as I hate using it."

Five pairs of eyes widened at the declaration. Lucretia crossed her arms under her chest. Her glare was oppressive and promised immense pain. "Is that so? And what trump do you have to keep you from getting butchered? I care not a whit for you, but the rest of them do."

Kai didn't say anything. Instead, he hooked a finger around the chain in his vest pocket and revealed its contents.

A brass pocket watch with a crystalline cover etched with a symbol any Livorian would recognize: the seal of the Royal House of Ardei.

The reaction was instant. Ione gasped, backing away until she toppled backwards onto a pile of grain sacks. Lucretia's breath hitched. She gawked at Kai as if meeting him for the first time. Orelia's staff clattered to the floor, a stupefied look on her face. Morgan's examined the watch with a blank stare, his confusion plain to see.

Maple was the only one who didn't react, which surprised Kai until he remembered she saw the watch in their first meeting.

After several minutes of bewildered silence, Lucretia finally found her voice. "Kai Travaldi, where in the winds did you get *that*!?"

Morgan raised a tentative hand and voiced a question that drew everyone's scrutiny.

"What's with the hysteria? It's just a watch."

CHAPTER XII

Being different was hard, and Kai knew that more than most.

Growing up the only Norzen in a village of humans, Kai was accustomed to the slurs and suspicious looks from those outside of his family. As he got older, he earned the village's respect, with notable exceptions. He also realized his uniqueness applied to other Norzen, a group he should've felt some manner of kinship with after his ostracization in Havenfall.

Compared to other faumen, Norzen outside of Duskmarsh were often bombastic and opportunistic. This was in part due to the excess discrimination they received from other tribes, coupled with a deep pride in their own history. But Kai wasn't like that either. Those that knew him described him as compassionate and resourceful, with only brief flashes of the traits often attributed to his tribe. To most Norzen, his willingness to help anyone in need was a betrayal.

Now, standing before the party, Kai came to terms with the fact that he would always be different, no matter how much he wanted to fit in. The watch in his hand was proof of that.

"You know, Kai," Lucretia said, pacing back and forth with a disappointed look. "You nearly had me fooled. I was beginning to hope you might be different from other Norzen. You showed reliability and honesty during our travels. But now, I see that it was all a lie."

Ione stood quaking between Orelia and Morgan. "Lucretia, please. The least we can do is let him explain."

The scholar's hand coiled around the hilt of her rapier. "Explain what, that at the very least, he is either a thief or scavenger? At worst, he is a murderer!"

Morgan questioned again why everyone was so disturbed by a watch.

"The only thing saving you, Morgan, is blissful ignorance. That isn't *just a watch*," Lucretia snapped. "It is the mark of Livoria's most prestigious order: The Exarch Knights."

Maple stood next to Kai with wings crossed, her irritation clear. "You're being too harsh. Who are you to say he didn't earn it legitimately?" Kai was unnerved by the grim smirk stretching across Maple's face. He refused to say anything for now. Opening his mouth might draw Lucretia's attention enough for her to stab him for once.

For the first time, the scholar burst into uproarious laughter. "Are you serious, Maple? In Livoria's entire existence, no Norzen has ever been named an Exarch!"

Maple dug around her pack, giving a triumphant chirp moments later. She clutched a thick scroll in her hands.

"What is that?" Lucretia asked.

"As an Archivist, you're the last one I'd expect to *not* have this. It's a list of all 55 active Exarchs. All local archives are required to carry and provide copies of it on request by royal decree," Maple replied. "Despite their unique status as nobles, Exarchs remain royal officers serving the Grand Duchess, so their names are supposed to be easily accessible. I requested this copy years ago; you never know when the information may be useful. This explains why Kai's name sounded familiar when I first met y'all."

Unfurling the scroll, Maple trailed a finger down each name, muttering to herself. After a few minutes, she released an excited trill, beckoning everyone over. Pointing at the final entry, there was Kai's name, written in plain Centric for the entire party to see. Along with his tribe and occupation, Kai's official Brand was shown: Gravebane. Kai rubbed his neck with a hesitant smile.

Completely paralyzed, Orelia stared at the entry. Moments later, the thin woman collapsed in a fit of laughter. "Oh, this is beautiful!" she shouted. "I'm going to assume Adalbard doesn't know any of this. If he did, he never would've been stupid enough to try striking you today."

Ione and Lucretia both turned pale, the scholar looking ill. Bowing her head, she apologized to Kai for her accusations.

Confusion was still plastered on Morgan's face. "I don't get it," he said. "Why does that make him stupid?"

Orelia conceded she never expected any bishop to make such a critical mistake. "He assaulted someone who, as an Exarch, is a representative and guardian of the Grand Duchess. He did this on church grounds, in a public hallway, in front of dozens of witnesses," the priestess explained. "Not even his ecclesiastic title can save him from that charge. Because of his position, he's *required* to know who every Exarch is. If Kai wanted, he could demand anything up to and including the bishop's head on a pike. Attacking an Exarch without cause is treated as seriously as assaulting the royal family.

"You're from Corlati, correct?" When Morgan nodded, Orelia grinned. "Imagine what would happen if someone in your country attempted to murder a Primal Abbot."

The sellsword blanched, the gravity of the situation hitting him. "Oh piss," he muttered. "Damn, 'pothy, why didn't you say anything?"

Kai shrugged the man's question off. "I'm not a fan of the attention. Most Exarchs I've met tend to be full of themselves. Everywhere they go, people lavish them with praise. That's not me. I'd rather be acknowledged for my actions, not a title. That's why a lot of people still don't realize I'm in the order. I specifically requested Her Grace not to make a huge ceremony out of it. Sometimes the other Exarchs need to be reminded I exist."

Everyone jumped when Orelia clapped, suggesting a visit to the battalion commander. Maple burst into laughter when the priestess said the commander would have to hear them out now. Not even an admiral would be foolish enough to brush off an Exarch, Norzen or not. The party followed Orelia back into West Ward.

Kai was impressed. Despite being from Galstein, the woman navigated the streets with the precision of a local. Orelia marched with a purposeful stride, making snappy pivots at each turn. Kai whispered to the others that if he tried to lead them back to the temple by this point, he'd be lost.

By the time the party stepped into an open area with four large warehouses, Kai's legs were cramped and sore. Each building was surrounded by sailors dressed in the crisp blue uniforms of the Royalist Navy, with more pouring in from the seaport on the far side. It looked as though a lake cropped up in the middle of the city.

Orelia tapped Kai's shoulder, motioning to the far-left warehouse. It was the only building with two sailors guarding the entrance. Clenching his fist, Kai approached the door. With a sharp clang, the guards' partisans crossed together and blocked Kai from entering.

The left guard sneered. "State your business, peltneck."

Feeling his eye twitch, Kai replied, "I have information for your commander. I'm requesting to speak with him." In response the right guard leaned forward, growling that the commander was a busy man. Kai ignored the man's attitude and replied that, since his information was about the Liberation Army, they might want to hear him out.

Now both guards loomed over Kai who found the attempt amusing. So much so, he couldn't hold back a chuckle. Compared to Grimghast, the two guards were as frightening as newborn lambs.

The guards brandished their weapons with a snarl, pointing the spears at Kai's heart when a barking voice came from behind.

"What's all the ruckus?"

Both guards turned and saluted the newcomer, a tall human male wearing a richly decorated uniform. A black cross was emblazoned on the front with the silver diamonds of a lieutenant commander on his epaulets. "Commander Poretti, sir! This peltneck was attempting to illegally enter the warehouse."

Lucretia strode behind Kai and leer at the pair. "Perhaps you two should try lying when not surrounded by people who can contradict your hogwash. All we want is to speak with the commanding officer."

The guards looked at each other, completely befuddled. "What did she say?" the left one asked.

"I think she said we're lying," his partner replied, his face blank.

Poretti told the pair to stand down, shaking his head. He apologized and introduced himself, beckoning the party to follow him. Inside the building was alive with action, as sailors bustled about setting up bed rolls or prying open crates of supplies. The commander led them to the back corner, where box sidings were erected into makeshift walls, creating a small room. A table sat in the center with maps and documents scattered around. It reminded Kai of the Hunter commander's office back in Havenfall.

Taking a seat and steepling his fingers together, Poretti regarded the party with interest. "I must confess, it isn't every day I find a Norzen requesting an audience. Judging by that vest, I'm guessing you're with the Hunter Corps. Now, what do you want? As you can see, we're rather busy preparing for battle."

"So you *do* know that the Liberators are coming?" When the officer nodded his assent, Kai continued, "Good, that saves us some time. How do you plan to evacuate or otherwise protect the citizens?"

Poretti's eyes pinched together, releasing an agitated huff. "Not that it's any of your business, but we are taking measures. Reinforcements are on their way from Whistlevale. Until the Libbies are dealt with, no one leaves this city. My men are sealing the gates at this moment. We will hold the city until support arrives and helps drive them back. Since the Hunters are official combat support, I'll be making use of you on the front lines."

Maple and Ione shot to their feet, fury blazing in their eyes. It was only Kai throwing an arm up that kept the two women from launching themselves at the officer.

"You get one warning," Kai hissed. "I have no intention of being a meat shield. So your plan is to trap the entire city inside the walls and wait for assistance?" Poretti nodded with eyes full of pride. To Kai's indignation, it was obvious he believed the plan was foolproof.

The apothecary pressured the man on when the reinforcements were arriving. Poretti claimed he didn't know. However, Kai noticed his eyes flitting to the junior officers along the wall, several of whom gripped their swords. Morgan stepped behind Kai, resting a hand on his own blade. The officers backed down.

Poretti surged up, knocking his chair over and sending documents to the floor. "Listen here, peltneck, I oversee this city's defenses now. Everything is under control, and no bloody Norzen is going to question my decisions. This plan will work. Now give me one damned good reason why I shouldn't have you thrown in the gaol," he shouted. Spittle flew into Kai's face, who swallowed his anger despite a burning desire to punch Poretti's nose in.

Kai turned to face Orelia when she tapped him on the shoulder wearing a wide grin. "Should we tell him?" she asked.

"Tell me what?" Poretti demanded.

Ignoring the provocation, Kai set his watch down before the officer without a word. He thought it hilarious when Poretti's face shifted through several colors like a kaleidoscope. Red, white, gray, then blue; the man was a veritable rainbow of expression.

"Wh-where did you get that? That can't be real," Poretti stammered. The junior officers drew their swords when Kai stood.

"I'm not one to usurp authority like this, but you're a fish out of water here. If something isn't done, your men and thousands of innocents are going to *die*," Kai said. A heavy rumble emitted from his chest as he set his knuckles on the table. "This watch is very real. You're welcome to verify Her Grace's official signature on the back. I am the Exarch and apothecary known as Gravebane. My sworn duty is to ensure the health and safety of *all* Her Grace's subjects, no matter their tribe or status. I do have a plan that should drive the Liberators out. And you're going to at least hear me out. Am. I. Clear?" Kai dilated his eyes and pinned the officer with a simmering glare.

Poretti tried to answer, but his voice refused to work. He dropped into his seat and nodded; the wind cut from his sails.

"It seems we finally understand one another. Now answer this: Do you know how many Liberators you're up against?" When Poretti admitted he didn't, Lucretia mumbled some choice words regarding the man's competence. Kai stared the commander down with a grim smile. "Consider yourself lucky because we do. An Aerivolk acquaintance of mine spotted them and says we're facing six thousand enemy soldiers."

Poretti looked ready to faint, his face sweating profusely and whitening to a pallid shade.

Kai continued, "Yes, and if you keep everyone trapped, what will happen when the Liberators set the city wall ablaze? They aren't well known for patience, after all."

The ramifications of his plan were laid bare; Poretti groaned in frustration. "Damn it all, every report from Runegard said the Liberator forces were maybe a thousand at best!" He looked up at Kai with unsure eyes. "What kind of plan could you have that can handle that many soldiers?"

Kai spread a map of the city over the table, used knives to pin the corners. Asking everyone to gather round, he described his plan in full. Individuals were divided into teams and a list was compiled with each team's objective. Some, like Morgan, thought the idea was crazy enough to work. Others, like Poretti, were hesitant.

"This seems risky," the commander commented. "I understand you're an Exarch, Sir Gravebane, but have you ever done anything like this before?"

Kai raised his eyes and grinned. "Not once." Poretti and his staff gaped at the Norzen, unable to speak. "Most Exarchs are members of the Navy, as you probably know," Kai continued, "but I'm an apothecary by trade, not a military strategist."

The sailors' eyes bulged. "You're a *what*? Then why are we doing this if you have no experience?"

Pulling his mace from its loop, Kai set it on the table. "I never said I don't know what I'm doing. In case you forgot, I'm also a Hunter. Most of you probably see us as backup soldiers, but we're quite uniquely skilled in one area that makes us dangerous compared to a common sailor. Anyone care to guess what that is?"

The first answer came in moments. "Setting traps?" suggested one sailor. Kai shook his head but complimented the sailor for a good guess.

Then another, "Tracking quarry?" Another shake. More guesses sprang forth, but none were correct.

Surprisingly, the answer came from the party. Lucretia nursed a stein of water before sending the Norzen a curious look. "You can adapt."

A wide grin split Kai's face from ear to ear. "Correct, Lucretia. The first thing young Hunters are taught is to use what you have. Bloody Nulyma, they teach us this almost from the moment we learn to walk. You won't always be in a good position. So you adapt, improvise, and alter the battlefield on your terms."

Poretti gazed around the table. "You know if this fails, we all die, correct?" Seeing the collective agreement, he presented Kai with one final question. "Are you sure they'll want to do this?"

Kai looked at Orelia, who answered with a single nod. "They'll do it. I'm positive the chance to pull one over on these bastards will be too juicy a fruit to pass up. Now let's get started. Our trap won't set itself."

As the officers leapt up and rushed to deliver orders, the party remained in place. No one moved or spoke. Finally, Maple crossed her wings and reviewed the map once more. "I'll admit, the commander has a point. This is a hell of a risk. What if they don't take the bait?"

"They will take it," Lucretia replied to everyone's surprise. "This plan is a massive gamble, but Kai, Ione, and I have all seen the Liberators in battle. For them to ignore a prize like that would defy all logic."

This would be the biggest risk Kai had ever taken. Tomorrow would tell if he placed his bets right.

The next morning, Kai rolled out of bed with nervous anticipation. The Liberators would be there before nightfall.

Poretti allowed the party to stay in the camp, which suited their purposes fine, while Orelia returned to Stahl Granz to tend to the orphanage.

Exiting the warehouse, Kai was surprised to see the priestess weaving her way through a throng of sailors setting up campfires for breakfast.

"You're up early," Kai mentioned as they greeted each other.

Orelia waved a small roll of parchment in Kai's face. "There are no lie-ins at the orphanage, I'm afraid. Those rascals get in enough trouble when I'm awake, as you well know. Besides, Poretti and I need to inform Bishop Adalbard and the headman of their roles in your little scheme," she explained with a small giggle. "But there is good news. I received a hawk this morning. My friend is back in the city. Wake the others, and I'll introduce you to him."

The pair reentered the warehouse and split up. Ione and Maple were already awake when Orelia arrived, but Lucretia had to be roused from bed. She was unhappy at being disturbed, though her mood visibly improved when she heard they would be meeting the man sailing them to Runegard. Ione in particular was happy at being put one step closer to returning home.

On the men's side, Kai found Morgan snoring like a war horn. Smirking, he snuck next to the man's head and did his best bison imitation, cutting loose with a loud bellow. The sound sent the sellsword rolling out of his cot and crashing to the floor. Several surrounding sailors watched the whole thing cackling, congratulating Kai on a brilliant prank. The rest gave him a wide berth and continued eating while keeping an eye on the Norzen. Morgan was less than pleased but admitted he would've done the same if the roles were reversed.

Once the party gathered, they joined the sailors for breakfast outside. Finding an empty spot was vexing, but they managed, and a small fire was soon crackling under their pot.

Seeing the Navy in action was a rare opportunity, and Kai noticed the battalion truly was a stew of people, filled with individuals representing every tribe and walk of life one could imagine. Nobles mixed freely with commoners, and members of all tribes came together to accomplish a mission. It was an eye-opening sight for Kai. He even noticed an occasional Norzen patrolling the camp in full uniform, tails swaying in the wind and ears poking from beneath their caps. It made him wish for a chance to truly talk with and get to know other members of his tribe.

Swiveling his ears, the apothecary listened in on nearby conversations and made mental notes of what he heard. More than a few were discussing the plan. Some thought the plan was a stroke of genius, while others were unsure and believed it a suicide mission. Kai admitted it was a valid concern. Facing off against an army four times your size would unnerve even hardened warriors. But if they could cut the size of that army before the real fighting started...their chances of victory would soar.

Kai's focus was dragged back when Maple popped him behind the head. Noticing Orelia frowning at him, Kai apologized. "As I was saying," the priestess said while giving Kai a dull stare, "we'll head to the underground docks after breakfast. Keep in mind, my friend can be a bit gruff when you first meet him, but he's a good man. He's also a bit smaller than other Soltauri, but don't let it fool you. He's stronger than he looks. Be respectful, and above all else, do *not* say anything about his height or horn!"

"What's wrong with his horn?" Morgan asked, only for Ione to clobber him with her pan. The sellsword whined she was going to break his brain if she kept hitting him.

Lucretia snorted. "After what you just asked, I am certain your brain was damaged when we first met you."

Morgan crossed his arms with a strange look. "You might be on to something. Mam always said Pops dropped me on my head a few times as a baby."

The scholar's mumbled reply of, "This explains so much," made everyone snicker.

The party descended into small talk for the remainder of breakfast. Ione apologized to Morgan, but he laughed it off, commenting that his parents tried teaching him tact growing up. The lessons just never stuck.

As always, after eating came the cleanup. Kai figured they would've finished in half the time if Morgan and Maple didn't keep begging Ione for extra helpings. Once Orelia threatened to overturn the pot over their heads and ring it with her staff, they decided to pick up the slack.

The party bid the sailors farewell as they passed. Poretti crossed their path accompanied by his assistant, inquiring where they were going.

"We have business at the docks, Commander," Orelia replied with a stiff bow. "Rest assured we will return once our business has concluded." The woman spun on her heel and led the party into the alley, towards the market road.

The scent of the river grew stronger, sending a tingle of nervousness through Kai's fur. If everything went smooth, they would be out of town tonight and on their way to Runegard before the Liberation Army knew what was happening. But to ensure that, there was one final thing to take care of.

They had a smuggler to meet.

Despite the lack of traffic on the river, the branch canal docks remained bustling with activity. Kai had seen a number of fish markets, but the catch just brought in from the seaport was unusual. Gone were the nets full of trout, moonfish, and sturgeon found within Livoria's numerous rivers. Instead, the market was overflowing with yellowtail bass, cobia, and black snapper hauled in from the ocean.

According to Morgan, it made sense. Even with boats forbidden from going downriver, people still needed to eat, and the anchor of any port town's diet was the local fish. Without access to the river, the fishermen adjusted and made for the open sea. It was more dangerous, but they had little choice.

Maple was in her element, flitting between stalls at a rapid clip, bartering for deals in her cheery drawl. Often, she would exchange some of her handcrafted accessories for food and other trinkets Kai found lovely to look at, though he knew nothing of their practical use. While the others marched ahead, Kai drifted behind her and listened as she inspected a large bass with the stall's Wasini shopkeeper leering from the side.

"Very discerning eye, miss," the snake-like faumen said. He had a smooth voice that, while it seemed charismatic, sent a chill through Kai's fur. "That's one of my finest catches today. Really put up a fight getting him out of the water. I'll let you have it for ten coppers a pound. A real steal!"

Maple hummed to herself, scrutinizing every inch of the fish. Turning it over, she side-eyed the shopkeeper and set the fish down. "I'll give ya four."

The man goggled and hissed at the merchant, his arms flailing. "Four?! Bloody Nulyma, girl, are you a blooming pirate under those feathers? That's robbery is what it is! Eight coppers a pound. You'll never find a better offer for such a pristine specimen."

How Maple managed to stay calm under the Wasini's belligerence, Kai couldn't imagine. He was curious as to why she would make such low offers, countering the shopkeeper's offer with five marks a pound. It was almost like she was trying to...his eyes widened when he took a closer look at the fish.

That cheeky bird!

"You seemed like a reputable businessman," Maple said, fingering her coin pouch, which the Wasini eyed with hunger. "But 'pristine' doesn't feel like a proper word for this fish. Look." She turned the fish on its back, exposing a jagged gash along the belly. "Obviously, you were a touch heavy-handed in getting him on the boat. I *was* going to overlook the damage, but your first offer forced my wing. What say we do six coppers a pound, dressing included, and call it a deal?"

She offered her hand to the shopkeeper, who frowned and cast a final longing look at the bass before shaking on it. Maple watched as the man dressed and weighed the fish before providing payment. Taking her prize in hand, she sauntered away with a smug grin.

Kai sidled alongside her and glanced back at the unhappy Wasini. "Remind me never to brass you off. You're ruthless, woman!"

"I can't stand sloppy business or dishonesty," Maple replied, her talons clicking on the cobblestones as they walked. She flashed a smile brimming with confidence. "Integrity is the cornerstone of a true merchant. Anyone can lie and lie and imitate success. But what happens when the lies catch up to them? Everything crashes down. Without honesty a merchant is naught, but a thief dressed in a shroud of duplicity."

There was passion in every word she spoke. Kai couldn't help but feel a kindling of inspiration listening to the ardent merchant. "You're something else, Maple," he commented. "I'm not sure how to describe it, but you've got a spark here." He raised a finger to Maple's heart. "You told me when we met you were going to be the most beloved merchant in all of Alezon, right?"

She nodded. Kai replied with a raised thumb, "Well call me convinced, because I have no doubt you can do it with that attitude." The smile on Maple's face was bright enough to light a cavern. No more words were shared as the two caught up to the rest of the party.

Orelia shot the pair an odd look before leading everyone to an alley loping around and down into a tunnel beneath the docks. The tunnel sloped down and opened into a maze of canals. The air was mustier than the main docks, with moss covering large portions of the brick walls like a shaggy blanket. The scent of salt was in the air, faint but strong enough to remind Kai of their proximity to the sea.

When asked how she knew where to go, Orelia remarked that the orphans taught her many things over the past two years. Such as navigating the deepest, darkest alleys of Faith Hollow and interacting with the people who thrived there. The further they traveled, the fainter the salty scent became.

After what felt like forever, Orelia led them into an intersection, with several canals branching off in various directions. Multicolored speckles coming from open holes in the ceiling provided a modicum of light, drawing Kai's curiosity until Orelia explained that they were currently beneath Stahl Granz. The light was reflecting off the temple's stained-glass windows, lighting up the underground canals.

Orelia explained that the system spread throughout the city's lower level like an irrigation line and helped ease the pressure from the river when the sluice gate was closed. Strolling along the path, the priestess pointed at the central point where all the canals met.

There, moored at a dilapidated dock that looked held together by the excessive application of rope, was a small towboat of ten yards laden with a steam engine. A deck barge twenty yards long was connected to the towboat by thick, tightly knotted ropes and loaded with crates covered by a leather tarp.

Standing at the towboat's helm was a Soltauri man leaning on a halberd and watching the party with apprehension. As Orelia mentioned, he was short for his tribe, standing only about two hands taller than Kai himself. His ears and chest were covered in bright white fur with scattered black spots. A spiraling horn half a yard in length protruded backwards from the left side of his head. Wincing, Kai realized why the priestess warned everyone about commenting on them: a fractured stump was all that remained of the right horn.

He wore a dusty, sleeveless ivory tunic tucked into black knee-length trousers. A black bowler hat with an upturned brim and yellow trim rested on his head. His arms bore black leather gauntlets stretching to just beneath his elbows, likely to protect his forearms from his own weapon's blade. His tail flicked behind him, ending in a small teardrop-shaped ball of white fur.

As the party approached, he leapt to the dock and tipped his hat. "Pleasant morning to you, Sister Orelia," the man called out in an eastern brogue, his voice deep and commanding. It reminded Kai of his father when the man was serious. Waving his halberd towards the party, the Soltauri asked, "Is this the group you told you me about?" The members of the party each greeted the man in turn and introduced themselves.

Orelia nodded with a clap of her hands. "That's correct, Teos. You truly are doing me a favor in helping these people."

"Bah!" Teos exclaimed, shrugging his shoulders. "Think nothing of it. You've saved my tail from the town guard more times than I can count. If anything, this just makes us a little more even."

Facing the party, his lips curled into a haughty grin as he looked them up and down. "You seem like an odd bunch, especially traveling to a place like Runegard. Let's see: a Norzen apothecary, an Archivist, a tavern girl, an Aerivolk merchant, and a Wasini mixblood in Corlatian armor. Feels like I'm staring at the beginning of a court fool's bawdy joke."

When a stunned Maple asked him how he was able to tell what their jobs were, Teos brayed with laughter and pointed out each item that gave them away: Kai's satchel, Lucretia's cloak emblem, Ione's dress, Maple's rucksack, and Morgan's armor.

Put that bluntly, Kai had to agree with the man. Under normal circumstances, the chances of any of them meeting, much less traveling together, were short of impossible. "I'm afraid we're a party of unfortunate circumstances. Other than Maple, all of us were caught up in the Liberators' invasion of Mistport," Kai explained.

Teos frowned. "Mistport? The Libbies really *did* attack that little port town?" Seeing everyone nod, he swore. "Damn it all, here I hoped those rumors were just that. I knew good people in that town. Those Libbie bastards are gonna pay."

Placing a comforting hand on Teos's shoulder, Orelia turned him to face her. "I know how you feel, my friend. This war has already caused so much senseless bloodshed. And more is sure to come. You may be able to get some revenge sooner than you think, though."

The Soltauri's eyes were full of curiosity. "Is that so? How?"

Orelia pointed at Kai. "Our resident apothecary here is to blame." The smuggler's eyes bulged at that. "He browbeat the commander of the city defenses into helping with his plan to not only create an opening for us to escape onto the Galen, but also cut the enemy down to a more manageable size."

"Now you've got my attention. What exactly are you planning?" Kai then outlined the plan, focusing on the party's role and what they would need from Teos. The barge captain howled with laughter when Kai revealed his plan for the Liberation Army. "Oh, that's beautiful! If this lunacy of yours works, I might just hug you."

Kai blushed, admitting that the plan hinged on a bit of luck. He changed topics and gestured towards the towboat. "This is an impressive vessel, Captain Teos. It's rare to see a steamboat this far north. I assume she's sturdy enough to weather a good drubbing?"

"Just Teos is fine. And you bet the winds, she is. Her name's *Gulley*, and she's the toughest boat I've ever ridden the Galen with, even if she is getting on in years. She and the barge both have teakwood frames and decks with oil-varnished cedar planking and aluminum plates to protect against arrows and flintlocks. She's a bit slow, but damned if she can't take a beating and keep on floating."

"Perfect," Kai said, "She'll need to be tough if we're going to get out of here. Once the plan is in motion, we'll meet you right here."

Teos tapped his halberd against the *Gulley*'s side. "We'll be here. Just be ready for some rough waters. If there's one thing you learn in this town, it's that the river waits for no one."

Chapter XIII

"That's a lot of soldiers."

Kai side-eyed Poretti before admitting the man had a point. Six thousand men loitered outside the walls of Faith Hollow, many jeering and hollering at the sparse defenders lining the allure. Their formations were shoddy and fragmented at best, but it remained a daunting sight. Kai knew even apex predators would hesitate against such an overwhelming disadvantage.

"Are the teams in position?" Kai asked. Poretti confirmed that everything was set up according to plan. The apothecary raised his spyglass to survey the army. The hood of his vest was up once more, concealing his ears. The last thing they wanted was the enemy attacking before they were ready. Seeing a Norzen in the battlements would no doubt spur the groups nearest the wall to charge.

Scanning the army, he found several units in the center bearing weapons that looked like flintlock pistols, but with a longer barrel than any firearm he'd ever seen. He also noticed a figure atop a wiroch in the rear, bedecked in shinier armor compared to the surrounding men. Kai couldn't shake the familiar feeling the man gave him.

Probably some snooty admiral I met when I visited Whistlevale, he thought.

An ensign whistled from below the allure. "Commander Poretti, the headman is in position and ready for our signal!" the man yelled.

"Excellent work," Poretti replied. "What about the market?" The ensign nodded, to Kai's relief. That meant the show was ready to start.

Tucking the spyglass away, Kai took a deep breath and unfurled his tails, allowing them to twitch freely. "Guess it's time for the curtain to rise on our little performance. Ready, commander?"

Poretti rolled his shoulders and drew his sword. "As ready as I'll ever be, I suppose. We'll be on your tail once they charge, so be quick. Now comes the real problem: How do we goad them into doing what we want?"

In response, Kai flipped his hood back and freed his ears, a sharkish grin on his face. "Allow me. I've wanted to do this ever since Mistport." He grabbed a war horn from a nearby guards and blew into it as hard as he could. The resulting blast caught the Liberators' attention, as six thousand startled faces turned to the wall.

Kai raised his tails into the air and waggled them at the Liberators before bellowing into the war horn. "You assholes couldn't pour piss out of a hat if you put it on!" he taunted, flashing a rude gesture before taking a running leap out of sight. The outcry and clang of metal from beyond the wall was exactly what Kai hoped for.

The defenders stared open-mouthed at the apothecary's audacity. Moments later, the crack of a flintlock pierced the din as an iron ball grazed Poretti's ear. Spurred into action, the officer shouted for everyone to fight back and leapt for the haystack beneath him. Rolling onto the street, he bolted after Kai. Dozens of arrows and bullets soared over the battlements, but none struck true. Poretti's sailors responded with volleys from their flintlocks and bows.

The men on the allure watched as the Liberators set up a battering ram and charged the southern gate. "Lower the barricade!" A lieutenant cried out. A sailor manning the gate winch slammed the latch open, letting its chain run free and dropping an iron portcullis behind the wooden gate. "Excellent job," the officer praised, "Everyone, fall back to the defensive positions."

A loud thud echoed through the courtyard as the battering ram pounded the outer doors. More arrows flew overhead, some with flickering rags tied to the heads. Several of these pierced the rooftops nearest the South Ward entrance. The report of flintlocks rang out again, toppling several men from the allure as the bullets found their marks. The sailors below called for water to extinguish the rooftop fires before they could spread.

Kai barreled through South Ward, the sounds of battle ringing behind him. Checking the surrounding buildings, he caught splashes of color on several corners. Paint was used to mark the different paths teams were required to take, with each team assigned a different color. He smiled when he saw a blot of crimson paint on one corner. Twisting his hip, he spun his body while leaping at the adjacent building, kicking off the wall and into the alley without losing speed.

The shouts of sailors grew louder as everyone raced through the alleys. He didn't have time to aid them, so he had to trust Poretti drilled his men well. Navigation was made simpler by the splotches of red marking which corner he needed to turn into. At times, he spotted faumen sailors crossing his path. Kai uttered a quick prayer for them, knowing the faumen of Faith Hollow had the toughest job in the plan.

By the time he reached his destination, Kai was exhausted, and his legs burned from overuse. The party was waiting at the bridge leading back to Temple Square. A sea of glimmering lights flickered across the bridge, where crowds of people huddled together outside Stahl Granz.

"What kept ya, 'pothy?" Morgan asked. "I was starting to wonder if you got snagged on the way. Is everything good to go?"

Kai raised his thumb before taking a swig from his canteen. "The battalion is moving into position. All we need now is to lure those bastards in."

With the sun almost set, Lucretia carried a torch to light their way. Kai saw dozens of families around campfires and oil lanterns, reminding him of the battalion camp that morning. Many civilians were evacuated via the seaport earlier that day, where they waited among the rocky seaside cliffs outside town. The ones that remained were those too ill or old to make the trip, along with their families. The battering ram's strikes were muffled by distance but could still be heard over the crowd's chattering.

Orelia waved everyone over to a squad of sailors. They surrounded a battery of cannons angled along the road. Poretti stood at their head, his sword shining in the light of the fires.

"Perfect timing," she said as they approached. "Sounds like the Liberators still can't break the gates down." A deafening crash shattered the calm and sent a wave of nervousness through the crowd.

Leveling the priestess with a dead stare, Lucretia quipped, "You were saying?"

It was to Orelia's credit that she didn't flounder under Lucretia's intense gaze. Instead, she rapped the nearest cannon with her staff. "You're up, boys," she called to the sailors. In unison, all fifteen cannons turned on the bridge.

"Bring it down!" Poretti bellowed.

The crowd covered their ears as the cannons erupted in flashes of flame and metal. Kai's teeth rattled from the intensity of their rapport. Their iron missiles smashed into the bridge, sending it crumbling to the canal floor in a shower of dust. The sailors cheered when the dust settled to reveal the annihilated bridge. One of the men broke off from the others and sent a firework into the air with a burst of orange sparks.

More blasts rang out from downriver, followed by additional fireworks showering sparks from above the southern bridges. Kai whooped in triumph. With every bridge out, they could begin the next act. Just in time too, as his ears picked up the growing shouts of the Liberators.

"Things are going smooth, now to keep it that way." Kai turned to the commander. "Let's get them in there, Poretti. Once the enemy is inside, give the signal. We're counting on you." Poretti nodded and shouted for his sailors to move.

Kai returned to the waiting party. Poretti and one of his men ran to the edge of the canal, waving an emerald flag. In moments, dozens of Vesikoi rose from the drainage openings lining the central canal's inner edge. Each was armed with rope and nets. Together, they hooked the nets over the stairwell entrances leading to the defenders' side.

Kai thanked Orelia for leading them to the barge.

"Think nothing of it," she replied. "You helped one of my children when you had no need to. Besides, if this crazy idea of yours works, the city may at least survive to see the war's end. Now let's get you all into the—"

An uproar sounded from within the crowd. "Sister Orelia," a woman cried, approaching the group. "The temple is on fire!" All eyes turned to Stahl Granz, where an eerie red glow came from the building's rear. The west wing, specifically.

Orelia gasped. "The orphanage! Sweet merciful Galen...the children!"

She broke into a full sprint towards the temple, the party trailing behind her. Kai ordered everyone to bring water from the city wells before following the others. Orelia threw herself against the door, but it didn't budge. She grabbed the handle and yanked, but it refused to give.

"It's locked! Someone barricaded the inside," she moaned. Orelia's face was furrowed, and the pleading look in her eyes was desperate.

Grabbing his mace, Kai tapped Morgan on the arm. "Break it down?"

The sellsword grinned. "I thought you'd never ask," he said, cracking his knuckles. The pair hammered at the door. With each successive blow, the door creaked and splintered, but it would not break.

"The hinges! Aim for the hinges," Kai instructed while throwing a swing at the lower hinge, knocking it loose with two blows. Morgan used his sword like a pry bar to tear the upper one loose. The men dug their fingers into the cracks between the door and frame, wrenching it out. A wooden crossbar fell to the ground with a thud.

Orelia shoved past, not waiting for the others as they followed her mad dash into the temple. Black smoke advanced from the back of the wing. The flicker of flames grew brighter the deeper into the hall they ran. Kai watched as Orelia entered the orphans' room across from the chapel, hoping the children were alright.

His heart shattered when he heard it: a wail of grief erupting from the room.

Kai and Morgan were pushed aside as the women rushed into the room. The men shared a grim look when more cries joined the tumult, drowning out the fire's crackle. Already having an idea of what they'd find, they entered the room.

The first thing Kai noticed was the blood. Not just the splatters of crimson covering the walls and floor, but the overwhelming stench of iron. It was enough to make the apothecary stumble backwards. Morgan placed a bracing palm against his back. Kai wondered how such small bodies could produce the amount of blood smeared across the room.

Worst of all was seeing the five bodies on the floor, partially hidden under blankets with Orelia sobbing over them. Lucretia wrapped her arms around Ione as the older woman wept into her shoulder. Maple looked utterly lost, slumped against the wall with tears streaming down her cheeks. Seeing the peppy merchant in such a state shook Kai to his core. Looking to the side, he saw even Morgan frozen in silence.

Orelia saw Kai and rushed into his arms, clawing at his vest. "Save them!" she cried. "You're an apothecary, right? Please, I'm begging you!" The wild look in her eye was one Kai knew all too well. And no matter how often he saw it, it always felt like a knife digging into his chest. He rested a hand on Orelia's shoulder and asked Maple to stay with her. The Aerivolk embraced Orelia as Kai stepped amidst the bodies and knelt. Pulling the blanket off the closest body, a feeling of rage simmered in his gut.

Wide-eyed and open-mouthed, Dannel's body lay unmoving in a pool of blood. Pressing his fingers to the boy's neck, Kai flinched. No pulse. He inspected the body, seeing several long, shallow cuts on the arms, hip, and upper leg. His chest was sliced open from the breastbone to the stomach. A deep purple bruise encircled his neck as well.

Seeing the kind boy's body like this sent images of Marko and the others through Kai's mind. Fighting back his own tears, he tried to ignore the familiarity of the scene.

Grimacing, he inspected the other children. With each pulseless body, the rage in Kai's belly grew and festered. All were dead, and all exhibited the same wounds as Dannel. He turned his gaze back to Orelia and shook his head. "I'm sorry."

"No!"

Orelia fell to her knees and wailed. An aura of despair permeated the group as the fire grew louder around them. Kai heard the shouts of people bailing water onto the fire from the outside. He called for everyone to head towards the barge. Orelia begged to know why they couldn't at least save the children's bodies. Lucretia reminded her that if they didn't hurry, the fire would trap them, and they would die as well.

Rising to his feet, Kai spotted Ione pointing at each body with a frown. "Wait, I only count five children. Aren't we missing one?"

Orelia spun and did her own count. Sure enough, there were only five bodies instead of the six that should've been there. Doing a mental tally, Kai realized who was missing.

"Where's Tuvi?"

"Looking for something?" a familiar voice barked from outside.

The party turned to see Bishop Adalbard blocking the chapel door with a malicious grin. The mitre was gone, exposing a balding head, and his vestment was stained red. Kai heard the clack of boots through the fire coming from behind the priest, but he ignored it for now.

Instead, he focused on what was in the bishop's hand: A bloody dagger pointed at a struggling Tuvi wrapped within his other arm.

"Tuvi!" Orelia cried, trying to rush forward only for Morgan to hold her back.

"Easy, Sister."

"Let me go, Morgan! I have to save her!"

Lucretia drew her rapier, pointing it at Adalbard. "What have you done?"

The old man twirled the blade in his hand with a surprising deftness. "I simply removed some unwanted garbage. See, there are certain truths many in the world are ignorant to." Adalbard's voice carried the passion of a priest delivering a sermon. "The winds of fortune are powerful, but they favor only those meant to do great things. Those worthy above all others."

"People like you," Ione said.

Adalbard cackled with delight. "Exactly, my dear! There is no fortune for those with no purpose. It's a simple fact. Those creatures are meant to serve and elevate the worthy! Creatures like this little peltneck wretch!" The priest gestured to Tuvi, who stared at the party with tears in her eyes. "And if they can't find purpose in that, then they must be culled to make room for those who know their place."

The longer Adalbard preached, the more Kai wanted to bash his head in. A familiar crimson haze settled over his eyes. "And what of those who overcome life's hardships?" he asked, fighting back the fog by sheer will. "What do you say of people who build themselves up from nothing to achieve an honorable and peaceful life?"

Adalbard pointed the dagger at Kai's heart. "Those of proper breeding know that great deeds in life are the only way to reach the gardens of Finyt. Faumen like you have none of that breeding. You're nothing but the stained lineage of the heretics our forefathers brought to heel centuries ago. And you Norzen have proven the worst of them all."

The bishop's eyes shone with pious fury. "You devil cats have been a plague on Alezon since the beginning, even before the sins of Cacovis! Creatures like you have no hope to embrace Finyt's light. This little one will serve some purpose, at least. I hear the Liberation Army pays good coin for you peltnecks."

Scarlet filled Kai's vision as he stomped forward, the others spitting curses at Adalbard. The party stepped back when Kai's foot came down hard enough to crack the stone floor, leaving a crater in its wake. "Choose your next words *very* carefully, priest," the Norzen warned. A hand gripped his arm tight, washing the red from his vision. A glance sideways revealed Maple holding onto him with concern in her eyes.

The bishop's laughter was high-pitched and screechy as he blathered about not fearing a pack of heretics. "The Wind Saints will protect me. All I do is for the glory of the church! Those orphans were an unnecessary burden. They deserved their fate. Don't worry, though. You'll be joining them very soon."

"You seem to be forgetting we outnumber you," Morgan reminded the priest.

Adalbard pressed the dagger against Tuvi's throat, growling for the party to stay back.

"He won't kill her." Everyone's eyes spun to Kai. "The Libbies only pay out for living Norzen. Adalbard's a disgusting monster, but he's also proven he's a greedy coward."

Orelia charged Adalbard with a scream of rage. The priest sidestepped and thrust his dagger at her ribs, only for the clumsy attack to be parried. She struck the man's wrist with the length of her staff, sending the dagger clattering to the floor. Sweeping the bishop's ankles from behind, Orelia dropped him onto his back, though he refused to relinquish his hold on Tuvi.

"You are nothing but a wretched, irredeemable beast." Orelia pinned Adalbard to the floor with her foot and held the tip of her staff against his throat. "You murder innocent children and claim it's for the glory of the church? You know nothing of the Eight Paths of Virtue, or the Wind Saints' true teachings. Even Cacovis was said to be a respected leader before the Desolation. If I knew you were capable of this, I would've killed you the day I arrived."

Gritting her teeth, Orelia raised her cudgel and swung down, intent on smashing the bishop's head. Adalbard raised his free hand to shield himself when sparks flew, Orelia's staff stopping short.

Everyone tensed. A longsword had appeared from the chapel door and blocked the priestess' strike. Orelia was shoved back, caught by Morgan before she could fall. A dirt-covered figure emerged, brandishing the sword. A figure with closely cropped hair and captain's leaves on his armor.

Kai groaned as Agosti's hate-filled eyes locked on him. "You can't be serious. How'd you get past that sinkhole in the mines?"

The officer laughed but didn't respond, preferring to grab Adalbard by his vestment and haul the older man up. "Move, cleric! Make yourself useful and get that brat somewhere secure." The bishop ran into the chapel as Tuvi struggled against his grip, screaming.

Orelia dashed after Adalbard, yelling for him to stop.

Agosti didn't bother lifting a finger to stop her, his eyes fully locked on Kai. "Not gonna lie, peltneck, I thought you bastards had me. It was fool's luck there was a second path that led to the other side. Now then," he twirled his sword like a fan, rattling the blade against the wall, "what do you say we finish this?"

Kai ordered the party to follow Orelia and reach the barge after saving Tuvi, handing his pack to Morgan. Ione begged him to come as well, but Kai promised to handle Agosti.

The captain stood in front of the chapel entrance. "You and I have a score to settle."

Giving his weapon a test swing, Kai grinned. He saw memories of Marko and Faust on that day, injured yet still facing off against the Liberator captain. "I was hoping you'd say that. I owe you a thrashing for what you and your men did to my friends in Mistport. Besides, that priest put me in a foul mood, so I guess I'll take my anger out on you."

The two men stared at each other before rushing forward in a clash of metal. Agosti's eyes widened when Kai's charge took him off his feet and carried him into the chapel, smashing a pew into splinters.

"By the winds, that's a lot of soldiers," Poretti muttered.

The man's assistant, a young Soltauri ensign, remained standing at attention. "Indeed, Commander. You've said that four times since they showed up."

Poretti had the decency to look abashed, although the ensign knew his superior had a point. The Liberators stood on the other side of the canal, braying insults at the defenders. Kai's party had not been gone long, but Poretti knew he needed to trust the young Exarch's plan. The city's Vesikoi lined the edge of the central canal, protecting the net-covered stairwells and screeching their own insults back at the Liberators.

Behind them, the citizens were working to extinguish the fires behind Stahl Granz. It was a monumental task, with the flames spreading fast due to piles of straw scattered across the building's foundation.

The Liberators expressed a rabid level of excitement, clanging their weapons together and flinging stones across the canal. An officer with shaggy auburn hair and wearing diamonds to match Poretti's pushed his way to the front, calling out through a war horn. "Listen, Royalist scum! You have no hope of victory. If you surrender now and swear fealty to the Conclave, my superiors promise your citizens will not be harmed. However, we demand you turn over the Norzen that so blatantly disrespected us earlier."

Poretti scowled and grabbed a horn of his own. "And if we refuse?"

"You seem intelligent," the enemy officer remarked. "I think you already know what will happen." As if to drive the point further, the Liberators began leering and hurling vulgar remarks towards the women in the crowd. Some even grabbed themselves and gyrated their hips in a bawdy manner.

Being from nobility, Poretti considered himself a gentleman, so the Liberators' actions rankled his core. He ordered his assistant to spread word through the battalion that, should the enemy break through, the women and children's safety took priority. A subtle shift rippled through the crowd as sailors and town guards put themselves between the citizens and the enemy.

"Your answer, Royalist?" the enemy commander asked.

Poretti smirked, waggling his pinkie. If they were going to die tonight, then at least he would get one verbal barb in. "I say your sister works a back-alley tavern and your father smells of thistletwill, you low-born, incompetent pebblewit!" The battalion exploded in laughter. Soon, a sea of waggling fingers was directed at the Liberators, with several children joining in.

The Liberator officer stood stock still, unable to comprehend what he heard. "M-my sister is a saint, you ruddy bastard!" he shrieked in an earsplitting voice. His face flush with rage, the commander drew his sword and ordered a charge. He took a running leap into the canal as his men followed. Several dozen stayed put, loading balls into the long flintlocks.

Poretti raised an arm. "They've got flints! Shielders, to the vanguard!" The thud of armored boots echoed as chainmail armored sailors marched in front. Each carried a thick aluminum wedge shield as tall as themselves. Standing shoulder to shoulder, the sailors formed a wall of metal as the opposing flintlocks roared. The shields held firm against the barrage, deflecting the incoming fire.

Rather than wait for the enemy to arrive, the Vesikoi dove into the open drainage ports, taking refuge within the aqueducts. The commander and his men barreled headfirst into the nets, hacking at the thick ropes with their swords.

A pained cry rang out when a Vesikoi thrust his spear through the opening and found a hole in an unfortunate Liberator's armor. The spear disappeared beneath the water before anyone could spot where it came from.

More Liberators dove into the canal with each second, and soon enough the entire river market, from Temple Square to the other side of Faith hollow, was flooded with soldiers. The men destroyed anything they could get ahold of. Stalls, ceramics, food. Everything was trampled under the Liberators' boots with many reaching into the drainage ports after the Vesikoi. It proved futile though as the Vesikoi's mucus-covered bodies proved impossible to grip in water.

Poretti watched from behind the shielders with a smirk. It was time. Signaling to the ensign, he grabbed a torch smeared with blue powder and rushed past the temple. He stopped a passing soldier begging for a sparker, which she provided. The moment the sparks touched the powder, the torch burst into a green flame. Several people watched as Poretti held the torch above his head and waved back and forth, his eyes focused on the sluice gate's engine house.

Soon, an identical green flame shone from the engine house and Poretti muttered a quiet prayer of thanks. The Royalist commander shouted for the cannoneers to fire into the canal, taking out anyone attempting to cut the nets. An older sailor approached and reported that the Liberators had made little progress on breaking through. The Vesikoi had done their job well: the nets overlapped and intertwined until they melded into an impossibly thick knot. The Royalists doubted even a cannonball could penetrate them.

A deafening groan of creaking metal overpowered the shouts of the battling armies. All eyes swiveled eastward, towards the sluice. A loud shout came from the engine house, followed by the shrill whistle of a steam engine and a loud crack. The sluice gate shuddered, then dropped in a deafening crash. Each of the branch canal gates dropped moments later. The river flooded into the market canal, rushing towards the Liberation Army.

Realizing the danger they were in, the Liberators abandoned their weapons and tried running back to the south side of the canal. Instead, the army dissolved into a riot with comrades pushing, shoving, and attacking each other to escape first. Those closest to the exits made it to safety, leaving those in the back to attempt a frenzied rush at the nets blocking them from Temple Square.

The sound of rushing water rumbled through the streets; the river was racing to fill as much of the canal as possible. Already, these closest to the sluice were being swept under the waves. The Liberators' shouts of anger and frustration shifted to cries of fear and hopelessness. Still fighting amongst themselves, many were dragged into the waves. The ones that weren't immediately crushed by the pressure were battered against the stone walls of the canal or impaled by debris before being pulled downriver.

Poretti raised a hand to shield his eyes from the splashing water and rising dust. He ordered the defenders to back away, lest they be hit by a cresting wave and carried away as well. Gazing south, he realized just how many soldiers were packed into the canal.

"Ensign," he said. His assistant jogged up and snapped a crisp salute. "Send runners to West Ward. That crazy Exarch's plan worked." The younger officer whooped in delight, running to carry out the order. The

Liberators scattered before his eyes. With many of their officers drowned in the waters of the Galen, they had no direction. Hopping onto a nearby pile of haystacks, he raised his voice above the din.

"Prepare yourselves, everyone! The real fight starts now!" he bellowed. The crowd cheered and rattled their weapons. Watching the flowing river, Poretti felt something he thought he lost leading up to the battle: a glimmer of hope.

The crack of a flintlock reverberated in the air. A sudden and unexpected pressure spread through Poretti's side. In moments, it was joined by a powerful burning that caused the commander's hands to clutch his hip. His side felt wet. A liquid flowed between his fingertips and down his uniform. Looking down, he noticed an expanding red splotch coloring the tunic's white segments. Bringing his hand up, he saw blood coating his palm. When had that happened?

Poretti's knees felt weak. He staggered a little and tried steadying himself. Moving his foot sideways, however, caught nothing but open air. Poretti could hear his men's shouts as he toppled from the stack. The air was knocked from his lungs when his back struck the ground, and he saw the blurry images of his assistant and several others standing over him. All at once, lying on the ground with the pain in his side swelling at a rapid pace, he realized what happened.

He had been shot. One of those damned Libbies shot him.

A low groan escaped his lips and several pairs of hands swarmed over him. He tilted his head and saw the temple; a smile lay etched on his face. "May the winds of fortune guide you, Gravebane," Poretti whispered. "Give those bastards a good licking for me."

The officer allowed himself to drift away as his blurred vision faded to black.

Kai ducked under Agosti's sword and kicked the man in the sternum, knocking him back against a pew. Near the altar, where a statue of Galen the Sage stood, Orelia directed the rest of the party through a trap door. The rug that once lay there was kicked aside, and the door thrown wide open, likely by Adalbard in his hasty escape. Kai could hear Tuvi's cries growing softer.

"For a peltneck," Agosti said, aiming another slash at Kai's neck, "you fight rather well. Then again, any beast is dangerous when backed into a corner."

Kai stepped back, letting the blade come up short, though he did lose some fur from his mane. He thrust his mace forward like a rapier, tagging Agosti's cheek. The man snarled, reaching forward to grab the apothecary by the vest before pulling him close.

Seeing the sword arcing towards him, Kai blocked it with the mace's shaft and stepped into the hold. Sliding a foot behind Agosti's, he threw his weight forward and knocked the man off balance to send them both onto the ground. Kai took advantage and rolled away, putting himself between the trap door and Agosti.

Smoke from the fire climbed to the top of the temple and Kai felt the stifling heat spread through the chapel. He needed to get down the trap door, and quick. However, Agosti was proving more skilled than he expected. The captain refused to give him any breathing room. Eyes darting around, Kai searched for anything he could use as a distraction. Looking back to the altar, one thought struck his mind like lightning.

Orelia's gonna tan my hide if she ever finds out about this, Kai thought as he backed up.

Agosti lumbered to his feet. Wooden beams from the scaffolding above cracked under the flames. One beam snapped loose and fell between the two men with a crash. Agosti threw an arm up to shield himself, giving Kai the moment he needed.

He turned and rained blows at the statue's legs. The stone shattered after half a dozen strikes, causing the statue to tilt. A shout told Kai his time was up. Seeing Agosti bolt in his direction, Kai ducked behind the statue and shoved it as hard as he could. The statue tipped forward but did not fall. Huffing, Kai backed up several yards and took a running leap at the effigy, throwing his full weight at the center of its back.

The statue toppled forward, aimed to land directly on Agosti. The man slid to a stop and beat a hasty retreat. A loud boom echoed through the chapel. The building shook from the impact, the vibrations causing additional beams to drop from the scaffolding. Agosti cursed and continued backpedaling to avoid the falling debris. When the dust settled, the Liberator bellowed, finding the chapel split in half by a wall of rubble.

Kai rubbed his shoulder, wincing at the pain shooting through it. *I really need to quit doing that, but at least now he can't follow me.*

Ignoring Agosti's rage-fueled shouts, Kai grabbed hold of the trap door and pulled it shut after him, escaping into the lower level.

Lit torches lined the stairs leading into the underground channels. Kai was unsure of who lit them, but he was grateful for it. The stairs soon led to a short hall, ending at a door. Kai gave a tentative pull. It wasn't locked. Sighing in relief, he continued down the path until he heard rising voices further down. Pivoting his ears, he recognized the voices as Maple and Ione. They sounded angry.

Slipping into a jog, Kai hurried towards the voices. The path led him to the canal intersection, where the *Gulley* awaited. Maple was arguing with Teos, Ione standing behind her with a dour scowl on her face.

"Just give him a little more time!" Maple shouted. "Kai will be here; I know he will!"

Teos sighed and hopped onto the dock, untying the mooring rope. "He has two minutes, then we go. If the sounds from up there are any indication, that sluice gate is about to open. We need to get the *Gulley* in position to ride the waves out."

"We understand that," Ione replied, "but we can't just abandon him."

Hearing the women argue on his behalf brought a smile to Kai's face. Before meeting this group, he couldn't remember the last time anyone outside the Hunters or his family had defended him. It felt nice.

Kai shouted for them to get moving. The party spun around in shock. Maple howled with glee, swearing she knew all along he would make it. Everyone leapt into action, hauling themselves onto the barge.

Teos threw the mooring rope onto the deck and hopped on. "Time to set sail!" he shouted, rushing to the pilot house and firing the *Gulley's* engine up. The smokestack emitted a growing cloud of steam, and the barge pulled away from the dock.

A loud groan resounded. The walls seemed to shake, a veil of dust floating in the air. Rushing water could be heard through the stone walls. "The gate is opening! We better get out of here," shouted Kai.

"We need a bit more power!" Teos called back. "One of you needs to come up and load the boiler. That way I can steer the old girl and keep her from hitting a wall!"

To everyone's surprise, Ione pushed past and climbed up to the boiler. Rolling her sleeves up, she grabbed the shovel and kicked the door open before hoisting the coal inside.

Teos looked at the woman with a calculating smile. Before long, the barge was coasting into the branch canal. "Well I'll be damned," the smuggler remarked. "Ma'am, where in Finyt did you learn to do that?"

Ione gave a confident wink and threw another load of coal into the boiler. "Are you kidding? I carried heavy plates all day for years back in the tavern. A few shovels of coal are nothing." Teos fought to keep the ship straight as the water grew in intensity.

Kai saw Orelia sitting alone among a pile of crates, her head in her hands. Frowning, he trudged over and collapsed next to her. The priestess sniffled and leaned against Kai's shoulder, weeping. "She's gone," Orelia whispered. "He got away, Kai. Tuvi's gone and it's my fault."

"You did everything you could, Orelia. We'll get her back," offered Kai. "I don't know when or how, but we'll save her and make that bastard pay. I didn't know Dannel and the others as well as you, obviously, but they were good kids. Nobody deserves what happened."

"I swear," Orelia muttered, her tone low and harsh. Her sapphire eyes burned with fury. "When I find that bastard, I'm going to destroy him. Even if I didn't give birth to them, those were *my children*."

The apothecary nodded. "Fair point. Just don't lose yourself in that anger. The kids wouldn't want you to fall into darkness on their behalf. Still, that man is living on borrowed time. You of all people know the church's stance on harming children. The real question is where he went." The only thing Kai knew was that Adalbard would take his captive to the Liberators.

Orelia cast a forlorn look at the underground channel. "That's the problem. He could have gone anywhere. There are secret paths here Teos and I never found. I swear, though, on my honor as a Windbringer priestess," stated Orelia, "Adalbard will pay for his crimes with his life. Murdering a child carries an automatic death penalty, and since we caught him in the act, no trial would even be needed."

Kai was very aware of that law. Children were precious in the eyes of the Windbringer church. To harm one was a grievous sin. He still thought of his squad's mission before their ill-fated encounter with Grimghast. Duarte faced execution for his role in that incident, if captured.

He regretted thinking about those days almost immediately as he saw his squad mates' looks of fear before their deaths flashing before his eyes once more. Cradling his head in his hands, Kai tried to focus on anything else, but his mind kept returning to those terror-filled eyes.

Teos hollered over the rushing river and engine's whistle, "Brace yourselves, we're hitting the river!" Kai's eyes flew open, all thoughts of his squad gone as he looked ahead. The shadows of the dimly lit sewers gave way to the flare of the torches on both sides of the canal. The pump system groaned as it switched gears, forcing a pressure change in the channel. This caused it to surge forward, carrying the *Gulley* into the rushing river.

Everyone grabbed hold of whatever was nearby, shouting as Teos spun the pilot's wheel. The *Gulley* banked hard coming out of the channel and barely avoided slamming into the canal wall. The barge, however, wasn't so lucky.

Kai grabbed hold of Orelia's arm with one hand and a rope with the other. He saw Morgan holding onto Lucretia and Maple, while Ione stayed in the pilot house with Teos.

The barge rocked and rolled, forcing Kai to keep a firm grip on the rope. The rapport of flintlocks split the air as the Liberators' bullets peppered the deck. The water carried them too fast for any of the shots to hit. Sailors on the Royalist side fired back in earnest. Men on both sides fell to bullet and arrow alike. Soon, the *Gulley* passed under the city wall's arch, reaching the river proper.

Once they passed the city wall, the river's flow leveled off to a tolerable speed. The party emerged from their cover. The sounds of battle faded behind them, and turning southward, the plains of Livoria stretched beyond the horizon.

Everyone let out a cheer. Even Lucretia was laughing and whooping alongside Morgan, which brought a smile to Kai's face. Calling out to Teos, he raised his arm in an informal salute. "Thank you, Teos. We owe you a lot for this."

Teos grinned, returning the gesture. "Don't mention it. Like I said, I owed Orelia a favor, and being able to stick it in the Libbies' craw as they saw us get away felt damn good."

Slumping against a crate, Kai felt himself drifting to sleep, completely exhausted. He stretched out as the others join him and Orelia. The priestess' eyes were red and brimming with tears. Maple nestled herself between Kai and Orelia, wrapping her wings around the other woman in a protective embrace.

With a loud thump, Teos dropped from the pilot house and approached the group with Ione. Kai wondered about the safety of leaving the wheel but noticed the stretch of river ahead was long and straight, so it was likely they would be safe for now.

"What happened back there, Orelia?" the smuggler asked. "I've never seen you like this." The sluice gates opened as Orelia erupted into a fresh wave of tears. Teos sat on her other side and took her hand in his.

She threw herself against the Soltauri and beat her hands against his chest. "I failed them, Teos! Adalbard is taking Tuvi to those Libbie bastards and the others are—" she cried. She couldn't bring herself to finish. Teos met Kai's gaze and the apothecary explained what happened at the temple.

A dark scowl covered the smuggler's face. "I always thought there was something off about that priest," Teos muttered. Clutching Orelia tight, he whispered, "He'll pay one of these days, I swear it."

The air grew heavy with gloom as everyone shared despondent looks. Kai noted the marks left behind by the Liberators' weapons. He asked if anyone had injuries from the escape he needed to fix, sighing in relief when each of them admitted they were unharmed.

"We were lucky," said Lucretia. "But now that we are on the river, it is only a matter of days before we reach Runegard."

"Indeed," replied Ione. "I'm thankful that we're all safe. Luopari be praised." The tavern maid clasped her hands together in prayer. "Now perhaps we should get some sleep. The captain has offered us blankets for the remainder of our voyage. We need the rest." Teos nodded his assent, gesturing to the hold's door before returning to the pilot house.

The party muttered sleepily as Ione opened the barge's cargo hold, handing everyone a blanket. They nestled into their own spaces and allowed sleep to claim them, the sounds of the night echoing in the air.

CHAPTER XIV

The carrier hawk sat on Razarr's desk patiently, holding a leg out for the forge master to relieve it of its load. The desk looked even more untidy than during Doulterre's visit. Piles of documents lay scattered, some covered in illegible scribbles. The forge master reviewed one of them, humming to himself before scrawling a signature at the bottom. Mirabell fluttered about, dusting the bookshelves with a quiet diligence.

Removing his spectacles, Razarr finally decided to relieve the hawk of its letters. "This better be good," he muttered. Parchment in hand, he slid a bowl of water to the hawk, letting it drink before it shot through the open window.

Razarr opened the first letter after seeing it was from Doulterre. The general's scratchy handwriting was unmistakable. The last time he heard from him, the Liberation Army was halfway to Faith Hollow. That was eight days ago. Razarr wondered if a reminder was needed on the importance of frequent reports, lest he rethink their agreement.

It seemed Doulterre was sending word of his victory at last. Nice to see his investment was showing profits.

Reading through the missive, he frowned. The more he read, the greater his fury grew. The picture Doulterre painted was not pleasant. The Liberation Army attacked Faith Hollow with a full brigade's worth of men. More than half of those were conscripts from western Livoria shipped over following the Mistport attack. The army faced a defense force containing a single Royalist battalion, plus the town guard. It should have been a bloodbath, with the third largest city in Livoria destroyed and the Royalists utterly demoralized.

It had been a bloodbath, alright, but not in the way Razarr wanted.

Instead of crushing the defenders in a wave of force, over half of Doulterre's army was swept away, drowning in the Galen after being lured into a simple but effective trap. As for the survivors, they were so shaken by the ruse that they were driven out of the city with ease. That the Liberators had double their opponent's numbers *after* the setback and still got their bells rung made the defeat more humiliating.

Razarr gave a silent salute to the trap's perpetrator, whomever they were. They played the Liberators' terrorist ideology like a fiddle and dealt him a ruinous blow. Despite his anger at being on the receiving end, Razarr couldn't help but be impressed by the ploy's ingenuity.

That didn't mean he enjoyed knowing Doulterre failed in every way possible. If his report was correct, the army was rallying southwest of the city. Razarr hoped Doulterre wasn't stupid enough to make a second attempt on Faith Hollow. He would be sending the general a reply insinuating such. He was better served attacking smaller targets to the south and east to rebuild morale. After this embarrassment, Doulterre didn't have much choice in the matter.

Another defeat like that and the Liberation Army would be finished. Bloody Berelmir, the war was barely three moons old!

The report's plea for better weapons and more sellswords was blood boiling. While it was true sellswords were a marked improvement over untrained conscripts, the fact remained that they cost money. And ludicrous amounts of it, especially at the numbers Doulterre requested.

"It appears I need to impress upon the good general that when I enter an agreement, I expect results, not excuses," said Razarr. Mirabell winced but said nothing. He hated getting his hands dirty, but sometimes it was needed to get desired results. Perhaps some old-fashioned torture was in order. He still couldn't wrap his head around Doulterre losing with such an overwhelming edge. "Mirabell, you used to travel before entering my service. How long would it take to reach Livoria?"

The girl pondered the question before giving the forge master a blank stare. "That depends on where you wish to go, Master. Simply reaching the border will take two moons by carriage, but that's if you go north around the mountains. If you prefer to visit the Conclave in Shineford, then it would take three moons."

Razarr nodded. "That sounds in line with my expectations. If I'm lucky, Doulterre can hold out long enough for me to arrive. It really has been far too long since my last trip there. About twenty years, in fact."

"22 to be precise, Master. You've only agonized over it since before we first met."

"Don't you sass me, Mirabell," Razarr sneered. "You know what happened last time." The young woman nodded and went about her duties with a demure apology.

Watching the woman work, Razarr turned back to the letter with a huff. He needed to jot down his priorities. Realigning Mirabell's attitude was now on his list. The girl did exceptional work, but she still had far too much cheek, even after ten years.

Tossing the first report onto his ever-increasing pile, he read the next one. This contained most of what Doulterre deemed secondary concerns, though still relevant to his mission. To Razarr, the contents were of minimal interest. But it painted a clearer picture of the army's situation, so he endured if only so he could devise a way to salvage Doulterre's mess.

Let's see...we have supply expenses. Scouting reports on the Royalist's movements. That might be useful. A captain encountered a Norzen carrying an Exarch's watch. Odd, but intriguing. Recruitment efforts are picking— wait, what was that last one?!

Razarr's eyes bulged as he re-read the report. He heard the rumors, but his true knowledge of the order was limited. "Mirabell," he called, "you're a native Livorian, correct?" Seeing the girl nod, he pressed on. "What can you tell me about the Exarch Knights?"

Mirabell quirked an eyebrow. "They are legally considered nobles of the Duchy. Unlike traditional titles, however, their Brands are unique and cannot be passed down family lines. The process for acquiring a Brand involves being nominated by two individuals outside the person's family."

Waving his hand, Razarr beckoned Mirabell to continue. "Not just any-one can be selected, either. The individual must accomplish a great or noble deed in service to the realm. That action is reviewed and approved by the Grand Duchess herself.

"Most often, these deeds occur in battle, so most Exarchs are members of the Royalist Navy. Because of this, they are often said to be the Grand Duchess's most skilled warriors. The order comprises mostly humans, with few exceptions. I do remember hearing of a Wasini priest Branded fifteen years ago for saving a bunch of children during a bandit raid in Hornmire."

"What of a Norzen? Is there any record of one being an Exarch?"

Mirabell stared at her master before bursting into titters. "Master, I wasn't aware you could joke. To my knowledge, a Norzen has never been Branded in history, though there have been attempts. Why would you ask such a ridiculous question?"

Razarr explained what he saw in Doulterre's report. The maid admitted the Norzen in question would've been Branded in the last ten years if it were true. "I haven't been back to Livoria since you took me in, Master. I wouldn't know of any new Exarchs since that time."

Rising to his feet, Razarr paced the study muttering to himself. If the report were true, and a Norzen was ensconced in such an order, then perhaps he could make use of that. A Norzen Exarch would have superior knowledge of other Norzen in the Duchy, especially those in Duskmarsh. If he could tap that knowledge, then locating his quarry would be much easier.

"Mirabell, find Dilmear," Razarr commanded. "Tell him to prepare the carriage and pack provisions for three moons. You and I shall journey to Livoria."

The woman dropped her duster to the floor. "Master, you plan to bring me along?"

"Of course. You're the most reliable servant I have. Do you expect me to take Dilmear? I'll admit the man is organized, but outside of that, he's useless. Stupid fool couldn't navigate his way out of an open crate. Besides, your knowledge and skills will prove more valuable."

Sighing, Mirabell acquiesced reached for the door. But Razarr wasn't quite done doling out orders. "Oh, and Mirabell?"

The maid winced. "Yes, Master?"

"Bring your *other* uniform. I'm certain you'll make use of it at some point while we're away." Mirabell said nothing but fled the room at a brisk walk.

Razarr found it amusing that, even after ten years, the girl had such qualms about performing certain duties. He remembered the day he took her in as if it were yesterday and, in some ways, she was still the same timid waif he pulled from the slums. But training her was well worth the effort.

The forge master slammed a palm on the desk. Now wasn't the time to reminisce! He had no need for such frivolous thoughts. He had work to do, and no half-witted incompetent like Doulterre would stop him from achieving his life's goal.

He would find those two brats, even if he had to raze all Livoria to do it.

Vizent sneezed. He wondered if someone was thinking about him. Reflecting on the past day's events and his last report, the general shuddered. If anyone was thinking about him, chances were high it was Razarr. Worse, he knew the man would not be pleased with the results at Faith Hollow.

Wiping an arm across his face, he observed the men loading their captured Norzen. They had captured far more roaming the grasslands compared to Faith Hollow. Some were submissive and entered the carts with little resistance. Others, however, were more belligerent and needed a sound beating before being thrown in.

A familiar head of cropped hair stepped into Vizent's view, prompting a sigh of relief. The last time he saw Agosti was when he sent the man out with a scouting party, watching for Royalist forces on the path to Faith

Hollow. He hadn't heard from the man since, leading Vizent to believe he was captured or killed.

It was a relief to see the young captain alive. He was impulsive but had a good head for combat and the men were growing to like him, despite his hotheadedness. Or perhaps even *because* of it.

Vizent blinked when he saw Agosti leading an older man towards the carts. This was strange. The man was dressed in scruffy cleric's garb and pulling a struggling Norzen child with filthy blonde hair along by the arm. A female, judging by her high-pitched shrieks. Vizent could see by Agosti's crimson face he was ready to do something foolish, so the general marched towards them.

"Let me go, you old bat!" the girl shouted. She punched and kicked at the old man to no avail. "When Sister Orelia finds us, you'll wish you were never born!"

"Silence!" Agosti roared, yanking the girl away and holding her up by the throat. Her eyes widen in fear as she clawed at Agosti's gauntleted arm. "Now listen, you little brat. Either shut your peltneck mouth, or I'll cut your hand off and give you a reason to cry!"

Vizent cleared his throat, drawing the men's attention. "That's enough, captain." Stepping forward, he took the girl from the irate officer by her hand but kept a firm hold. "Now then, who is this gentleman that you've brought back?"

The old man bowed in the traditional church greeting. "Greetings, sir. My name is Adalbard Salviso, former bishop of Stahl Granz Temple."

A hearty chuckle rumbled from Vizent. "'Former' bishop...?"

"Indeed. I daresay the church will revoke my title once they learn I brought that little furball here." The priest jerked a thumb at the scowling girl.

Now Vizent broke into a full belly laugh. "I must confess, I never would've imagined we'd have friends in such high places within the church. And who might you be?" The general turned his eyes on the girl, who met the officer's gaze with no fear.

"Tuvi."

"I see. And where are your parents, Tuvi?"

"Don't know. The sisters said I was left on the temple stairs when I was a baby. All I remember is the temple." She looked Vizent up and down before sticking her tongue out at him. "And even if I did know where they were, I wouldn't tell you."

Vizent quirked an eyebrow. "She's got spunk, I'll give her that."

"Are you sure I can't just break her neck?" Agosti asked, sneering at Tuvi.

"Absolutely not. You know Razarr wants these pests alive, though why I couldn't guess. Regardless, load her up and take our priest to get his payment."

Tuvi strained as Agosti tossed her over his shoulder but earned nothing but a growl from the irate captain. "You jerks will be sorry," Tuvi grumbled, flailing her limbs about. "Sister Orelia and Mr. Kai will find me and beat you up!" Vizent's eyes swung to the child in stunned silence.

There's no bloody way...

Snarling, Agosti threw the girl to the ground, pressing her face into the dirt. Vizent snapped a warning to his subordinate, but Agosti ignored it, looming over Tuvi with a vicious grin. "You ever mention that peltneck bastard again, little bitch, and I won't care about my punishment; I'll gag your mouth shut and bury you alive." The girl stared at the man in terror, nodding her head.

Vizent asked what Agosti was talking about. "She's talking about that damned Norzen what escaped me back in Mistport, the one with an Exarch watch. I fought him at the temple and could've taken him down, but the slippery bastard still got away." The captain explained the events leading up to his fight with Kai, including losing his men in the sinkhole at the mines.

"Interesting," Vizent replied, threading his fingers through his beard. In his mind, he was sweating. There was no way it could be the same Norzen. "I'll need to inform Razarr of these incidents. This peltneck may prove to be more of a bother than he should." Glancing at the frightened Tuvi, he smirked. "We may be able to make use of this one. Razarr did say he preferred the young adults, so I think we can get away with using a runt to snatch the bigger prize."

Adalbard cocked his head. "Are you suggesting that we—"

"Use her for bait? Of course. Secure her, Agosti. We'll be taking her with us instead of sending her with the others. And don't worry, priest, you'll still get your payment. I'll pay you for this boon out of my own coffers, rather than the army's." Vizent rolled his eyes at the visible relief in Adalbard's eyes.

Agosti emitted a dark chuckle before leering at Tuvi. "Trust me, girl. You'll be wishing we'd sent you with the rest of your kind, soon enough. Your precious Sister Orelia? You're going to make sure she comes right to us, then we'll kill her and that bastard before your eyes!"

"No!" Tuvi screamed, blinking back tears. She pulled and yanked as hard as she could to get away, but Agosti's grip refused to budge. He lifted her up and backhanded Tuvi across the face, knocking her out.

"Finally," Adalbard whispered, "never thought that brat would shut up."

"You really need to learn some restraint, Captain. Now secure her, for Galen's sake. We need to decide our next move, so tell me everything that happened. Perhaps we can lure her friends where we want them sooner rather than later."

CHAPTER XV

On a normal day, Fusette would feel relaxed by the musical chirping of the wirochs pulling her carriage. Outside of the lute in her hands, there were few things that made the Grand Duchess as happy as listening to wirochs sing.

Music was Fusette's escape from the crushing responsibility of her title. Whether that music came from her own hands, or the sounds of the world around her, it didn't matter. Plucking a few strings, Fusette did her best to match the wirochs' tune, though the instrument proved to have a lower tone compared to the large birds. The notes reverberated in the large carriage.

"If I may be so bold, Your Grace, you seem distracted," Saredi commented, his crisp voice cutting through the lute's sound. A small barrel of water sat next to the chamberlain. As with most Vesikoi, they needed to keep their skin wet to prevent drying out. Fusette ordered the large carriage they sat in custom built for the sole purpose of hauling Saredi's water supply.

"My apologies, Saredi. I've been pondering last night's message." A dainty hand reached into the folds of her robe and removed a furled scroll. Opening it, Fusette read it once more. It was a report from the headman of Faith Hollow. Mere days ago, the Liberation Army attempted to seize the city with overwhelming force. Even now, Fusette had trouble believing the Liberators could amass that many men so fast.

Luck was on their side, however, as the headman was happy to report that the enemy was driven off by the combined forces of the town guard and a Navy battalion sent to defend the city.

Something about the report seemed strange, though. "I can't under-stand, Saredi. From what we've been told, the Liberation Army outnum-bered us four to one at Faith Hollow. How could the city defenses have been so effective?"

"Perhaps the commander had exceptional tactical skills?"

Fusette shook her head. "No, I don't believe that's it. The report said Commander Poretti was injured in the battle. Shot in the rib by an enemy marksman. If he were the tactical leader, losing him would've destroyed morale." This puzzle was proving to be quite the conundrum, though the duchess would admit she enjoyed a challenge.

"That's true. Will he survive, at least?"

"He will." Fusette plucked a few strings, creating a cheerful chord. "The headman says Poretti shall make a full recovery, though he won't be see-ing battle for quite some time. The real question is how we accomplished such a miraculous victory."

"Does the method truly matter? After all, Sir Hanblum will be ecstatic to learn we achieved our goal so quickly."

The duchess continued plucking the lute with deft fingers, a smile creeping across her face. In a sense, she understood Saredi's reasoning. Knowing how the Navy achieved victory didn't matter in a grander war. The victory itself was the vital piece, securing Galstein's aid in the battle ahead. Once her message back to Whistlevale reached Hanblum, it would only be a matter of time before he presented the case to Queen Isolde for aid.

But Fusette prided herself on her curiosity, and not knowing the full story was maddening.

A knock on the carriage's wall pulled Fusette from her thoughts. Some-one in the box was requesting permission to speak. Replying with a knock of her own, the carriage slowed to a full stop. Saredi bowed and offered to inspect the goings on.

Before Fusette could reply, the door opened to reveal the conductor, a young Aerivolk man with red feathers. A small carrier hawk sat on the man's shoulder, and he held an unfurled scroll. "Begging your pardon,

Your Grace, but this message just arrived. It says it's from someone named Poretti in Faith Hollow."

A bright smile stretched Fusette's lips. "That's wonderful news!" she exclaimed, playing a few cheerful notes. The wirochs responded to the lute in kind with happy chirps of their own. "Perhaps our esteemed officer can shed some light on what happened during the battle. You did well for bringing this. Thank you." The conductor turned his eyes away with a red tint to his cheeks as he handed the parchment to Fusette.

"You truly are like a stray dog with a bone in these matters, milady," Saredi commented. "What do you hope to find in that missive? It's not as if the information will be world-shattering."

"I'm not sure how to describe it, Saredi. I just feel something in my bones. It's like my heart and body are telling me that this is important. I know it sounds mad, but I'd like you to trust me on this."

The chamberlain bowed, reminding Fusette his trust and loyalty were never in doubt. With shaking fingers, she opened the parchment and read at a sedate pace. The more she read, the brighter her smile grew.

"I assume the commander's letter brings good news?" Saredi asked, one eyebrow cocked in amusement.

Flashing the noble a smug grin, Fusette's body wriggled with excitement. "Oh, this news couldn't be any better. It appears that our wayward Hunter has made a new appearance. According to Poretti, the Navy's entire defensive strategy was concocted by a Hunter that arrived from Mistport. Lord Kendela is going to pitch a fit when I throw this in his face."

"I'm afraid you've lost me, milady. What does Kendela have to do with this? I'll admit the man is a boor when it comes to his mercantile interests, but why would he care about some Hunter from the backwoods of Havenfall?"

Fusette's grin grew until it threatened to split her face in two. "Because, my dear Saredi, this Hunter happens to be a Norzen. More importantly, he's also my most recent Exarch, who Kendela swore up and down the Parliament floor would be the greatest mistake of my rule."

Seeing Saredi's face light up in recognition sent a rumble of satisfaction through Fusette's chest. "I see you know exactly who I'm talking about."

"Your Grace, are you positive the Hunter is question was Gravebane?"

"Without a doubt. Poretti mentions him by Brand. Of course, the commander confessed to being snappish with Gravebane at the beginning. I swear, this wouldn't be such a problem if he allowed us to hold the public Branding ceremony in the first place."

Stroking his chin, Saredi paced back and forth. "That's true, but from what I remember, Gravebane is a very private man. The moment you mentioned a ceremony in his honor, the poor lad turned so pale, I thought he'd been cut open and drained of every drop of blood."

Fusette giggled. "I remember that. Still, if this is true, then it only proves that I was correct in Branding him. His defeat of that beast six years ago showed only a glimpse of the things he's capable of. From the letter, it seems Gravebane has gathered an interesting group of companions since Mistport. They are currently enroute to Runegard. If the winds smile upon us, we'll cross paths there."

"If I may be so bold as to ask, Your Grace, but what exactly are we going to be doing once we arrive in Runegard?"

Rolling the parchment and tucking it away, Fusette cast a somber smile at the chamberlain. "Our goal is to acquire help for the war effort and conduct research to dig up why the Liberation Army is capturing faumen. Every report we've received thus far has mentioned that any faumen they come across are captured and shipped off to parts unknown."

"And you believe we can find information in Runegard?"

"I do. There's something tying all this together. The Liberators and their strange path through the realm, the faumen, the beast that appeared in Mistport...there's a thread somewhere connecting them all; I just have to find it."

Saredi asked if the scouts located the creature responsible for the Hunters' deaths. "No, and that's the strangest thing. From the description, the beast is massive and loud. Finding it should be simple. However, no one has spotted it once since Mistport. It's almost as if the creature vanished without a trace."

"Perhaps it left the area in search of food?"

Pondering the idea, Fusette strummed the lute again to play a soothing melody. "That may be. Considering what we know, it has a voracious appetite. Perhaps it decided to follow the Liberation Army, hoping to pick off stragglers."

"If that is the case, it's very possible Gravebane and his companions may encounter that monster again." The duchess blanched at Saredi's words. "I am unsure if the winds of fortune will shine on them a second time. Gravebane has proven his mettle against a Great Beast in the past, but this may be out of his depth."

Fusette was aware of her Exarch's ability. The Great Beasts were considered the six most dangerous animal species in all of Alezon, from Livoria to the far coasts of the Belomas Highlands. Only one was native to Livoria: the bulwark deer. And Gravebane was one of three Exarchs, and the youngest at that, to fell a Great Beast in battle single handed; no one alive was known to have defeated a second. His defeat of a Great Beast at the age of seventeen for no other purpose than protecting his village was the primary reason she Branded him in the first place. The last known person to defeat more than one of the monsters on their own was the warrior scholar, Dolmaru, the Wind Saint of Courage.

For Saredi to question this particular Exarch's ability against a dangerous creature suggested a possible need to name a seventh Great Beast. Assuming they figured out what it is.

"Then let us make haste for Runegard," Fusette proclaimed, tucking the parchment into her robes. "I shall pray for both our and Gravebane's safe arrival. Every hair of my body is telling me we need to find him."

Saredi bowed and waved for the conductor to get them on the road again. "Your instincts are strong, Your Grace. Luopari willing, they will guide us to the right path. I do have my reservations, however. Gravebane is a Norzen, after all."

Huffing to herself, Fusette settled back into the carriage as they continued on their way. One thought kept echoing in the back of her mind, despite Saredi's concerns.

Norzen could be rather clever when necessary. It was something Saredi should know better than anyone.

Chapter XVI

Despite being on the run, Kai felt the last two days passed in relative peace. Teos confessed the trip downriver would be extended by two additional days. After their escape, the smuggler checked the *Gulley*'s supplies and discovered over half their coal missing; more than likely fallen overboard during their escape. The party would need to stop at one of the river's numerous refueling stations by morning. If they didn't, the rest of the trip was a dream at best.

He knew the tranquility couldn't last forever. The Liberators wouldn't spend too long licking their wounds after the debacle at Faith Hollow. No, they'd be madder than a kicked hornet's nest and seeking revenge.

Leaning against a makeshift cushion fashioned from blankets, Kai took in the colorful sunset. By tomorrow, they would enter the central forests where Runegard lay. The thought of returning to the forest filled Kai with contentment. He could already hear the sounds in his mind. The twittering of birds, the low grunts of the deer, and rustling leaves in the wind.

Thinking back, he realized the last time he was in a forest was five moons ago. Gazing at the passing trees, he thought about the moons his squad spent tromping in the grasslands before Mistport. Thinking of the squad sent Kai's thoughts into another downward spiral. His shoulders drooped, his body slumping against the crate.

Kai reached for his watch, tightening his grip on it. The timepiece felt like a heavy anchor on his chest whenever he thought of Grimghast. Did he really deserve his Brand after what happened? He should've been able to stop that monster. But he couldn't.

He failed.

"Everything alright, 'pothy?" Kai jumped hearing Morgan's voice behind him. The sellsword gave a barking laugh, sitting down next to the Norzen. "You look like a dead ringer for my Pop after Mam passed on. What's eating ya?"

Side eying Morgan, Kai's fist clenched. "My mind keeps going back to what happened at Mistport," he started. "As far as we knew, it should have been a routine disposal mission. Find out what was attacking people and exterminate it. We'd done dozens of missions like it before. Instead, we ended up facing something never seen before."

"Aye," said Morgan. "I'll remember that bloody monster till the day I die. Whatever that Grimghast is, it's unnatural. You going to go back to kill it one day?"

Kai admitted he thought about it. The situation was out of his hands now, considering he sent a carrier hawk back to Havenfall while at Faith Hollow. The final decision was up to the Hunter Corps' commander. Kai guessed they wouldn't be able to deal with Grimghast until after the war.

Assuming the Royalists won, of course.

A thud from above drew the men's attention upwards, where Maple stared at them. "You boys look way too serious. Relax. We have a few more days together, so chin up," she chirped. Maple beckoned the others to join them.

"I must confess, I hoped we would reach our destination sooner, but there is not much we can do," said Lucretia with a discouraged sigh. Ione rested a hand on the other woman's shoulder, reminding her they would be there soon.

Orelia rapped her fingers on the deck, her face twisted into a fierce scowl. "I spent two years serving in that temple. I spoke with Adalbard almost every day. How could I be so blind? None of those children had to die. And who knows what those monsters will do to Tuvi."

Everyone refused to look the priestess in the eye. Everyone except Kai.

The apothecary tucked his watch into its pocket and told Orelia she was in no way responsible for the bishop's actions. "The only person responsible for what Adalbard did is Adalbard. You didn't force him to kill those children or take Tuvi, so don't waste time or energy blaming yourself. Besides, he'll get his soon enough."

"For once, I agree with him." Everyone stared at Lucretia in silence. "That bastard shall pay for his sins in the void of Nulyma. For now, all we can do is reach Runegard. If it is the will of the Saints, we will find Tuvi along the way and save her from those beasts."

Morgan crowed in agreement, praising the priestess' willingness to chase after Adalbard to make sure justice was carried out. "I'll admit," said the sellsword, "I ain't ever met a holy woman who could swing a staff the way you do. Where'd you learn to fight like that?"

"From my brothers," said Orelia with a cocky grin. "They're both officers in the Galstan Royal Navy and made sure I knew how to protect myself. I never beat either of them in a spar growing up, but I gave as good as I got anyway."

Ione emitted a slow whistle, staring at Orelia in awe. "That's impressive. I do hope they're proud of you."

"Not bloody likely," the priestess admitted to everyone's shock. "Father wanted me to join the Navy too, but that's not the life for me. I'd much rather do what I can tending to the common folk. Believe it or not, I ran away from home to join the church. I'm certain if Father weren't so busy with his duties, he'd be trying to find me just to drag me back home."

A loud curse from the *Gulley* brought the party to the barge's bow. From the helm, Teos stared at something on the shore, his face pale. Following his line of sight, a wave of shock rippled through the party. Lying half-sunk in the water was the mangled wreck of a twin-masted river frigate.

The ship was beyond repair. Both masts were snapped like dry twigs, their sails shredded. Chunks of the deck and hull appeared to be torn out, leaving enormous holes. Bits and planks of broken wood floated nearby. There was a reddish tint to the water surrounding the wreckage.

"What in bloody Nulyma?" asked Teos. The party was unsure what to make of the sight. Kai stood at the deck's edge, peering at the mutilated ship's bow.

"I think I can read the name. That ship was called the *Fallbrook*."

Teos sent a surprised look towards the Norzen. "Are you absolutely certain?" Kai took a second look before nodding. Maple confirmed it from her perch on the crates. Teos swore and kicked the coal pile, sending dust everywhere. Grabbing the wheel, he steered the *Gulley* towards the wreck. "I don't like this, not one bit! The *Fallbrook* is a known river pirate vessel."

Morgan glanced at the ship in concern. "If so, then why in hoarfrost are we sailing *towards* a beached ship that may still have pirates on it?" The others muttered in agreement.

"If there were men on that vessel, they'd be making a devil of a rumpus." Teos brought the *Gulley* alongside the wreck. "River pirates treat their ships better than their own mothers. I can't imagine them not squealing about this much damage. No, something ain't right, and we need to find out what."

A sense of dread pervaded the air. Maple spoke up, "Do we have to? What if the Liberation Army is respon—" Anything else the merchant wanted to say was cut short by Ione's scream of terror. The whistle of metal sang out as everyone drew their weapons. Morgan stood in front of the tavern maid, who pointed past him at the *Fallbrook*'s helm.

A single hand was clutched tight around a wheel spoke, but the rest of the body past the elbow was missing. Kai saw the flesh torn ragged where the arm was separated from the rest of its owner.

Ione bent over the barge's side and vomited. Everyone else stood frozen, unnerved by the sight. "By the winds," Lucretia stuttered, "what could have done that?"

Staring at the torn arm, Kai's gut felt like a sinking anchor.

"Impossible." He called out to Teos, requesting the smuggler get as close as possible.

Ione glowered and wiped her mouth on a nearby blanket. "What's the matter with you, Kai?" she asked. "What reason do you of all people have to investigate?"

"This feels like a bad omen. I doubt the Libbies did it, either. They would've looted the vessel and captured the crew, not torn them apart.

Worse, every instinct in my belly is shrieking that we need to know what happened. I have an idea, but I really hope I'm wrong. Wait here until I come back."

With a grim smile, Kai leapt onto the *Fallbrook*'s deck. Maple followed him despite his calls to go back, using her talons to grip the shroud. "I hate water with a passion, but I'm not letting you do this alone," Maple whispered. "You're never alone." Kai's chest tightened, his face flushing red.

He scanned the broken deck and gestured to the helm. Maple drew her bow, nocking an arrow. Together, the pair eased their way to the ship's stern.

The setting sun cast a dark tinge over the river as the pair crept over the deck. Kai prayed he wouldn't be taking an unwanted dip, his legs wobbling on the shifting boards. Though he didn't say it aloud, Maple's presence was comforting. Even now, the merchant kept flashing him a peppy smile. Seeing her willingness to brave the wreck despite her fear rejuvenated his spirit.

Reaching the wheel, Kai examined the separated arm. Kneeling, he inspected the wound and noted deep gashes on the limb itself. Maple's head was on a swivel, as were Kai's ears. The apothecary took a broken plank from the deck and used the sparkstone to make a small torch. He hovered the flame over the arm and took a deeper look at the torn flesh. What he saw made him recoil with a hiss.

A viscous lavender fluid covered the skin. Waving the torch in a circle, he saw several puddles of the liquid surrounding the helm.

"*Taen!*" Kai reached over and took Maple's arm in a firm grip. "We need to leave. Now."

Eyes sweeping the deck, the fluid's presence was painfully obvious, and Kai kicked himself for not telling Teos to sail past the *Fallbrook* at the first chance.

"Kai, what's going on? I've never seen you like this," asked Maple as they shuffled back to the edge of the deck.

The apothecary debated if he could get away with carrying Maple out, but the added weight might collapse the deck. "Maple, I'm certain I know what did this now, and we do *not* want to be here if it comes back," he replied. Kai felt a lump in his throat. He swore to Tapimor he wouldn't let anyone else he cared about suffer his squad's fate.

The images of their torn bodies assaulted him again, but Kai bit his tongue and willed those thoughts away. He had to protect Maple!

Sensing her nervousness, he helped the merchant hop over a hole near the front mast, only for the floor to give way. Maple shrieked, flailing her arms for anything to grab onto. Kai snatched her arm before she could vanish into the darkness. Swinging his mace over the deck's wall, he drove it into the hull to brace himself.

Maple's fingers dug into his forearm tight enough to draw blood. He looked down to see her gasping for breath, her eyes wide and scared as they stared into the abyss below. Kai heard the party yelling from the barge, but he tuned the noise out. He had more important things to focus on.

"Look at me, Maple!" Kai commanded. Her eyes swung upward and the two locked eyes. "That's it," he murmured, "keep your eyes on me and take slow, deep breaths. I won't let you fall."

The merchant closed her eyes and swallowed a deep breath before returning Kai's gaze. "You promise?" The apothecary nodded with a slanted, toothy grin. He tested the mace's grip on the hull and swung the arm holding Maple sideways.

Realizing his intention, Maple reached with her talons to snag the torn ropes above. The rope drew taut but held firm under her weight. With a deep breath, she hauled herself up and allowed Kai to pull her back with a powerful yank.

Kai felt the wind forced from his lungs as Maple's body struck his chest. He pulled his arm free and wrapped it around her, clutching tight.

The pair ignored the excited cheers coming from the *Gulley*. Kai blushed as Maple's wings encircled him. He didn't dare move or even speak. Looking down, her face was buried in his mane, her body shivering. Peering into the black depths below, he empathized. Considering they were standing on what used to be a pirate ship, there was no telling what rested down there.

Chancing a look back at the barge, Kai noticed everyone watching with smug curiosity all over their faces. Morgan was giving the apothecary a thumbs up. He rolled his eyes and settled for rubbing Maple's back. "We should get back to the *Gulley*. It's not safe."

A muffled grumble of agreement from the woman made Kai chuckle. He guided her back to the edge when a thunderous roar blared from longgrass on the shore. A roar that still haunted Kai's nightmares.

The Norzen swore and hooked an arm around Maple's waist, plucking the merchant off the ground with a twist. He ignored her startled squawk and took a running jump onto the barge.

"What in the five hells of Nulyma was that!?" Teos snapped, casting a terror-filled look at the grass.

"Pray it is too far away for you to find out," answered Lucretia, her face paling to an ivory sheen.

After asking Orelia to help check Maple for injuries, Kai shouted for Teos to get the *Gulley* back in the middle of the river at once. The smuggler kicked the engine into reverse while spinning the wheel. With a whistle, the *Gulley* backed away from the wreck. Ione grabbed the shovel and began heaving coal into the open boiler.

A loud thud rumbled from the shore. The grass shifted, as if something were walking through it. Kai hefted his mace, ordering everyone to find cover. Another thud rang out, sending the party into a scramble. Before long, they were huddled between crates along the deck.

The thuds grew louder and more frequent with every second. The *Gulley* was halfway to the center of the river, which made Kai nervous. They weren't quite safe yet. The river was at its deepest, and thus safest, near the center. Sweeping the grass, the sunset cast enough light to notice movement in the air near the *Fallbrook*'s stern.

"Stay still," Kai instructed. "No moving, no noise. Whatever you do, don't draw attention. Winds willing, it can't swim." The others shared wary glances before turning back to the wreck.

The grass stopped moving. The thuds went quiet. A small flock of birds fluttered from the trees and flew down river. Nothing moved other than the *Gulley* and her cargo puffing downriver.

Giving a huff from the wheel, Teos leered at the huddled party. "I swear, Kai," he growled, "if this is your idea of a fool's prank, I'll tie you to an anchor and dump your furry ass in the river myself."

The sound of sloshing water cut the silence like a blade. Facing the *Fallbrook*, Kai saw ripples extending from a point near the stern. Pressing a finger to his lips, Kai slid out from his cover and brought his spyglass up. He examined the epicenter of the ripples and felt his breath hitch when he realized the problem.

The water was shifting around a large spot where the ripples were coming from. There was something there. Something they couldn't see.

He moved to slip the spyglass back into his satchel, but his fingers refused to stop twitching. He lost his grip, the scope falling to the deck with a loud clatter. Six pairs of eyes swung to Kai when a loud growl resonated from the wreckage. The water rippled to the sides as if something were swimming towards them.

Taen. It can swim, Kai thought.

Morgan glared at Kai. "What the hoarfrost is going on? I don't see anything. You sure there's something there, 'pothy?" Kai simply nodded once, not trusting his voice.

"Remember when you told us the monster that killed your comrades appeared out of nowhere?" Lucretia asked. Morgan nodded while shooting the scholar a hesitant leer. "That's because it was there the entire time." Morgan's eyes bulged.

The air above the rippling water shimmered to everyone's surprise. Before their eyes, the hulking figure of Grimghast melted into existence. Its beady crimson eyes locked on the retreating barge and even in the dim light, Kai could see the beast's thick saliva dripping into the water.

"*Bermwel zorfahrek!*" gasped Maple in what Kai assumed was Aerian, the Aerivolk's native language. He remembered hearing a few traveling Aerivolk back in Havenfall speaking Aerian, and to his ear it had a strange guttural sound. The words were sharp and intense, but Maple somehow still gave them a melodic tune. If the merchant felt fear before after nearly falling into the *Fallbrook*'s deck, it was nothing compared to the primal horror in her eyes seeing the monster before them.

"Blessed ancestors, indeed," Lucretia breathed. Kai blinked, staring at the woman in confusion. Was that a translation of what Maple said? If so, how could she understand Aerian?

With a bellow, Grimghast burst from the river with a single leap and soared towards the prone barge. Kai shouted for everyone to brace themselves before it hit the water astride them. The *Gulley* was almost capsized by the surging waves but stayed upright, chugging along.

Shouts and curses rang out as the party scrambled back. A mangy paw reached up and hit the barge deck with a bang. Grimghast's head soon followed, snapping at anything that moved. Lucretia narrowly avoided getting caught in the creature's maw.

Kai grabbed an iron bar jutting from a damaged crate, throwing it like a javelin to the barge's stern, away from the party. It clanged against the floor, drawing the beast's attention. With a grim smirk, Kai took advantage and swung the mace down onto Grimghast's paw. It roared in pain and pulled back, sinking into the water. The apothecary called for everyone to stand in the middle of the barge.

When Morgan demanded to know why, Kai retorted he was welcome to stand near the edge when the beast came back up for a snack. The warning snapped the sellsword's jaw shut.

Glancing at the wheel, Kai saw Teos and Ione busy manning the pilot house that kept them moving downriver. That would have to be enough to keep them safe for now. Kai directed the party to stand shoulder to shoulder in a line, each member alternating facing east and west.

"You're doing great so far!" Kai praised the group. "This thing is tough as iron, so stay focused. This is what we need to do: I don't care what it takes, but when that thing shows its ugly face, stay defensive. Use anything on board as a weapon. It hunts by smell and hearing, so loud noises will disorient it. Parry the claws if they get close. Aim for the jaw or eyes if it tries to bite. And for the love of Luopari, *don't* let it bite you. The saliva is venomous."

"Sounds easy. Got any other ideas, 'pothy?" Morgan asked from the Norzen's right.

Kai jabbed an elbow into the mixblood's rib. "This one's for you, Morgan: Don't die."

The two grinned, sharing a nervous laugh when the barge shook. A geyser of water erupted from the barge's port side. With a howl, the creature threw its full weight onto the deck, scattering the party.

Morgan gave a war cry and slashed at Grimghast's shoulder, but its bony armor deflected the blade and sent him stumbling back. Before he got back up, the beast raised its paw and hammered it on Morgan's chest, slamming him onto the deck. The man groaned and tried wriggling free, but Grimghast responded by putting more weight on him.

Charging from behind, Kai and Lucretia tried to cut the hind legs. However, every time they got within striking distance, a foot lashed out and knocked them away. Dodging another kick, Kai covered his ears with a wince when Grimghast broke open a crate and sent a pile of shields clattering to the deck. Lucretia landed a hit, digging her rapier into the heel. Grimghast roared in pain, landing a kick on her chest to send the scholar flying. Kai used his body as a wall to keep Lucretia from being thrown into the river.

The twang of a bow sang as an arrow pierced the creature's cheek. Grimghast shrieked, twisting to face the pilot house atop which Maple stood, nocking another arrow. It advanced towards the towboat on all fours, ignoring every blow they threw at it.

Morgan wheezed while wobbling to his feet. Leaning against another crate, he stumbled when the large box slid overboard, no longer tied down to the deck. Orelia helped the sellsword steady himself, and both watched as Grimghast stalked towards the *Gulley*. Morgan reached for the pile of shields and grabbed a circular one, holding it outstretched and parallel to his forearm like a discus. With a practiced twirl, Morgan hurled the shield to the left of Grimghast's body. It curved at an arc, catching the beast in the temple.

Nostrils flared, Grimghast spun see what hit it but tripped over its own feet on the slick deck. It crashed to the floor, sending more crates and debris skidding into the river. Kai shouted for everyone to stay back. Morgan was emboldened by his attack, however, charging with his falchion raised.

Grimghast attempted to untangle its own legs, which left it prone. Morgan approached from the rear and hacked at the hind quarters. He wasn't prepared for Grimghast to emit an odd hissing sound before hurling a glob of saliva at him. Shocked, he stepped back enough for the attack to fall short. Unfortunately, Grimghast used the distraction to heave itself up, rocking the barge portside.

The unexpected movement caused Morgan to slide directly into the saliva. He slipped backward and fell into Grimghast's path. The beast lunged. He made to roll away, but its jaws clamped around his armored forearm. Grimghast lifted Morgan off the ground, causing him to release his sword. It rolled its head, trying to tear the man's arm off. Morgan shouted in pain and struggled to free himself. He kicked the beast in the side of the head while trying to unhook the vambrace from his arm.

Lucretia and Orelia grabbed Morgan's legs to try pulling him down. Kai tied a strip of cloth over his ears before choosing a shield from the deck. He banged his mace against it, creating a loud clang that stung his ears, despite the cover. The noise infuriated Grimghast judging from its snarls. It tried to grab the struggling Morgan and lift him into its mouth.

Kai saw movement on the towboat behind Grimghast but didn't have time to see who it was. He charged and threw a heavy swing into the beast's bone-plated ribs. Grimghast brushed the hit off and grabbed Morgan around the waist. It threw the man aside, tearing the vambrace off. Morgan crashed into Kai, leaving both men lying on the deck. Lucretia and Orelia raced to their sides and pulled Morgan off the prone apothecary.

A loud rattle came from the boat, followed by a snicker. Grimghast turned back to the *Gulley*, where Teos shoved the ship's anchor through a hole in the deck wall. Following the anchor's chain, Kai saw that Ione and Maple had knotted the other end around Grimghast's back leg. The two women rushed into the pilot house as the anchor dropped, sending the chain disappearing into the river. The smuggler fell to his knees and covered his ears when Grimghast roared, diving for the four on the barge with a manic look in its eye.

Morgan shouted a warning, jumping in front of the others. Grimghast hit the sellsword full force, pinning him against the deck floor with a massive paw.

He reached back for his sword with his good arm, but it was just out of reach. Grimghast lowered its head to stare at Morgan, its saliva dripping onto his chest. "You need a mint leaf, mate," Morgan growled while punching the beast square in its snout. "Your breath is horrid!"

Clambering back to the storage hatch, Kai threw the door open and reached inside. Feeling around, he felt his hand grip solid wood. Grinning, Kai pulled the loaded crossbow and swung into a kneeling position, taking aim at Grimghast's face. "Let's see how you like this, you bastard," Kai hissed. The barge shifted as he squeezed the trigger, sending the bolt off-course and into the beast's shoulder rather than its head. Kai swore and tossed the crossbow aside. He needed to get that thing off Morgan before—

A snap rang out as the anchor chain pulled taut, yanking Grimghast back towards the *Gulley*. A howl of pain came from Morgan. His breast-plate was torn off by the beast's claws, leaving a bloody gash down his chest. Kai darted to the man's side and removed his tunic, tearing it into strips and wrapping the wound. Grimghast flailed wildly, its paws grasping for any stability as it was dragged into the river.

Orelia and Lucretia leapt onto the *Gulley*'s opposite side, hiding behind the pilot house. Teos took his halberd and thrust it towards the monster's neck. He swore loudly when it snarled at the new wound, digging its claws into the *Gulley*. Boards were ripped apart the farther it was pulled, creating a massive hole in the deck.

Teos scrambled to the wheel and tried steering the opposite direction, but the vessel shuddered a bit before stopping. The smuggler cursed, slamming a palm against the wheel. A loud crash, followed by splashing and frantic howling, drew everyone's attention to Grimghast. It held fast to the deck wall, a futile action as the anchor's weight dragged it over the edge. Grimghast's claws brought a chunk of the hull with it before vanishing into the depths.

The *Gulley* began to tilt as water rushed in through the holes. "Damn it all!" Teos shouted. "She's going down. Abandon ship!"

Maple rushed to help Kai lift Morgan, but he instructed her to grab what she could from the packs and glide to the opposite shore, sending her running for the hatch. Orelia and Lucretia followed and helped pull items from the sacks. The two tossed everything they grabbed into a pair of wool blankets and tied them into bundles.

Back on the *Gulley*, Teos propped Ione onto his back. He took a running jump into the water, swimming for shore as fast as he could. Kai did the same with Morgan, draping the injured sellsword over his shoulders like a scarf before jumping. Lucretia and Orelia followed suit with the packs they grabbed.

Maple climbed atop the pilot house with her bundle and leaped, the sack clutched in her talons. Opening her wings, she took a calming breath and allowed herself to glide most of the way to shore. She didn't have enough height to make the full distance, causing her body to shiver. Looking to the side, she saw multiple rocks jutting from the water. Tilting her body, Maple angled herself to land on the first rock before jumping the moment her talons touched it. Using them as platforms, she made it to shore dry but weary from gliding with the heavy bundle. She collapsed in a heap on the riverbank.

Before long, everyone was safe on shore. Soaked, exhausted, and sore, the seven allowed themselves a brief respite. Kai was the only one moving much as he checked Morgan's wound, wanting to check the wrap before resting. He muttered a curse seeing the cracked scales surrounding the gash; Grimghast's claws tore through Morgan's scales like paper. The others lay prone, gulping down deep breaths.

Looking out onto the river, Kai frowned at the *Gulley* sinking into the river. The wrecked barge was pulled under behind it.

"I think...we are getting better at this," said Lucretia, rolling onto her belly and pushing herself to her knees.

"What in Nulyma do you mean by that?" Teos demanded. Lucretia glared at the smuggler and explained their last encounter with Grimghast back in Mistport. Ione agreed and said that compared to last time, they came out in much better shape, if drained.

Morgan groaned in pain, putting pressure on his wound. "I knew that thing was uglier than sin, but the whole trick where it popped up out of nothing was freaky!"

Shaking his head, Kai admitted that seeing Grimghast appear like that was unnerving. "Some of us have seen that trick before. I am curious as to why it doesn't use the ability while fighting. Maybe it has to focus in order to conceal itself. I suppose we should count our blessings. No one died this time."

"Easy for you to say, 'pothy," Morgan growled, "This cut hurts like that damn Nulyma place you all keep blabbering about!"

"Be grateful it didn't bite anything exposed like I warned you," Kai retorted. "You're damned lucky it bit your vambrace and not a shoulder. Otherwise, that venom would've made sure you weren't here to bitch about the pain." With those words, the reality of their experience seemed to hit everyone at once. An eerie calm settled over them all, as well as a realization of how lucky they were to walk away alive.

Ione pushed herself to a sitting position and wrung the water from her dirndl. "So now what?" she asked. "That barge was our best chance to reach Runegard."

Morgan beckoned for Kai to help him sit up as well. The apothecary leaned him against a nearby boulder. "Did you ladies get anything useful before jumping ship?" he asked.

A groaning Maple rolled onto her back and confessed to snagging a few camping supplies, as well as the money pouches and her crafting tools. Orelia and Lucretia mentioned grabbing food and clothing.

"Great," said Teos, "guess we rest for now and dry off. We're not going anywhere until then. At least we drowned that abomination. The Galen has got to be fifty yards deep in the center, so that bastard is dead for sure. Damn thing deserved it for doing that to my boat. My whole life was on that barge." When Ione asked if he was going to walk back to Faith Hollow, Teos laughed. "Nah. Nothing waiting for me back there, to tell you the truth. Besides, I promised Orelia I'd get you to Runegard, and that's what I'll do, boat or no boat. Where she goes, I go."

A ruckus on the opposite shore drew Kai's attention. There was movement in the grass, and several familiar animals calls broke the silence. It seemed like the wildlife was moving again with Grimghast gone. For now, he planned on catching his breath and making sure Morgan didn't succumb to his wounds. He was confident the stubborn mixblood would pull through.

They could check supplies and chart a new path after some well-deserved rest. Then again, they weren't the only ones who could rest. "Well boys," Kai whispered, "maybe you can be at peace now." Forcing himself to his feet, the Norzen went about building a campfire for everyone to gather around and dry off.

A sense of dread shot through his spine, giving him pause. Perhaps there was more to Grimghast than he thought. There was also the panicked look in its eyes when it saw the anchor falling into the river. Almost as if it understood what was happening.

That's impossible, Kai thought. *Most animals are incapable of logical thinking like that. The only ones that intelligent are the Great Beasts. I should know...*

He shrugged the feeling off and reminded himself that the beast was dead, gone, and buried. It couldn't hurt anyone anymore. There was no way it could survive drowning.

All they had to worry about now was the Liberation Army.

Chapter XVII

K ai liked to think he was prepared for hardship. This was part necessity, given the troubles that followed any Norzen. Considering his unique status as a Hunter and Exarch, and the public scrutiny that came with those positions, he needed the ability to adapt to any situation imaginable.

His Hunter training instilled a level of survival instinct above and beyond the common Norzen bandits he was familiar with. He also learned camaraderie and duty. Studying the apothecary trade taught him observation skills and built a breadth of knowledge capable of keeping himself and others alive in critical situations.

He was well aware that the Norzen in faumen-centered cities like Faith Hollow or even Duskmarsh had to be different from nomadic bandits, but they tended to keep to themselves from what he heard. Still, he hoped to someday meet an adult Norzen that wasn't a criminal or beggar.

Nothing he learned over the years, however, could've prepared Kai for traveling with people thrown into his life by pure chance. Even now, sitting in a corner table with his six companions at a roadside inn two days after the sinking of the *Gulley*, Kai still felt his experiences over the last moon were too surreal.

Thinking back, a niggling at the back of Kai's mind wondered if the Wind Saints brought them together for some specific purpose. They certainly would not have met under normal circumstances, that's for sure. Even to the most open-minded philosophers of Alezon, they made for an odd spectacle.

Across from him, Teos slammed back another stein of ale and scanned the table with bloodshot eyes, several empty mugs around his plate. Seeing him like this reminded Kai of Marko's drinking binges. The smuggler was not taking the *Gulley's* loss well. Lucretia glared at the scattered steins, taking a sip of water. "You should learn some restraint, Teos," the scholar reprimanded. "The last thing we need is for you to cause trouble in a drunken stupor."

"Ah, boil your tongue, woman. I'm a grown man, so if I want to get drunk, then by the winds, I'm gonna get drunk!"

Putting herself between the two, Orelia threatened to send them to their rooms if they were going to act like children. Lucretia turned a stupefied look to the priestess before scoffing and turning away. Kai concealed a smirk behind his stein of mead, hearing their scholar grumble that Teos wasn't worth the humiliation.

Glancing at Maple, sitting next to him and nursing a mead of her own, Kai couldn't help but be impressed. He was grateful for her foresight in grabbing the money pouches before they could sink with the barge. It was only through that foresight that they were able to secure their current lodging and food. When asked why the coin pouches had been her priority, her mercantile response wasn't surprising in the least.

She said, "Wits and knowledge are the currency of nature, but that wouldn't help us a lick in the wilds of business. There, you need cold, hard coin." The more he thought about it, he realized it was a valid point.

Morgan's wound was healing nicely thanks to his stitching, though Kai warned it would scar. The sellsword wasn't upset too much by that, deciding the story behind it was worth the pain. More than once, someone had to remind the Wasini mixblood not to exert himself, lest he rip the stitches open and invite Kai's painful policy on the matter.

Before arriving at the inn, he reminded everyone, "If I ever have to stitch the same wound more than once, you can be damn sure you won't get the benefit of a soporific the second time. Maybe then you'll learn." Not even Lucretia was willing to risk the apothecary's needlework without a sleeping draught. And their travels earned them more than their fair share of cuts and scrapes up to this point.

Kai's tails tingled; a sure sign he was being watched. Scanning the table, he saw Teos staring with a curious expression. Kai knew he wasn't familiar enough with the Soltauri to guess what was going through his mind.

Slamming his stein on the table, Teos jabbed a finger at Kai. "Alright, listen up. I'll be the first to admit I'm not the brightest flame on the candle," he growled, "but it seems to me like most of our band of misfits are following your lead, and something about that bothers me."

A quick glance at several glowering faces forced him to continue, "As crazy as it sounds, it's not because you're a Norzen. By the winds, I've met at least a dozen Norzen in my line of work I respect. Might even go so far as to call them friends. No, what strikes me as odd is that you seem rather young compared to the rest of us. How old are you exactly?"

Kai shrugged. He didn't see the harm in answering. "I turned 23 four moons ago."

Silence reigned, the ruckus from the other patrons nothing but a dull buzz in their ears. "Bloody Nulyma," Teos muttered, "we're marching to the tune of a kid twenty years my junior. Knowing what I do of the Hunters, that means you passed your Trial, what, six years ago?" Teos groaned and took another draw of ale when Kai nodded.

Maple's face burned crimson as she regarded Kai with interest. "That's a surprise. That makes you five years younger than me. I honestly believed you were in your thirties and just had a youthful face."

The sound of laughter drew everyone's eyes to Orelia. "Guess that means I'm the only one here younger than our esteemed leader. I just turned twenty last moon. Wait." Now the priestess was staring at Kai in awe, as if seeing him for the first time. "That would make you the youngest Exarch in history."

Teos, in the middle of another drink, sprayed his ale all over the table. "Hold the hawk, Orelia," he coughed out. "Did you say this whelp's an Exarch? That's impossi—" The smuggler's rant was cut short when Kai removed the watch, setting it in front of him. Teos stared at it, eyes wide and unfocused. Finally, he leaned back and rubbed his temple. Fixing Kai with a blank stare, he uttered a single word.

"Explain."

The others shared nervous glances, unsure of how to respond. Ione took a draw from her own stein before replying, "Teos, have you lost your kettle? That's an extremely rude and personal question. An Exarch is Branded by the approval of Lady Fusette herself. To demand a reason for their selection is to question her judgment! Are you not aware of how much of an insult that is?" Now Teos found the contents of his cup far more interesting, a contemplative look in his eyes.

Kai cleared his throat and confessed Teos was far from the first person to question his Branding. "I'll admit I feel unworthy of the title more often than not. By the winds, I've felt that way ever since I was Branded!

"However," he continued, "we've been through a lot on this journey. There's no telling how much longer we'll travel together, but until the day comes we forge our own paths, we need to rely on and trust one another. I think if anyone deserves to know the whole story, it's you six. Besides, I already promised Maple I'd share. Now seems as good a time as any."

Without another word, Kai unbuttoned his vest and slid his left arm out. He heard gasps from the women, even Lucretia, at the sight of a large circular scar just below his shoulder.

"What in Galen's holy name did that?" Orelia choked.

Kai traced the edge of the scar with his finger. "I earned this during my Trial of Ascension; our annual ceremony to anoint those seventeen years of age as full-fledged Hunters. This was my very first kill. Nobody ever figured out how it got into the forests around Havenfall, but during the Trial, the other candidates and I ran afoul of an adult nettleboar."

Several at the table erupted into a clamor, with Morgan and Lucretia the most vocal. "I think me ears are going bad, 'pothy," Morgan babbled, the twang of his accent becoming more pronounced, "but I swear you just said ya ran into a nettleboar!"

Maple raised a hesitant wing and looked at the others. "This might be a stupid question, but what exactly *is* a nettleboar?"

Lucretia slumped against her chair and pounded a fist into her upper lip. "One of the six Great Beasts. Think of a wild hog, the kind you would see near the mountains." Seeing the merchant nod, she continued, "Now imagine it ten times bigger and smarter, and fifty times as vicious, with a muzzle of venom-tipped quills. They are native to the Corlatian savannahs and considered dangerous enough that a full squad of knights is needed to bring down a small one."

"You're kidding, right?" Maple asked. Lucretia shook her head. The merchant faced Kai and grabbed him by the vest. "How in Finyt are you still alive?!"

Placing his hands over hers, Kai eased her grip and gave a shy smile. "If we're being honest, a lot of dumb luck and a stubbornness my Da says can only come from being Norzen. I got the scar when it gored my arm with a tusk. Damned thing pinned me against a tree."

"Again," Maple pressed, "how are you alive? A wound like that should have been a death sentence."

"I got a lucky hit and took an eye out with my mace. The tusk snapped in two after getting stuck in the tree trunk. That kept the wound plugged until I could get it treated. I was able to drive the boar into the river while it was still writhing about in pain. Thankfully, nettleboars are too bulky to swim worth a damn and it wore itself out trying to escape. Finishing the job after that was simple enough, but I'll admit I was terrified the entire time."

Leaning back, Morgan raised his cup and regarded Kai with a look of respect. "You gotta be either the bravest or craziest man I've ever met, 'pothy. Anyone with the stones to fight a grown nettleboar alone deserves the title of warrior."

Kai shook his head with a frown. "I wouldn't go that far. While we were running from it, the nettleboar killed Sal, one of the other candidates and my squad mate Marko's best friend at the time. I'll be honest, before our Trial, Marko pretty much hated me. It wasn't until after I saved him from getting gored and we got put on a squad together that we learned to get along. If that thing ran free in Havenfall, though, my family could've been hurt or killed. I wasn't going to let that happen and did what any other Hunter would've in that situation." It still hurt talking about Marko, but sharing the story helped ease the pain a bit.

"Well," said Ione while raising her stein, "I for one am grateful you survived. After all, we wouldn't be here tonight if not for you." The others agreed and raised their cups in solidarity, barring Lucretia.

Turning his attention back to his meal, Teos asked how they were planning on getting to Runegard. Their map, after all, was now at the bottom of the river. Maple offered to ask the innkeeper if he knew where to procure a new map before getting up to do just that.

The party ate in silence until Maple returned. Downcast, she reported the nearest village with a cartography shop was a day's journey back upriver. Kai frowned, replying they would be better off following the river south until they reached Runegard. Backtracking would cost them at least two extra days travel time. Time they couldn't afford to waste.

"I suppose it is fortunate the Galen River flows straight to Runegard," said Lucretia as the group polished off the last of their meals.

Waving for a tavern maid to remove their plates, Ione leaned forward and whispered, "That's true, but we also need to be wary of the Liberation Army. Don't forget, five of you are faumen, with two mixbloods. If they catch us out there, we'll be run down!"

"Three mixbloods, actually," Maple murmured.

Six heads swung to face the merchant in shock. "You're a mix?" Kai asked with a quirked eyebrow. "Could've fooled me."

She giggled and gestured to her body. "I can tell y'all don't meet too many Aerivolk. I'm one-quarter human on Papa's side. My grandmother. If you put me next to a fullblood, I'm at least a head or two taller than most," she explained.

"Now that you mention it, ya got a bigger set o' melons on ya than any Aerivolk I've ever seen too," Morgan added with his loud, braying laugh. Maple's face turned scarlet, wrapping her wings around herself with a downcast frown. Kai scowled and reached over to smack Morgan behind the head, earning him a nod of approval from the women.

"Papa says I take after Grammy a lot. She was rather tall and gifted with womanly charms, as they liked to say," Maple replied, her eyes focusing on anything except the others. "I don't like thinking about it too much. The girls back home poked fun at me for a lot of things, especially my looks." A lone tear trailed down her cheek.

Clenching his fist, Kai gave Maple's shoulder a squeeze. When she met his gaze, he smiled and brushed the tear away. "Well they're the biggest fools of all, if you ask me," he said, his voice calm and tender. "You've already proven yourself brave, intelligent, kind, beautiful, and above all else, forthright. Maybe even a little sneaky," he admitted with a sly grin.

She couldn't hold back the tears and giggle bubbling up from her chest. "Oh for Ausrina's sake, Kai, you know how to make a gal cry," said Maple with a tiny hiccup.

Now everyone turned to Kai, who stammered that he never meant to upset her. Ione ribbed the apothecary, asking if he was planning to make Lucretia and Orelia cry as well, since he'd already made her do so when they first met.

Kai blushed and babbled incoherently. He wasn't sure how the conversation flipped on him, but now he was confused and worried he offended the ladies in some way. It was only when the table exploded in laughter that he realized they were jerking his chain.

The bang of a door shattered the inn's ambience, drawing the crowd's eyes to the entrance. Three men stood in the doorway, knees bent, and bodies slouched as they surveyed the crowd. One of the men pulled a sheet of parchment from his coat, glancing at it before scanning the room once more. The trio emitted an eerie chattering laugh the moment their eyes landed on the party. With a skulking walk, they lumbering to the corner table where the seven travelers pretended the newcomers weren't there.

"What do we have here, boys?" asked the tallest of the three, a lanky man with a large, hooked nose. Kai didn't know what his name was and didn't care beyond naming him Beak in his mind. "Looks like we found some wayward faumen. Don't you folks know it's dangerous to be on the road these days?" Beak's slick manner of speaking and pretentious accent reminded Kai of a snooty noble, despite his scruffy appearance.

The second man, average in height but with a stocky build and dusky wrinkled skin, guffawed while running a finger along the edge of his scabbard. Kai dubbed him Bark for his skin's tree-like appearance. "Aye, they must be very brave," he growled in a hoarse voice. "Or very stupid."

A high-pitched cackle joined in as the shortest man, who was shorter than even Maple, with crooked teeth and foul breath that caused everyone to reel back in disgust. Kai aptly dubbed this one Bile. "Not that it matters," he said with a nasally tone, pulling a long knife from his belt. The other patrons scrambled away.

The innkeeper tried moving towards the door when the crack of a flintlock went off, a bullet grazing his nose. Beak tucked the pistol back into his tunic. "Don't go getting any stupid ideas, friend."

All three men turned to the party with sneers on their faces. "Now then, I think you know what we're here for," said Bile.

Morgan made a show of holding his stein to his face and peering into it, as if searching for the last drop of booze. "It's a funny thing, fellas. We don't. Been busy trying to not die, you see. So forgive us if we have no clue what you're making such a racket about."

Snarling, Bile held the tip of his knife to Morgan's neck. "Don't play stupid with us, chimera! You should've known bounty hunters would be after your heads one of these days." Bile then ripped the parchment from Bark's hand and slammed it on the table. It was a reward poster, offering varying amounts of marks for bringing captured faumen to the Liberation Army.

"First of all," replied Lucretia, "it is rather rude of you to be waving that knife around. And second, I am afraid Morgan is not playing. He really is that stupid."

Morgan's cry of "Hey!" was ignored as the rest of the party chuckled. The trio of bounty hunters weren't amused.

Bark grabbed Kai by the tunic, dragging the Norzen to his feet. The apothecary met his assailant's glowering face with a blank stare. "Let me make this simple enough for a rock. There's a nice little price for any Norzen that gets brought to the Libbies. There are even prices on all chimeras and other faumen that get turned in. So we're going on a little trip."

"And if we refuse? We have better things to do than cater to a pack of third-rate bounty hunters," replied Kai.

"Now what makes you think you have much choice in the matter?"

The click of several flintlocks in succession behind the bounty hunters made them pause.

"That's quite enough of that," a crisp voice sounded. The trio turned and found themselves facing four Royalist sailors, each pointing a pistol at the men's chests. At the front was an older Wasini wearing a decorated uniform coat with admiral stars on his epaulets. The top of his serpentine tail was covered in rust-colored scales. His neck-length brown hair was thicker and shaggier than a typical sailor, but still neatly combed with bangs that perfectly framed his amber eyes.

Beak sneered at the admiral, drawing an axe from his belt. "We ain't afraid of some damned snake bastard and a pack of half-wit sailors. Now stay out of this." Kai was impressed with their bravado, but doubted they knew who they were talking to.

The Wasini officer coiled his tail beneath his torso and drew himself taller than Beak by two hands, scowling at the bounty hunter. "You do realize you're claiming intention to sell Livorian citizens to the Liberation Army, correct? Such an action would be considered a direct benefit to a known enemy of the Duchy. If I wanted, I could have all three of you in the gallows and hanged for treason before the sun rises."

"I'd love to see you try. Even if you don't agree with our methods, we're Livorian citizens too. That means you bastards have to arrest us first and send us to a magistrate," Bark snapped. He gripped his sword's hilt and tried to puff his chest out. "We need food on our plates, the same as any other poor sod. If you're so worried about them Libbies, then maybe you oughta be out looking for them instead of hounding us!"

The admiral chuckled. "Perhaps we already are. Regardless, you'd best leave before I'm forced to deal with you in an official capacity. No magistrate would let you free, despite your bluster. Not in these parts."

Bile turned back to the party and eyed the women with a shady leer. "We're not going anywhere. We haven't even had a chance to get friendly with the ladies here. The half-breeds may have their uses, though. The Aerivolk might make a nice snack if you know what I'm saying."

Maple stepped back in revulsion. Lucretia tried to draw her rapier, clearly wanting to skewer the bounty hunter, only for Teos to pin her arms in place. Around the tavern, the patrons swore and cursed at the three men. Lucretia opted to spit at their feet, calling them an affront to every woman in Alezon.

The short man cackled. "Don't knock it till you try it, sweetheart. Tear the wings off that little chicken, fry 'em in fresh oil, and they'll taste delicious! Maybe we'll even have some fun with you human girls while we eat." Maple's face switched from disgust to horror as everyone stared at Bile in stunned silence.

Morgan was the first to move, striding forward while reaching for his blade. "You little runt, I'm gonna—" The admiral and his men all readied their pistols, expecting a brawl.

Everyone was stopped short by Kai's hand snatching Morgan's wrist in an iron grip, keeping him from drawing the falchion. The sellsword glared. "Let go, 'pothy."

Kai tilted his head and stared blankly at Morgan. He stopped the sellsword from attacking, true, but that was more to draw his focus away from the storm of emotions roiling in his chest.

Ultimately, it didn't work.

Rage, malice, horror, bewilderment. These and many other feelings churned and bubbled within him. Kai was reminded of the soldier he killed back in Mistport, and the Aerivolk family the man killed just before his own demise. He thought about Tuvi, and the fear in her eyes as Adalbard carried her away. The same red haze from Mistport spread over his vision.

After a few moments of being held in place with his eyes locked on Kai's, Morgan's demeanor shifted from anger to confusion, then fear. His fingers released the hilt as if it were on fire and Morgan tore his hand away from Kai, stumbling backwards. The others stood baffled, wondering what could cause such a dramatic shift in the emotional mixblood.

Morgan turned to face the bounty hunters and sailors before slumping his shoulders. "I don't know who you sailors are, but you boys had best step back. As for you three," he gave the trio a grim smile, "you better hope you've made peace with whatever god you kneel to."

When Beak scowled and asked what he meant by that, Morgan jerked a thumb at the trembling apothecary. "Cause you idiots picked the wrong Norzen to brass off."

Without a word, Kai darted to Bile's side, being the closest of the trio, raising his arm and hammering the short man across the cheek with a vicious backhand. A loud snap rang out and the bounty hunter was blasted through the inn's wall, leaving a sizable hole. The other two goggled at the damage, foolishly forgetting for a moment they were being attacked.

That moment was all Kai needed. Like before, he sensed a wall between his mind and body. His thoughts within the haze were clear, but his body moved of its own accord. It was as if his body was being wielded like a weapon by the maelstrom of emotion surging inside his heart.

He plucked his mace from its loop and flayed Beak in the spine with a double-handed swing. The man had no chance to shout before his lifeless body crashed into a table, leaving it a pile of splintered wood.

Bark realized too late that he needed to fight back. He reached for his own weapon but couldn't reach the hilt before Kai kicked his feet out from underneath him. Tumbling onto his back, Bark finally managed to draw his sword. Kai raised the mace overhead while Bark held the flat side of the blade up to block. The apothecary's muscles tensed, bulging as the mace came down, sending sparks through the air when the weapons collided.

The sword was unable to withstand the attack, shattering into pieces. Kai's mace wasn't slowed in the least, crushing the bounty hunter's chest and sending him through the wooden floor into the cellar. The crowd gaped.

Kai noticed the other sailors aiming their flintlocks at his chest when the admiral ordered them to stand down. The haze began clearing, allowing Kai to stumble back and grab his aching head. His arms felt shaky, and he could feel blood pulsing through his veins. The same uneven feeling he remembered from Mistport wracked his body. Unable to maintain his grip, the mace clattered to the floor. Kai's body wobbled on uneasy legs before tilting backwards. He would've collapsed, had Ione and Maple not caught him by the arms before he could hit the ground.

"What...what happened?" asked Kai.

Her breath racing, Lucretia cocked her head at the Norzen while watching the others. "I assume you all saw the same thing I did, correct?" They nodded.

The admiral cleared his throat and waited for everyone in the inn to face him before speaking. "As much as it pains me to admit, legally I should have you arrested for murder."

Kai groaned. He really couldn't afford to be put in the gaol after making it this far. Looking at the others, he was stunned to see each of them glowering at the admiral and tense, ready to fight.

The Wasini held up a hand. "I understand your anger but let me finish. Now, that's what I *should* do, were this a normal situation. However, you're quite a lucky Norzen."

Kai quirked an eyebrow at the older man. "And why do you say that?" Any other words died in his throat when the admiral pulled a familiar brass watch from his uniform pocket.

"Because I know *exactly* who you are, Gravebane, even if we've never been properly introduced. Allow me to rectify that oversight. I am Admiral Larimanz, commander of the Royalist Navy's Marine Cavalry Fleet. However, I am also known by my Brand: Waveweaver."

Chapter XVIII

5. The number rolled around Kai's head like a tumbleweed from the deserts of the northern Rodekan Empire. It was estimated that Livoria contained a little under two million inhabitants. Of that vast number, only 55 were deemed exceptional enough to be Branded an Exarch Knight. The number of faumen within that already low number was more striking, with only sixteen current faumen Exarchs after his own Branding six years ago.

As Kai stared at the smirking Admiral Larimanz, it baffled him that he never knew just how little he truly understood about the order. He never knew, never suspected, that the regal Wasini in front of him was an Exarch.

If I ever have an audience with Her Grace again, Kai thought, *I really should suggest the Exarchs have routine meetings. Even if I don't like the attention, it would keep me from being blindsided.*

Larimanz broke out into booming laughter. "No need to look so serious, Gravebane! We're comrades, so please relax your guard." Kai was captivated by the older man. Wasini were already a rarity, and he remembered the stories from his childhood. Despite coming from a supposed tribe of ruthless warriors, Larimanz appeared jovial.

The admiral ordered the bodies of the bounty hunters buried while everyone helped repair the damages to the inn. He even handed the innkeeper a sack of marks to cover the material cost. Now, Larimanz and his entourage stood in the back corner with the party.

One of the sailors standing behind the admiral saluted. "Sir, are you certain that we should ignore the murder of those men? Detestable as they were, they still had a point about being sent to a magistrate."

"That is true, Lieutenant," replied Larimanz, "but consider this: It was obvious they were about to commit multiple serious crimes. Not just in selling citizens to the Liberators, but they insinuated they weren't above violating women and indulging in cannibalism. The only thing I saw was an Exarch performing his sacred duty to protect our people."

The sailors looked over Kai with skepticism written in their eyes. "I...wasn't aware there was a Norzen in the order, Admiral," one of them confessed.

Larimanz clapped a beefy hand on Kai's back, knocking him off-balance. "Gravebane is a bit odd from the reports I've read, but he's a legitimate Exarch. First apothecary to be Branded as well if I remember correct."

All three sailors stepped back. "An apothecary? Sir, I've never seen an apothecary dispense death as easily as they do their tonics."

Holding up his hands up with palms out, Kai gave a weak chuckle. "As strange as this sounds, I don't know what happened. All I remember is seeing red after hearing those bastards say those things. Everything got foggy after that. Even though I could see and hear what was happening to a point, I had no control over my body. When I came to, it was over."

Larimanz nodded. "Interesting. The more I talk to you, the more intriguing you become, Gravebane. It's rare for a Norzen to not be aware of the Frenzy Haze."

A gasp emitted from behind. Kai turned to see Lucretia staring at Larimanz with wide eyes. "You truly believe that was a Frenzy Haze?"

"Indeed. The symptoms line up, and it sounds like episodes I had when I was younger and more...aggressive. Not that I remember much about them myself. Regrettably, partial memory blanks are almost guaranteed."

Ione raised a hand and cast a nervous look. "Forgive me, but what is this Frenzy Haze you're talking about?"

It was Morgan that explained, "It's a nasty thing. My grandpap taught me about it. All faumen can slip into a Haze, but some tribes are more vulnerable. Even mixbloods can do it, but their human blood tends to lower their chances by a large amount."

"I assume Norzen are very vulnerable to it?"

Larimanz lowered his body and allowed his tail to coil into a circle, like a chair. "They are. The Citadel has researched the condition, and according to their results, the five tribes have an order of vulnerability to the Haze. From highest to lowest risk, the order is as such: Norzen, Wasini, Soltauri, Vesikoi, and Aerivolk."

Kai felt his legs crumple beneath him as Teos helped him into a chair. "I... I never knew. I suppose it's because I was raised by humans. I never even met another Norzen until I was ten. The only other time something like this happened was back at Mistport."

All eyes turned to Kai. "This happened to you in Mistport?" Lucretia questioned. "Explain, please. Keep in mind, I still cannot fully trust you, but I am trying to give you the benefit of the doubt. What you say here may have severe consequences."

"My memory of what happened is fuzzy as you can guess. All I remember is heading back to the *Sunken Anchor* to look for Marko and Faust. This was in the middle of the attack, so I was trying to avoid attention. Then I heard a little Aerivolk girl crying in an alley nearby. She was begging her parents to get up."

Hearing Maple's gasp caused the apothecary to flinch. Kai refused to meet her gaze, preferring to stare at his knees. "I heard someone else there. A Liberator. He had this cold laugh, like he was enjoying what was going on around him. That bastard, h-he cut down that little girl, just like her parents. I was too far away; I couldn't do anything to stop him.

"Once I realized what he did, that red fog came over me. It felt so strange, like my body and mind were separated by a wall. I could recognize some of the thoughts, but my mind was racing, and everything was a blur. My legs just moved. I had no control. Before I realized what happened, the Liberator was lying dead at my feet, and there was a bloody mace in my hand."

"Holy Finyt," Teos groaned. "That sounds like the Haze, alright. And you've never once experienced it before Mistport?" Kai shook his head. It was a strange enough feeling that he knew he would have recognized it. "The admiral is right: You're an odd one," the smuggler continued, "I've never met a Norzen who had their first Haze this old. Usually they start slipping as kids, from what my Norzen buddies used to tell me."

That idea made Kai slouch further into his chair. Great, something else to mark him as different. If the other Norzen knew of this, he was certain they'd call him a freak.

"Maybe it means Kai has a stronger will," Ione piped up, drawing everyone's attention to her. "I can think of several reasons why Kai has never been through this Frenzy Haze until now, but right now it doesn't matter. That's not our concern. We still need to get to Runegard."

Lucretia agreed and asked Larimanz if the Navy could assist. The admiral snapped his fingers, ordering a sailor to return to camp for supplies. Beckoning the sailor close, the admiral whispered something in his ear before sending the man off. When questioned, Larimanz smiled and said it was a surprise. "Our camp is a tad further up the river and tucked into the woods, but we brought wirochs so it shouldn't take too long for him to return. We didn't want to disturb the inn's business too much which is why I brought only three retainers tonight."

When Morgan asked why bother coming in the first place, the admiral blushed. "To be frank, I've grown sick of hardtack, beans, and porridge and wanted a home-cooked meal. I need real food, damn it! You can only take so much of the stuff before you never want to see it again. But such is the military life."

The party exploded in laughter, which made Larimanz's face burn even brighter. As they waited for the sailor to return, everyone settled into a comfortable rapport. Larimanz asked Lucretia why she had trouble trusting Kai. "He's easily the calmest Norzen I've ever met," the admiral admitted. "In fact, I'd say he's probably the calmest Exarch in the entire order, and that includes me!"

"All I will say on the matter is that Norzen bandits are the reason why I haven't spoken to my brother, or anyone else in my family really, outside of carrier hawks for years."

"Fair enough," Larimanz replied. "You've got your reasons, but you kids should take some advice from an old war viper: not everything in Nixtral is made of black and white. There's plenty of grey to find between the seams if you bother to look."

Maple asked Lucretia how she understood what she said back on the *Gulley* when Grimghast first showed up.

"Oh, that's true," Ione piped up. "I didn't know you understood Aerian, Lucretia."

The scholar blushed. "Aerian is not the only other language I know. I studied several languages while at the Citadel. You would be surprised at how much easier it is to learn new things from tomes by knowing how to read them in the original language." A wave of agreement passed through the party.

As the night carried on, stories were shared, jokes were made, and as Kai looked around the table at each of his companions, he realized something.

Traveling with this group was proving to be more fun than anything he ever did during his Hunter career. He enjoyed the work, sure, but with the Hunters there was always a sense of formality and rigidity that he couldn't ignore, despite how much his squad toed that line. Being here, among this group thrown together by the worst and strangest of circumstances...it felt nice.

Larimanz muttered something to another of his retainers and the sailor rummaged through his pack. Finally, he brought out a long, thin package and set it on the table. The admiral cleared his throat. "Kai, as a Hunter you're familiar with flintlocks, I assume?"

Kai nodded and replied that, while he knew his way around a flintlock and could use one, he rarely did. The Hunters as a rule preferred more traditional long-range weapons like bows.

"I figured that was the case. Tell me, what do you make of this?" Larimanz opened the package to reveal an unusual flintlock. While built in the same manner as a pistol, with the lock plate and firing mechanisms all identical, the stock and barrel were longer and thicker. The wood used to make the stock had a reddish tint that made it look as if it were varnished with blood. A slender metal rod was slotted into place just beneath the muzzle.

"This looks like the flints some of the Libbies were using during the Battle of Faith Hollow. Before I saw those, I wasn't aware any were made like this," said Kai.

Picking the weapon up, Larimanz said they acquired it from a Liberator scout they encountered. "I've sent a carrier hawk back to Whistlevale asking for a deeper investigation. The scout we got this from called it a musket. The Liberation Army must be procuring them from somewhere. They don't have a crafting industry able to produce these on their own."

"You believe they are receiving outside help?" asked Lucretia.

"I'm almost certain of it. Corlati would be my first guess, but I have no evidence," the admiral bemoaned.

Kai inspected the weapon, turning it over in his hands after ensuring it was unloaded. He ran a claw over the stock and peered at the indentation left behind. "This entire 'musket' as they call it is evidence Corlati is backing the Liberators."

Maple examined the weapon herself and, after a few moments, clicked her tongue. "Kai's right. There's no way this thing was crafted in Livoria," said the merchant turning her gaze on Teos. "You know how smugglers operate, Teos. Would it be profitable for someone to smuggle large amounts of wood or logs?"

Teos scratched the base of his horn with a curious look. "Only under two conditions: the wood needs to be something sufficiently rare or have a unique use and thus expensive, and it would have to be cut into small enough pieces to store below deck. Otherwise, the elements would damage it. If either of those are missing, then it'd be pointless."

After muttering to herself, Maple set the musket down and palmed her chin. "Well the second condition is easy enough for this, but would this be worth the risk to smuggle?"

"Absolutely not." Everyone turned to Kai, who regarded the weapon with disdain. "The red tint alone would be enough of a giveaway. This musket was crafted from rhubarb cypress. It's a tree with red tinted wood reminiscent of rhubarb stalks, hence the name. The wood is dense enough to use in weapon stocks and shafts but still easy to carve, similar to pine."

"So what makes you think that's proof of Corlati's involvement?" Orelia asked. "Even the accusation of interference would be enough to draw Galstein into the war backing the Royalists, to say nothing of Rodekan or Belomas! Now that I think about it, couldn't we use Morgan's presence as proof as well? He's from Corlati, after all."

The sellsword held up his hands. "Hey now, don't bring me into this. Sellswords will take any job if the price is right. To my knowledge, all we did was transport weapons into Mistport. That's what we were contracted to do. We weren't allowed to fight unless in self-defense."

Kai turned the weapon over and ran a finger along the wood's grain. "Focus on the musket. First, no tree native to Livoria has this distinct color. Rhubarb cypress grows in one place: the Corlatian plains. It needs a specific type of soil that can only be found there."

It was then Maple that took over. "More importantly, rhubarb cypress is the Federation's national tree. Last I heard, it's against Corlatian law to export the wood, though they are known for using it in a lot of their crafts to give them that nice red shade without the use of dyes."

Lucretia raised her hand. "Would that not provide a viable reason for smugglers to sneak it over the border? I only ask because we need to think of every possible option."

With a gruff chuckle, Teos replied, "No worries, it's a good question. But to answer you, that alone doesn't make it worth smuggling out. Only a fool would want to smuggle something that sticks out the way this does. Besides, there's nothing the wood can be used for that is truly unique to justify the risk of smuggling. Livorian craftsmen can use native trees for the exact same things and for cheaper."

Maple gestured to the musket. "Using flintlocks as an example, Livoria has multiple trees that could be used for stock wood which are both more durable than rhubarb cypress and easier to get. I've traded a few flintlocks in the past, and the most common woods used are black myrtle and

Livorian walnut. I wouldn't be surprised if a quarter of this forest is made of those trees."

"So we have strong evidence Corlati is backing the Liberation Army from the shadows," pondered Larimanz. "That helps explain a few things. They certainly have a motive for it, knowing their views on faumen in general."

"Sorry, but what does it explain? I'm lost" Morgan asked.

"We've been getting information from scouts we have stationed in the western regions controlled by the Liberation Army. According to their reports, the faumen in the west are being captured and shipped elsewhere. The only problem is, we haven't figured out where that is. I will say one thing about the Libbies: They're a slick bunch."

Kai leaned back, mulling over the new information. What reason would the Liberators have for transporting faumen? From what he'd seen, they acted as if they wanted to wipe all the tribes out, like yanking a weed up by the roots. Suddenly, his thoughts raced back to Mistport.

"This might sound crazy, but what if the Libbies are gathering faumen to send them to Corlati?" Glancing around the table, he noted their reactions ranged from Lucretia's quiet curiosity to Maple's paling cheeks and Teos's smoldering rage.

Orelia and Teos each slammed a fist on the table. "You can't be serious, Kai!" Orelia snapped. "Why would they do that? The Liberation Army's leaders have made it known their focus is on ridding Livoria of every single faumen."

"That's just it, they want to *get rid* of them. That doesn't necessarily mean killing them. Think about it. What do the Corlatians do with all their faumen?"

It was Teos that answered. "They enslave them. If your theory is correct, the Liberation Army could be selling thousands of faumen into the Corlatian slave trade."

Ione dug her fingers into her scalp, worry etched on her face. "That must be why the Corlatians are supplying the Liberators. In exchange for weapons and supplies, they're handing over captured faumen to use as slaves."

"That would explain why that captain was so determined to capture me back at Mistport and in Faith Hollow," Kai added. "They mentioned a bounty of thirty golds for every Norzen they bring in alive. That's what those three idiots were after."

Orelia paled. "That's why Adalbard took Tuvi. He was turning her in for the bounty."

Larimanz's eyebrows shot upwards. "That's a hefty sum. That alone would suggest outside support. The Liberators won't have so much gold on hand to pay such an amount for every Norzen caught on top of what they pay out for other faumen. But if Corlati is paying the bounty, it makes more sense."

There was no way Kai could fault that line of reasoning. The vast majority of Livorians made less than thirty golds over an entire year. That was three thousand marks a head. It would be a tantalizing incentive for even those terrified of his tribe's reputation.

The aura at the table settled into an uncomfortable silence. Teos was holding onto a new stein so tight Kai was certain he'd break the handle. Maple's face had regained a little of its color, but when she met his eyes, she shook her head and busied herself with inspecting her feathers. Kai grimaced and reminded himself to ask about it later.

A familiar voice rose from the clamor, "Well I'll be a turkey's uncle. We really need to stop meeting like this." The apothecary turned with wide eyes to the source of the familiar voice. He'd know those white feathers anywhere.

"Locke! Nice to see you in good health, my friend," Kai exclaimed.

"I'm not sure if good health is what I would call it. It's only because of a traveling merchant that I reached this far. I simply disembarked to rest for the evening. I wasn't expecting to run into you again. Regardless, this old body is still kicking somehow," Locke replied with a hacking cough.

Taking a closer look, Kai noticed more pronounced wrinkles around the forlorn Aerivolk's eyes, and his cheeks had a deeper sag than when they met at Faith Hollow. "I suppose you're right. Would you like me to examine you? Free of charge."

"Oh there's no need for that," Locke declined, waving the invitation off. "I'm afraid I've been like this ever since boyhood. Not a single apothecary has managed to determine what my affliction is, so I've learned to live with it. For as long as my body holds out, that is."

With a somber nod, Kai accepted the man's words as everyone else watched with interest. Instead, he offered a seat at the table with the rest of them.

"Again, I'm afraid I must decline. You look as though you're talking about serious matters. I'd hate to intrude. However, I do have a useful tidbit of information you might find useful." When urged, Locke continued, "Word on the trails say the Liberators are taking ideas from Corlati's methods against Galstein back in the Fifty Years War. Any town they overrun is razed to the ground after they snatch every bit of food and supplies for themselves. You'd best stay ahead of them if you want to avoid the same fate."

The two sailors with Larimanz loomed over Locke with intense sneers. "And how exactly do you know of this?"

Locke smiled and patted the two men on the shoulder. "Despite my ailment, I do quite a bit of traveling thanks to friendly passersby and have more than a few connections because of that. Besides, I'm a rather skilled cook, and we all know people are more apt to share stories over good food. More so in these trying times, with more people traveling out of a desire to survive."

The admiral laughed and clapped his subordinates on their backs, "You have a good point, Locke. I do thank you for the information. Any little bit helps."

"Indeed, Admiral. Keep in mind this tactic is also serving to weaken the supply lines of the Royalist Navy. If they decided to start blocking the rivers, things could turn nasty."

Lucretia regarded the Aerivolk with a sly smile. "You seem to know a lot for a simple traveler. Who are you?"

His face flushing, Locke shivered under the woman's hawkish eyes. "I've always made it a point to know as much as I can. I grew up wanting to be a Citadel scholar." Lucretia's eyes widened. "However, my illness made that impossible, as I could never pass the required health examination. So, instead, I became a self-taught wanderer, performing odd jobs wherever I go to keep food on my plate. It's not a glamorous life, but it keeps me going."

"I suppose as long as you're happy, that's the most important thing," said Ione. Locke's lips tightened as he shrugged.

Suddenly the door burst open to reveal the sailor Larimanz sent out earlier. Kai took a quick glance at the clock and blinked, unsure if he had read it right.

Bloody Cacovis, it's that late already? What a night, he thought. Somehow several hours had passed without his being aware. *I suppose Ma was right. Time has a way of slipping away if you aren't careful.*

"Apologies Admiral, for taking so long," the sailor pleaded, "but you'll be pleased to know that I secured everything you requested. Shall I have it brought inside?"

Larimanz waved a dismissive hand. "Not yet, Lieutenant. Arrange with the innkeeper to have it stored in the barn for the night. I suspect our friends are on their last legs."

Kai scanned the table and agreed with the admiral's assessment. The rest of the party was beginning to nod off, their eyes heavy. He clapped an open palm on the desk that jolted everyone awake.

"Alright, you lot know I'm not one for throwing orders around, but I think it's best we tuck in. We'll inventory our supplies in the morning, decide what we can carry, and make for Runegard after breakfast. Understood?" The others mumbled in what Kai assumed was consent. He and Larimanz shared an amused smile. "Then head for your rooms. I'll settle the tab and see you bright and early."

Orelia waved her staff at the apothecary threateningly and muttered, "Not this little fishy, good sir. Just because I always had to be up early at the orphanage doesn't mean I like it. If you want bright-eyed and bushy-tailed at first light, go find a squirrel."

Trying to ignore Larimanz's uproarious cackling and bite his own tongue, Kai chuckled, "I'll make note of it, Orelia. But thank you for putting up with this. All of you."

"Don't mention it," the priestess replied, "all of us have something worth fighting for. Now don't stay up too late, you hear." She gave the apothecary a firm smirk.

Kai snapped to attention and saluted. "Yes, ma'am!"

The party broke out into laughter and headed upstairs, leaving Kai with Larimanz.

"You've got a good party with you," said the admiral. "Take care of them, lad."

"I intend to," Kai retorted. "Even if it costs my life, Waveweaver. By Cacovis, I'll make sure they get out of this mess alive."

Chapter XIX

I t was a groggy Kai that stumbled out of bed the next morning. Whatever rush the Frenzy Haze stoked within his body the night before was long gone. All that remained were sore muscles and a splitting headache. It reminded Kai of his early Hunter training. "Ugh, I need some tea," he murmured while rummaging through his satchel for clothes. A splash of red caught his attention. Lifting the garb, he felt a smile grow.

His apothecary robes.

He remembered receiving the custom garment upon completing his apprenticeship. Blood-red with ivory tundra wolf fur sewn to the waist and collar, the top was sewn into two separate halves that connected at the waist. It was looser than his Hunter's vest and allowed freer movement. Shedding his tunic, he pulled on a black leather undershirt with holes cut into the front and back that exposed his chest and back muscles before slipping into the robes. He allowed the left side of the robe to hang free, only wearing the right half over his chest. Content with his appearance, he went downstairs.

None of the others had woken, so the tables were empty except for a pair of travelers on the far end. Giving them a friendly wave and receiving cold stares in return, Kai trudged to the bar and asked the innkeeper to let his companions know he would be outside when they arrived.

"Hey," said the innkeeper as Kai turned away, "your friend, the scruffy Aerivolk; he wanted me to tell you he's already left. Caught the first boat going downriver and hopped on before the sun was up."

Kai nodded his thanks and slapped five coppers into the man's burly hands before strolling outside.

Stepping into the warmth of nature made Kai feel at ease. Gazing around, he saw the trees swaying in the autumn breeze. While winter was still more than a moon away, the wind carried a slight sting that prickled Kai's exposed skin. He was grateful for his mane's protection from the biting wind. Gathering wood from the inn's pile, he settled on an empty spot of sand near the river. Dropping his supplies, Kai built a small campfire. He would have a fresh pot of tea, one way or another.

The burble of the river, combined with the rustling wind and the crackle of the growing fire, had a distinct calming effect. The sounds reminded Kai of Havenfall and gave him a burning desire to see home again.

He filled the kettle and set it on a collapsible stand above the fire. While waiting for the water to boil, Kai plucked vials and bottles of herbs from his satchel. Setting them in a line, the Norzen regarded them with intense concentration. *I want something that can help with this headache, but also provides an energy boost. I have a feeling we'll need it for the road.*

His goal set, Kai scanned each container. As the water came to a rolling boil, he had five bottles next to his mortar while he inspected a sixth vial, the last one in the line. He hummed to himself, staring at the bottle with a frown. Finally, he separated it from the other five. The rest of the vials were returned to the satchel. Kai removed the kettle and set it on a flat stone.

Next, he added herbs from the first five bottles into a mortar and mixed them. Once done, the mixture was dumped into the kettle and allowed to steep. Kai then procured small cups and put seven in a circle around the kettle before popping the cork off the sixth vial. He grabbed a single cup and tapped the vial's bottom until two drops of liquid fell into the cup. Reinserting the cork, Kai set all the vials back in the satchel and waited for the tea to finish. The cup with the liquid, he kept at his side.

"Good morning!" a familiar voice sang out. Kai turned with a smile as Ione approached at a light jog. "The innkeeper said you were out here. Isn't it a little early for teatime?" she asked jabbing an elbow into the Norzen's exposed ribs. Realizing his new attire, Ione blushed scarlet, averting her eyes.

Kai laughed, rubbing the spot where Ione had struck him. "My dear Ione, there is no such thing as too early for tea. It perks me up in the morning, and I thought we could use that. We've got a long march ahead."

"I reckon you got a fair point. I see you're also wearing something new." Settling onto her knees, Ione took the top off the kettle and inhaled. "You never cease to amaze me, Kai. That smells divine."

Kai accepted the thanks and noticed the others lumbering outside. He asked Ione to wave them over while he finished. As she strolled back, he strained the tea into each cup.

A loud, booming laugh echoed that drew Kai's eyes towards the main road. The familiar form of Larimanz slithered towards the party, his face split by a wide grin. "I had a feeling in my tail you lot would be up early. Rested up for the day's journey?"

"As well as we'll ever be, Admiral," said Maple while perching on a nearby fence. Kai offered her a cup and a small jar of honey. She graciously took the cup and smiled at the jar, her cheeks tinted red while trying not to stare at Kai's chest. "And here I figured I was the only person that enjoyed honey with tea. You truly are a sweetheart." Scooping a large dab of the golden sweet into her cup, she nodded her thanks and brushed her wing against Kai's cheek.

Morgan howled with laughter, "Feathers, if either of you turn any redder, we're gonna see steam pop out of both your ears!" True to his word, Kai and Maple's cheeks were the shade of a fresh tomato as the apothecary turned away from the cackling sellsword.

Lucretia rolled her eyes and admonished the sellsword for his abrasive shouting. "Some of us prefer to have peace in the morning, Morgan. So I would appreciate it if you kept your voice down. Thank you," said the scholar, accepting a cup.

Soon, everyone was enjoying their tea. The aromatic brew received praise all around. Even Larimanz was able to partake as he carried his own cup. "Never know when you'll need the silly thing," he explained. "Now, before we part ways, my men and I will ensure you're properly equipped. There should be more than enough to last you through to Runegard. We'll even loan you some wirochs to make the journey easier on your feet." This offer was met with relieved cries of joy. "Just take them to the Navy stables in Runegard after you arrive."

Once they finished their tea, Larimanz led them to the inn's barn, where a squad of sailors presented each of them with a new rucksack and allowed them to forage through a pile of supplies. At the same time, Larimanz ordered another group to saddle a flock of wirochs. Kai reminded everyone to pack light. It wouldn't do any good to have their mounts so bogged down they wore themselves out before the day was half done.

Soon, the new packs were laden and secured as the party mounted their wirochs. Kai and Larimanz shook hands, the Wasini admiral pulling the Norzen into a brotherly embrace. "It was a pleasure to meet you, Gravebane. Winds willing, the two of us will have plenty more time to talk after the war."

"I'd like that, Waveweaver. May the winds bless you with safe travels," replied Kai with a demure grin.

A huffy Lucretia shouted for Kai to hurry, prompting him to hop into the saddle and urge his wiroch forward. The sailors waved goodbye to the party as they sidled up to the main road. Kai felt a sense of relief well up in his chest. They were ready to begin the next leg of their journey.

Nothing would get in their way this time.

A desperate shout came from the forest on the other side of the inn, bringing Kai's thoughts to a grinding halt. Everyone spun to see a single sailor in a tattered uniform burst from the trees, scrambling towards Larimanz as fast as he could.

"Admiral! It's the Liberation Army, they're here!" he shouted. Larimanz frowned and slithered towards the sailor.

"Where's the rest of the fleet? And the enemy?" the admiral demanded.

"The fleet is preparing for battle, sir! The Libbies are on—" The loud rapport of a gunshot breached the air before the sailor finished speaking. His hands flew to his back as he cried out, stumbling to the ground dead. A red stain spread over his tunic. The sudden noise spooked the wirochs, forcing the party to guide the birds into the trees for safety.

"Bloody Nulyma!" exclaimed Larimanz, his head swiveling to find where the shot came from. He raised the thick metal buckler strapped to his arm while moving back towards the trees. His men were scrambling for cover and loading their pistols at the same time.

A clamor across the river drew Kai's attention, where the trees were rustling more than they should, given the low strength of the wind. "Maple, what's on the opposite bank?" he asked. The merchant poked her head around the tree her wiroch was hiding behind and confirmed a large crowd of people was moving amongst the trees. Another crack rang out and Maple ducked back behind the tree, the bullet biting into its trunk. Kai shouted a warning to Larimanz.

"I think it's safe to say they're Liberators," she commented in a snarky tone.

Jerking his thumb at the splintered wood, Morgan quipped, "If that's safe, I'd hate to see what you think dangerous is."

Kai watched as Larimanz deflected the bullets with his buckler while urging his men to the safety of the forest. Turning towards the party, the admiral called out, "You go on ahead. We'll deal with these Libbie bastards!" Everyone exchanged uneasy looks before deciding to heed the man's order. They spurred their wirochs into the trees.

A multitude of jeers and screams came from across the river. Kai saw the Liberation Army barreling towards the bridge behind the inn. Thoughts of the kindly innkeeper and his family jumped out to Kai's mind, but he had to trust Larimanz would protect them.

Despite wanting to help, he knew he had no chance against the Liberation Army on his own. Better to let the Navy handle that part of the fighting.

"Are you sure we should leave them behind?" asked Ione.

Lucretia ducked her head at the sound of another bullet smacking into a nearby trunk. "Do not worry, Ione! We would just get in their way. The Marine Cavalry Fleet is one of the most decorated units in the Navy. Only the most capable sailors are allowed entry."

"Besides," Kai continued, "Larimanz knows what he's doing. Despite his age, he didn't earn a Brand for nothing. We need to trust him. Right now, we should put as much distance between us and the Libbies as possible." No one disagreed with his plan.

The party readied their weapons as the wirochs weaved in an erratic pattern. The group was spaced out enough to still be within earshot, while also giving themselves room to move.

Everything flew past in a blur. The only way Kai knew they were still heading in the right direction was because he kept the river in his sights. Without time to consult the map Larimanz gave them, they would have to use the river as their compass. The roar of gunfire rent the air, making the Norzen flinch. Sometimes he detested his sensitive ears. While useful for tracking, they were proving a hindrance in the fires of war.

"We've got company," Maple warned from his left. "We've got four riders on our tails. What do we do?"

Chancing a glance backwards, Kai saw them. Four figures in pursuit, winding through the tree trunks. Their wirochs were scraggly in comparison to the party's, but the Liberators were pushing them hard to keep up. He called back out to Maple. "Think you can pick them off? I can't fire my crossbow straight while riding."

She responded with a cocky smirk. Kai watched Maple nock an arrow while twisting in the saddle. Taking aim, she fired, and a shout of rage followed. Looking back, the apothecary saw one of the men clutching at his shoulder, a long shaft protruding from an open space in his armor. "Nice shot! Hopefully, they don't have any of those blasted muskets," said Kai.

As if to prove him wrong, a series of cracks rang out as bullets sped past Kai's head, slapping into the trees. "Why'd I have to open my big mouth?" he questioned.

"The next time you want to ask something stupid, Kai," Orelia shouted from the end of the line, "do us a favor and *don't*!"

"Look at it this way," said Morgan, "at least there's only a few of them following us and not the whole bleeding army. All things considered; it can't get much worse—"

Cutting the sellsword off, an ear-shattering roar echoed from within the forest, a roar the party hoped they'd never hear again. All the wirochs skidded to a stop. A massive flock of birds burst from the treetops, flying away. The Liberators were so unprepared for the sudden halt that all four were sent flying from their mounts.

Kai blanched, giving the others a terror-filled gaze as they spun in circles. "Impossible. There's no way," he whispered. How in the five hells of Nulyma could Grimghast be alive?

"By the winds," Lucretia spat. "Did we not drown that thing in the river? Please tell me I was not hallucinating."

The others confirmed they had all seen Grimghast dragged under with the *Gulley*. How it survived, no one could figure out. Kai ordered the party to close ranks and form a circle. The wirochs refused to follow directions, however. It was obvious the birds were spooked and desperate in their desire to flee. If Kai was honest, he empathized with them. His instincts were screaming at him to run.

The Liberators shouted at each other and tried corralling their own wirochs but were left stranded when the birds broke free, scampering away in a chorus of frightened squawks. The four men began reloading their muskets while standing in a haphazard formation. None of them seemed concerned about the roar that sent their best hope of escape tearing through the forest.

Trying to calm his breathing, Kai gestured for the party to quiet down and allowed his ears to turn outwards. His pupils expanded ever so slightly, giving a crispness to the surrounding woods. "Stay sharp, everyone," he murmured, "and remember: if you see any movement, be defensive. If you can get a clean hit, do not hesitate. No dumb risks. I want all of you alive and kicking when this is over." Six heads nodded in agreement.

A loud thump reverberated from the left. Kai's head snapped in that direction, eyes wide. Even the Liberators took note of the sound and scattered for cover. The thumps grew louder with each one. A deep low rumble, like a far-away stampede, seemed to come from all around. The Liberators' heads twisted in confusion, unable to see the source of the noise.

Kai knew his parents would tan his hide for thinking this way, but he had no intention of warning the four of the danger. His Da always implored him to do what he could to help others, and his Ma was one of the sweetest people he ever knew. Still, he felt no sympathy for anyone trying to kill them. Not after what he'd seen them capable of.

One of the men, stocky and unkempt, turned to the group and scowled. He drew his sword and stalked towards them, but he put little effort into being stealthy. Twigs and dried leaves crackled beneath his feet. Kai followed the man's progress while maintaining focus on the forest around him. The wirochs thrashed against their reins, emitting terrified shrieks.

"Kai how are we going to hear it coming? These birds are making too much noise," Teos hissed. His halberd was tilted at an angle, poised to swing in any direction at the slightest twitch of his arm.

"Keep your eyes open," instructed Maple. "It's true it can blend into the surroundings, but it's not perfect. The air moves around its body, so watch for any ripples above the ground."

The Liberator snapped at them, demanding to know what was going on while brandishing his sword. Kai returned the man's glare and gestured for him to be quiet while keeping his mace in position to block any attacks. The soldier balked, shouting and stamping his feet. His comrades all wore nervous expressions and begged the man to calm down.

"No," the man screamed. "I will not calm down! I deserve to know what's going on. And what is that incessant thumping?" His arms were flailing about as he screamed, spittle flying from his lips. Were the situation not so serious, Kai would find the man's reactions hilarious.

The soldier's rant was cut short when a glob of liquid splattered onto his head. Groaning in disgust, he tried wiping the fluid off. Instead, all he did was spread it around his hands and clothes. "What is this slop? It smells horrendous! And why is my skin prickling?"

Kai winced and cast an uneasy glance at the others. He noticed Maple and Ione staring at the soldier, eyes wide with fear. Turning back, he saw it.

The shimmer in the air, right on top of the unfortunate soldier.

The wirochs swung their heads in a panic, their squawks unbearable to Kai's ears. Orelia suggested they make a break for it. Weighing the idea for a few moments, Kai agreed. The moment Grimghast made its move, they would cut and run.

"Oi, what are you bastards whispering about?" asked the soldier. "You aren't going anywhere!"

Morgan chuffed. "Oh yes, we are. What's more, it's better than where you're going, that's for sure."

Confusion bloomed over the man's face. "And where exactly am I going?"

Ione pointed the tip of her dagger above the soldier's head. "I'd wager on that thing's belly, because it looks damned hungry."

Blinking, the man turned around to see his comrades backing away. Their faces were gaping upwards, eyes filled with uneasiness at the shimmering air. He chased after them but stopped when he ran into something blocking the path. Another glob of liquid spilled on his head, sending him into another cursing fit. Grumbling, he wiped the sludge from his face and glanced up.

Kai cursed at the now familiar scene. The air melted away into Grimghast's hideous form. The soldier blanched, stumbling backwards as he tried crawling away from the great beast.

Its beady eyes examined the soldier. Each heavy breath sounded like the throaty growl of an angry bull. Towering on its hind legs, Kai was reminded of how massive the beast was, despite its wiry body.

Peering at the leg Teos tied the anchor to back on the *Gulley*, Kai noticed the scarring above its ankle. The skin looked raw and new, with patches of dried blood caked onto the fur. Somehow, it had ripped the anchor chain off its leg, tearing its own skin in the process.

The three Liberators behind Grimghast screamed before bolting as fast as their legs could carry them. The noise had the expected effect, causing Grimghast to roar in the rough soldier's face. The last soldier attempted to push himself up to flee. He didn't make it that far as Grimghast snatched him up, crushing his torso with one bite.

"Now!" Kai snapped, jerking his wiroch's reins. "Follow the river!"

The others trailed after Kai, leading their mounts stampeding through the trees while Grimghast devoured the hapless Liberator. Looking back, Kai saw the beast swallow the man whole before turning its attention to the other soldiers.

"Perfect, it's chasing them!" Ione cheered.

"Of course it is," Teos replied, "they're closer and slower than us. Any moderately intelligent animal goes for easy prey, and their armor can't withstand its bite."

"Don't get comfortable," warned Kai. "That thing has already proven it's stronger and faster than it looks. The best way to survive is to just not be near it."

"I don't understand, Kai," said Morgan, "that monster killed your team back at Mistport. It also wiped out my company. We should stand and fight!" The sound of a terrified scream tore through the woods, followed by an unmistakable crunch.

Morgan's face turned a pale shade of green. "Never mind."

Kai grimaced. His heart was pounding in his ears. His fingers tightened around the reins and urged his wiroch to speed up. "Let me tell you something, Morgan, and any apothecary worth their salt will tell you the same thing. Learn to pick your battles. You'll live longer. I want to kill that thing so much. By the winds, I want that monster dead more than anything. But last time, we sunk it in the river with an anchor. By all logic, Grimghast should be a rotting corpse on the riverbed, yet it *still won't die*!

"If we're lucky, Larimanz and his men might be able to take it down if they cross it. Not even that beast could take down the entire Marine Cavalry. If it escapes again, then we can track it later and hit it with a full brigade of men."

Lucretia cast a worried glance at Kai. "Would that even work?"

"No, the idea has merit," Orelia replied. "You see it in nature all the time. Ants will swarm a much larger opponent and kill it through sheer numbers." Kai was impressed. It wasn't often he met someone aware of such things.

Grimghast's roar cut their conversation off. Kai looked back. That sounded way too close. The wirochs were stirred into a frenzy. All seven slid to a stop and began trying to fling their riders off.

Ione was the first to topple, unable to hold her grip before being tossed from the saddle. She hit the ground with a thud. When Maple tried to reach down and help, her wiroch took advantage and swung the merchant off.

Kai stretched for the free birds' reins, only to be knocked to the ground when he lost sight of a low-hanging branch. For his inattention, he caught a blow to the sternum. He struck the ground wheezing. "That's gonna hurt in the morning," he muttered.

Assuming he lived long enough to see the next sunrise.

By the time Kai hauled himself to his feet, everyone had been sent to the ground in some way and the wirochs sprinted into the forest. Swearing under his breath, Kai did a quick count, sighing in relief that everyone kept hold of their packs.

He beckoned the party to keep moving. The faster they put distance between themselves and Grimghast, the better their chances of survival.

Thump! The sound of the beast's footfalls rumbled nearby, sending everyone into a panic. "Bloody Nulyma, I refuse to die to some scraggly, mange-ridden bear. Not today, not ever," Teos snapped. He dropped his pack and twirled his halberd in one hand before sliding into a stance.

Waving his arms, Kai warned the smuggler not to worry about fighting. "We should distract it and run. We don't have the options to face it on even ground that we did on the *Gulley.*"

A scream from behind caused Kai to spin in place. His face paled seeing Grimghast appear out of nowhere, looming over Ione and Maple. Grabbing his crossbow, he tossed his pack aside and swung the weapon up, shouting a challenge to the beast. It ignored him, advancing on the women with hunger in its eyes.

"Not this time, you Nulymian abomination," Kai growled. Taking aim, he fired and watched with grim satisfaction as the bolt struck Grimghast behind the ear. That got its attention. It backed away with a pained bellow, clawing at the bolt. The women ran past while everyone readied their weapons.

Grimghast tore the bolt free and swung to face Kai. Blazing crimson eyes met stormy grey as the two stared at each other, the woods silent except for the party's movements. The apothecary saw something as the beast tilted its head to the sides while watching him, like a puppy investigating a new toy. It sniffed the air, observing Kai with an odd glimmer in its eye.

Can it...can Grimghast recognize me? Kai wondered. The more he watched the beast's movements, the more he considered the possibility. *But that would mean it is more intelligent than we thought. Maybe even on par with the Great Beasts. Not good, not good at all.*

Grimghast lowered its body, standing on all four paws and roaring a challenge. Orelia shouted for Kai to move when it charged, surging forward in a leap that carried it the full twenty yards between them.

Kai could only brace himself as the beast's head slammed into his chest, sending him careening into a nearby tree. He heard the others shouting, Teos and Morgan putting themselves between him and Grimghast. The two aimed slashes at Grimghast's legs, only for it to back away and swat them aside.

He propped himself against the tree and stood on shaky legs, only for a sudden wrenching sensation to erupt from his gut. *Taen, not now! Damn it, it hurts!* The pain in his stomach flared, feeling as though his organs were being tied into knots and boiled in oil. A stabbing pain shot up from his stomach and into his throat. Kai dropped to his knees and clutched his pain-riddled gut while Grimghast advanced towards him.

In the back of Kai's mind, he heard the others screaming, but the pain made any sort of thinking hard. A dark shadow appeared above him, and from its heavy breathing, Kai knew what it was. Clenching his mace, he stood as straight as he could and met the beast's intense eyes. With a tree to his back and Grimghast blocking any escape, he knew he wouldn't be walking away alive.

"Well," Kai grumbled, "if I'm going out, I'm not going without a fight." His friends' shouts faded to a faint buzzing in his ears. All his focus was on the beast in front of him. Smirking, Kai inhaled deeply, his face scrunching up. With no hesitation, he spat a wad of saliva into Grimghast's eye. The beast reared up, wiping an arm across its eyes. Kai released a war cry and hammered Grimghast in the ribs. A bony piece of rib armor cracked under the blow, falling to the ground with a thud.

Stunned at what he just did, Kai stared at the object in bewilderment and spotted the glint of nails emerging from one side. *Wait a tic...that bone was nailed into its body? But how?!*

Kai felt an immense pressure cover his body when Grimghast swung down and snatched him in a crushing grip. He struggled to escape, but the pressure was too painful combined with the fire in his stomach. One of Grimghast's claws pierced his side, drawing a hiss as he fought the pain. It felt like his Trial was playing out all over again. Kai shouted for the others to escape while they could. He thought he heard Morgan yelling a reply, but between all the swear words the sellsword was spewing, he wasn't certain. Orelia shouted something at Maple, but he couldn't see the two women around Grimghast's body.

Staring into its face, Kai gave the creature a cocky grin. "You are one *ugly* son of a bitch, you know that?" The beast's lips curled into a snarl, smashing Kai's back against the tree, and pinning him there. He wheezed, unable to breathe.

Looking around, there was a sense of familiarity. *I really should stop getting into these situations. Oh well, I suppose I couldn't expect to get lucky twice in a row.* Seeing Grimghast's maw open wide, Kai closed his eyes and waited for the pain of its bite.

What he didn't expect was a shrill screech to come from above, causing him and Grimghast to flinch. Unable to move his arms, Kai flattened his ears and turned his head towards the sound's origin. His eyes widened.

Maple stood on a high branch, her nostrils flared and eyes full of what Kai could only describe as unbridled rage. She spread her arms wide, opening her impressive wingspan and bending at the knees.

A prickle of fear lanced through Kai's mind when he realized her plan. "Oh no," he whispered. "Don't do it, you idiot. For the love of the Saints, no."

Unable to hear the warning, Maple launched herself from the tree, tucking into a falcon-like dive. Approaching fast, she pulled up and crashed into Grimghast's head talons first. "Put. Him. Down!" she shrieked.

From his brief experiences with Aerivolk, Kai knew their claws were sharp. He learned that well enough when he first met Maple. Now he saw upfront how dangerous an angered Aerivolk could be. Maple's talons shredded the beast's ears, tearing one off. The other went for Grimghast's eye, but came up short, catching it on the cheek. The daggerlike talons dug deep, leaving a line of bloody gashes down the side of its face. She flapped her wings in its eyes, throwing unsteady punches into its snout.

Grimghast roared in pain, trying to swing Maple into its maw. All it managed was to send her airborne when she kicked off its shoulder. It's grip on Kai loosened enough for him to pull free. Fighting the growing pain in his stomach, he dangled from the beast's arm rather than let himself drop to the ground.

With one limb occupied, Grimghast reached out with its other paw and grabbed Maple by the legs. The others fanned out in a circle surrounding it. Morgan hefted a large rock and hurled it with a spin, landing a lucky blow to the beast's chest. The hit staggered Grimghast, cracking several rib plates, but its hold on Maple refused to yield. It raised the Aerivolk up and opened its jaw wide, bringing her close. Even Ione fought back, using her dagger to stab the beast in the ankle. Grimghast shrieked, kicking the tavern maid aside and sending her rolling across the dirt.

Seeing Maple about to be torn apart, Kai felt his grip on his emotions snap. The recognizable fog of the Frenzy Haze encompassed him, but something felt off. Different. There was a clarity not there before. It also felt like time was slowing. He watched Grimghast holding Maple like a chicken ready for slaughter, but its movements were sluggish. The pain in his belly remained, but he found himself able to brush it aside now.

Even the way his body reacted was different. The wall separating his mind from his body shifted into a raging current, increasing his focus. Kai tested his arm, swinging the mace back and forth. The movement felt smoother, more controlled. He also sensed more control over his tails. Kai turned his gaze on Grimghast and tensed. He felt the muscles in his limbs coiling in preparation. His eyes latched onto Maple's terrified face and his mind was flooded with images of the last time he saw that look, back at Mistport.

Calvino. Faust. Marko. The fear in their eyes that day would forever be ingrained in his memory. He swore not to let it happen again.

A flood of power swelled in his chest. Taking a deep breath, Kai released a booming roar filled with every drop of frustration and fury built up since Mistport. Grimghast's head jerked to face him. He shot the beast a malicious grin, grabbing hold of its shoulder with his right hand while raising the mace in his left.

"Get away from her!" Kai bellowed. He slammed the mace into Grimghast's eye. The weapon became a blur, its flanges rupturing the soft orb in an explosion of blood.

Grimghast brayed and released Maple, the merchant's back hitting the ground hard. Kai swayed on Grimghast's shoulder and took a wild backhanded swing. This one struck the beast in the upper jaw, breaking a massive fang off.

Diving to the ground, he scooped Maple into his arms. Even as the Haze cleared, Kai knew he needed distance before Grimghast resumed its attack. Rushing to the group, he felt Maple curl closer to his chest and tightened his grip. He hoped it was enough to calm her. The winds only knew how scared she was. Being so close to death would drain even a battle-hardened warrior.

"No bloody way," Teos muttered. Twisting around, Kai was stunned to see Grimghast regarding him with hesitance. Its remaining eye was locked on the apothecary and filled with a mix of fear and rage. Blood gushed from its mouth where its broken fang once sat. Huffing and growling, it spat a glob of saliva at the party that fell well short before turning tail and rumbling away, back towards the fighting. Trees were knocked askew, and bushes lay trampled in its retreat. Soon, the forest grew silent once more. The only sound remaining was the far-off noise of the battle.

Finally spent, Kai slumped against the nearest trunk and let himself slide into a seated position. The sting of his injured side returned, leaving him gasping for air. His arms were still wrapped around Maple, and he was aware the others were staring in unabashed shock. "What?" the Norzen grumbled.

The party stepped back as if slapped. "What do you mean, 'pothy? You just drove that beastie off and took its eye and tooth as payment! What in hoarfrost was that?" Morgan shouted.

Maple's body shivered in Kai's arms. He pinned the sellsword in place with a glare. He could already feel the shakes settling in with the rush of battle fading away. The burning pain in his stomach was also growing. "We've already lost too many people to Grimghast. Morgan, you know that better than anyone else except Ione and Lucretia. I refuse to let it happen again. I promised myself I would make sure you all get home alive. I'm not in the habit of being a liar."

Kneeling next to the prone Norzen, Lucretia cocked an eyebrow. "And what if it had been me in the beast's grasp? We haven't exactly been good friends."

Kai shrugged. "Nothing would change. We may not always agree, but you're still a member of this party until we split ways. Besides, your knowledge of maps and history is better than anyone else's. We never would've progressed so fast without you telling us where to go. For that, I thank you. I made this promise for *all* of you, and no disagreements we may have will hinder that. I'd even make that oath on Cacovis's name, if necessary."

An audible gasp came from Ione. Kai could see the dread in her face, and he couldn't fault that. It was no secret that, as a devotee of Luopari, hearing him invoke Cacovis would be a shock. Morgan cocked his head and looked at the tavern maid in befuddlement. "What's got you so spooked, lass?"

"My apologies, Morgan, I often forget you're a Cadist," Ione replied. "Many of the Windbringer faith consider it a bad omen to invoke Cacovis's name. Most Norzen refuse to do so, despite her being a member of their tribe."

"Was she really that bad?" he asked.

Lucretia took over, "She was responsible for the Desolation, an event which as you know ended in Livoria's independence from Galstein. There's a reason why she is known as the Shadow. Many associate her with war and death." Glancing at Kai, she grimaced. "It makes me wonder why *you* of all people would invoke her name."

Kai shrugged. He understood the confusion, but he'd come to terms with the unique quirks of his life. "You said it yourself: Cacovis is an avatar of death. Death is another facet of the cycle of life, one I'm quite familiar with. You know I'm an apothecary as well, right?"

Seeing them nod, he continued, "Well, don't forget I'm *also* a Hunter. And both trades are intimately tied to this natural cycle. One whose oath seeks to induce death, and the other to protect life. It's a matter of maintaining the balance of nature."

The scholar gazed at Kai in silence, her eyes wide. It was obvious the thought never crossed her mind of the inherent conflicts in his work.

Ignoring the stares, Kai set Maple down and rubbed her back, asking in a whisper if she was injured. He asked for his satchel, thanking Orelia when she set it by his side.

The merchant shook her head, unable to speak. She met Kai's gaze. Her eyes were full of emotion, but Kai couldn't pinpoint exactly which ones. Perhaps admiration, or graciousness. "Ya saved me," she murmured. The fear was bringing Maple's drawl out, and Kai felt her natural accent suited her more than the deliberate city one.

Letting a soft chuckle escape, he gave her a warm smile. "First of all, you saved me first. Next, I hope you didn't think I'd leave you there. We're friends, and friends don't leave each other behind."

A soft thump sounded. Glancing down, he saw the fang and rib he knocked loose from Grimghast. He looked back up and saw Teos smirking. "Figured you'd want a trophy after all that. Our first tussle with this damned thing felt like a draw if you ask me. We did lose my barge, after all. This time, I think it's safe to say we eked out a win."

Wrapping his fingers around the fang, Kai agreed with the smuggler. Up to now, they'd been fighting Grimghast on the back foot, unable to do much else besides parry its advances and scramble away in fear. Today, they managed to deal visible damage to it. And if there was one thing he learned as a Hunter, it was one irrefutable fact: If it bled, it could be killed. And now, staring at the bloody fang, Kai felt relief. Even if they didn't finish the job, they proved Grimghast wasn't invincible. It was a small victory, sure.

But it was a victory that provided a beacon of hope for the future.

Chapter XX

V izent continued muttering curses under his breath. Their last battle was unanticipated and cost more men than he could afford. After the written thrashing he received from Razarr following Faith Hollow, he knew he needed results. More so because of the forge master's intentions to travel to Livoria himself. His head still throbbed in pain when he thought about it. Of course, the pounding rain outside did little to alleviate his headache, either. The tent shielding them from the elements wasn't what he was used to, but it was far better than the pitiable covers his men were using.

I suppose I've weathered worse than this, Vizent thought.

While he considered it a positive their forces managed a draw against the Marine Cavalry Fleet, it was still close. The only reason they weren't wiped out was because they caught the Royalists by surprise. Then there were rumors floating about saying the beast from Mistport made another appearance. He didn't want to imagine the implications of that thing running loose.

"You seemed stressed, General," said Obram from across the table. The faumen's ears twitched. Triangular with fur lining the inside, they made Vizent believe the man a Norzen with unusual ears, but Obram didn't carry himself the way a typical Norzen did. Plus, he gnashed his teeth whenever the feline tribe was mentioned. Vizent noted that he never saw the distinctive pair of tails that marked the Norzen tribe. Instead, he saw a large bulge in the back of the man's cloak, suggesting either a larger tail or some other body part not normally seen on faumen.

So not a Norzen, but what else could he be? A mixblood banished from the tribe, perhaps? Or perhaps even a tribe we've never seen before.

"Even a dead man would stress in this situation, Obram," Vizent growled. "Outside the initial invasion, our only victories are against piddling villages that scatter like rats the moment we approach. A victory at Faith Hollow would have given us the morale boost to march on Whistlevale, but that was a catastrophe."

Obram burst into maniacal laughter. "Oh Vizent, you don't truly believe that, do you? Even if you won Faith Hollow, your men are still far too unprepared. They deflected the Marine Cavalry today by pure chance alone. Be grateful you didn't cross their commander. I saw him in battle today, and the man would have butchered you for sure."

Vizent growled a warning. He was aware of Larimanz's reputation. He'd earned his Brand ten-fold, and Vizent respected the man's skill, even if he was a Wasini. The general knew how lucky he was. His fingers tightened around his quill, snapping it in two before he slammed a palm on the table.

"We aren't getting anywhere like this," shouted Vizent, "We need a big victory. The men need more training. We need so much but have few methods to get it."

Obram agreed, reminding the officer these things took time. "You must remember, not all problems can be solved through force. You of all people know this."

Hearing that from an outsider made Vizent's blood boil. The fact it came from a faumen made the reprimand worse. "As much as I loathe it, I cannot disagree. When will the new weapon be ready? Razarr's muskets are useful for long range, but we have far too few of them."

"Don't worry your pretty little head," Obram elucidated, pouring a glass of wine to Vizent's irritation. The man enjoyed making himself at home, though it was rare for him to do much besides criticize the war effort and eat the general's food. "The weapon is being built as we speak. Master Razarr expects it to be at least spring before it's ready for battle tests. Even if you get your bells rung by the Royalists before then, we'll make sure things work out. Though you'd best avoid that, as I know Razarr would be...most displeased with you. Hate me all you want, General, but believe me when I say angering him is your worst option. I've seen what my employer does to those he deems expendable."

Remembering his initial visit with the forge master sent an involuntary shudder down Vizent's spine. No craftsman was surrounded by an aura of death like Razarr's, which terrified the general. That type of aura was something you saw in seasoned warriors and assassins; individuals intimate enough with death, it seeped into their very presence.

Through the pouring rain, Vizent heard familiar voices outside the tent. He scowled, hoping they had a damned good reason for bothering him. Otherwise, he'd let Obram have some fun. If anything, the strange faumen proved a deft hand at doling out punishment.

"Where are you taking me, you brutes?" a childish voice said. Vizent watched as Tuvi, the Norzen girl they acquired after Faith Hollow, was shoved inside, followed by Captain Agosti and the bishop that brought them the girl in the first place. Adalbard, if he remembered right. The priest's robe was tattered and covered with claw marks.

"Quit your whining, brat, or I'll put your face in the dirt," Agosti snapped, pulling the girl around by her hair. She cried out, tears streaming down her face when Agosti pushed her into a chair. The one next to Obram.

The faumen looked over the child with a sneer, as if she were a slug. "I must confess, Doulterre, I wasn't aware you dealt with children." Obram's gaze swiveled to Adalbard, where his sneer deepened. "And why do you allow your priests to look so slovenly? Even the lowest of Cadist monks take better care of themselves than this."

"Shut your dirty mouth, peltneck," Adalbard barked while wringing water from his robe. Vizent chuckled at Adalbard's audacity. He watched Obram wordlessly smack the priest in the nose with an open palm, grab him by the back of his thinning hair, and smash his face against the table. Tuvi screamed and fell out of her chair, scurrying away.

In one smooth motion, the faumen put a knife to Adalbard's neck and whispered, "Listen well, priest, because you won't get a second chance. Don't ever call me a peltneck again like I'm some dirty Norzen. If you do, I'll skin your hide for a new satchel to give my old lady back home. Am I clear?"

Despite his distaste for Obram, Vizent couldn't help but be impressed and took notes on his technique as Adalbard pled for mercy. Not one word was yelled, but the man's voice carried such an edge that any fool would know Obram had no qualms carrying out the threat.

He let go of Adalbard and returned to his seat, making a show of using his knife to pick between his teeth. "Good dog. He's all yours, General."

Inhaling deep, Vizent reminded himself that arguing with Obram was not in his best interest. Instead, he directed his ire at the two men who brough the girl into his command tent. "Why have you fools not broken this girl yet? She's a damned child!" Tuvi stuck her tongue out at Vizent. Were she not so infuriating, the general would find her determination amusing.

"She's a stubborn one, general," Adalbard stammered. "We've tried every method I can think of to break her resistance, but she refuses to back down."

"Perhaps I was too lenient in allowing you to handle this alone," Vizent admitted. "There are other methods to make her submit. Obram, any ideas you want to share? I assume you have some tricks up your sleeve."

Obram looked between the general and the girl for a few moments before snickering. "As much as I'd love flaying a Norzen, I have no desire to assist. My duty is to observe and guide. I'm not some fledgling soldier you can order about."

Tuvi sighed in relief, tucking herself into the corner while the men bickered.

Vizent grumbled, returning his gaze to the map on the table. He would worry about the girl later. Right now, he needed to figure out how to turn things around before the Liberation Army was finished. His eyes flickered to Adalbard, and an idea formed in his mind.

"It seems we may have some use for you after all, priest." Adalbard faced Vizent, eyes glazed with confusion. "I'd like for you to work on seeking out those who might be receptive to our cause. After all, the more people are sympathetic to us, the fewer we'll have to cull once we oust the Grand Duchess from her throne."

A loud commotion from outside cut off anything else the general wanted to say. "Obram! Damn it all, Obram, where in hoarfrost are you?" a gruff voice bellowed. Tuvi covered her ears in the corner and ducked under a nearby table. Vizent glanced at the faumen and noticed grim acceptance in his features.

With a groan, Obram shouted back, "Quit your bellyaching, Duarte. Get in here before I cut your tongue out for my evening stew!"

Vizent raised an eyebrow. "Are you always so abrasive towards your allies? If I didn't know better, I'd swear your sole purpose is to piss off everyone you meet."

A hoarse chuckle came from behind. "That's normal for Obram. I've seen nettleboars less prickly than this bastard," spoke a massive, soaked Soltauri coming into the tent. Vizent wasn't surprised the man had to bend at the waist to fit.

"I don't believe we've been introduced. Vizent Doulterre, General of the Livorian Liberation Army," spoke the officer, holding out his hand. He had trouble restraining his disdain, but appearances needed to be kept.

The Soltauri stared at the appendage before grasping it in a hesitant handshake. "Pleasure, I'm sure. The name's Duarte, personal bodyguard to the man you know as Master Razarr. Don't bother calling me sir, either. You humans are a vile lot, but I hate standing on ceremony with anyone. Gives me the heebies if you know what I mean."

Vizent couldn't help but laugh at the man's forthright way of speaking. "I do know what you mean, Duarte, as odd as it sounds. One of the big reasons I left the Navy was my frustration with the pomp of the Royalist court. I didn't have to deal with it very often in my previous work, but when I did, it was so stifling. Like wearing a fur coat in the summertime."

"That's exactly what it feels like!" Duarte exclaimed, a wide grin stretching from ear to ear. "Oh, Cadell be praised, someone who understands me! You may be the first human I could grow to tolerate."

For the general, the feeling was mutual. It was refreshing for Vizent to meet someone who detested formalities as much as himself. Still, he knew those of influence thrived on it, and so he tolerated the decorum as best he could.

He couldn't help but wonder if, in Duarte, he'd found a kindred spirit after so many years. It reminded him of days long past. It was a pity the man was a damned faumen and Cadist heretic. Then again, no one was perfect. Not even himself.

"Knock it off, you two. You'll have plenty of time to share peasant stories over a campfire soon enough," Obram snapped. The faumen's face was flush with drunkenness as he poured another glass of wine.

Duarte loomed over the other faumen and smirked. "Don't get your silky unmentionables in a twist, Obram. And don't act so superior. We both work for Master. And at least I'm not a drunkard."

"Aye, but I'm here to enforce Razarr's will. You're nothing but extra muscle to make sure certain jobs get done."

A meaty fist snatched Obram by the tunic, lifting him to meet the Soltauri eye to eye. "Say that again, you walking rug."

Vizent drew his pistol and fired out of the tent. A loud thump followed by frightened yells for an apothecary came from outside. The two bickering faumen stared at the general in confusion.

"Enough! If you two wish to beat the shit out of each other, do it after we accomplish our mission. Speaking of, we need to decide on our next course. Runegard is the next major city along the path, but I want to hear what you all think."

Obram removed himself from Duarte's grip. "Your army is in no condition to take Runegard. Not after the hammering you took at Faith Hollow and this morning's battle with the Marine Cavalry. You're better off training your rabble further east. If anything, it might draw the Navy away from the capital if they decide to pursue you. According to the map, there's a large settlement in the southeast called Thorncrest. That might be a good target."

Adalbard spoke up, regaining his voice, "You can't simply ignore Runegard, however. The Citadel is a powerful tool in the Duchess's satchel. Perhaps a small group could infiltrate the city and sow discord from within. If the Citadel is fractured, it would be one less obstacle for you to deal with when we attack Whistlevale."

Agosti raised a tentative hand. "The priest makes a good point. With your approval, General, I'd volunteer to lead a squad to accomplish this goal."

"You, Captain Agosti?" Vizent questioned. He admired the young officer's initiative, but he didn't like overworking his men if he could help it. "Are you sure you can handle another mission so soon?"

"Absolutely, sir!" exclaimed Agosti. "I must admit, however, I do have another reason for wanting this. I have a bone to grind with the peltneck I told you about. He's escaped me three times now. From what we've gleaned from the brat, he and his band are heading to Runegard. They had an Archivist among their number, and they're likely trying to return her to the Citadel. There's also the Vesikoi priestess from the orphanage we plucked the kid out of. If I get an opportunity, I'll snatch them both for sure." Vizent rolled his eyes. He could sympathize with the man's frustration, but he wondered if Agosti was focusing too much on a single Norzen. Especially if it was the one he was thinking of.

Duarte chuckled, lowering himself into a seated position with legs crossed. "Can't stand having unfinished business, eh?" At Agosti's uneasy nod, he continued, "I know the feeling myself. There's a Norzen I met back in Mistport who owes me a good fight. Tough bastard too. Last I saw him, he was wearing a brown vest and swung a mace better than any gladiator I ever—" Vizent's eyes shot towards Duarte in shock.

Agosti jumped to his feet, shifting the table and sending documents flying everywhere. "Wait a tic, did you say a mace?" Duarte nodded. A sense of foreboding grew inside Vizent's stomach, churning it in knots.

It couldn't possibly be him, the general thought.

"Was he wearing vials all over his vest?" Agosti asked. Another nod. "Bloody Nulyma, Soltauri, I think you and I are after the same damned peltneck."

Saints be damned, it is him. Vizent groaned and rubbed his temples, leading the others in the tent to look at him in concern. "You idiots really know how to bungle things. Of all the Norzen in the bloody duchy, you *both* picked a fight with the one best left alone!"

Duarte raised an eyebrow. "Why are you overreacting? It's one Norzen. They can't cause too much trouble on their own, can they?"

Scoffing, Agosti muttered, "The scars this peltneck gave me suggest otherwise."

Realizing just how uninformed the rest of the group was, Vizent straightened his back. "I can understand your ignorance, Duarte. You and Obram hail from Corlati, correct?" Duarte confessed he was a native Livorian but came to Corlati as a boy.

Obram scoffed. "I would be embarrassed to admit coming from a third-rate nation like Corlati. I'm not even Alezonian." This information shocked the other four. "I'm a sellsword from the northern continent, Feswili."

If Vizent's curiosity about the strange faumen hadn't been stoked before, it was now. *I heard the realms of Feswili preferred to isolate themselves from the rest of the world. What possible purpose would Obram have being here then?*

Shaking his head, the general knew he had to get the conversation back on track. "Regardless, you don't know who you're up against. I have knowledge of this Norzen, but the rumors alone are enough to justify caution. For one thing, that Exarch watch you found on him is likely legitimate, Agosti." The captain paled. "Take my word for it. He's dangerous in ways you don't understand, and if you've provoked him, you may not walk away alive."

It was an agitated Adalbard that spoke up next. "I think I know which peltneck you're talking about. One of my priestesses gave him and his ruffians beds for the short time they were in Faith Hollow. He and that pack of his were the reason I snatched the girl while I could still use her as a hostage. What's so dangerous about this peltneck, General?"

"The worrisome part is that he's a Hunter, which is concerning on its own. I've dealt with Hunters, and they're the Duchess's warriors of last resort alongside the Exarchs for a reason. A Norzen with that kind of training under his mane is going to be damned hard to take down." Rubbing his chin, Vizent mulled over his options while tuning out the others' arguing. He couldn't send too many men to Runegard, lest he alert the Royalists. Deciding on a course of action, he slammed a fist on the table.

He gestured to Duarte, ordering him to sneak into Runegard with Adalbard in tow. When the priest asked why he had to go, Vizent smirked. "Why Bishop, this mission was your idea in the first place," he said, his voice like silk. "Besides, as a former member of the clergy, you have the best chance of dividing the Citadel. Reach out to anyone you suspect leans towards our sentiments. Use that silver tongue of yours."

Turning towards Duarte, he fixed him with a pointed glare. "As for you, I'd prefer it if you caused as much chaos as possible while assisting Adalbard. If you run into that Norzen, do not engage unless you're certain you can surprise him. If it does turn into a fight, *never* let him out of your sight! A Hunter is no easy prey, even alone. If his comrades have any level of skill, you'll be on the back foot before you can blink."

Resting a hand on the head of his axe, Duarte thanked Vizent for the warning and promised they would leave immediately. The Soltauri nodded to Obram, and the pair left the tent, not bothering with cover as the rain abated during their planning. Duarte shouted for Adalbard to hurry up.

Sneering at the retreating faumen, Agosti glanced at his commander. "With all due respect, sir, why do we cater to those beasts? Would it not be better to slaughter them now?" Adalbard nodded in agreement and expressed the same sentiment.

Vizent clicked his tongue. Sometimes being in charge was so difficult. "Because, you two, those brutes have the ear of our primary supplier and financier. And from my brief time speaking with him, Razarr is not a man to cross without good reason. No, we bide our time and wait for our chance. Even if it can't be done until after the war is won, we will return this humiliation ten-fold one day, mark my words."

"And what would have me do, sir, since I haven't been given leave to join the priest's mission?"

"You will be helping me with our preparations for Thorncrest. Obram was right about one thing: our army needs improvement before we can take the fight to Whistlevale. The men are growing to respect you, Agosti, and I need you here to spread that spark of passion you have."

It was a grinning Agosti that grabbed Tuvi by the arm and forced her out from her hiding place. The captain leered at the girl, holding her up by the limb. "Thank you, sir, for the compliment. Priest, take this brat with you. With any luck, you can make good use of her."

Adalbard slumped into an empty chair. "Why bother? The little witch refuses to cooperate and no matter how many times we beat her, nothing has changed."

A low rumble came from Agosti as he chuckled darkly. "She can be a useful bargaining chip. After all, the priestess who raised her is with that Norzen. If you come across them, you'll have the advantage."

"And if they refuse to negotiate?" Vizent asked.

Agosti drew his sword and licked the blade with a deranged look in his eye. He cackled at the look of terror in Tuvi's eyes.

"Simple. If the kid can't get us what we want, we kill her. Now hold her still."

CHAPTER XXI

A dalbard pulled his hood tight as he navigated Runegard's streets. The sprawling city was larger and more spread out than Faith Hollow, with the massive Citadel encompassing the center of town. As the largest and most famous learning academy in eastern Alezon, it made sense the Citadel was the largest building in the city, outstripping even the city headman's station in height by three or four times.

Considering his last visit to Runegard was years ago, Adalbard repeated what he knew about the academy in his mind.

Back before Livoria was its own nation, the Citadel was said to be the home of a thriving warlord that ruled these lands, the priest thought. The history tomes were divided on what happened to the warlord. The prevailing theory, which Adalbard agreed with, was that he was killed in the Desolation, he and his entire army wiped out by Cacovis. *Yet another reason we should eradicate those damned Norzen.* There was no telling how powerful Livoria could have become if the warlord had retained control of the fledgling nation.

It always struck Adalbard as odd for the Wind Saints to convert a fortress into a school, with most of the upper floors and towers dedicated to dormitories or storage. From his vantage point near the north wall, the former bishop could still see the entire top half of the building. Adalbard felt the Citadel would have been put to better use in its original purpose: a military structure.

As far as he knew, the only building in Livoria that was larger was the Royal Palace.

Shaking the thoughts from his head, Adalbard sidled up to a nearby shop, tilting his head in respect to the proprietor, who nodded back before ignoring the man. He removed a folded parchment from inside his cloak, studied it for a few moments, then tucked it away once more.

"It should be a bit further down this street, assuming I was given correct information. I should ask for assistance, just to be safe," he murmured.

The skies were still dark this early in the morning, with just a tinge of sunlight peeking above the horizon. Because of the surrounding buildings, the light it provided was minimal, leaving the priest surrounded by shifting shadows.

Raising a tentative hand, Adalbard beckoned the shopkeeper over. "Pardon me, my good man, but would you happen to know where I can find Branclor's Bounty? It's been some time since my last trip to Runegard, so I'm rather lost."

The shopkeeper snickered, pointing further down the road. "Don't worry, it happens to everyone. Even the locals still get lost sometimes. Price you pay for living in such a big city, I guess. The place you want is maybe fifty or sixty yards that way. You can't miss it. Look for the huge gold-plated shield over the door."

Adalbard shook the man's hand. "Many thanks, my friend! May the winds bring you fortune."

"Same to you, traveler. May the winds guide you."

Slinging his sack over one shoulder, Adalbard marched on after tipping the shopkeeper a few bronze marks. He was grateful to be so close to his goal. At his age, he felt more suited for the comforts of the church over traveling. With any luck, he would be back at Stahl Granz after this dreadful war ended.

As the shopkeeper said, Adalbard found a giant shield hanging from the wall, the words "Branclor's Bounty" etched into it. The priest stepped inside, shouting a greeting.

Despite the darkness outside, the shop was well-lit and filled with merchandise. One half was littered with all types of weapons and armor. The other contained shelves full of shiny baubles and various artifacts, most of which Adalbard didn't have the faintest clue what they were for. So he ignored them in favor of moving towards the large table in the rear.

"Excuse me," he shouted again, "is anyone here?"

A throaty voice barked out from behind a curtain, "Hold yer horses, ya old bat, I'm coming!" A large hand emerged, followed by the wiry frame of a well-muscled Soltauri woman. Compared to Duarte, the woman was short, but she still towered over Adalbard. "What ya looking fer? I'm guessing you ain't in the market for a weapon," she asked with a cocky grin.

The priest was struck dumb. Doulterre's instructions didn't mention anything about this. "Uh, my apologies. I was told to meet with someone here. Are you...Branclor, by any chance?"

The woman stared at Adalbard, her eyes traveling up and down the old man's body. "You ain't from around here, that's for damn sure. Branclor was my husband, least before he kicked the bucket. The name's Pekalda, and I own this shop now. You said you're here for a meeting?"

Adalbard nodded, not trusting his voice. He was certain this woman could break him in half if provoked.

"You must be the one I was told to watch for. The name's Adalbard, right?" The priest nodded again. "Perfect! I gotta admit, they didn't give me a good description, so I wasn't expecting someone with one foot in the grave." Adalbard bristled. He was no spring chicken, but he still had a few good years left.

Provided he didn't botch this meeting.

Pekalda burst into laughter. "Come on, I'll take you down below. The man you're looking for is already waiting."

Adalbard followed Pekalda into the back room. It looked to be a workshop, with several tables covered in trinkets and tools. "So what do you sell here, if I may ask?" the priest asked.

"Eh, a little of everything, so long as it can make some marks," replied the merchant. "Most of my wares come from what we call abandoned estates. You'll get an old noble that hoarded too much in life. Once they kick it, the family wants to get rid of the crap they don't want. That's where I come in. I usually get first pickings ahead of the other merchants because I don't bother asking too many questions. That's why a lot of folks use my cellar for meetings. If you got the coin, your business ain't none of my business."

It seemed unusual to Adalbard, but he was raised in a traditional household. Still, he couldn't help but be impressed with the woman's dedication to her principles. After all, those principles were benefiting him at the moment.

Pekalda stopped near the workshop's back corner, kneeling to open a hidden door. A thin staircase was revealed. The room at the bottom was dimly lit. "I'll stay here and keep the door locked while you two talk. I already told the other fella, but when you're ready to come back up, knock three times.

The priest nodded. Three times, simple enough. He eased himself down the stairway. The flickering light brightened the further he descended. Reaching the bottom, he stepped into a large open room lit by a single lantern. A single table sat in the center. Judging by the boxes, chairs and tables pressed against the walls, Adalbard guessed the room was used for storage.

At the center table were two chairs, one of which was occupied by a figure in a gray cloak. Adalbard assumed it was a man judging by the broad shoulders. The figure's brown eyes were the only thing visible. Their face from the nose down was covered by a cloth mask. When he spoke, it was in a low, clipped tone. "I was beginning to wonder if you would show up," said the figure.

"Apologies," replied Adalbard, "as you can tell, I'm not a young man, so travel is slow going. Now who do I have the pleasure of speaking with?" The figure's voice was familiar, but Adalbard couldn't quite remember where he'd heard it.

The man waved off the question and reminded the former bishop they were there for a reason. "We have important issues to discuss, and socializing isn't one of them."

Adalbard ignored the snappish tone, pulling a roll of parchment and quill from his sack. "Understood. I must confess I wasn't given much information on what this meeting would entail. All General Doulterre said was you were a good contact for accomplishing our goals. Would you enlighten me?"

The figure emitted a frustrated groan. "Doulterre, you bastard," he breathed. "This is why I can't trust those Liberator mongrels. This is nothing against you. Damnation, you're as much a victim here as me. Unfortunately, your leaders seem to be deathly allergic to sharing useful information with potential allies."

Adalbard chuckled. He wasn't sure if it was an intentional slight on Doulterre's part or if the man was scatterbrained from too much work. Leading an army of amateur soldiers couldn't be easy.

"Regardless," the figure continued, "we're supposed to discuss your plans for Runegard. Doulterre mentioned fracturing the Citadel."

For the first time since his retreat from Faith Hollow, Adalbard felt invigorated. "That is the basic idea. My intention is to spread rumors among the scholar divisions, perhaps even convincing some of them to join our cause."

The man's eyes flickered with amusement. "An ambitious plan. I can work on spreading some rumors. It shouldn't be hard, especially since the Citadel is having a problem with disappearing students."

"Disappearing, you say?" Adalbard questioned. This sounded like useful intelligence. "How is that possible?"

"That's the problem. They can't determine the cause. And there's no discernable pattern to the missing students, either. Faumen. Human. Male. Female. It's like they're vanishing at random."

The priest was writing at a furious pace. This was perfect! "In that case, causing chaos should be simple. Spread a few false rumors about the missing students and who could be responsible. That should have the divisions fighting amongst themselves. Then we can bring the frustrated into the fold."

The figure's head nodded. "That's all well and good, but there's something else."

"Oh?"

Leaning in close, the man whispered, "Word on the river says the Citadel is getting a special visitor as soon as this morning. One that could be a *royal* thorn in your side if you catch my meaning."

Eyes wide, Adalbard's body slumped against the chair. That could only mean one thing. "The Grand Duchess..." Glancing up at his companion, the priest racked his brain trying to remember why the voice was so familiar. Only the senior scholars and staff would have early knowledge of a visit by Lady Fusette.

"Aye. It's been all smoke and mirrors trying to figure out why she's leaving the capital now. Our best guess is it has to do with the war. However, it might be something you can use to your advantage. Just be warned, she'll be under guard for certain. It might be better to ignore her and focus on splitting the divisions. You need to turn as many as you can before she conscripts the whole damn academy."

Adalbard couldn't disagree with the suggestion. Making any sort of direct move against the Grand Duchess would be suicide. She would have at least several high-ranking sailors, or possibly even an Exarch, guarding her. "I'll bring this information to my comrades and handle the aftermath. If you and your allies can spread rumors for the time being, that will be more than enough to work with. There is one last thing."

"And what would that be?" the figure asked, tapping a finger against his chin.

Removing a scroll from his sack, Adalbard unfurled it and pushed it forward. "We've been having a bit of trouble with a group of travelers led by a Hunter. A Norzen Hunter."

The figure's eyebrows shot upwards. "Well that is strange. What would you have us do? Tracking a Hunter is a fool's errand."

"That's the beauty of it. They'll come to us," Adalbard gloated. "We have reason to believe they're heading for Runegard if they haven't already entered the city. Should we encounter them ourselves, we have a bargaining chip to keep them nice and docile. Among their group, however, is a Citadel scholar. An Archivist stationed in Mistport during the invasion."

A grim chuckle came from the figure. "Mistport, you say? I think I know who that is, which makes this rather amusing. Very well, if we come across this group, we will stall or deal with them."

A gracious Adalbard bowed to the figure, thanking them for taking the time to meet with him. "It feels as though things might be turning around," he said.

"I agree. I'm quite interested in seeing what the former bishop of Stahl Granz is capable of." Adalbard's mind skidded to a halt. He had come to the meeting wearing nothing but a simple peasant's tunic and trousers, with none of the religious garments or accoutrements he was used to. He asked the figure how they knew who he was.

"That's simple. I have quite a few friends in high places. In fact, I work within the Highmaster's office. Lots of useful, *unprotected*, information flitting about up there." With a hearty laugh, the figure reached up and removed their hood and mask. Adalbard's breath hitched in his throat.

"Well, I can't say I was expecting this. It's been a while, old friend."

Constant travel was never Kai's favorite part of being a Hunter. Most of the children back home liked to wax poetic about the wonderful sights that came with being on the road. To an extent, Kai could agree. In six years, he'd seen many things he never would've experienced while trapped in Havenfall.

But, as expected, he also saw a lot that was unsettling. He would never trade his experiences for anything, but at the same time he yearned for his warm bed back home and his sister's cheerful smile. The glimmering sunset spreading across the horizon only deepened his desire for a real bed.

Despite losing their wirochs while fighting Grimghast, the party continued their trek on foot. After traveling for two days, Runegard was now within sight. Not for the first time, Kai was grateful he asked everyone to limit their supplies. They would never have progressed so fast weighed down by everything Larimanz offered them. At their current pace, Kai estimated that they would reach the city before lunch tomorrow, if they got an early start.

Even with lighter packs, the journey was harsh on Orelia and Ione, who weren't used to traveling long distances. Shifting from the flat northern grasslands to the forests' uneven terrain also made the journey much more rigorous.

In the interest of ensuring everyone was well rested, it was decided to set up camp now.

The party split up to work on their own tasks. Morgan and Teos hauled in some fish for dinner. Lucretia led the women in setting up the tents and campfire. On his own, Kai ventured into the woods to gather herbs for his depleted stocks.

The apothecary knelt by a large oak, inspecting a bundle of flowering plants in the tree's shade. Snapping off one of the light blue flowers, he brought it to his nose for a careful whiff. The scent was reminiscent of lavender, mixed with a touch of mint. "Never thought I'd find cexmeg all the way out here," he whispered. Wild cexmeg was a rarity this time of year. He never had it in stock back home as Havenfall was too far south for the herb to grow. Kai took a small sickle, digging the bundle out by the roots. He stuffed it into his satchel. Looking around, he saw several more bundles and snatched them up with a grin.

Humming a tune, Kai crept along the forest floor. Some plants he took only small samples of, others he harvested everything he found. Before long, his satchel was overflowing. He returned to camp with a wide smile that grew when he saw the line of fish the other men pulled from the river.

"You look like the cat that ate the cardinal, 'pothy," chortled Morgan.

With shrug, Kai admitted his harvesting went much better than expected. "Autumn is an irritating time of year to harvest wild herbs," he said,

"The most useful ones tend to wither away in the cooling temperatures. I did find some cexmeg if you can believe it."

"Cexmeg? What in the winds is that?" asked Orelia.

"An herb that grows in the shade of large trees. It has powerful healing traits, being a known remedy for nausea, infections, and fever. Of course, it also helps boost the body's ability to ward off illness, so I'll be adding some to our dinner tonight," explained Kai as he sat between Maple and Ione, setting up a small board from his pack.

Twirling a knife, the apothecary emptied the satchel and busied himself with chopping and pruning with a deft hand. Piles were separated between leaves, flowers, nuts, and roots. Some were tossed into the mortar and crushed into a fine powder, while most were left chopped and simply scooped into empty vials.

From the corner of his eye, Kai saw the others watching in silent fascination. Even Lucretia kept a civil tongue, preferring to observe from a distance with her nose buried in a tome. Morgan was the first to lose interest, though Kai guessed it was due to hunger. The sellsword was setting up his own space to dress the fish.

Kai asked Teos and Lucretia to fill the cauldron with water and stoke the fire. Orelia asked if she could help, and Kai nodded while tossing her a handful of vials. He explained which herbs would be used tonight. Turning to Maple and Ione, he tasked them with vegetable prep. Both women attacked the assignment with gusto. Ione in particular had grown more confident with her dagger, wielding it with the skill of a professional chef.

It felt nice to see the party working together, Kai realized. With all the recent stress, being able to sit down and enjoy a quiet evening was relaxing in a way they couldn't enjoy until now. The past few nights were trying enough with everyone worrying whether Grimghast would ambush them while they slept. To prevent that, the party took turns standing watch during the night in pairs. Kai was used to working on less sleep, so he offered to take an extra shift with the remaining person.

As the one with the most kitchen experience, Ione took charge of dinner prep. Kai worked alongside her, separating herbs and suggesting mixtures to bring out the flavor of the trout stew. A dash of flour to thicken the broth, the tiniest pinch of cappara pepper for a jolt of heat without making it overpowering.

Before long, the smell of fish stew permeated the campsite. A salivating Morgan tried sneaking an early taste, only to make a pained shout when Ione thwacked the offending hand with her ladle. The others laughed as the sellsword nursed his fingers, Ione shooting him an unamused smirk. The stew was soon ready, and everyone cheered as the tavern maid filled their bowls.

In the fading sunlight, the seven sat around the fire enjoying a warm meal while sharing their hopes for the future once the war ended. Whether that would happen in several moons or several years was left unmentioned.

Some of their ideas were a bit surprising to Kai. Orelia was considering traveling back to Galstein and opening an orphanage. After her experiences at Stahl Granz, the priestess said she discovered joy in caring for children.

Morgan said he wanted to travel across Alezon. With his old comrades gone thanks to Grimghast and the rest of his family long passed, the sellsword admitted there was nothing tying him back to Corlati, so he wanted to see the world.

"You know, Morgan," said Maple after hearing his plan, "you say your family is gone, but the way I see it, we're your new family." Lucretia scoffed and replied that they were far too different to be any sort of family. The scholar carried a slender tome in one hand as always, which she read from while using her other hand to spoon her stew.

Kai mulled over the idea as the others debated. "Honestly, what Maple says makes sense," he replied. Teos asked him to elaborate. "In the Hunters, one thing we're taught early on is that your squad is like family, though there's always a sense of formality we can't avoid. A squad does everything together on a mission. They watch each other's backs, no matter what.

"Da used to tell me and my sister something an old squad mate of his said: 'Your friends are the family you choose.' That idea always resonated with me, despite the fact that I've always been a bit of an outsider. I still think it fits us in a way." The others looked at each other with a spark of renewed interest.

"I guess, when you consider it, each of us are outsiders in our own way," Ione commented. Brushing her hair out of her face, she gazed at each member of the party with her kind and gentle smile. "All of us have something that sets us outside the mold of everyone else we know. We're all misfits in a way, but we've also had to learn to have faith in each other just to survive this long. I believe that faith will shield us as we continue forward, for however long we remain together. If you ask me, that makes us as good as family."

After a couple minutes, Orelia quipped, "I don't know about you all, but this is the strangest family I've ever seen." The circle exploded into raucous laughter.

A wave of disappointment washed over Kai once the sun went down and the sluggishness of full stomachs sent everyone to their tents. Only Orelia stayed awake, as the priestess offered to stand first watch with him. Kai would also be taking the final watch with Maple before dawn.

At least the watch wouldn't be boring. Orelia and Maple were always pleasant to talk to.

If Kai was grateful for one thing, it was not having to sleep through Morgan's snoring for the rest of the night. The man sounded like a mix of an angry bull and a carpenter's saw when sleeping off a night of drinking. How the man always had a flask of liquor on hand was a mystery Kai wasn't sure he'd ever figure out.

He and Maple spent their watch perched on top of a fallen beech tree overlooking the camp. Shooting a sideways glance at the merchant, Kai pointed at the sellsword's tent. He then cupped both hands to his mouth and imitated a cow's low. It sounded close enough to Morgan's snoring that Maple choked on her water.

"That was mean, you ass," she coughed out.

Kai couldn't hold back his chuckle. "Maybe, but you have to admit it was funny."

Maple smacked Kai in the face with her wing. He leaned back and feigned spitting feathers from his mouth, flailing his arms in mock agony. It was enough to provoke a giggle.

"Kai, I've been thinking about something." Maple's voice sounded nervous and unsure.

The Norzen calmed himself, settling into a more serious frame of mind before meeting her gaze. "Hmm? What is it?"

Maple reached up and curled her fingers around a dorsal feather, sending Kai a shy smile. "I never got a chance to thank you. For everything."

Exhaling, Kai felt a wave of relief. He never knew what to expect when women spoke in that tone. "You don't have to thank me, Maple. If anything, you saved my hide back in the forest. So I should be thanking you, more than anything."

"You still saved me from that monster just as much. But I'm talking about our whole journey. I've tried to hide it, but I was scared in the days leading up to when we met. I've been traveling alone for a while, and when the war started, I was terrified."

Kai agreed. "That's not a surprise. I'm certain any faumen traveling alone would be nervous. Especially once the Libbies invaded Mistport and brought the fight to us."

Maple let out a yawn while stretching her wings. Kai noticed the moonlight reflecting off her feathers, giving them an ethereal glow. "I know you might hear this all the time, but you're rather unusual," she admitted, "and not just for a Norzen."

Kai's ears flattened against his head. He did hear it often, but having it pointed out was never fun. "Aye, I do. Growing up, so many strangers that visited Havenfall told me to go back to Duskmarsh. What they don't understand is that I've never been there. Not once. Worse yet, I'm certain the Norzen would all brand me a freak, just like everyone else." The apothecary found the words rolling off his tongue, though he never shared this with anyone back home. Not even his sister knew of these thoughts. In a sense, he saw parts of himself in Maple. Even through the cheerful smiles, there was a hint of pain hidden there that called to him.

After pushing his problems aside for so long, having them mentioned by someone else made holding back impossible. It was as if the cork keeping his thoughts from the surface popped off, like a shaken wine bottle.

The pinch of fingers digging into his cheeks yanked him from his thoughts as Maple twisted his head to face hers. "Don't ever listen to those bastards," she hissed. Her violet eyes brimmed with simmering anger. "You are in no way a freak. If there's one thing I learned, it's that people attack anyone or anything different from themselves. But here's the thing. Different isn't bad. Remember when I said you were one of the Norzen's good berries?"

Kai nodded. It seemed an eternity ago since their first meeting, but the merchant's words still stuck to his mind like mortar.

Maple's smile grew wide and bright. The pain was still there, but it was overshadowed by the merriment dancing in her eyes. "That hasn't changed one bit. You're one of the kindest men I've ever met, and considering how long I've traveled, that says something," she chirped.

It was impossible for Kai to hold back the blush spreading over his cheeks. "Thanks," he murmured, "That means a lot to me. Not many people outside my family ever say such things."

"Let's just say I know how you feel...from personal experience."

Kai's curiosity was piqued. He remembered her mentioning trouble with other girls growing up, but it was hard to imagine anyone haranguing Maple. There was only one reason he could think of for why anyone would take issue with the congenial merchant.

"Did people hurt you for being a mixblood?" he asked.

"They tried," said Maple. "I was lucky to grow up in a town where only a select few believed such drivel, but of course the ones who hated us most were the Aerivolk elder and his family. Papa and I were the only mixbloods in Shiverhill, which is split into the Aerivolk district on the upper cliffs with everyone else further down the slope. Shiverhill began as an Aerivolk town, so we tended to do things our own way." Maple tried maintaining her smile, but Kai knew her heart wasn't in it.

Ruffling her feathers, she continued, "Elder Reed was always a pompous ass, and his daughter Peppra was just as bad, if not worse. She and the drones that followed her everywhere called me Mount Melons because of my height and chest size compared to the other Aerivolk." Maple crossed her arms under her chest and pouted. "I'm sure you know Aerivolk are too heavy to truly fly, so we glide when we need to move fast. Well, as you can probably guess, my chest made gliding hard for me."

Kai winced. "That's why you reacted so bad to what Morgan said at the inn."

"Aye. I know Morgan's not a bad person and didn't mean it, but those words cut deep. It reminded me of days I'd rather forget. I can't even go back home because of that vulture."

That was certainly not something the apothecary expected to hear. Blinking, he took a moment to calm himself. Whatever the full story was, he had a sinking feeling he wouldn't like what he heard. "Would you care to explain what you mean by that? I understand if it's too painful—"

"No, it's part of who I am, and I've spent years avoiding it. When I was thirteen, I was chosen as the lead dancer in the annual harvest festival. Merchants from all around came to sell their wares and watch the performances. Those festivals were what inspired me to be a merchant. To make people happy by providing them with their heart's desires.

"The night of the festival, Peppra and her friends did something horrible. I stood up to their taunts earlier that day, so they wanted revenge. Instead of coming after me, they...they attacked my best friend, Clove. They beat her nearly to death and tore all her feathers out." Kai's face turned sallow. He knew little of Aerivolk culture, but he remembered meeting one as a boy who told him pulling an Aerivolk's feathers was a horrendous insult.

"Clove had the most beautiful blue and silver feathers you've ever seen, but just like that, they were gone. Taken because they knew it would hurt me. We couldn't even request judgment from the elder's council. Reed had them all under his wing. So I did the only thing I could."

Thinking of Maple's reaction to Grimghast nearly killing him, Kai had an idea of what she did. "Please tell me you beat her ass."

Maple snickered and flashed Kai a wink. "Damn right I did. I beat her ass like a rawhide drum. Even if it got me exiled, I'd do it again. No hesitation."

Kai gasped. Exiled? That meant Maple was forced to completely look out for herself at such a young age. "Wow. That's...horrible. If anything though, it proves something about you I've thought of for a while." Seeing her eyes sparkle with curiosity, he smiled. "You're one of the bravest and strongest people I've ever known."

Maple's face burned red as she swatted him again. "Hush, you. You're not allowed to be this charming. Besides, being exiled did have its benefits." Kai's eyebrow rose as she flashed him a tilted smile. "It put me on the path that brought us together." She gave a loud yawn as her body leaned over, resting against Kai's side. The apothecary's face reddened as she nuzzled against him.

"Anyway, I'm still a bit tired. I'll rest my eyes for a few if that's okay."

"That's fine." She emitted a content trill and closed her eyes. "Just don't fall—" He glanced down where, sure enough, Maple was snoring. "And she's gone. Of course."

Still blushing, Kai was unsure how to proceed, but he couldn't hold back his smile. He knew his experience with women was lacking and having one so close outside of a health exam was disconcerting. He tried inching away, only to be stopped when Maple's talon reached over and grabbed his foot, giving it a firm squeeze. He looked to see if she had woken, but the snores kept coming.

The scarlet tinge in his face intensified when she nuzzled closer, burying her nose in his mane. "You're doing this on purpose, aren't you?" he whispered.

There was no movement, just the gentle sound of her snores and what he swore was a soft giggle. Shaking his head, Kai allowed himself to lean against her and enjoyed the rising sun, keeping his ears on a swivel for anything approaching.

Still...this feels nice. I know we can't be any closer, but I can't really think of anyone else I'd be so comfortable with. Reaching down, Kai brushed her hair aside, prompting Maple to press her face a little deeper into his mane.

She truly is something special.

Tomorrow, it was possible their little family would part ways. Best to savor the time they had left while he still could.

Chapter XXII

"**I** forgot how big this city is," said Kai. He fought the urge to stare up at the massive buildings around them. He felt out of place in such a massive city, and he noticed his apothecary robes earning a few stares. The scarlet cloth and white fur stood out against the vibrant colors of the surrounding crowd. How they kept their clothes clean with all the smoke billowing from the chimneys, he chalked up as a local secret.

It was Lucretia who grabbed him by the ear and twisted, eliciting a yelp from the Norzen. "Enough, Kai. You look like a country bumpkin with your gawking. Now move!"

Rubbing his ear, Kai stuck his tongue out. "In case you've forgotten, madam, I *am* a country bumpkin. Havenfall isn't the largest town out there and is off the beaten path for most folks." Havenfall also didn't have a building with walls over 150 yards tall and towers that stretched to almost 200 at their tips, but Kai bit his tongue on that. Very few buildings in Livoria dominated a city like the Citadel did.

Orelia stepped between the two and grabbed their shoulders. "Don't make me separate you two like children. By the winds, can't you get along for more than five minutes?"

Lucretia tapped her chin and looked Kai up and down. He took an involuntary step back. She was staring at him like a farmer judging a bull on whether it would become that week's dinner. "Doubtful. While I respect his ability, he is still a Norzen. That is not something you can change like a bad habit."

Everyone groaned at that. "One of these days, you two might have to work together, then what's going to happen?" inquired Orelia. Lucretia huffed and reminded everyone that she would be parting ways from them after today.

Putting herself in the center of the group, Ione held her hands up. "Now, now, let's not fight today. We've finally achieved our goal. We should be celebrating."

"I shall celebrate once I am back in my office," snapped Lucretia. "However, I do have something to say." Six pairs of eyes watched the scholar. She sucked in a breath and held a hand towards Kai, though it looked like the action physically pained her.

"Kai, when we first met, I was certain you were nothing but a vagrant." Kai rolled his eyes at the description but stayed quiet. He knew this was hard for the proud scholar. "When you risked your life to save Ione and myself from Grimghast and the Liberators, I wondered if you had hidden motives. But you have proven yourself different since that day.

"Everywhere we have been, you risked your life to protect others in a way I never believed possible for a Norzen. I doubt I can ever fully trust your tribe. I have my reasons for this. Still, I appreciate your assistance in helping me make it home alive. Not many would have done the same. And so, I thank you."

The party listened in rapt silence. None of the travelers had a dry eye between them. Kai bowed at the waist. "Coming from you, I consider it praise of the highest order. At times, I forget I'm a Norzen, but then I always have you to remind me of that fact." Lucretia stifled a chuckle. "We may not be the best of friends, but your knowledge and calm mind have been an inspiration and taught me I still have room to grow." Kai gripped the scholar's hand in a firm shake and nodded in respect.

Morgan gave a barking laugh and threw his arms around the two. "Aww, it's about time you two made up! Now come on, let's get our little bookworm home."

Finding the Citadel was the easy part. Teos quipped that not even a blind man could miss the enormous building, with its five towers looming over Runegard. One tower was located at each corner of the outer wall, with the tallest sitting at the direct center.

The difficult part was navigating the labyrinthine streets without getting separated. Orelia wondered aloud if it would be safer to tie themselves together, but Lucretia was adamant in her refusal. The pointed glare she shot at Kai with a hand gripping her rapier perfectly expressed her feelings about that idea.

Instead, the party allowed Lucretia to lead while attempting to stay within eyesight. Being midday, the roads were filled with carriages and people on foot, packed together like fish in a barrel. Teos and Kai kept their ears flattened to drown out the deafening noise around them, while Maple covered her own feathery ears with her wings. More than once, Ione had to be rescued before she could be dragged away in the throng pushing and shoving their way down the road. Kai swore he heard Orelia threatening to smack a man with her staff for brushing against her in a way she didn't like.

"Damn it all, this is getting tiresome," growled Teos. A group of Vesikoi almost knocked him over rushing to catch a canal boat. Maple asked why the party couldn't follow their lead.

Lucretia clicked her tongue. "Sadly, the canals aren't an effective method of travel for normal folk like they are in Faith Hollow. Their primary use is to transport goods throughout the city from merchant ships on the Galen River. They also serve as the city's Vesikoi district."

"Ooh, that makes sense," Maple replied. "The canals make it easier to move wares via the river instead of unloading it all onto a bunch of carriages when the roads are already so crowded."

An unusually bright smile spread over Lucretia's face. "Precisely! Now, we should be getting close. Perhaps another ten minutes of walking."

"I hope so," Morgan replied, "cause that building's getting a lot bigger. We better be close." Looking up, Kai saw the Citadel looming like a threatening monolith. Even in the bright sunlight, the dark building cast a large shadow over the area, emitting a gloomy aura that made Kai's fur stand on end.

"Be grateful you do not have to go inside," said Lucretia, "It took me years to learn where everything was once I began my apprenticeship."

Lucretia pressed forward, pulling away from the party. Kai could see a cheerful gleam in her eye as she marched through the throng with each purposeful step. He understood that feeling, the excitement of coming home after a long time away. He knew the sensation for Lucretia would be enhanced by the hardships they faced getting here.

Before long, the stairway leading up to the academy was in sight. Before anyone could stop her, Lucretia broke into a sprint, clearing the stairs two at a time. Kai looked at the others, shrugging his shoulders. They followed at a more sedate pace.

By the time the party made it halfway to the top, Lucretia was already at the front door, speaking to the guards while waving her hands. If he didn't already know she'd smack him for it, Kai would have burst out laughing at the manic look in Lucretia's eyes when her head turned in their direction.

Once they reached the landing, however, Kai grew concerned. He thought the woman's expressiveness was a result of glee at being home. As they approached, he noticed more. Eyes that contained not happiness, but confusion. Her arms were shaking. Even at this distance, he could hear short, repeated breaths, as if she couldn't breathe. The guards looked unamused, their posture defensive and threatening.

"Something's very wrong," Kai claimed as he took longer strides. He shifted to a straighter posture and allowed his muscles to tense in preparation. His eyes pinched together; his mouth settled into a straight line.

From the corner of his eye, Kai saw the others matching his pace. Some, like Ione and Teos, looked worried. Others looked brassed off, like Morgan. Without speaking, everyone shared a look and nodded. No matter what was going on, they would provide support.

"This does not make any sense!" Lucretia cried out, her hands clenching as if she wanted to reach out and grab the guards' arms. Considering they both held vicious-looking spears crossed together to block her entrance, doing that would've been foolish. Instead, she tore the emblem from her cloak and held it up to the left guard's face. "I am Lucretia Dineri, Archivist Division. This is my certification crest. Now cease this foolishness at once and let me in!"

The guards shared a look before spewing a cruel laugh. "I don't think so," said the right guard. "What makes you think we would allow an oathbreaker into these sacred halls?"

Lucretia's sienna skin turned alabaster at the guard's words, and Kai noticed the others inching their fingers towards their weapons.

Shaking his head, he stepped forward. "I hope you have a damned good reason for saying something so severe," Kai growled. "Because if you don't, there will be repercussions."

The guards thrust their spears out, pointing them at the apothecary's heart. "Stay out of this, peltneck. You have no business or authority on these grounds. Now leave, or we'll turn you into a pincushion for the local knitting circle."

Kai's eye twitched. He brushed the spears aside, only for Lucretia to throw herself between the three and push the Norzen back. "Hold still, Kai. The last thing we need is you causing a scene." Turning back to the guards, she tucked a stray bang away from her face and took a deep breath. "Now, I think I deserve to know why you call me an oathbreaker. I have done nothing to warrant such an insult."

The guards kept their weapons pointed at Kai's chest. "Do you take us for fools? How can someone not know why they were deemed an oathbreaker?"

Lucretia's stare was so cold, that Kai was shocked the guards didn't turn to ice. "Let us assume I have received no such notice. After all, I have been on the road for many days since Mistport was destroyed, with little access to carrier hawks."

Running their eyes up and down Kai, the two sneered. "We can see that. It's funny; we heard stories about you, and all of them say you loath Norzen from the depths of your spirit. So what's with this one?"

"That has no bearing on the matter. If you must know, however, he and the others behind us helped me get back. I was in no condition to make the journey on my own with the war going on."

Somehow, Kai felt the guards' sneers became more sinister. "And that there is the problem, ain't it? You weren't permitted to come back." Confusion bloomed over Lucretia's face. "It was reported you abandoned your duties before receiving a return order. As such, you were deemed an oathbreaker and therefore are excommunicated from the Citadel."

With that statement, Lucretia's entire body sagged, and her eyes turned lifeless. It was as if all the intensity was drained from her body in one swoop, leaving a listless husk. "W-what about my things? My personal belongings?"

The left guard tittered and waggled a finger at the scholar. "What belongings? According to orders from Highmaster Nerod's office, everything in your former quarters was burned. The only reason we don't set your cloak aflame right now is because setting a person on fire in public is against city law, no matter how detestable they are."

A heartrending wail came from Lucretia, who dropped to her knees in tears. The women huddled around, helping her up as Kai herded the group away from the gate.

A look up told Kai that Morgan and Teos were furious. Both men glowered at the cackling guards, the sellsword cracking his knuckles as he stepped forward. Throwing his arm out, Kai stopped him from doing anything foolish. "Not here," he whispered to Morgan.

"What in hoarfrost are you saying? We're not going to do anything?"

"I didn't say that," said Kai. Teos leaned over to whisper in the apothecary's ear, prompting him to smirk. "But we do need to be crafty. I may be an Exarch, but I doubt the Grand Duchess would appreciate hearing I thrashed the Citadel's guards and tore the gate down. No, we do this by the tome and *when*, not if, they tell us to pound cobbles, we'll have a legitimate reason for what we're planning."

Urging the two to stay quiet and just back him up, he strode up to the guards. "Didn't we already tell you to get lost, peltneck?" snapped the guard on the right. "You want to meet ol' Cacovis that soon?"

The apothecary held up a hand. "I am submitting a formal request to meet with the Highmaster to appeal this decision on behalf of Miss Dineri. Per official protocol, one of you must immediately bring me to someone who may arrange this meeting, or you must bring them here to the gate."

The guards looked at each other and gave a sputtering laugh, one leaning on the other's shoulder. They looked as if they had heard the most hilarious joke. "Are you sure you're not a court fool?" asked the left guard. "What makes you think we're going to acknowledge any request coming from a peltneck?"

Teos cleared his throat and glared at the two. "Perhaps you should remember that you are still required to follow the law, which states that any formal request made for disciplinary appeal must be acknowledged and addressed as swiftly as possible, without regard to the requestor's tribe, gender, age, or religious affiliation." Kai and Morgan gaped at the smuggler, whose face shifted into a confident grin.

Snarling, the two guards ranted at the three men, claiming that there was no way they would be meeting with the Highmaster, now or ever. The right guard stomped forward and jabbed his spear forward, its tip pressing into Kai's chest just above his heart.

Near the staircase, Lucretia let out a small hiccup and tried to stand, leaning against Orelia. Maple reached around for her bow only to stop when Kai looked back and shook his head.

Turning back to the guards, Kai's face showed indifference. Inside, he was furious. There were rumors of classist factions within the Citadel, but this was worse than he thought. He felt no remorse about his plan to deal with this insult. He and Lucretia may not get along great, but she was still a comrade.

And any insult against someone under his protection, especially one as vile as this, deserved a sufficiently blistering response.

Kai wrapped his index finger around the shaft of the spear pointed at him, letting the thumb rest flat against the wood just beneath the iron spearhead. With a grim smile he pushed his thumb forward, snapping the spearhead off and letting it fall into his palm. The guards' eyes bulged, and Kai clenched his hand around the spearhead. A crunching sound resounded until Kai's fist was tight. Letting his hand relax, the Norzen tipped it over and allowed the crushed blade to clang on the cobbles.

"Just so you gentlemen know, and I'm being very loose with that term," said Kai as he tapped the broken piece of metal with his toe, "there is an Exarch among us. And they've heard everything you just said to me. Think about that." Inclining his head as if tipping a hat to the paling pair, he pivoted on his heels and marched back towards the women, Teos and Morgan following close behind.

"Uh, 'pothy?" whispered Morgan. "I know I'm not the smartest guy around, but why didn't you mention that *you're* the Exarch?"

Teos clapped the sellsword on the back and told Morgan to think about it. "The guards already proved that they hate Norzen with that horrid attitude. What do you think they would say if Kai told them straight that he is an Exarch?"

"They...wouldn't believe him?"

The smuggler nodded. "Exactly! But by telling them the Exarch is *among* us, Kai made the threat more credible because they don't know who it is. It could be me; it could be Maple. They don't know. And not having knowledge about a very real threat can be terrifying."

Morgan found himself nodding and looked at Kai with a mix of respect and fear. "You're scary sometimes, ya know that, 'pothy?" Rather than say anything, Kai glanced at Morgan and grinned, his fangs glimmering in the sunlight.

"By the way, Teos," Kai remarked as they strolled towards the women. "How do you know so much about protocol and disciplinary procedures?"

The smuggler responded with a smirk. "Got an uncle on my father's side who's a constable back home in Hornmire. He used to always lecture me and my cousins on etiquette and protocol when we got into trouble until my Maman threatened to beat him over the head with his own club. Besides, nine tenths of breaking the law is knowing it just so you know where to toe the line."

The three approached the ladies, still gathered at the top of the stairs. "What were you thinking?" asked Lucretia. She still showed obvious signs of distress. The teary eyes, quick breaths, her entire body shivering as she leaned against Orelia. "I told you not to cause a scene. What is going to happen if those two call the constables?"

Orelia whispered to the scholar that stressing over it would only worsen her health. Despite the constant vitriol that Lucretia normally directed at him, Kai found it disturbing to see the fiery woman so defeated. He knew she was passionate about her job, in a way that seemed almost obsessive.

"It hurts, doesn't it?" Kai muttered. She looked at him, stunned. "You're one of the most ardent and dedicated people I've ever met, Lucretia. I mean it. So having everything you've ever known torn away like this, it must be brutal. I can't say I've experienced the same situation, but I can imagine how I would feel if it were me in your boots. And honestly, I'd be spitting mad about it. Bloody Nulyma, I *am* spitting mad about it!"

Lucretia turned away and rubbed her nose, a small sniffle escaping. "What can we even do? I have nothing now. You heard what they said, my entire life went up in flames. It's over."

"You still have us, for what that's worth. And it's over when we *all* say it's over," said Kai. "I ain't letting you quit now. Not after coming this far. No, we're sneaking into that building and you're going to demand a full appeal."

Kai knew the Citadel had special rules but as a certified Archivist, Lucretia was still a government official and allowed to appeal any form of disciplinary action. Kai knew the original law was pushed by noble families to allow themselves a way of evading punishment, but he had every intention of milking it to Lucretia's benefit.

The others muttered among themselves, wondering aloud if that would work. "Wouldn't we just get arrested and tossed in the gaol for trespassing?" Ione asked.

Pulling his watch from its pocket, Kai twirled it around his finger by its chain. "That would cause them more headaches than they want. They're already on the dock for several things that could get some high-ranking people in big trouble. I'm naming this an official investigation. There's something fishy about this whole mess, and it's not the stew we had last night."

"Very well. You haven't steered us wrong yet, Kai. What do we do first?" Orelia asked.

"First, we find a nearby inn and settle in for a couple days while we wait. They'll be expecting something now, so better to let them relax their guard. Then, we strike."

"Okay birdy, spill it," said Orelia as the women sat in a circle within their shared room.

Maple tilted her head, staring at the priestess blankly. "Spill what? I didn't bring anything to drink." In the back of her mind, Maple suspected what Orelia wanted to talk about, but she was *not* ready for that conversation.

"Do not think you can escape by playing the fool, Maple," snapped Lucretia. "Only Morgan would be taken seriously in that regard. I think it is time you confess. What exactly is going on between you and our fur-ridden leader?"

The merchant flinched. *Damn.* "I have no idea what you're talking about. Kai is a wonderful friend, possibly even my best friend, and that's all there is to it."

Ione tsked and wrapped an arm around the younger woman's shoulders. Maple detected the scent of sweat and food coming off the tavern maid. "You and I both know that's a lie, Maple. We're not judging you." Lucretia scoffed. "Okay, *most* of us aren't judging you, but it would be better to realize just what you're getting into. You know how the church feels about those types of relations."

"And what makes you believe I feel that way about Kai? I'd swear on Vadako herself that we've never done anything other than hug!" The other three women shared a hesitant look. Vadako, as the Wind Saint associated with love and marriage, was commonly invoked when swearing oaths regarding relationships. Maple knew they'd have to take her seriously.

With a flat stare, Ione pinched Maple's cheek. "I don't believe, I know. And I know because you look at that man the same way I looked at Athos when he was still alive, may Galen rest his soul. Besides, I saw you two sitting in the tree together when I awoke."

Maple wilted. *Is it really that obvious?*

She coiled a dorsal feather around her finger, tears pricking at her eyes. "So what if it's true? He's unlike any other man I've ever met. I didn't mean to fall for him, it just...happened. I know what the church says about marriages between the tribes, so why would I even bother? Nulyma, if my Papa knew I was saying this, his heart would stop!"

"Hmm, I wonder why," murmured Lucretia.

Orelia leveled a frown at the scholar before taking Maple's hands in hers. "As a priestess, I know what I'm officially supposed to tell you in regard to this." Maple's face fell, tears beginning to show. "Every single Windbringer cleric would say the two of you can never be together and that to even attempt it is an affront to the Saints themselves."

Unable to hold back, Maple let her tears flow freely, wiping a wing across her eyes. A soft touch on her face drew her eyes back up to Orelia's. "That's what I'm *supposed* to tell you. However, as a fellow woman and, more importantly, as your friend...I'm happy you could find someone who makes you feel this way. Many go their entire lives without finding that special someone. If you decide to take things further with Kai, I won't say anything to stop you. And neither will anyone in this room," Orelia declared, side eyeing Lucretia. The scholar snorted and replied that she had better things to do than concern herself with Maple's questionable tastes.

"Thank you," Maple sniffed, drying her tears. "That really means a lot. But I still need to sort out my feelings on my own later. We have too much going on with the Libbies and helping Lucretia. I want to approach this without anything else dragging me down." In her heart, Maple knew it was just an excuse. The thought of admitting her feelings *terrified* her.

She only hoped she could pluck up her courage before it was too late.

Kai was beginning to question his decision to wait before sneaking into the Citadel. While a sound tactical idea, he failed to consider the consequences of having the party holed up in an inn for three days. He was rather surprised Orelia hadn't clubbed anyone with her staff yet with all the arguments breaking out.

Despite knowing the plan and agreeing with it, Lucretia still looked like a kicked puppy. Maple and Ione took charge trying to perk the woman's spirits back up. Morgan offered to help as well, but changed his mind when Lucretia threw her rapier at him like a javelin, just missing his groin.

The party tried getting Lucretia drunk the first night to take her mind off the situation, which ended up a total disaster. Instead of forgetting her troubles, Lucretia found herself in a fistfight at the meadhouse with a local drunk that made the mistake of grabbing her rear. Kai and the barkeep gave the woman a wide berth after watching her shoulder throw the drunkard, slamming him onto a table.

Worse, Kai allowed Teos and Morgan, both experienced drinkers, to press him into imbibing too much ale. If Ione was to be believed, he, Maple, and Orelia all ended up crocked and on top of the bar, singing sea shanties to the whole meadhouse. Teos brayed about it the next morning as Kai nursed a hangover, praising their performance.

The next day didn't fare much better. If anything, the apothecary preferred to forget yesterday ever happened. He still felt the occasional twitch from all the shaking his body went through that day. His stomach was racked with pain once again and the frequent vomiting forced him to wash his mouth out at least once an hour. He glanced over at his satchel next to the bed, glaring at it. One thing was for certain: he'd never look at a roast duck the same way again.

At least the pain and nausea were gone. Trudging downstairs, he helped himself to a hearty breakfast while waiting for the others to wake and mulled everything over. They needed to make their move tonight. He'd lose the plot otherwise.

The heavy clomp of hooves reached Kai's ears. He turned an eye to see Teos strolling to the table. Giving his order to a nearby maid, the Soltauri sat next to Kai.

The ladies shuffled downstairs, moving Kai to call for a tavern maid to take their orders. Soon, everyone was enjoying a full plate.

With one exception.

"Has anyone checked on Morgan yet?" asked Maple. "I swear, if we gave him half a chance, that man would sleep the day away."

"Someone mention me?" asked Morgan as he stumbled down the stairs. His hair was askew, and his clothes rumpled, making him look a vagrant. Everyone laughed, prompting the sellsword to glance down at himself. "Uh oh. Maybe I should've changed clothes before coming down."

"Indeed," said Lucretia. "Go make yourself presentable, for Galen's sake. We have much to do today. We cannot afford to wait around for you."

Cheeks burning, Morgan stammered his order to a tavern maid before rushing back upstairs to change clothes. The maid blushed, bustling back to the kitchen while Maple looked between the kitchen door and the stairs. She and the other women huddled together, though Kai heard their conversation all the same.

"You don't think...?" Ione blushed at the question while Orelia snickered, a wide grin on her face.

Lucretia's eyes furrowed, her eyes flashing towards Maple. "I certainly hope not, though I suppose there is no assessing someone's tastes in that matter." Everyone dropped that line of thought. Whatever Morgan decided to do at night in his room was his own business.

Once the party left the tavern, Kai heard a gasp from his left. "Well this is a surprise. Lucretia, is that you?" The group turned to see a dainty woman in ivory scholar robes, only with a scarlet overcoat compared to Lucretia's cobalt. "Praise Luopari, it is you! I almost didn't believe it was true."

The woman rushed forward and embraced Lucretia, who stiffened at the sudden contact. "Ria, what in Finyt are you doing here?" she asked, wrapping her arms around the newcomer. Lucretia faced the others, her cheeks flushed. "Apologies, everyone. This is Rialta, a fellow scholar from the Citadel who works in the Novelist Division. We have known each other since we were children." Lucretia introduced each member of the party to Rialta, whose eyes lingered on Kai.

Maple shook the woman's hand. "Pleasure to meet ya! What's a Novelist do in the Citadel? I've never heard of that job before."

Rialta's smile brightened. "Oh we're the ones that write new tomes. A lot of what we do depends on the work of the other scholars."

"How many divisions are there?" Ione asked. Kai admitted he was curious as it was rare for Lucretia to discuss what life was like at the Citadel, and his own knowledge was limited.

"Oh, that sounds like Lu, alright. She's a sweetheart under all those thorns, but she keeps to herself. To tell you the truth, I'm shocked to see she's been traveling with a Norzen. Her thoughts on them are well established. To make it simple, the Citadel is split into four Divisions, each with their own area of expertise and represented by different colored cloaks.

"Archivists like Lu wear blue and are responsible for collecting knowledge from around Livoria, as well as repairing damaged tomes. Then there's the Inventors, who wear yellow. They conduct research to develop new knowledge and methods of accomplishing daily tasks. Next are the Curators. They wear green and are responsible for stockpiling and organizing all tomes and scrolls within the Citadel and other libraries around the realm. Last is my Division, the Novelists. We wear red cloaks and oversee the compilation of all knowledge gathered by the other three divisions, molding it into new tomes."

The party listened in rapt attention while Lucretia blushed. It was clear she wasn't used to being the center of attention. "Wow, Lucretia, I had no idea your job was so important!" exclaimed Maple. She gazed at the scholar in awe.

"Indeed, all scholars are important in their own way. What's more amazing is the Citadel requires everyone to have their own personal research focus. This way each scholar has something to contribute to. As an example, I specialize in researching agriculture to improve our methods of growing food. Lucretia, by comparison, is an expert in ancient languages. Besides Centric, she's fluent in four languages considered dead or endangered."

Six heads turned to the scholar with wide eyes. "Damn," Teos muttered, "I knew you were a smart biscuit, but that's impressive."

Feeling a tug on his robe, Kai turned to find Maple leaning up to his ear and whispering. The Norzen's eyes widened before giving her a nod.

"Excuse me, Miss Rialta," Kai began, prompting Lucretia to frown, "but would you happen to know of a way to earn an audience with the Highmaster? It's imperative that we speak with him."

The young woman's face fell before shaking her head. "If this is about Lucretia's excommunication, you shouldn't bother. Word among the senior scholars says the Highmaster has started wiping Lucretia's existence from the records. As it is, the Citadel is in a pinch with the divisions arguing with each other the past few days. It's gotten so bad; I'm amazed nobody has come to blows yet."

Kai smirked. "Oh, really? Would you be willing to testify that before a magistrate if it cleared Lucretia's name?" Having someone on the inside to collaborate rumors within the Citadel would be perfect.

Rialta threw her arms around Lucretia once more, sobbing into the other woman's shoulder. "Of course I would! Lu is my best friend. Security is locked tight, though, but there's a way in through the canals only a few know about. If the seniors find out I said anything, there's no telling what they'll do."

Pulling his watch out, Kai showed it to the shocked scholar. "Consider yourself under official protection. Anyone retaliating against you would be taking direct action to interfere with an Exarch's investigation. And I'm rather serious about my duties."

The apothecary tucked the watch away. "Now then, tell us everything you know about this canal entrance. We're sneaking in. Tonight."

Chapter XXIII

The moons shimmered high above the Citadel, casting a gentle glow over the building. Few lanterns were lit along the streets, leaving much of the streets shrouded in darkness. The moonlight caused the rippling water to sparkle like tiny gems in the night. With the shifting waves, every walkway was filled with shadows moving in an eerie dance.

It was on one of these walkways where Rialta led the party on a winding path beneath the wall of the Citadel. A tiny torch in her hand offered just enough light to guide them.

Kai noticed her moving with practiced ease, as if she made this same trip countless times. Every step, every surreptitious glance around a corner looked natural. A quick look to Lucretia showed she wasn't at all surprised by her friend's ability to navigate the walkways with the grace and agility of a cat.

Kai inquired how much further they had to go. "We're already underneath the wall," Rialta replied, "so it isn't much further. This path leads to a stairway that goes to the back of the kitchen. We'll split up once we reach the central gardens."

Nodding, Kai pressed against the wall, beckoning the others to go ahead. As his friends slipped past, Kai counted them off and swiveled his ears. The only sounds beyond their footsteps on the cobbles were of the waves below and the occasional cricket. Once everyone was accounted for, Kai took one last look back. He couldn't see anything, but something felt off. The skin beneath his mane tingled, like he was missing something. He needed focus if they wanted to pull this off.

A door creaked. Kai's ears twitched to the front, watching Rialta wave the party through the opening. Scanning the walkways one last time, he ducked inside. Rialta eased the door shut, rushing back to the front of the group.

"The kitchens are at the end of this hall. Stay in a straight line and follow me," Rialta instructed. "And for the winds' sake, don't touch anything."

Nobody dared to talk. Lucretia pushed everyone into a line before standing behind Maple, who she placed at the front between the two scholars. Kai was the rear guard, eyes and ears always moving. Once everyone was in place, Rialta gestured them forward, leading the way down the hall.

This place must not be used much, judging by all the dust, Kai thought. He brushed a stray cobweb out of his mane. *Maybe it's an escape route for emergencies, or an unused path for food delivery from the canal. It does lead to the kitchens, after all.*

The further they walked, the brighter it became. Soon, they stepped into a massive kitchen. Several torches were lit around the walls, providing better visibility. Pots and pans of varying sizes were stacked across one shelf on the left side. The right side was dominated by barrels, strings, and sacks of vegetables. A pile of food lay on a long table on that side, next to a line of knives, possibly set aside for tomorrow's breakfast. Morgan muttered about the Citadel having enough food to feed an army.

Rialta shushed the man before replying, "It may as well be. The Citadel houses at least five hundred scholars, plus another two hundred students, and a hundred staff. The numbers are only an estimate, but there's roughly half a battalion's worth of people living here."

Morgan let out a low whistle, only for Orelia to clamp a hand over his mouth and look at him with death in her eyes. "Are you stupid?" she whispered. "You're gonna get us caught!" The sellsword gulped and nodded when Orelia waved her staff at him. The entire party shivered at the sight of it.

Rialta watched the exchange with interest and muttered, "Impressive. Where can I get one of those?"

The priestess shook her head and smirked a little, mouthing that they would talk later. Kai sighed in relief. They couldn't waste too much time considering their time limit. It was late enough for most people to be asleep, but their target was an exception. Lucretia and Rialta collaborated that the Highmaster and several senior scholars enjoyed having a night-cap in their quarters every night. Though it was a gamble on how late the man would stay awake, they hoped to catch him before he retired to bed. Waking a drunk was never easy or quiet.

Kai kept an eye on the knives and utensils hanging on the wall. They swayed in the breeze flowing from the windows. If any of those fell, there would be trouble.

A loud thump echoed through the kitchen, freezing Kai in place. He swerved his head and watched a lone potato rolling along the floor. Scanning the area, he saw everyone else stiff as well. Looking at the offending item, he traced its path back to a quaking Ione, who looked at him, shaking her head in terror.

"Oi, you hear something?" a muffled voice asked from the front of the kitchen. Rialta pointed to the wall separating the prep area from the main kitchen. There was a shadowy area in the lower part of the wall, allowing the party to hide in the dark. Maple's talons clacked on the stone floor, distinct from the tapping sound of everyone else's boots.

A second voice came from the same area, this one deeper and coarser. "You heard it too? Blast, I thought me hearing was going bad. What is it, you reckon?"

"Judging by the clicking, I'd say mice," answered the first voice.

Kai and the others released a collective breath. Huddling together, he whispered, "We're not going far with guards hanging around. Do they normally stand watch at the kitchens?"

Both scholars answered in the negative. "Chances are they're in the middle of patrol. If we wait long enough, they'll go somewhere else," explained Rialta.

Kai twitched his ears, listening to the guards discussing whether they should investigate the sound. "I don't think they're leaving any time soon. We need to distract them somehow."

The apothecary bit his tongue when Lucretia grabbed his ear and tugged hard. "And how do you suggest we do that?" she hissed. Kai pulled away, rubbing his ear.

Gazing at the floor, he held up a finger to his lips. His eyes darted back and forth, searching for something. With knees bent and arms spread, Kai lowered himself closer to the ground. Suddenly, before anyone could ask what he was doing, he *moved*. His hand snapped to the floor like a viper before coming up with a tiny form struggling in the gloved fist.

A small mouse.

The rodent squeaked in terror, swinging its head about trying to bite the fingers holding it. Kai's gloves were thick enough he didn't feel a thing as it sunk its teeth into the tough leather.

Lucretia moved to strangle Kai but was held back by Teos and Rialta. "Are you serious?" she spat. "We are about to be caught and you waste time grabbing a snack?!"

Kai leveled a flat stare at the woman. "You can't think I'm going to eat this. You've tasted my cooking." Lucretia blushed, remembering the meals he helped Ione make during their travels. Putting herself between the two, Ione asked Kai what he was planning to do.

"Just watch. Get ready to run." Holding the mouse in one hand and scooping the potato into the other, Kai tossed the mouse onto a string of onions hanging from an overhead beam. Everyone looked on in confusion. Then, taking aim, he pitched the potato at a pile of vegetables on the table. The potato struck the pile with a thwack and enough force to bring the entire mountain rolling down.

Lucretia turned on Kai in a flash, nostrils flaring and a hand reaching for his throat. He grabbed her wrist and tilted his head to the collapsing pile. The sound of thundering footsteps rumbled as the doors flew open. The two guards held their spears ready, rushing to the mass of rolling vegetables.

"Who's in there? Show yourself!" the first guard commanded. They spun in place, unable to spot the party hidden in the shadows to their side. A frantic squeaking came from the pile, drawing the guards' attention to the mouse crawling over the food.

The second guard scratched his head. "You gotta be bleeding joking. All that rumpus and it just a stupid mouse like we thought?"

"You mean like I thought," the first guard replied. "You're the one that's always thinking that we got thieves crawling all over the place when this is the only thing skulking around. You're gonna make yourself sick with all that worrying!"

Kai raised a hand and gestured for everyone to run for the exit. With the guards focused elsewhere, this was their best chance. He held Maple back as the others dashed for the door. She tilted her head in confusion. Kai pointed to her talons and turned around, holding his arms straight across behind his back while dropping to one knee.

She hopped up, perching on his arms and holding tight. Kai stood and rushed for the open door. Peeking back, he bit his tongue as the guards argued over what to do with the mouse, which was running for a hole in the wall. Both men were making a token effort to poke the pest with their spears, the weapons clanging against the floor. The second guard was questioning if they could place it under arrest, to the first's agitation.

"Arrest a mouse...? How much bloody ale did you drink, man?!" he shouted. "We'd be the laughingstock of the platoon. The commander would have our hides if we went to him with this. Just shut your mouth and help me clean this up. If the head chef finds this mess, we'll be the meat portion in tomorrow's stew!"

Kai and Maple shared an amused look and caught up with the others. Rialta shot them a curious glance as Maple hopped down and thanked Kai. Even in the dark, Kai could see the intricate paintings and tapestries covering the walls. Some depicted stories of the Windbringer church Kai knew by heart. A curving staircase leading to the second floor sat surrounding the door across from them. Pedestals bearing colorful vases sat at the stairs' base.

At the center of the hall, he saw a sculpture of a Wasini. It was a man Kai knew of, but not to the extent he felt he should. A plaque was nailed in at the statue's base that read, "Knowledge carries no bias at its start; Its winds of flight rely on the heart."

"That's Dolmaru, the patron of scholars, isn't it?" asked Teos. The Livorians all nodded, but Morgan stared at the statue in abject shock.

"Hold on a tic. One of your precious Wind Saints was a Wasini?" the sellsword babbled.

Lucretia smirked and whispered to Morgan as they walked past the statue towards the door underneath the staircase. "Is it truly that odd? I must confess, it surprises me how little you Corlatians know of our church despite being at odds with us since before the Desolation Wars. Of the eight Wind Saints, only two were human: Galen the Sage and Tapimor the Lifeweaver. The remaining six were all faumen.

"Ausrina the Wanderer and Edeval the Bandit Lord were both Aerivolk. Cacovis as you know was a Norzen. Luopari the Oracle was a Vesikoi, and Vadako the Maiden was a Soltauri. Dolmaru just happened to be the group's Wasini representative. He was known as the Quillblade, infamous for his sharp wit and intelligence, as well as his skill with a sword."

Gazing at the sculpture, Morgan smiled. "Well I'll be. I feel like my grandpap would be proud to see a tribe member revered like this. Most people just think we're barbarians."

"We can discuss this later," Ione murmured. Her eyes were everywhere, twitching at the slightest movement. "We should get this over with and get back to the inn. I suppose the Highmaster is in one of the towers?" she asked, looking to the scholars.

They nodded. "Correct," answered Rialta, "Highmaster Nerod lives at the top of the central tower. This is the main hall of the east wing. It's a bit of a walk upstairs, so we better move. There's no telling how long the guards will be kept busy, and we may run into more yet."

"Indeed," Lucretia continued. "The quicker we reach the Highmaster, the quicker we find out what is going on. This still makes little sense. The

Highmaster has always praised my work before. For him to mark me an oathbreaker is strange."

The guards' grumbling was still heard coming from the kitchens. Kai knew they needed to make tracks, so he guided everyone to the door leading into the central courtyard.

"Kai, there's someone on the battlements!" Morgan whispered once they stepped into the open air. Everyone's eyes veered up to where the sellsword was pointing. A shadowy figure was strolling across the northern battlement. Before they could get a clear look, they leapt through a window in the north tower.

"Think it could be a guard?" asked Maple. "Even in this light, I couldn't see them well. I think I caught a tail."

Kai shook his head. "Can't be a guard. It didn't sound like they were wearing the same plate armor. It would make some sort of noise at that speed. But it is likely they're faumen. It's just too far for us to tell who or what it is." A jolt went down Kai's tails. The situation reminded him of Mistport, and that made him nervous.

The courtyard was more well-lit than the inner halls. Not surprising given it was nighttime. Glass lanterns on poles sat evenly spaced around the garden edge. The brick walkways connecting each side of the main building to the central tower were wide enough to allow several columns of people to walk along.

There also seemed to be no guards. When Kai asked why, Rialta answered, "Highmaster Nerod is very particular about appearances. I suppose it comes from his noble upbringing. He can't stand the sight of guards tromping about the gardens, so he forbids them to come out here unless there's an incident requiring their attention."

Looking around, Kai could see the reasoning. Even in the dim light of the lanterns, the gardens were impressive. Rows of ornamental flowers like marigolds, roses, and begonias lined the walkways. Various wildflowers were scattered amongst the garden, while berry-bearing bushes created a wall behind the ornamentals. Large red oaks were the centerpieces of each segment, providing shade and a sense of passion in their crimson leaves. Circular patches of vibrant tulips surrounded each tree. In Kai's estimation, this garden would rival those of the most opulent noble manors.

"Questionable decisions aside, I will agree with Nerod on one thing," Kai muttered, earning a complaint from Lucretia at not using the man's title. "These gardens are too beautiful to have a band of armored ruffians lumbering about."

From out of nowhere, a calm, feminine voice came from the pillar to the right, "So very true. It's one of the things I love most about this place." Kai tensed and whirled around, putting himself at the vanguard of the party. The others reached for their weapons while Rialta backed away trembling.

A pair of hooded figures emerged before them, one noticeably taller than the other. Their eyes gleamed in the moonlight; their faces covered by scarves. A dainty cough came from the smaller figure, a female judging by her slender figure. Something about her voice felt familiar. It resonated in Kai, like a recognizable tune that he couldn't remember the name of.

"Hold now, there's no need for weapons," sighed a voice from the taller one, causing everyone to pause. This one was male, his voice low and confident. "We mean you no harm, at least not yet. Though I am curious who you all are and what you're doing skulking about the Citadel at night. While armed, no less. You seem like a rather odd group."

Whoever the pair was, they weren't looking for a fight. Their stances were relaxed and calm. A quick glance at their arms confirmed they weren't holding weapons. It was possible they had some concealed in their cloaks but reaching them would be difficult. Taking a closer look, Kai realized the cloaks were well made. *Very* well made. The material shimmered in the light, with a smooth sheen suggesting silk.

Nobles, Kai thought, *but what would a pair of nobles be doing wandering here of all places, and at night? Could I have met them while in Whistlevale, and that's why they feel so familiar?*

Standing up straight, he made a slight bow. "There seems to be an impasse. You don't know who we are, and we don't know you. The most I can say is that we do have a reason for being here. We're on a mission to correct an offense against one of our number, preferably in a non-violent manner."

"Is that so?" asked the male. "Then why have you not filed an official grievance with the local magistrate? Or petitioned the Highmaster, considering the problem seems to originate from the Citadel? If so, we might be able to secure a meeting with him come morning."

Lucretia stepped forward and bowed, her arms crossed. "With all due respect, we made an official request to meet with Highmaster Nerod earlier today. However, the guards turned us away with insults and laughter. I know there are other methods we could use, but I worry that the Highmaster was influenced in some way. Time is of the essence."

The smaller figure tilted her head. "Influenced? How so?"

Lucretia froze, her eyes bulging. The sting of the news must have still been too fresh. "I-I...well," she stammered.

Stepping forward, Kai put a hand on Lucretia's shoulder and pulled her back. She frowned but allowed Rialta to give her a comforting hug. "This young lady was branded an oathbreaker on what I believe to be flimsy or false evidence. I can tell that you're both nobles, so I assume you know what that means."

The pair stepped back as if physically struck. "Oath breaking?" the female whispered. She interlocked her fingers, clenching them together. "As I recall, there are protocols to be followed before anyone can be convicted of such an offense. And any such conviction, along with all relevant investigation and trial transcripts, are to be filed with the Grand Magistrate in Whistlevale. This is disturbing news."

Kai's tails tingled. These two were highly familiar with protocol, even for nobles. Something was off. There was also the way the woman weaved her fingers together. He knew he'd seen it before.

The clomp of a hoof sounded as Teos sidled next to Kai. "We might want to move. I smell another Norzen. They're close, too. I can't get a decent track on the scent, though. It might be the figure we saw entering the north tower."

The pair looked at each other. "A Norzen, you say? And not the, uh, gentleman with you, I presume?" the male asked. Teos answered no while twisting his head from side to side.

Kai watched the two. The aura they gave off was peaceful and not aggressive in the least, but feigned harmlessness invited complacency. More than one Hunter squad got themselves killed that way. Plus, the sense of familiarity was driving him crazy.

"That could pose a problem. We should seek shelter before something untoward happens," the woman said. "However, we cannot leave you here. Perhaps you should accompany us. I swear on my honor, we will secure you an audience with Nerod first thing tomorrow. In fact, we'll even petition the man on your behalf."

Everyone shared a confused look. "Pardon my candor, milady," replied Kai, "but would Nerod even consider the testimony of a noble in a case like this?"

"Oh, he'll have no choice," the man answered. "For him to dismiss either of us would be a foolish decision on his part."

Kai slid a foot back. That statement and the tone in which it was said made his mane stand on end. "I see. I must admit, you have me on the back foot." Reaching into his pocket while holding his other hand up as a sign of peace, he tugged his watch and exposed it to the pair. Their eyes widened and the woman's hand shot towards her mouth. "This grants me a decent amount of authority, but I've never had to reveal it to someone as high-ranking as Nerod. A Navy officer is one thing, but the Citadel Highmaster is a different barrel of fish."

The woman began shaking and emitting an odd sound. "Milady?" the man queried, raising a hand to her shoulder. Before he could make contact, the woman burst into giggles. Her scarf fell to the ground and Kai could make out her pointed nose and fair skin. Trying to hold back her laughter, the woman's cheeks puffed out like a chipmunk and nearly caused Kai to lose himself in laughter as well.

"I-I cannot believe this! This is either exceptional luck, or the Saints themselves are having a bit of fun at our expense," said the woman. The party tensed. What was she talking about?

Maple stepped forward and ruffled her feathers. "I think I speak for all of us when I say that this is confusing. Just who in Finyt are you?"

The woman quirked an eyebrow at the merchant before her gaze swung to Kai. "I must admit, I was worried after we received word of a Hunter squad being wiped out in the Mistport attack." Kai gaped at the woman, his hand tightening into a fist. How did she—? "But you seem to have done fine since then. You've formed quite the team, Sir Gravebane."

Everyone choked. "By the winds, how do you know that name? Are you also an Exarch?" asked Orelia. Her hold on her staff faltered letting it clatter to the walkway.

Kai racked his mind trying to think of which female Exarchs he knew well enough to recognize him, but none of the names fit the woman before him. Then, like a beam of sunlight breaking through the clouds, he remembered.

His eyes shot up to the woman in shock. *That explains a lot. But why would she of all people be here?*

"Oh, that's easy," the man replied. "Because she's the one that granted him that name." He tugged his hood back and lowered his scarf. To the party's shock, the man was a Vesikoi, with slicked back ebony hair and pale skin.

"Why did you have to spoil the surprise, old friend?" the woman chastised with a mirthful smile. Reaching up, she ignored the gasp from her companion and flipped her hood back, revealing a head concealed by an ivory veil that accentuating her shining eyes. She reached up and unhooked the pin holding her cloak together and allowed it to fall open. Underneath was a chartreuse robe with gold accents. On her breastbone stood an emblem known to any Livorian.

The crest of the Royal House Ardei.

Maple's jaw went slack as she staggered back, only kept from falling when Kai braced her with his arm. "Y-you're..." The woman smiled and lowered herself into a slight bow while everyone scrambled to drop to one knee and lower their heads.

"I don't believe we've been formally introduced," she intoned, "My name is Fusette Ardei, Grand Duchess of Livoria. And the man with me is my Lord Chamberlain, Saredi Bastion."

Chapter XXIV

O f all the people in the duchy Kai expected to run into on this mission, the Grand Duchess herself was not one of them. From his place before her, the apothecary pondered what could have brought her all the way to Runegard, leaving the safety of the palace. What confused him most was that the pair appeared to be without guards.

A stray thought flitted across his mind. *On the bright side, she's the one person that could get us an audience with Nerod whenever we want. Only one recourse available, in that case.*

"Your Grace," said Kai, "if you would have us, we shall accompany you in whatever duty you are performing." Glancing back, he saw a look of betrayal in Lucretia's eyes. He gave the scholar a wink before continuing. "In return, I request a boon. Two, to be honest. First, I ask you to secure an audience with the Highmaster to appeal Archivist Dineri's conviction. Second, I would like you to hear my report concerning a beast that has terrorized Livoria since the beginning of the war."

Having said his piece, Kai waited with bated breath. He was confident the Duchess would grant his boon, considering her earlier offer. However, making the request formal and binding was proper. Besides, Lord Saredi was there as well. As the Duchess's chief advisor, following protocol in his presence was safest.

He was surprised to hear Fusette laugh and soon felt a hand on his shoulder, pulling him to his feet. Raising his eyes, he saw hers shining with glee. "Relax, Gravebane, there is no need for formality. And don't worry, we shall deal with Miss Dineri's situation. No boon required. Consider it a reward for making it this far. I will say, when I received word your squad was killed in action, I prayed many nights for you to still be alive. You were the only Hunter whose identity marker was never recovered. I'm assuming the report you mentioned is regarding the beast responsible. Still, it's wonderful to see my prayers answered."

The blush spreading over Kai's face was bright enough to elicit chuckles from the others. "I appreciate the gesture, Your Grace. You are too kind."

"Oh think nothing of it. Also, I give you all leave to call me Fusette, and Saredi won't say a thing. This makes everything simpler if you think about it," replied Fusette. "Your party no longer has to sneak around, while Saredi and I gain an Exarch to guard us."

Orelia stepped forward and bowed, introducing herself. "Lady Fusette, it's an honor to meet you. Forgive my forwardness, but what has brought you to Runegard? Would it not be safer back in the capital?" The priestess looked contrite and clutched her staff, eyes cast downward.

From his few encounters with the duchess, Kai distinctly remembered her as fair-minded and tranquil. Unlike most nobles within the Parliament, Fusette never came across as strict about protocol despite most doing it out of respect. Then again, he remembered the incident with a Rodekan noble during his last visit to the capital. Kai still couldn't think about it without crossing his legs.

"You aren't being forward at all, Sister. Considering your garb, it's safe to say you're a Windbringer priestess, correct?" Seeing Orelia nod, she pressed on. "As for why we're here, there's two reasons. First, I am here to conscript scholars to assist in the war effort, specifically those with an interest in or knowledge of military history and tactics."

No one could fault that. The Liberation Army was primarily land-based unlike the river pirates the Navy usually fought, so the scholars' insight would be useful to develop more effective tactics.

"Second of all, I'm seeking information to determine what the Liberation Army is up to. My scouts within Liberator territory are sending back disturbing reports. It appears as though they are shipping captured faumen to secret locations scattered throughout the western territories."

The party shared an uneasy look. "That lines up with what that Locke fellow told us. Perhaps they *are* preparing to sell them to Corlati in exchange for support." said Teos. Saredi paled while Fusette gazed at them with obvious interest.

"I'm curious as to how you lot figured that out," the Duchess responded with an even tone.

"It wasn't until we met Admiral Larimanz that the pieces came together. And to be honest, all we have are theories, even if they are backed by convincing evidence." Kai went on to explain the musket that Larimanz showed them and how they considered the ways each piece fit the puzzle.

Mulling over what she heard, Fusette gave a slight bow. "This is frustrating, to say the least. And your theories might be on the mark. When you think about it, a lot makes sense. The scouts have sent some interesting reports on how they treat their captives as well."

Morgan raised a hand, asking where they were going. Saredi answered that they were heading for the base of the central tower. "We won't have to go up the stairs, either. Going down, however, is another story."

The party glanced at each other. This night was getting stranger every second. "Very well, Your Grace," said Ione, "we shall do our utmost to assist you."

Fusette gave a soft cheer before reminding the tavern maid to use her given name. The pair led the group towards the central tower. At thirty yards across, it was the widest of the five towers. Without anyone blocking the path, it was easy to reach the entrance. Saredi raised a fist and knocked twice on the door. A grumbling voice was heard inside, and it opened within moments.

"Who the hell is it and what do you want? It's almost midnight!" An irritated Wasini guard growled, only for his face to whiten once he realized who was at the door. His tail spread out in a wide coil, dropping down into a sprawling bow. "Your Grace, what are you and the Lord Chamberlain doing here so late? We don't get many visitors to the tower during the evening. Please forgive my rudeness!"

Saredi clicked his tongue and reprimanded the guard for his attitude, warning him to always endeavor to be cheerful when greeting guests, no matter how trivial their reasons for coming. "Now then, Her Grace and I have business to attend in the tower tonight. Our bodyguards here will accompany us. If you would, please return to your quarters for the time being. The work we are doing can be witnessed only by Her Grace and those she permits. We shall send for you to return when our business is concluded." The guard blabbered his appreciation and tripped over his own tail rushing away.

It was here that Rialta raised a shaking hand. "Um, I'm afraid I was here to assist Lucretia. I don't feel I deserve to be involved with whatever important work you're doing. Therefore, I request permission to take my leave. I can't think of anywhere else my best friend could be kept safe." Fusette gazed at the young woman and acquiesced. Rialta released a heavy breath and bid the party good night before leaving towards the west tower.

Fusette scanned the area and led the party inside. Saredi whispered in the duchess's ear before strolling to the shelves beneath the staircase. Kai and the others spread out, watching for any movement.

"Let's see," Saredi muttered under his breath, "it should be fourth from the right, third shelf." The man reached up and grabbed a tome, pulling it back by the top of its spine.

While watching Saredi from the corner of his eye, Kai's ears twitched when a click came from behind the wall. The party stood in fascination when Saredi hooked his fingers around the edge of the shelf and pulled it open like a door. Stepping forward, Kai peered inside and saw a spiraling staircase like the one above them, leading into the darkness.

"A hidden passage behind the shelf. I like it," said Teos. Snapping her fingers, Fusette ordered three of the party to grab hanging lanterns. The rest would focus on guarding.

When Morgan asked if anything was waiting for them down there, Orelia thumped him with her staff and reminded him, "Don't say that! Don't you know that's a bad omen?" The sellsword rubbed his new bump but stayed silent, giving the priestess a lopsided smile.

Kai suggested Lucretia, Ione, and Teos take the lanterns and stand at the front, middle, and rear of the group, respectively. Maple, as the party member with the best eyesight, would be near the front with Saredi. Morgan would guard Fusette. Lastly, Kai and Orelia would watch the rear. Pleased with the organization, Saredi led the way down the staircase.

As they traveled downstairs, the air grew thick with dust and smelled musty. Kai saw miniscule cracks growing along the walls. Cobwebs were everywhere, like the passage they snuck into the Citadel through. Other than their footsteps, it was as quiet as a grave. The stillness unnerved Kai, and he noticed the hesitance in his companions. Looking towards the front, he saw a door with the royal crest engraved on it.

"Your Grace," said Kai as Saredi led them through the door. He flinched at the disappointed look she gave him. "Um, Fusette...what are we looking for?"

"Knowledge, Gravebane. Knowledge," Fusette replied. "These are the Royal Archives. The preservation and advancement of knowledge are the lifeblood of any great nation." Lucretia gave a hum of approval as the duchess spoke. "This depository contains almost every major piece of written knowledge created since the Desolation Wars. Possibly even before that when this region was still the Galstan province of Liboda."

Kai heard Lucretia gasp when they stepped into a massive library. A labyrinth of shelves three yards high towered over them. Each was filled with neatly organized scrolls and tomes, their topics engraved in metal plates nailed to the shelf. Tight-fitting glass doors covered each shelf. Lucretia shook in excitement. A point Fusette noticed at once.

"Saredi, I do believe our scholar looks like she's found Finyt itself," she proclaimed. For Kai, it was good to see such a look of overwhelming joy on Lucretia's face. Her spark had returned. The woman was exercising an immense amount of restraint to keep from wandering into the labyrinth.

Lucretia turned to Fusette with hope in her eyes. "Your Grace, you say this place holds most of the written knowledge in Livorian history?" The duchess nodded. "Then, is there a specific topic you're here to investigate?"

Another nod. "Indeed. We're looking for any recent research on our relations with Corlati. Anything that mentions the Norzen would be most helpful. And do call me Fusette, Lucretia. I insist on it."

Lucretia's face fell. "Norzen? Why the focus on them?"

"Because we've received word that the Liberation Army's Norzen captives are separated from the other tribes and sent elsewhere. The problem is, we don't know *where* they're being taken. Or any of them for that matter."

Saredi chimed in, "The evidence points towards Corlati, as you mentioned, but we haven't caught anything being transported over the border. We also have no idea why they would want just the Norzen separated and not the other tribes. It would be simpler to transport them at the same time."

Morgan raised his hand. "This might be a crazy idea, but what if it ain't the Federation government backing the Liberators?"

Everyone turned to the sellsword. "But what about the musket Admiral Larimanz showed us?" asked Ione. "I thought we verified it was made in Corlati."

"Aye, we did," Morgan acquiesced, "but I remembered something. My old company, the Scarlet Spears. We were hired to transport crates of weapons to Mistport, but we only took the one shipment before we were wiped out. No other companies were involved at all." He paced back and forth, running his fingers through his beard. "What if, maybe, there's a few very rich jackasses in Corlati paying for the whole thing, and they're using sellsword companies as mules to move the equipment they trade with the Liberators?"

Fusette paled. "By the winds, we never considered that. Perhaps we should research high-ranking merchants and senators in Corlati instead. The most recent trade records and scouting reports should be a good place to start. If we're lucky, the records our scouts crafted will contain some useful information. Even something as simple as large numbers of Norzen being brought into certain Corlatian cities."

Uneasy looks passed between the group. Orelia suggested they split up to cover more ground. Saredi expressed uncertainty about the idea until Kai offered to stay with Fusette the entire time, citing his Exarch status. The Lord Chamberlain agreed, so long as everyone stayed within earshot.

Walking next to the Grand Duchess was more nerve-racking than Kai imagined. The only time he remembered being this close to her was his Branding ceremony. And now she was right next to him! "I-I hope you aren't too perturbed by having a Norzen as your bodyguard, Milady," said the apothecary.

Her hand reached up and gripped him by the chin, twisting his face to meet hers. It reminded Kai of his talk with Maple the night before they reached the city. He saw several emotions roiling in her eyes. "That's quite enough of that," said Fusette. Using her hands, she manipulated Kai's body as she wished. Straightening his posture, tilting his head up, rolling the shoulders back. Soon enough, he was standing at attention like a common sailor.

"There we go," Fusette murmured. "I have no issues whatsoever with you being a Norzen, Kaigo Travaldi, and it is high time you stand tall and be proud of who you are! There is nothing wrong with being a Norzen, and I'm aware of your unique situation. However, do not let it define you."

The apothecary's fist clenched. He asked Fusette if she knew what the nobles said about her decision to Brand him. Rumors of how she only Branded Kai in order to curry favor with Duskmarsh, when he happened to be the only Norzen to accomplish anything notable at the time.

The Duchess waved off his concerns. "Of course I've heard them, but you cannot take stock in the foolish ramblings of nobles. If I learned anything since my father began my etiquette lessons, it's that nobles have an irritating ability to take any problem, make it about them, and assign the worst possible outcome or reasoning to it. If it weren't so exasperating, I'd be impressed at the inherent talent."

Kai chuckled. From his past experiences, he could understand what she meant. "Regardless," Fusette continued, "I Branded you because of your noble heart. Not to mention your skill at taking a disadvantageous situation and coming out on top. That's not something anyone can lay claim to. Come, I wish to show you something."

Curious, Kai followed the duchess through the aisles. They could still hear the others riffling through tomes on the other side of the shelf. Fusette plucked a wooden stool from the ground without breaking stride and marched forward.

Able to keep up due to his longer strides, Kai took time to look at some of the listed topics on the shelf plates: Crop yield reports, manorial records, receipts of sale. Soon enough, Kai noticed the topics shifting to more ecclesiastical records such as anointments, priest rolls, and donations to the church.

Suddenly, Fusette emitted a squeak of triumph and set her stool down before stepping up. Browsing through a line of tomes, she found what she was looking for and slid a thin handbound volume from its place. She brushed off a layer of dust from the tome. The duchess stared at the book in adoration, like a favored child. Kai found his curiosity building. Coming down, she held her prize out for Kai to take. When he gestured to make sure it was okay, she pressed the tome against his chest.

Kai gazed at it, not seeing anything overtly interesting, other than its apparent age. It had no writing or symbols on the cover. No markings or notations to explained the contents. Flipping through it, he realized it was a journal of some sort. Scratching at his mane, Kai pondered why Fusette handed him this of all the tomes in the archives.

"Look at the first page," Fusette instructed. Without a word, Kai thumbed back to the front and read. It was written in archaic Centric, with the script more rounded and flowing compared to the sharp, blocky lettering of modern Centric. Still, reading it wasn't difficult. In moments, Kai nearly dropped the tome in shock.

Looking at Fusette, he snapped the tome shut and inhaled deeply, coughing from the floating dust. "I-Is this real?" whispered Kai. The young ruler nodded. "Then that means...I'm holding the personal journal of Master Galen himself." It was hard not to think of the stories he heard at Havenfall's small church growing up.

Galen Degelhart, also known by his epithet, the Sage. An aging warrior monk from Galstein who offered to stand against the warlord that conquered most of Liboda and its neighboring provinces, ruling them with an iron grip. Together, he and seven others infiltrated the warlord's fortress where the Citadel now stood and put it to the flame.

In response, the warlord went on a murderous rampage, tracking Galen and his party to the forests in the southernmost part of the provinces. All who stood in his way were cut down without mercy. It was in those forests where Cacovis brought about the Desolation and created the area now known as the Voidlands. Nothing was truly known, but it was suspected the warlord and his army were wiped out along with the forest.

In the aftermath, it was decided that the warlord's former lands would be granted independence instead of returning to Galstan rule. Galen and his party were given their title of Wind Saints and revered as heroes both in Galstein and the new nation. And thus, the Grand Duchy of Livoria was born, with young Tebalect Ardei crowned as the first Grand Duke, selected by the Wind Saints themselves.

Kai was pulled from his thoughts when Fusette touched his shoulder. Apologizing, he flipped through pages at random, reading of Galen's thoughts and worries while traveling. "This is incredible, Your Grace. Truly," said the apothecary, yelping when the Duchess flicked him in the ear. "I'm sorry! Fusette, right. I must ask though, why share this with me? And why keep something so important down here in an archive?"

Fusette sighed, leaning against the shelves. "Unfortunately, this journal was deemed a historical relic by Parliament and forced to be kept here. A catastrophe would have to occur for me to have a legitimate reason to remove it."

Humming to himself, Kai climbed the stool and went through the tomes on the same shelf where the journal had sat. None of them were of particular interest, which Kai felt was odd. The area brightened when Kai noticed a lantern rising above the shelf behind him. Listening closely, he chuckled at hearing Lucretia's excited babbling about the variety of tomes.

Turning back to his own search, Kai was stunned when a bright flash blinded him from the back of the shelf. He hissed and reached for the shelf with his free hand, using the journal to shield his eyes. His feet inched backwards, but Fusette rushed forward and pressed on his back to keep him from toppling off the stool.

"Thanks," Kai mumbled. Fusette asked him what happened, and the apothecary mentioned the blinding light. Frowning, he saw Lucretia's lantern dip back behind the shelf and turned to pull several tomes off the shelf. Easing his hand to the back, he felt the soft touch of leather. Lambskin, if he was guessing the texture right. He pulled a moderately thick tome out, turning it in his hand. A silver buckle was sewn onto the cover. Kai would wager a moon's rations the plain piece of metal was what blinded him a moment ago.

"What's that?" asked Fusette.

"Not sure," Kai replied. His ears prickled the longer he gazed at the book. Opening the buckle, he thumbed through it, only to find himself baffled. "What the...? I can't read any of this!"

Stepping down, he showed the pages of the strange tome to the Duchess, aware of raised voices coming from the shelf behind them. Together, they marveled at the flowing script. The symbols were woven together like a tapestry written in ink. While they couldn't understand what the symbols said, both appreciated the writing's beauty.

"I don't know who wrote this, but their penmanship is exquisite," Fusette praised. The shuffle of boots on stone drew Kai's vision to the rest of the party approaching.

Shooting the duchess a firm look, Saredi turned to Kai. "We heard you say you found a tome whose contents you can't read?" When the apothecary nodded, the Vesikoi noble extended a hand. Kai passed the book along, and everyone watched as Saredi inspected the contents with focused determination. After a few minutes, his eyes pinched together in frustration until he tossed the tome back into Kai's arms. "I feel like I've seen the script before, but by the winds, I can't bloody remember it."

"May I?" asked Lucretia, holding out her own hand. Kai handed the tome over, muttering that it felt like they were playing a game of hot rock toss. "Oh hush. I know several languages, so I might recognize the script at least. Now let me see." After running her fingers over the page, her face sunk. Kai watched as the light in her eyes ebbed away. Without warning, those eyes swung up to meet his and Lucretia asked a single question.

"Kai, where did you find a tome written in High Norzen?"

Everyone gaped at Lucretia and Kai felt the blood drain from his face. High Norzen? Only the inhabitants of Duskmarsh used the ancient Norzen language any longer. And few, if any, of their tomes ever saw the light of day outside those swamps.

Morgan side-eyed the scholar. "I think the better question is: How in hoarfrost can *you* read High Norzen? You hate the Norzen!"

With a huff, Lucretia's piercing gaze turned on the sellsword. "I will only say this. To defeat one's enemy, then you must know your enemy in every way possible." Returning her attention to the tome, the scholar continued reading. Every few seconds, she would flip to a random page, and with each successive one, her eyes widened a little bit more.

"It is a journal," she whispered. "A chronicle of someone's journeys, and from the context it seems like this is from the time of the Desolation Wars. Wait."

Finally, she dug her finger into the tome and turned back to the first page, just as Kai did with Galen's journal. Her eyes swept over the symbols on the page. Just then, her face turned the color of fresh snow. With a scream, she flung the tome and struck a baffled Kai square in the nose with it. Lucretia stumbled back in a blind panic. Ione and Orelia grabbed hold of her and helped the young woman steady herself.

Nursing his bleeding nose, Kai managed to croak out, "You better explain what in Tapimor's hairy ass that was all about, Lucretia. That bloody hurt!"

"You have no damned idea what you picked up, do you?"

Kai's face went stoic. "Whatever could have given you that idea? Oh, wait. Maybe it's because *I can't read it!*"

Teos sent the tome a worried glance, asking Lucretia why she was so terrified of a book.

"I was curious as to why some of the entries mentioned the Wind Saints. It was as if the writer had known them. That concerned me. Then I looked to see who the writer was, and now I wish I stayed ignorant. That thing was written by the only Norzen who would have traveled with the Wind Saints before the Desolation.

Kai's face turned ashen. "You mean...?"

"Yes," confirmed Lucretia, "that tome is the travel log of Cacovis the Shadow herself. The fallen Saint of Pride."

CHAPTER XXV

If anyone told Kai before today he would see Lucretia Dineri terrified of a book, he would have questioned their sanity. Her entire life revolved around written knowledge, and as far as he knew, nothing made her happier than a new tome. Seeing her now, staring at Cacovis's journal in Kai's hands as if it were Grimghast, seemed unnatural.

Given the dubious look Morgan was sending her way, he was thinking the same thing. "Hey, you okay lass?" he asked.

Lucretia's remained on the ground, her entire body shivering. "That tome should be destroyed. Anything written in that woman's hand can cause nothing but pain!" Kneeling next to her friend, Ione did her best to calm the scholar down, though her own face had taken a sickly pallor.

Even though he couldn't read it, Kai continued thumbing through the journal. Something in the deepest part of his mind compelled him to do so. Perhaps it was knowing that, despite the person who wrote it, the tome was a tangible connection to a piece of himself he still had trouble accepting.

"Even if you say that Lucretia, doesn't the scholar's creed say that knowledge itself isn't good or evil? It's the will of the wielder that's important," said Maple.

Fusette and Saredi nodded their agreement. "Wise words, indeed," said Saredi. "Cacovis did horrific things in her life, but the information in this journal could be invaluable. By the winds, there was never any evidence of this tome existing in the first place!"

After finally allowing Ione to help her to her feet, Lucretia glared at the innocuous tome. "So you had no idea it was here?" Fusette and

Saredi shook their heads, with the duchess admitting that, in reviewing her ancestors' records, nothing about a journal written by Cacovis was ever mentioned.

Maple eyed the tome with a mercantile gleam. "There's a lot of potential to be found, I think. A handwritten relic from the Shadow herself? I doubt anyone could put a price on the value of what she wrote in there! That tome could contain information about the Desolation Wars not recorded otherwise."

Raising his eyes to meet Lucretia's, Kai held the journal towards her, only for the scholar to flinch and back away. "Listen, I'm sure this is hard for you considering your feelings about Norzen, but you're the only one here who can translate it. Unless, of course, you know someone else that reads High Norzen. Our only other recourse would be to take it to Duskmarsh, and it's a gamble on how bad the Norzen would react to us bringing something like *this* to them."

With a solemn face, Lucretia replied that the Archivist who taught her the language during her apprenticeship passed away years ago.

"Do I have to?" she asked.

"Think of it this way," replied Kai, "it's like Maple said: there could be knowledge in here about the Desolation that nobody ever knew. This is an eyewitness record of the events that form the foundation of our country, our religion, our very way of life!" The Norzen's face burned with a passion that he hadn't felt since his apothecary training. "I understand I'm asking a lot, but at very least, could you translate the final entries and see if there's anything worthwhile?"

The sharp rap of wood on stone drew everyone's eyes to Orelia, who looked at Kai in amazement. "Sweet merciful Galen, you may be onto something. Not even the Wind Saints knew how or why Cacovis caused the Desolation. Or if they did, they never admitted it. This journal is a once-in-a-lifetime find if there's anything about her reasoning." Now the priestess turned on Lucretia with hope clear as day on her face. The scholar hesitated, seeing everyone staring at her so earnestly.

"B-but…oh, very well! I shall do it," she grumbled. Reaching out, she plucked the journal from Kai's outstretched hand.

Maple cheered and hugged the despondent woman. Lucretia couldn't stop a small smile from finding its way to her face. Settling into a comfortable spot against a shelf, she flipped to the back of the journal and read.

While curious at what Lucretia would discover, Kai also felt nervous. With everything they were taught about Cacovis, it was surreal to think he'd be finding out more about the mysterious Saint's past. Few records remained concerning her life. Even when she was alive, Cacovis was infamous for avoiding the spotlight.

A rather amusing thought, considering her ultimate place in history.

The library was silent as the party waited for Lucretia to finish. Kai grew more concerned as he watched various emotions flash across the woman's face. At first, she showed glimmers of sadness, then shock. Her face returned to the same pale sheen from when she first learned whose journal they found. With her mouth gaping open, Lucretia let her arms hang limp.

"Is it that bad?" asked Orelia.

"This book," murmured Lucretia, "I suppose I must translate it in its entirety at some point. Just the last few entries are enough to turn the entire Windbringer faith on its head. I can only imagine what the rest contains."

It was Fusette that stepped forward and took the journal from Lucretia. "Then we must endeavor to protect it at all costs. What did you find?"

Lucretia shot a withering glance at the book and released a deep breath. "If the journal is truly written by Cacovis, then it appears much of what we know of her has been warped, twisted, and banished to the darkness. Were any of you aware she was a mother?"

The party stepped back as if slapped.

"Cacovis had a child?" Maple blurted out.

"She had two sons: Erklaus and Tobiris."

Kai noticed Fusette enraptured by the information. Looking closer, he saw an expression of pure bliss on the duchess's face. *I shouldn't be surprised,* Kai thought. *Ever since taking the throne, she's pushed for more equal treatment for every tribe, particularly Norzen. This tome could help her bring about real change.*

Galvanized by the information, Teos asked what Cacovis mentioned about the war and the Desolation.

She answered, "From the little I read, it seems as though Cacovis joined the Saints in order to protect her children. The war was bleak for the Saints by the time the final entries were written. Cacovis' own husband was an early victim of the warlord, whose name appears to be Berelmir. He was destroying everything in his path while pursuing the Saints southward. According to Cacovis, thousands lost their lives either by fire or cut down by Berelmir's army.

"It was near the southern mountains when Cacovis broke off from the other Saints and continued on alone. Her final request to Master Galen was that he and the others hide her sons from their enemy's allies. While they escaped, she led Berelmir further, to the village where she was born. Supposedly, she knew of a powerful weapon there capable of destroying Berelmir, but she does not say what the weapon was explicitly. We can assume Cacovis gave her journal to Galen before they separated. It mentions nothing of her travels southward or of the final conflict."

Stroking his beard, Morgan let out a huff. "That makes sense. The book is still here, after all. If she kept it, it would've been burned to a crisp. Well that's a damn shame. Whatever weapon she used against Berelmir, it obviously did what it was supposed to."

"Perhaps a bit *too* well," retorted Ione, "considering she lost her own life in the process, and the surrounding area was reduced to an inhabitable wasteland."

Kai's fist clenched as he mulled over Lucretia's translation. "In a way," he said, "I can understand her reasoning." The others looked at him flabbergasted. "Think about it: if someone threatened to hurt your family, or even just someone you dearly cared for, how far would you go to protect them? Cacovis didn't hesitate to make the ultimate sacrifice to defend what was precious to her."

Maple sauntered next to him and gave the Norzen a playful punch to the shoulder. "You always were good at arguing a point. And after our last tussle with Grimghast, I think you've made it clear you'd do the same for any of us." Kai couldn't stop the blush spreading across his cheeks, to the others' amusement. He also realized Fusette giving him a strange look, like she was trying to put together a puzzle.

A sudden breeze blew through the aisles, ruffling Kai's mane. Surprised by the unexpected rush of air, he spun on his heel and swiveled his ears. "We've got company. Someone's opened the door." That was the only reason the air would be circulating.

Teos peered around the shelf's corner and inhaled through his nose. "Bollocks! I'm picking up that Norzen smell again. It must be the shadow we saw in the gardens. How in Nulyma did I miss it? What a night for me to lose focus."

Drawing her rapier, Lucretia side-eyed the smuggler. "And how do you know it isn't Kai that you smell?"

"The best way to describe it is that the scent is cleaner. No other smells are mixed in. I know Kai washes regularly, but he's been an apothecary so long, his scent is infused with an aroma of leaves, moss, and soil."

Everyone's eyes swung to Kai, who lifted an arm to his nose and sniffed. "He's got a point. I do kinda smell like the tika moss common back home, even if it is faint."

Saredi admonished the two and ordered everyone to stay alert. The party formed a defensive circle around the nobles, drawing their weapons. From the corner of his eye, Kai saw Fusette back up to the shelf where they found the journals and shuffle through the tomes. *Why is she—oh, she's hiding the journals. Smart move.*

The sound of footfalls echoed through the archive. Shifting his ears, Kai couldn't detect the sound's origin. The open ceiling above carried the noise and made it sound like it was coming from all around. He advised the others to watch every angle. The intruder could come from either side.

"Do you reckon they saw us come down here and we didn't notice?" asked Maple, an arrow nocked to her bow and ready to fly.

"That's possible," Saredi answered. "Only a select few know about these archives."

A deep chuckle reverberated nearby. Kai's finger pointed to his left and everyone turned to see a large shadow rounding the corner.

"Or," a loud, nasally voice rang out, "it could be that we received word there were sneaks scuttling about the academy." The party saw two men trudging towards them.

Lucretia gasped when the shorter man raised his lantern, illuminating both their faces.

"Highmaster Nerod and Viscount Savo," the scholar whispered.

Taking in the Highmaster's corpulent figure, it was easy to see Nerod never knew hunger or hard labor. He wore a creme scholar's overcloak with black accents. His grey collared shirt strained to contain his impressive gut, which hung over the top of his breeches. His legs were short and stocky, while his arms were thick with wide, meaty hands.

Nerod's balding head was chubby and gnarled like a potato, with a thick walrus-like mustache and barely any neck, and two beady eyes that reminded Kai too much of Grimghast.

The second man, Savo, had a thin, wiry waist with broad shoulders, a head of bushy hair, and sunken cheeks. He wore a red tailcoat over a white ruffled shirt and black breeches, all of which looked well-tailored.

When Kai asked who the shorter man was, Lucretia looked ready to hit him. "Viscount Savo is the Highmaster's assistant, responsible for his correspondence and verifying anyone wishing to meet him. He has a reputation for being a harsh taskmaster, but he is efficient in his duties."

The smaller noble had piercing brown eyes like a hawk, constantly moving and watching everything around him. Those same eyes shifted to Fusette as Nerod released a full belly laugh. "Well I'll be! If it isn't the Grand Duchess herself! What in Finyt are you doing here of all places, Your Grace, and in such questionable company too?"

"You are not in a place to question my choice of bodyguards, Nerod," Fusette snapped back. "As it stands, you're facing investigation and possible discipline for severe breach of protocol and abuse of authority."

The Highmaster took on a look of dismay while Savo sputtered with eyes widened in shock. "Your Grace, that is the most preposterous thing I've heard in a solstice! Who dares sully the Highmaster's good reputation with such balderdash?"

"Is that so?" Kai spoke up, bringing the man's eyes to him, "Then is it a mere rumor you branded Lucretia an oathbreaker and banished her?"

"Rumor? My dear Norzen, that is cold, hard truth," Savo answered.

Now Saredi drew himself up with a look of fury. "Would you care to explain why protocol was not followed? All accusations of oathbreaking require a trial, do they not?"

"We tried the little witch in absentia." A quick glance told Kai that Lucretia was struggling to control her emotions under Savo's verbal assault. "Not a soul knew where she was, only that she fled her duties before being recalled. I received multiple reports addressed to the Highmaster that she was spotted wandering the grasslands instead of returning at once."

Kai's ears twitched. "Funny how you accuse the Duchess of keeping questionable company, when now I find myself wondering just who you've been speaking with."

"Why is that?" Saredi asked.

A smug grin spread across Kai's lips. "Because the reason Lucretia left Mistport was due to the Liberator invasion. They would be the only ones who knew she was there outside of her direct superiors. And that's if they even knew who she was." Savo's eyes bulged. "Then you also have the Grimghast attack, which is a whole different barrel of fish."

"You've mentioned the name Grimghast twice now," Fusette observed. "Who is that?"

"Not who...what."

The party explained in gruesome detail what Grimghast was and of their battles against it. The Grand Duchess listened open-mouthed as Kai described the pain of watching his squad torn apart by the beast before he, Lucretia, and Ione escaped.

"Then that means Madams Dineri and Rasina left Mistport under your direct care, is that correct?" Saredi asked. Kai nodded.

After hearing that, Fusette flashed an exultant smile. "Well, that makes things simple. I've heard all I need to. Lucretia Dineri! By royal decree, your conviction of oathbreaking is hereby overturned and you are returned to full standing as an Archivist."

"Your Grace, have you lost your kettle?!" the Highmaster blubbered. The sound of singing steel rang out as Saredi drew his sword on the portly noble. Kai pointed the tip of his mace at Nerod's head.

"You want to take it out of his hide, Lord Chamberlain, or shall I do the honors?" asked Kai. Saredi chuckled and swore he'd run the man through himself.

Savo squawked in outrage. "Norzen, I can have you sent to the gallows for this! Master Nerod spoke out of turn, yes, but a person of your status drawing a weapon on a noble is a hanging offense."

Tired of hearing the viscount talk, Kai drew his watch and dangled it in front of the gaping pair.

"I'm quite certain this signifies I'm a special class of noble myself, leaving your argument invalid. Now I want answers. Who gave you the information on Lucretia?"

Nerod made an excuse of having hidden contacts around the duchy in many positions, with a need to protect their identities. Kai watched the man like a hawk. He noted Nerod's wild hand gestures and shifting facial expressions.

Saredi rapped his sword against the wooden shelf. "You have the gall to lie to Her Grace in front of me, Nerod?"

Putting himself between Saredi and the Highmaster, Savo pleaded for Fusette to listen. "One of the reports was from a bishop, Your Grace! Bishop Adalbard of Stahl Granz Temple provided us a detailed account of the trouble caused by Dineri and these ruffians. They even set the temple itself ablaze."

Cries of outrage flew from the party, but none as loud as the contempt spewing from Orelia's mouth. "Adalbard!" she shrieked. "You trusted the word of that filthy, child-murdering traitor? How stupid are you?"

Now it was Nerod who looked stunned. "What are you talking about? Child murderer?"

"Oh, did he not mention it? I'm not surprised. He was too much of a coward to fight us himself, preferring to slaughter most of the children in the orphanage under my charge before kidnapping one and leaving us to burn in the temple!"

Teos pointed his halberd at Savo's chest. "The fact that you're trading information with a man who kills and sells children into slavery means you have no good faith. If anything, it makes you accomplices, with all Adalbard has done."

A deep chortle rumbled from Nerod, who was resting his hands on his belly as it shook. Maple whispered in Kai's ear, drawing his gaze to Nerod's face. Despite his expressive movements just before, he wasn't sweating. Nor was he winded.

"Well, this is a fine mess," the Highmaster spoke. "I never did have the best attendance in church, but I suppose it's time to make a true leap of faith like my old friend Adalbard used to say. Why be an accomplice to treason and murder when I can make a full run of it, no?"

Savo paled, asking Nerod what he meant.

"Savo, my friend, you always were eager to make my life comfortable. Unfortunately, you're also as naïve as a young maiden and thought no one would have reason to lie to you. Getting rid of Dineri was supposed to be simple, but these pests refuse to roll over."

"What are you talking about, Highmaster? Are you saying you *were* trying to dispose of Dineri? And you used me as a pawn to do so?" the viscount shouted, gripping Nerod by his overcloak. Nerod looked down at his assistant and smirked.

Kai saw the flash of metal, but before he could move, Savo emitted a cry of pain. He stumbled away from Nerod, spinning to face the party. The broad handle of a dagger was buried deep in his stomach, his shirt now stained scarlet.

"*Taen!*" Kai blurted out. He pulled Savo over and removed the dagger. The viscount bit his lip and hissed as the curved blade came out with ragged bits of flesh covering a line of serrated indentions on the edge. "Damn it all, blood grooves. Lord Saredi!"

Saredi rushed to Kai's side and the apothecary handed him a thick rag, ordering him to keep pressure on the wound. "I'll try to sew the wound closed but I need time."

A bloody hand clasped down on Kai's arm. Looking down, he saw Savo looking at him with tears in his eyes.

"Why?" Savo gasped. "Why are you helping me, after everything I said? After helping him for so long?"

"I'm an apothecary sir. Norzen or not, my oath is to save lives. Besides, even a court fool can see you were taken advantage of. You wanted to help someone you thought was a good person. It would be a failure of my duty to hold that against you."

Savo stared at Kai in astonishment. Whether it was because of Kai's words, or he still couldn't comprehend a Norzen helping him, it was hard to say. Finally, his grip on Kai's arm tightened and he pushed the Norzen's hand away.

"What are you doing!? If we don't put pressure on that wound, you'll die."

"Then at least let me die with dignity." The viscount gave a weak chuckle. "Don't misunderstand me. I'm not saying this because you are a Norzen. But I have committed grave sins in being blind to the truth. Death truly provides the greatest clarity and shall be my atonement. Looking back, I should've seen the signs, but I ignored them because I let myself be blinded by my respect for Nerod's position. Just promise me something." Savo stopped to take a shaky breath while a pool of blood gathered below him.

"Don't make the same mistake I did. And if you do, don't hold onto that false hope. Some people are so far gone that logic, trust, and faith will never reach them."

With a final shudder, Savo relaxed his body and went still. The rest of the party lowered their heads in a moment of silence.

Kai pressed two fingers to the base of his neck and whispered, "May Cacovis guide you on this final journey."

Turning back to face Nerod, Kai took a calming breath. "I suppose there's no going back for you."

"There never was, boy. I did come here with a purpose, after all."

"Wait," said Ione, "I just realized something: Who told him we were down here? Did the guard at the tower door go blubbering?"

Nerod's lips curled into an ominous grin, setting Kai's fur on end. He didn't like that smile one bit. The Highmaster waved his arm with a flourish and stepped to the side, revealing someone behind him. With a gasp, Lucretia dropped her rapier.

It was Rialta.

"Ria," Lucretia whispered. "W-what is going on?"

"I'm sorry, Lu. The guards saw me returning to the tower and took me to the Highmaster's chambers. I-I couldn't..."

Kai's hand tightened around his mace. The only thing in Rialta's eyes at that moment was terror. Her robes were torn, and bruises dotted her arms and face.

Nerod sneered and backhanded Rialta in the cheek, sending her careening into the shelves. The woman's head snapped to the side and Kai saw a line of blood dribble down her face.

"Shut your damn mouth, girl! You already know what disobedience brings. After all, I gave you a personal lesson before we came down. Be grateful I still have a use for you, or I would've handed you to Adalbard and those fools he's cavorting with."

Lucretia hooked the toe of her boot under the fallen rapier, kicking it up to her waiting hand. With a twirl, she rushed and made a lunging stab at Nerod's throat. The noble shrieked and sidestepped the attack.

The Archivist snarled, "You bastard. Keep your filthy hands off my best friend!" She lunged again, grazing the Highmaster's cheek before he shoved her backwards. Lucretia gasped in pain, stumbling back before falling on her rump.

"You have some nerve, girl," Nerod grumbled. "Hey! What are you bastards waiting for? You're supposed to be protecting me!"

"Apologies, Nerod. Our surprise hasn't been the most cooperative," came a gruff voice from behind Nerod. Kai wasn't surprised to see Orelia spitting nails when Adalbard revealed himself, carrying a new staff with a spiked head. The apothecary's vision was tinted red when he saw the priest dragging Tuvi behind him, the Norzen girl struggling listlessly against his grip. He nearly lost control what he saw Tuvi's right arm.

Her hand was cut off at the wrist and bound in leather, leaving a rounded stump.

"Tuvi!" Teos grabbed Orelia by the waist to keep her from rushing the priest. "Let me go, Teos! I'm gonna kill that bastard!" Orelia shouted. The rest of the party jumped in to hold back the enraged priestess.

"Sister Orelia!" Tuvi cried out, throwing punches and kicks at Adalbard. "Let me go!"

The priest pressed the spiked head of his staff against Tuvi's neck. "Keep screeching, you little brat, and I'll smash your head over the floor like a melon. The general already gave me leave, since they don't need your worthless hide for anything."

"Take it easy, Sister," the smuggler replied while glaring daggers at Adalbard. "You can't run in there half-nocked, or you'll get yourself killed. Worse yet, he'll hurt Tuvi."

Orelia slumped in Teos's arms, looking at the girl with devastation.

"My, my, Your Grace," Nerod's voiced echoed. Everyone turned to find him missing, hidden somewhere in the maze of shelves. "Your bodyguards are rather violent, aren't they? Makes you wonder where they learned such brutish manners. But then, you'd know all about that, wouldn't you?"

Pushing himself to the front, Saredi peered around the nearest corner and shouted, "I'm warning you, Nerod. You tread a dangerous line."

"Whatever do you mean, Saredi? These ruffians are only taking their cues from the worst monster of them all. Not that they know of the secrets their precious Grand Duchess hides. Her secrets put all of Livoria at risk.

If the common people were privy to what I know, the war would be an afterthought as the duchy tears itself apart from the roots up."

Secrets? Kai glanced at Fusette to see her recoiling in fear. "I won't pretend to know what you're talking about Nerod, but I doubt Her Grace has done anything near as disgusting as what you've done." Turning back, Kai hissed and let out a curse. While he was distracted, Adalbard escaped into the labyrinth with Tuvi.

What Kai wasn't expecting was for the grandiose noble to explode into laughter. "This is rich! She never even bothered to tell *you* her greatest secret. Everyone in Whistlevale knows she has a soft spot for you, the Exarch Knights' greatest outcast. Of course, there's more reason for that than meets the eye."

Now Kai was really confused. "What does that have to do with anything?" Out of the corner of his eye, he saw Fusette staring at him in terror. Saredi's face somehow turned even paler than it naturally was.

Nerod's laughter became more high-pitched, like the cackle of a parrot. "Allow me to enlighten you, then. Your Grace, remove your veil and cloak. Show them the scars of your family's past. Reveal just who these fools pledge their loyalty to.

Saredi lambasted Nerod for his impudence in ordering the Grand Duchess to do anything.

Kai would admit he was always curious about what was under Fusette's veil, but he would never presume himself brave enough to ask directly. Only a suicidal moron would dare to do so. Still, it was obvious that Fusette, Saredi, and Nerod believed it to be of paramount importance. Thinking about the possibilities and their implications, something spoke to Kai in the back of his mind. A pair of phrases his parents told him growing up. It left only one option.

"Fusette, I think you should do as he says."

The rest of the party looked at Kai as if he had grown a second head. "Now I am sure you *have* lost your kettle!" Lucretia snapped. "Why would you dare ask Her Grace to follow the orders of that lunatic?"

"It's obvious they consider what's under that veil important. So much so that Fusette is terrified of it. But my Da always used to say something if me or my sister ever lied to him: A secret holds more power the longer it's kept in the darkness. Only the light of truth can take away the fear a secret like that leaves in a person." Turning to Fusette, Kai gave her a crooked smile and tapped his temple.

"You've never given me any reason to doubt you, milady. I reckon what's under there won't change anything."

From her place next the duchess, Maple shot her a smirk. "Kai's a good judge of character, so I'll trust his word to the grave. And I'd wager my feathers the others will do the same, even our prickly little scholar. Don't ya reckon it's time to free yourself?"

Saredi continued shaking his head, but Fusette reached up to grasp the cloth. "Your father is a wise man, Gravebane. I'd much like to meet him one day. Assuming, of course, you don't change your mind after this."

Using one hand to unhook her cloak's clasp and the other to grip her veil, she pulled back and allowed both to fall.

Everyone stepped back with wide eyes. Kai's breath stopped. How could it not, seeing a pair of long tails emerge from the back of her robes and two pointed fluffy ears atop the woman's head. Taking a closer look, Kai realized that Fusette's eyes were the same stormy grey as his own.

Fusette Ardei, the Grand Duchess of Livoria, was a Norzen.

Chapter XXVI

Seeing Fusette like this left Kai with an odd feeling of relief and befuddlement.

When Nerod mentioned that the Grand Duchess was keeping dangerous secrets, Kai admitted his original thoughts were of assassinating political enemies or performing experiments on people. Things that might result in riots if revealed to the public.

Compared to those, discovering that the Duchess was a Norzen felt mild. It was like expecting the heated sting of cappara on your meal but finding out it was an ordinary sweet pepper.

There was no sign of Nerod or Adalbard either. Both men were hesitant to rise from their hiding places.

I'd wager the only reason the others haven't run after those two yet is to make sense of what's going on, Kai thought.

Teos and Morgan alone would have been enough to drag them out, but both stood in uneasy stances, preferring to stare at the Grand Duchess.

Fusette crossed her arms and looked away with downcast eyes. Taking a glance, Kai noticed Lucretia's flabbergasted expression. If the situation were less serious, and his stomach wasn't still tender from cramping last night, he would be laughing. As it was, he restrained the urge.

Wait, someone *was* laughing. Kai swiveled his ears and heard Nerod cackling in whatever hole he'd hidden in. It sounded like he was hammering a fist against the wall, so it was obvious he reveled in the shock resonating through the room. "This is beautiful!" the noble proclaimed. "Now you see your precious Grand Duchess for the beast she truly is. What do you have to say now, Dineri?"

"This can't be real," Lucretia gasped. She slumped against the shelf and slid down into a seated position. "The Grand Duchess is...a Norzen? How is this possible? How has no one found this out before now?"

Slumping against the shelves, Saredi cupped his head in his hands. "Only a few high-ranking individuals in the realm are permitted to know this about the royal family. Not even Parliament knows the truth. It's why the only palace staff that directly serve Her Grace are Norzen. We allow Parliament and the nobles to believe that it's to remind the Norzen of their place, but in reality it's to protect Her Grace."

Ione dropped to her knees, a blank look on her face. "But, if this is true, then how are heirs born? Are the midwives in on it as well?"

"We make use of Norzen midwives from Duskmarsh. That's usually also where we procure partners for the sitting Grand Duke or Duchess to obtain an heir. Her Grace's mother was a jewel artisan that Duke Vonlo grew quite taken with during his many trips to the city. Once Lady Fusette was born, she was brought to Whistlevale and anointed as the future Grand Duchess. Her mother remained in Duskmarsh with no one the wiser. Sadly, Her Grace was never permitted to travel to the city whilst her father was alive, and Parliament has ensured there are too many issues to handle across the duchy for Lady Fusette to travel to Duskmarsh herself."

"Then," Kai spoke up, "Does that mean...?" His eyes shifted to meet Fusette's solemn gaze.

"Yes, Her Grace has never been able to meet her own mother. Ever. It's one of the reasons Duskmarsh has grown so irritable in recent years. No monarch has ever gone so long without visiting Duskmarsh after their ascension to the throne. Her Grace must visit the city before her thirtieth birthday, if only to decide on a partner to ensure the Ardei line continues."

Morgan stroked his beard, staring at Nerod. "Something bothers me about this. If Nerod is a Libbie sympathizer and knew this information, why not reveal it the moment he found out?"

"I'll admit it was a tempting idea," Nerod confessed. "However, I decided to hold onto the information for when I could cause some true damage with it. This war presented me with the perfect opportunity. My intention is to sell these secrets to the Liberation Army. The wonderful thing for you is that it gets worse. Being the Highmaster comes with useful privileges, like knowing the true story behind our royal family." Fusette's whole body shook, staring at Lucretia with wide eyes. "It turns out that bitch Cacovis had a son. After the Desolation, the Wind Saints decided to hide the brat. His name was changed, and he was hidden in plain sight, right under everyone's noses. Take a guess as to where they put him."

Maple turned to Fusette wide-eyed. "Wait a tic. Does he mean..."

The Highmaster's laughter grew in intensity until the man started wheezing. "Correct, featherbrain. She's the last living descendant of Cacovis! To think, all these years we've been worshipping the offspring of that disgusting creature." There wasn't a peep from Adalbard, who was likely as stunned as the party was.

"Are you done yet?" The simple question from Kai brought Nerod's laughter to a halt. "I'll admit, finding out Fusette is a Norzen, and descended from a Wind Saint at that, is surprising. But, when you stop and think, it doesn't matter."

After hauling herself to her feet again, Lucretia stomped over and jabbed a finger in Kai's mane. "What are you bloody talking about? Of course it matters! The entire royal family has been lying to us for three hundred years. What's worse, the Wind Saints themselves were in on it! That's not something that can easily be forgotten. Forget what we learned earlier; *this* will bring the entire church and our realm to ruin!"

Kai couldn't help but smirk. For a scholar, Lucretia had horrible near-sightedness when it came to Norzen. "What about all the good things the royal family has done over the years?" At everyone's confused looks, Kai raised three fingers and counted off.

He lowered the first finger. "Livoria has enjoyed unprecedented peace compared to the other realms of Alezon. Other than this current war, our only major conflicts have been the border scuffles with Corlati."

The second finger came down. "The Ardei family promoted the creation of new technologies and even shared them with other realms. Fusette's grandfather was the one to finance the invention of the steam engine and irrigation lines, after all."

The third finger. "And last, while there are issues, Livoria is still considered the Alezonian realm with the greatest opportunities for faumen. Even now, Galstein still refuses to grant noble titles to mixbloods. Here, any faumen, full- or mixblood, can advance in rank if they make suitable contributions to the good of the nation."

"That is true," Lucretia retorted, "but why keep it a secret for so long?"

Kai shrugged. "My best guess is the royal family fell into a cycle of tradition. Remember, rights for Norzen were much more constricted following the Desolation compared to now. Even I know this. It's possible they were worried about causing a panic, so preferred to keep everything under lock and key."

With her ears folded down, Fusette chimed in, "Gravebane is correct. It's one of the reasons I have argued so much for Norzen rights. Even though I've never been able to visit Duskmarsh, not a day goes by that I don't think about it. I hate that my family has kept this secret for so long. But Nerod is right. Once this gets out, our side will turn on itself and the war will fall to the Liberators."

It was Ione that stomped her foot down and thumped the duchess over the head with her fist, to Saredi's visible shock. "None of that, now." The tavern maid berated Fusette for assuming the worst outcome. "Anyone with a lick of sense can see that you've worked hard to serve the Livorian people."

"That won't matter, girl," Adalbard interrupted from somewhere in the maze. Tuvi's muffled screams could be heard as well. "No one will desire a Norzen on the throne, no matter how noble her intentions. Many will call for her head."

It became apparent Orelia was at her breaking point when she snatched Kai's loaded crossbow from his side and moved to wander into the archives in search of the former bishop.

Deciding it was safer to stop her, Kai held the priestess back with one arm. Teos met his glance and took hold of Orelia while Kai turned back to

Fusette. "Don't listen to that blowhard. And don't let the fact that you're Norzen hold you down. The circumstances of someone's birth have little bearing on their future. Their identity is determined by how one chooses to live their life. And from what I've seen, you've proven beyond a doubt your kindness and generosity."

Ignoring Nerod and Adalbard's indignant scoffs, Kai dropped to one knee, his mace head-down on the floor. "It wouldn't matter a whit if you were Norzen, Aerivolk, human, or anything else. Even knowing the truth, you're still the rightful Grand Duchess and the best person to lead us. Thus, as an Exarch Knight, my duty is to serve and protect you and our people to the best of my ability."

The rest of the party, sans Lucretia, raised their weapons and cheered. The boisterous ovation echoed in the labyrinth. Morgan moved over to Lucretia and patted her shoulder. "Hey lass, I know yer feeling pretty stung right now." The scholar glowered and shoved his hand off. "Look, the way I see it, ya can either sit on your rump and let your beef with the Norzen eat at ya, or ya can let it go long enough for us to get out of here."

Without responding, Lucretia stared straight ahead, glaring at the tomes on the shelf as if they had offended her. After almost a minute, she stood straight and faced Fusette. "I want to discuss this further after we have escaped. For now, I will put my thoughts aside so we may get everyone to safety." The duchess thanked Lucretia for her assistance.

"How sweet," Nerod chortled, stepping out from behind a shelf on the far end of the aisle. "What a shame none of you will leave here alive."

A dark laugh came from Teos. "In case you've forgotten, we outnumber and outmatch you, Nerod."

From behind Nerod came another voice. "Outnumbered, perhaps. But I'd like to see how well you can stand against *me* in battle." It was a deep baritone that sent shivers down Kai's spine. He knew that voice.

"Bloody Nulyma," Kai hissed, seeing Duarte's hulking form step into the light. "And here I was hoping things would be simple." The Soltauri towered over Nerod, and even looked to be a full head and a half taller than Teos.

He never expected to see Lucretia and Rialta run to the front, eyes bulging as they stared at the monk. "Duarte?!" the women yelled. "I-Is that you?"

Tilting his head to the side, Duarte examined the two before surprise spread over his face. "Sweet Cadell...Lu? Ria? Why are you both here?"

"What the piss, do you two know this guy?" Morgan fumed. Kai was also curious, but wary of allowing anyone to get within arm's reach of Duarte.

"We were all childhood friends," Lucretia explained. She explained that Duarte and his family worked the Citadel grounds back when she and Rialta were new students. "We played together on the canal walkways when he wasn't working with his parents. They left without saying a word not long after Nerod took over as Highmaster ten years ago."

The burly Soltauri turned to Nerod with a dead look in his eye. "Indeed. I certainly remember you. For someone who likes to gloat of your knowledge, you're remarkably ignorant."

A chill permeated the air as Nerod tapped the tip of his lantern pole against Duarte's chest. "You'd best watch your mouth, boy. Just because the Liberation Army sent you to help doesn't permit you to disrespect me like that."

"Is that so? I suppose it's unfortunate for you that I don't work for the Liberation Army. They're nothing but convenient allies that happen to hate me just for being different, much like you. And I shouldn't be surprised by your assistance to them thus far. It fits your history."

Rialta tried to push her way towards Duarte, demanding to know what he was talking about, only for Ione to hold her back. Morgan grabbed hold of Orelia, who swore up a storm when Adalbard scuttled out from around the corner, Tuvi still in his grasp and his staff pressed against her head. Orelia hissed but stayed still, earning a smug smirk from the priest.

Kai watched Duarte yank the pole from Nerod's hands in one pull. The monk then craned his neck to meet Rialta's gaze. "I assume you've heard the rumors of students disappearing since the war started."

She nodded. "That's because of this pathetic waste. He's been dipping his fingers into the slave trade by abducting students and staff, selling them to Corlati and the Liberators."

Lucretia's hands flew to her mouth with a gasp, her rapier clattering to the floor. Rialta staggered backwards and fell on her rear while taking short, heavy breaths. "H-he was going to sell me to them."

Teos and Orelia growled and had to be pulled back by Kai. He warned them to calm down and wait for a better chance to deal with Nerod.

"It's rather pitiful, and not the first time he's done it either," Duarte continued.

"What do you mean?" Fusette asked.

"Why do you think I left the Citadel ten years ago?" Everyone paled. "Yes, the Highmaster decided he had no more use for my family and sold us to the slave traders. I never saw my parents again after they threw us in separate crates and sent us to the slave houses. It was several moons before my master took me in and saved me from the overseers."

A soft thump sounded when Lucretia dropped to her knees. Her eyes looked dead and void. Kai swore and knelt by her side, calling her name. There was no response. "Damn it," he whispered. "She's had too many shocks. Her mind's gone numb!"

Ione grabbed Lucretia by the shoulders and shook her, pleading with the younger woman to say something. The scholar's head bobbled around, but she didn't respond.

Shaking his head, Duarte scowled at Nerod. "You always were a lowlife. How the Parliament put you in the Highmaster's chair, I'll never know."

"I've always had friends in high places," Nerod responded. "They helped get me here, and in return I allowed their children to breeze through the Citadel's training unimpeded. Besides, some noble families needed help acquiring fresh slaves, and this was the perfect place to set up shop. Training them can be a pain, but it pays handsomely."

"Which proves your depravity and ignorance. You focus too much on immediate benefits without bothering to notice the deeper consequences. Much like your limited knowledge of the royal family."

Now everyone turned towards Duarte. "What are you blabbering about?" Nerod asked.

"My master has done extensive research on the Cacovis bloodline. Enough to learn the fates of both her sons, instead of just one."

"What!? What do you mean *both sons*?" Nerod looked as though he'd been trout slapped.

The monk fingered the lantern pole in his hands, giving Nerod a cocky smirk. "I fail to see why it concerns you. After all..." Before anyone could move, Duarte grabbed Nerod by the throat and rammed the spade at the bottom of the pole through the Highmaster's chest. The spade exploded from Nerod's back in a spray of crimson, with the pole's lantern clanging to the ground. Nerod choked out a gasp as the makeshift spear pierced him.

"You won't be alive long enough to care."

The library echoed with the clamor coming from everyone. Adalbard blubbered, unable to tear his eyes from the gruesome scene. His grip on Tuvi loosened enough for the girl to bite down on the priest's arm. He shrieked in pain and clutched at the wound as Tuvi barreled into Orelia's waiting arms. The two held each other and sobbed, Teos putting himself between them and the priest.

"That little wretch! I'll kill her!" Adalbard shouted, waving his staff at the party.

Nerod gurgled while struggling against Duarte's iron grip. A red stain bloomed over his shirt while his face turned blue.

Kai watched as Nerod was lifted, legs kicking out to no avail, only to be thrown like a child's doll against a shelf with a crash. The entire shelf tipped over and collapsed, sending glass and hundreds of tomes and scrolls scattering across the floor. The party covered their eyes from the wave of dust washing over them.

The area around Kai darkened. Looking up, he saw Maple spreading her arms, using her wings as a shield. After the dust subsided, the air became still. Kai saw Duarte standing over Nerod's body, his arms clapped together as he whispered. The corpulent scholar didn't twitch.

After a moment, Duarte turned to face the party with a confident smirk. "I've wanted to do that for ten years. Now that the waste has been dealt with," he said, "we can continue. Master discovered the travel logs of a Wind Saint laying amongst a pile of dusty old tomes in Corlati. Dolmaru, if my memory is correct." Fusette's eyes widened. "In it, he described how the Saints wished for Erklaus, Cacovis's eldest, to assume the throne as he was already a grown man with a family. However, he refused and took his family into the swamps of Livoria with the other Norzen, where they founded the city of Duskmarsh. After Erklaus left, it was left to Tobiris, the younger son, to take the mantle his brother refused. According to the logs, the new Grand Duke was only fifteen years of age when he took the throne. Afterwards, the brothers never spoke again."

Kai and Fusette shared a look but said nothing. The longer Duarte talked, the longer they had to devise a plan.

"After reading the log, Master made subtle inquiries within Duskmarsh, trying to discover where Erklaus's line ended. He passed himself off as a historian performing research to evade suspicion. It was fortunate that Norzen are so proud of their heritage. It was easy to use that to his advantage. Even though Master never met Erklaus's descendant at first, his fellow Norzen were aware of the man's lineage and outed him without a second thought. Master told me he was amused to find Ulfrik, the last adult of Erklaus' direct line, slaving away as a weaver of all things."

"Very interesting history lesson," said Saredi, "but it makes no difference to us. What does it matter how the man earned his keep?"

"Oh, his profession wasn't what Master was interested in. What he cared about was the man's family. Including a wife and infant son."

Striding forward, Fusette stood next to Saredi, pulling a small dagger from her belt. "Why was your benefactor searching for the descendants of Cacovis? I mean, it's clear he knows where I am, but why search out Erklaus's family?"

Duarte chuckled. "That happens to lead into why he sent me here in the first place. See, my true mission is to bring any and all heirs of Cacovis back. He'd prefer you alive, of course, but I'm permitted to kill if you resist too much. That blithering fool Nerod also let slip that the journal of another Wind Saint was hidden in the Citadel. I'll be taking that as well."

Kai and Saredi crossed their weapons in front of Fusette. The duchess held the tome in her arms tight, eyes darting back and forth. "You better be prepared for a fight then. I'm not the same person I was back at Mistport," Kai challenged.

When he saw the others staring in confusion, Kai admitted that he and Duarte fought just before the invasion.

"Oh don't worry, Kaigo, you'll be coming as well."

"Eh?" Kai's tails twitched as he processed what he heard.

Maple raised her bow and aimed at Duarte's head; her feathers ruffled. "What in bloody Nulyma are you talking about?" she demanded.

"I informed Master about you after our battle. He found you rather fascinating. Especially when I mentioned you were raised in Havenfall by humans."

A sinking feeling grew in Kai's gut. "Why would he care about that?"

Duarte reached for his axe and twirled it in one hand like a stick. "Because after he found Ulfrik, my master offered him more prestigious work. When the man refused, Master hunted him down like an animal. The fool fled into the forests with his family. After several days of running with little rest, they were caught near the Great Ardei River. My master killed Ulfrik and his wife…but was unable to find any evidence of the boy."

Kai's face turned pallid, and his stomach felt as if it were tied into a bowknot.

"I see you understand. The evidence suggests that *you* are the lucky child who escaped my master's blade 22 years ago."

Kai would be the first to admit he harbored a curiosity about where he came from. Things like who his real parents were and what they did. He loved the Travaldi family, but that niggling sense of abandonment followed him for years. Like a hound that refused to give up the chase.

Now he wondered whether that curiosity was worth it to learn the truth like this.

"Kaigo, just as the Grand Duchess is the last descendant of Tobiris, you are the last of the Erklaus line."

CHAPTER XXVII

The Royal Archives were as silent as a grave after the latest revelation. Seven pairs of eyes locked onto Kai, as Lucretia remained nonresponsive on the ground. The apothecary stood still, reflecting on the new information. Finding out he was likely related to the most infamous heretic of the church was jarring. Ever since he was old enough to realize how different he was from everyone else, Kai imagined how he would react should he ever discover the truth about his birth parents.

If Duarte's information was correct, and Kai had little logical reason to refute it, many of the answers he agonized over for much of his life lay in the pages of the journal Fusette hid behind them. Part of him was desperate to know the journal's contents at once. The rest of him was scared of what truths he might find.

"You're rather quiet," Duarte noted. "How does it feel, knowing you're descended from someone your entire country deems a heretic and a monster?"

"Yes, it's a shock. The most shocking part is learning the Grand Duchess is a distant relative. However, I fail to see how my feelings are your concern. You do work for the man who supposedly murdered my parents, after all," Kai replied. He had no intention of revealing what they learned from the small bit of the journal Lucretia translated.

The others whispered amongst each other, some of them shooting Kai odd looks. Kai's ears twitched, picking up soft muttering from Lucretia. The others shook her by the shoulders, trying to snap her from her shocked state.

"You know, Kaigo, my master took meticulous notes during his research. If you come quietly, I could inquire on your behalf for him to share them. I might even be able to convince him to spare you and the duchess. You proved a worthy adversary. As a warrior, I appreciate a good sparring partner. It'd be a shame to see you slaughtered, as I suspect my master wishes."

Kai's eyes shifted to the party. They were all watching, and he couldn't blame them. On the surface, it sounded like a good deal. He questioned the notes' authenticity, but the chance to learn the tiniest bit of his past was tantalizing.

His gaze met Ione's and he was stricken dumb. The tavern maid looked at him with tears streaming down her cheeks. She mouthed "Please" over and over. Sweeping over the rest of the party, they all watched in nervous anticipation, except for Lucretia. Seeing her so lifeless was disconcerting. Kai wondered how they could reach her.

Tuvi stared at him in wonder, and his thoughts returned to when he first met her at Stahl Granz. The image of her and Dannel playing together wracked his mind, and he fought to blink back tears of his own. He saw the stump where her hand once was and grit his teeth.

A quiet sniffle tickled his ears, turning his eyes towards Maple at the end of the line. The merchant smiled, her eyes shining. Kai bit his own tongue to keep quiet.

Suddenly, he heard it. Her voice was soft and gentle, like a touch of cotton in his ears. Three simple, but powerful, words:

"I trust you."

"Well, what's it going to be?" Duarte pressed. He stood over Nerod's corpse, tapping his hoof with arms crossed.

Kai knew he wouldn't get this chance again unless he somehow ran into Duarte's master. However, he also knew from the start what his answer would be. No matter how seductive the offer, his conviction refused to waver. He would never renege on his oath. "The offer is tempting, Duarte. However, I must decline."

The Soltauri monk chuckled. "A pity," he said, "and here I hoped you would see reason, but it appears you're just as much a fool as the man who sired you. I suppose I'll have to take you both back by force, along with the journal."

Fusette glanced down at the book in her hand. Kai wondered what was going through her mind, and why she opted to hold onto Galen's journal while hiding Cacovis'. Would she hand it over? He doubted it.

What he wasn't prepared for was for Fusette to lash out with her dagger and strike the lantern frame in Saredi's hand with the pommel. Shattered glass flew everywhere. Duarte slid into a stance, but the Duchess ignored him and snatched the thick candle from the frame. She matched Duarte's gaze and held the candle under the tome, just far enough away to keep the journal from catching fire.

"You say your master wants this? Perhaps I should turn it into ash," Fusette warned.

Duarte blanched. "You wouldn't dare!"

Dropping to his knee, Saredi pleaded with Fusette to stop. "Your Grace, what are you thinking?" he asked in a desperate tone. "That journal is a sacred relic of our history! You can't destroy it."

"I'd rather see it burned than fall into the hands of these monsters."

"You play a dangerous game woman," Duarte cautioned. "If you damage that tome, I can't be responsible for what happens."

The tension in the air was thicker than lard. Fusette stared hard at Kai, who matched her gaze until she tilted her head towards the party. Taking the hint, he joined the others and continued trying to revive Lucretia.

On the opposite end of the aisle, Duarte and Adalbard muttered to each other. Kai could hear bits and pieces of their argument over how to retrieve the journal. The only undamaged lanterns left were with Teos and Ione, leaving Duarte's side of the aisle in the fading light of their broken torch.

"Damn it all," Kai snapped. No matter what he tried, Lucretia wouldn't respond to any stimulus. He'd tried pinching, poking, shaking, even smelling salts, yet nothing worked. "I'm almost out of options."

He felt a soft breeze when Morgan leaned in and whispered an idea in Kai's ear. The apothecary's eyes furrowed, and he gave Morgan an unamused stare. "No way. I may be a lot of things, but stupid isn't one of them. You do it. If I did that and it worked, I wouldn't have to worry about Duarte, because *she'd* kill me first!"

The sellsword shrugged. "Fair point. Turn her towards me."

A heavy clomp rang through the aisle. Kai spun to see Duarte marching towards Fusette. He ordered the party to prepare for escape. He would help the duchess. The moment Kai started running, he heard a deafening slap echo as Morgan struck Lucretia's cheek with an open palm. Judging by the enraged screams now coming from the scholar, Kai was willing to admit the sellsword's unorthodox treatment worked.

Taking a step back, Fusette ordered Duarte to stop. The monk's response was to throw all caution to the wind and continue advancing with a huff. Smirking, Fusette lifted the candle and watched the tome's corner burst into flame.

The reaction was immediate. Duarte charged with a furious roar, head lowered and intent on trampling Fusette. Rather than stand still, Fusette dove sideways while flinging the burning tome down the aisle. The journal hit the floor with a smack, sliding into the wall.

Duarte proved more agile than his frame suggested. He pivoted on one hoof and leapt over the prone duchess. His strides were long and powerful, taking him the full 30 yards in moments. He scooped the tome up and slapped it against his trouser legs, desperate to extinguish the fire.

With Adalbard opting to observe from afar, Kai had no one blocking him from Fusette. He helped her up, scanning for injuries. Other than dust and dirt on her clothes and cheeks, she looked fine.

"Ow! Enough, you daft woman! That hurts!" Morgan cried out while trying to shield himself from the furious Archivist chasing him with a massive brick of a tome, a bright red handprint covering her cheek. Kai's eyes bulged. *How in the winds can she swing that?*

Lucretia didn't seem too bothered by the weight, considering she easily kept up with the fleeing mixblood, swinging the book at his head. "Get back here and take your beating like a man!" she shouted. "I will teach you what real pain is!"

When Saredi put himself between the two, Kai felt his respect for the noble go up. It took stones to face Lucretia's temper at its peak. "Enough! You can discuss this after we escape. Until then, you will acquit yourselves like adults or you'll answer to me. Understood?" Kai was stunned to see both nodding with lowered heads.

He lost his footing, almost toppling onto his face when Duarte gave a bellow and stomped hard enough to make the ground quake. He flung the burning tome over the shelves, his attempts to save the journal fruitless. A rush of air soon came from that direction, a plume of smoke rising above the shelves. Kai swore and shouted, "Fire! Run for the exit, the archives are on fire!"

Chest heaving, Duarte regarded the two Norzen with a fierce glare.

"You," he whispered. Every step forward was methodical and heavy. Dust rose in tiny clouds with each stomp. His eyes burned red like crackling coals.

Muttering a curse, Kai wondered if the monk had slipped into a Frenzy Haze.

Duarte raised his axe and pointed it at Fusette. "You just destroyed a valuable artifact, woman. One that was a vital objective for my mission. My master will not be pleased. I'm bringing you back alive, but don't think for a moment that you will go unharmed."

Inhaling deep, Kai settled his breathing and gave the mace a quick twirl. He slid in front of Fusette, rolling his shoulders back and slipping into a battle stance. It was a movement practiced hundreds of times over the years. The action felt natural and smooth after the frequent fighting he found himself in since Mistport.

"If you want *her*, Duarte, you'll have to step over my rotting corpse," Kai challenged.

"That can be arranged, Kaigo. Don't forget, you needed a tree to fend me off last time. That won't save you now."

"I don't need anything special to deal with you. Compared to Grimghast, you're just an old weed that needs pulling." Tilting his head, Kai commanded the party to protect Fusette and Saredi during their escape.

Maple's voice called back, "What about you? I refuse to leave you here!"

"I've got a bone to pick with this sorry bastard, Maple. And I'll ram it down his throat if I must. Now go! I'll be behind you soon." Saredi beckoned the group to follow, and everyone fled into the archives, leaving Kai facing Duarte and Adalbard alone.

A grim laugh came from the Soltauri monk. "You seem rather blood-thirsty compared to our previous meeting. Is your true fur showing through? Adalbard! I want you to delay those fools. Use the general's idea he gave you. We can afford to run wild." The priest nodded and hobbled after the party.

"I wouldn't say this is my true fur," Kai answered. He trusted the others could handle the old priest without his aid. "But there's a big difference between trying to kill me and going after my friends."

Duarte burst into heaving laughter, needling Kai for thinking there was any difference between the two. "Either way, you and your pathetic friends are all going to die tonight, though your end will be slow and painful."

Kai's response was to waggle his finger at the monk and utter two words. "Prove it."

Fusette found herself nestled between Saredi and Teos as the group maneuvered through the archives. The Lord Chamberlain muttered to himself at such a speed that, even with her strong hearing, Fusette could barely understand him. The rest of the party followed in a loose arch, Rialta sticking close to Lucretia and Orelia leading Tuvi along by her remaining hand.

The sounds of battle raged behind them. Sharp clangs rent the air. Fusette hadn't heard any pained shouts. With luck, that meant Kai was keeping up with Duarte. Thinking of their size difference, the duchess was impressed.

Such an odd turn of events this evening, Fusette thought. *I came here to enlist aid for the war effort and conduct research. Instead, I discover my top scholar is a traitor, who then gets murdered in front of me. More important, I may have found a family member I never knew of.*

She shivered thinking of the Highmaster's death. While she had attended a few executions during her reign, never had Fusette been so close to such a grisly scene. It unnerved her and made her wonder how Kai managed to hold himself together seeing so much blood.

If Kai *was* the last descendant of Erklaus, though, then perhaps she wasn't as alone in the world as she believed. Ever since her father's passing, there was an empty void in her heart. She had never met her mother, in part thanks to Parliament's constant squabbling. The only reason she believed her father chose the woman to bear his child was due to her great beauty among the tribe. All knowledge of her conception was kept absolute secret until after her birth. As soon as she was born, her mother was given no chance to ever hold her before Fusette was whisked off to Whistlevale under the cloak of darkness. Due to their secret, multiple heirs within the royal family were rare. Fusette knew suppressing the loneliness and heartache was foolish, but she allowed her royal duties to take precedence over any desire for true family.

And now, in a single night, everything she knew was flipped on its head.

"Get down, Fusette!" Teos shouted, throwing himself atop the young woman and shielding her. A loud crash rang out, followed by the prickling of broken glass falling around her. Fusette gazed up with wide eyes. A single arrow was lodged in a thick tome, level with the height of her head a moment ago. She noticed an expanding orange glow coming from the arrow, and a burning strip of cloth tied beneath the head.

Someone was shooting flaming arrows at them!

Adalbard's sharp voice came from around the corner. "Blast!" The old priest nocked another arrow and let fly, aiming at the prone duchess. Saredi shouted a warning, rushing in desperation to protect Fusette.

Clang!

Everyone stared at the iron pan in front of Fusette's face. Ione, eyes blazing in fury, had used it as a shield to deflect the arrow into the ground, where its flame sputtered out.

Fusette heard a growl and looked over. Orelia gripped her staff, barreling off in pursuit. Ione shouted for her to stop, but the priestess ignored the plea and continued sprinting after Adalbard, who fled in terror. Tuvi cried out for Orelia, her eyes flowing with tears. Fusette took the girl in her arms and held her close.

"Damn it all!" Saredi said. "Someone needs to go after her."

"I'll do it," Teos offered, helping Fusette to her feet. "Morgan, keep an eye on Lady Fusette and Tuvi. You've got the best reflexes of us all except Kai."

"I hear ya," Morgan replied. "Watch yerself. That bastard may be old, but he's damned sneaky when he wants to be." Teos nodded, dashing after Orelia.

Fusette asked her advisor where he was leading them. "Saredi, isn't the exit the other way? Why are we heading deeper into the archives with the fire spreading?"

"True, but one of the benefits of my position is knowing certain things even you aren't privy to, Your Grace. For example, an escape passage hidden in the Royal Archives. It was built by your ancestor, Duke Tebalect, for such an occasion as this. Knowledge of its existence has been entrusted to each Lord Chamberlain upon assuming the post and is why they're required to accompany the sitting monarch whenever they visit these archives."

A loud yelp sounded from behind, followed by a loud crash and feminine screams. "I think Teos found our holy woman," Morgan quipped. Orelia's enraged shouts echoed from labyrinth. "And she sounds pissed."

Clearing his throat, Saredi reminded the party they still needed to reach the exit. "We are not far now, but I'm unsure if the others can still make it."

Fusette grabbed Saredi by the ear and tugged hard. "Absolutely not! We are leaving together, understood?"

The Vesikoi noble pulled away from Fusette with a hiss, rubbing his now crimson ear. He scolded the duchess, warning her that if the fire spread too far, then getting everyone out would be nearly impossible. In the background, the sound of Orelia ordering Teos to put her down drowned out the fire's crackle.

Now we wait for Kai, Fusette thought.

"I know this is hard for you to believe, Saredi, but I trust Gravebane. In six years of service, despite every manner of trial put before him by Parliament, he hasn't failed me once. If anyone can win this, it's him."

"Very well, Your Grace. If you are willing to put your faith in him, then I shall do the same. Now perhaps we should assist Sir Teos before the good Sister Orelia pummels him with that staff of hers."

Fusette felt something tug at her cloak. Thinking it was Tuvi, she instead saw Ione twiddling her fingers together and staring at the floor. After seeing the older woman's intensity in protecting her from Adalbard's arrow, her current timid look was surprising.

"What's wrong, Ione?" Fusette asked.

"Um, Fusette, I hesitate to bring this up but... have you seen Maple?" Fusette blinked. Sweeping the aisle, she realized Ione was correct. The Aerivolk merchant was gone.

"Oh dear."

Sweat dripped into Kai's mane as he ducked beneath a double handed swing of Duarte's axe, shattering another shelf into splinters and shards of glass. The itch was maddening. It felt like having dozens of tiny bugs skittering inside his fur.

But he had no time to address it. Duarte's assault was relentless, keeping Kai on the defensive and unable to counter or breathe. Each swing of his mace was parried with ease. Not only that, but every blow that Kai parried in return left his bones ringing. The one fortunate thing was that Duarte was too slow to land a clean hit. After battling Grimghast, Kai's reflexes and agility were sharper than ever.

Whether that would be enough to bring Duarte down, he wasn't sure.

"You don't seem to be putting much effort into this," said the monk. "Perhaps you're not as strong as you believed."

"I'll be the first to admit there are many people stronger than me, yourself included" Kai replied, "but most battles are never won on strength alone. You make assumptions like that, Duarte, and you'll be proven an ass in the end."

Duarte shifted to a one-handed stance, freeing up his left arm to throw an awkward punch. Kai trailed back, using the mace to brush aside the flimsy attack. A jab from the monk's axe was stopped when Kai grabbed the spike, pushing it away.

Duarte smirked and yanked the axe back. With his fingers still wrapped around the spike, Kai was brought off-balance by the sudden change in momentum when his body moved forward. Duarte prepared another swing, raising his arm to split Kai's head like a melon.

Gritting his teeth, Kai tensed his leg and pushed off. Slamming his shoulder into Duarte's chest, the monk was pushed back enough for Kai to throw an underhanded swing at his knee. The attack connected with a loud crack. Duarte yowled in pain, giving Kai an opportunity he knew he couldn't waste.

He threw a wide right hook, striking the monk in the throat. The blow sent Duarte reeling back. Emboldened, Kai swung the mace again, this time just under the rib cage. The weapon dented Duarte's breastplate, jarring his kidney on that side and bringing him to his knees. Trying to gulp down large breaths, the monk bent over and retched all over the floor.

Kai took the chance to compose himself. He backed away, drinking deep from his canteen. Sweat dripped from his body. The fire was growing in intensity by the moment. Kai wasn't sure how long he could fight in this sweltering heat. He needed to end this!

A soft twang came from behind and Kai felt a sharp pinch in his right shoulder. Gritting his teeth, he reached back and felt the shaft of an arrow. He turned around and spotted Adalbard smirking, a recurve bow in his hands.

Damn it, I let my guard down!

Kai didn't have time to think before Duarte's roar rattled his ears and he felt the flat side of the Soltauri's axe smash into his side. His back struck a shelf before collapsing onto his belly, the air driven from his lungs. Kai bit his lip and gripped the arrow, tearing it from his shoulder. The coppery taste of blood spread through his mouth after his teeth tore his lip open.

The clop of Duarte's hoof stamping the ground was accompanied by the two men's dark laughter. "Not so tough, are you, peltneck?" Adalbard sneered.

"Oh sure," Kai responded, his eye twitching, "because everyone knows two against one is a fair shake. Also, I'm getting *real* sick of that word."

Kai's chest flared with pain when Duarte's hoof slammed into his sternum. The hit sent him rolling down the aisle. "I suggest you watch your tongue. Take that tone with Master, and he might just rip it from your mouth."

Reaching up to his battered ribs, he pressed a finger against the muscle and winced. *Well, at least one rib is broken. That's going to make fighting a pain. Taen! I refuse to go out like this.* He promised Maple and the others he would see them. He would not break that promise after making it so far! A muffled jingle reached his ears. Clutching at his waist, Kai felt the smooth stone of his vials hooked into the wolf fur. *Wait, that's it!*

Once again, the sound of Duarte's approach rang in Kai's ears. He tugged a vial from his robe and prayed to Tapimor that it was the right one. Opening his hand, he saw the marking and felt a spark of hope. A flick of the thumb popped the cork off as he downed a gulp of water from his canteen, followed by the vial's contents.

"Oh no, you don't!" Duarte taunted, wrapping a broad hand around Kai's throat and lifting him level with the monk's own face. "I'm not letting you take one of your damned tonics. Spit it out."

Puffing his cheeks, Kai clawed at Duarte's hand and tried forcing it open enough to let him breathe. His lungs burned and the pressure on his throat made thinking difficult. Everything turned blurry and the monk's nails dug into his throat like tiny razor blades.

"You're a stubborn one, aren't you? I said spit it out!"

Kai chuffed. If Duarte wanted it that badly, he'd get his wish. With some effort, he hooked both hands around the monk's arm and lifted himself. Grinning, Kai inhaled through his nose and spat a scarlet mist into Duarte's face.

The pressure on Kai's throat vanished. Duarte clawed at his eyes, screaming and thrashing about. His axe lay forgotten on the stone floor. Adalbard's exuberance turned into horror as the monk's bellows grew louder. Duarte pulled his hands away long enough for Kai to see his eyes blazing red and inflamed. Mucus oozed from his nose and tears streamed down his face in rivulets.

"My eyes! My eyes are on fire! What did you do to me, you fucking bastard!" His fingers dug gashes into the skin around his eyes, sending splatters of blood over the ground. Unable to see, he lashed out with one arm trying to hit Kai, but none of his wild blows landed.

Kai's ears twitched. The sound of an arrow being drawn back reminded him of the other threat. Grabbing the nearest tome and holding it close, he spun and felt his hands pushed back when the arrow buried into the leather and parchment. The pain in his rib flared, but Kai refused to let the old priest see him flinch.

"What did you do, you filthy peltneck?" Adalbard demanded.

"Hey, he told me to spit it out. Don't blame me because he didn't know I had cappara dust in my mouth."

The priest shouted an expletive while reaching for another arrow, swearing to kill Kai if it was the last thing he did.

An angered trill echoed from behind. "I don't think so!"

Adalbard twisted towards the voice, snapping his arrow's shaft while pulling it from the quiver. He wasn't given another chance, as Maple crashed into the priest talons-first.

Her weight carried Adalbard into the wall. Kicking off, she shredded the priest's robes, staining the floor with blood.

"Maple?!" asked Kai. "What are you doing here? I told you to escape."

"Well that's a fine howdy-do for someone who just saved your ass," she replied. Stomping forward, she grabbed Kai by the mane and pulled his face dangerously close to hers. He fought back the blush threatening to erupt on his cheeks. Maple's face was close enough he could see the texture of her lips. "Like I mentioned before, you're never alone. Besides, I *know* I said we weren't leaving without ya. Now sew your lip and let's get."

The sound of a blade scraping over stone rang out. The two turned to see Duarte lifting his axe and charging. "You aren't going anywhere except your graves," he roared.

Kai groaned. He gestured for Maple to step aside and faced the rampaging monk. Bending down, Kai dived into a roll that carried him under the Soltauri's wide swing. He bit his lip, fighting the swelling pain in his chest.

"Here's the thing, Duarte... I have no intention of letting you decide when I die!"

Still partially blinded, Duarte barreled headlong into the shelf. He turned and swung again but didn't come close to hitting his target. Kai threw an overhand swing with the mace, striking Duarte's shoulder. The blow staggered him, letting Kai press forward.

He knew Duarte was tough, and a single blow wouldn't be enough to finish him. Spinning into the monk's blind spot, Kai aimed for the same kidney as before and heard a satisfying clang when the flanges struck armor.

Duarte dropped to his knees, holding one hand against his battered side and the other wiping at his eyes. He was left defenseless when Kai gripped the mace in both hands and swung it dead center into Duarte's chest, sending him flying back. Adalbard swore and abandoned the monk, stumbling away towards the archive entrance.

All around them the inferno transformed the archives into a sea of red and yellow. The oppressive heat made Kai feel sluggish and he noticed Maple struggling to cope as well.

"Maple, I think you had the right idea. Let's pound dirt. I'd rather not become a broiled steak," said Kai.

"Thank the winds. The pan-fried chicken look doesn't suit me in the least. I think Saredi led them this way."

The pair dashed off, leaving the unconscious Duarte. With his injuries, Kai would be amazed if the man escaped the blaze alive. Plus the hit he landed on Duarte's shoulder would bring the monk bigger problems. The fire was growing at a pace even a healthy person would find difficult to evade.

Kai followed Maple through the burning aisles. The further they went, the more sporadic the fires. When he asked if she could view the archives from the air, she skidded to a stop. Kai tried to swerve himself around her, but the distance between them was too short. He crashed into Maple, and both tumbled to the ground.

"Ouch. That stung. Sorry, Maple," Kai apologized. He wondered why the fall didn't hurt as much as expected.

"No, I should be the one who's sorry. I was so surprised I forgot you were right behind me. Could you do me a favor, though?"

"Sure, anything."

"I reckon I'll hold you to that later, but could ya get up please? You're kinda heavy."

Only then did Kai realize he had fallen on top of the prone merchant. His cheeks crimson, Kai's mind drifted back to their first meeting.

"We really need to stop ending up like this," groaned Kai. Scrambling to his feet, he pulled Maple up, using his free hand to nurse his injured rib.

"Agreed. Now as for your idea, I could spot them from the air, but I'd need to get on top of the shelves first. I can stay in the air for a few seconds at most, if I have height to start with."

"I thought Aerivolk could stay in the air for almost a minute."

"Fullbloods can. Given my family, I'm a fair amount heavier, so my body is harder to keep airborne. Most fullbloods are at least a head shorter and a stone lighter than me."

Kai's face burned red. "Apologies. I should've realized that."

The merchant giggled, tapping Kai on the nose with a long finger. "Quit that. I'm not mad. We taught each other there's nothing wrong with being different. Now quit moping and help me get up."

"I'll do you one better. Hop on"

Maple tilted her head. In response, Kai dropped to one knee and patted his shoulders. He saw the eager spark in her eyes as she stepped into place and rested both talons on his shoulders.

Taking a breath, Kai ignored the sting in his ribs and stood, lifting Maple above his head. She spread her wings and jumped, giving a powerful flap. The gust kicked up a cloud of dust and embers. Kai watched her use her wings to spin her body in midair twice before giving a triumphant chirp and dropping back into his arms.

"I see them! They're at the very back. And it looks like everyone is together."

"They haven't left yet?"

"I reckon they're waiting for us. The good news is there's a clear path, so follow me." Maple giggled when Kai gave her a salute, his face split by a wide grin. "By the winds, you're still the same fool I met back in that grove."

"What do you mean by that?" he asked.

She looked at him with the same peppy, lopsided smile he remembered from that day. A small tremor traveled down his spine, arcing across his body and leaving a tingle in his fingertips. Maple tapped his cheek and stuck her tongue out before answering.

"Think about it."

"He has no idea how lucky he is. If anything happened to Maple because she went back for that idiot, I would have turned him into a rug!" Lucretia muttered to Rialta. Her voice was muffled by the fire, but Kai still heard her with little trouble. Rialta was doing her best to talk down the miffed scholar, but that only stoked Lucretia's ranting.

Following Maple's lead, the pair reached the others with little trouble. The only thing keeping them from leaving was Saredi searching for the right brick in the wall to open the escape passage.

When Kai whispered to Maple what Lucretia said, she scoffed. "For someone so smart, she sure acts dumb when it comes to you. If you ask me, I reckon we need to get that woman a man of her own. Maybe that'd get the stick out of her rear," she muttered. Kai fought to hold back the laughter in his gut. A small snicker still passed his lips, drawing Lucretia's sharp gaze for a moment.

Rather than risk saying anything that would get him in trouble, Kai decided to help Saredi. Strolling next to him, Kai asked how he could help.

"Actually, there is a lever in that direction, now that I think about it," said the noble, pointing off to the left. "If you would be so kind as to pull it while I locate the exit, I would appreciate it." Kai jogged along the wall, scanning the area.

Finding the lever was easy. It was a long, wooden pole built into a thin slot in the wall, a yard above the ground. Kai grabbed hold of the handle and pulled down. It didn't budge, but his rib started to complain about the movement.

Frowning, Kai gripped with both hands and yanked, throwing his whole weight behind it. Not only did the lever *not* move but Kai's hold slipped, sending him slamming onto the ground. He hissed and clutched at his rib.

"This might be harder than I thought," Kai grumbled. "Hey Teos, I need an extra hand over here!"

An amused chuckle came from the smuggler, who ran over and asked what Kai was having trouble with.

"The damned lever is stuck."

"Stuck?" asked Teos. "Shove off and let me try." Grabbing hold, Teos pulled down hard. His hand slipped, just as Kai's had, but his position caused him to lurch forward and hit the wall with his head.

"Gah! Son of a land-sucking *gresaro*!" the smuggler hissed, nursing his reddening forehead.

Kai couldn't hold back his cackles. "Harder than it looks, right? Also, what in Finyt is a *gresaro*?" A shout of victory came from Saredi as he found the right brick.

"It's Soltish, the tongue of my tribe," Teos answered as the pair grabbed the lever together. "As for what it means, let's just say it's not a word for polite company." Leaning over, the smuggler whispered the meaning into Kai's ear.

Eyes widening, Kai shot Teos an incredulous grin. "And you kiss your mother with that mouth?"

"Trust me, if my Maman knew I said that, she'd drown me." The two men shared a look before laughing. Kai felt the tension leave his body. Even in this precarious situation, having something to laugh about helped him believe they'd get out fine.

Together, they pulled with all their might. Kai inhaled through his nose, straining against the lever. After a few seconds, the handle twitched downward.

"Just a bit more," said Teos. Kai felt his sweat beading in his mane as the fire inched towards them.

The party came running with Fusette and Saredi at the front. "Hey, quit slacking, you two. What's the trouble?" Orelia said. Kai muttered that the lever was stuck.

"We better hurry," Ione added, pointing to the encroaching flames. "If we don't leave soon, we're going to burn alive in here."

Tuvi wrapped her arms around Fusette and whimpered. "We're not gonna die, are we?" she asked.

Pulling the young Norzen close, Fusette whispered that everything would be fine.

"Morgan, get your ass over here and help!" Teos called. Before the sellsword could wrap a hand around the handle, Saredi stopped him.

"Perhaps I should have provided better instruction. That was my mistake, and I apologize."

Finally letting go of the lever and taking deep gulps of air, Kai and Teos shared a glance before turning on the chamberlain. "What are you talking about?"

"Observe." Without another word, Saredi grabbed the lever and pulled it *out* at an angle. The lever lowered with no effort after that.

That's why we couldn't get that thing to budge? Kai screamed at himself.

The women broke out into hysterics. Maple reached up and ruffled Kai's hair, but her smile was so contagious he couldn't bring himself to be upset, despite Tuvi pointing at him while laughing.

A low rumbling echoed through the room. Everyone stopped and spun in circles, searching for the noise's source.

"Don't be alarmed," said Fusette. "Look above us."

The party glanced up and saw a web of curved metal pipes stretching over the archives' ceiling. The central pipe was a yard across and reached from the back wall to the opposite end. Multiple smaller pipes half a yard across branched off from the central one every two yards with even smaller pipes branching from them. Lucretia peered at the pipes from different angles before recognizing the pattern.

"It looks like an irrigation line."

Fusette clapped her hands together with a smile. "Excellent observation, Lucretia. That's precisely what it is. Watch what happens."

The sound of rushing water reverberated in Kai's ears. Soon, tiny droplets fell from the spaces between the branch pipes and central pipe as water flooded the line. The open ends of the branches shook as water gushed out, raining over the fire.

"Wait, wait, what about all the tomes and scrolls? Won't the water ruin them?" Lucretia asked in open-mouthed shock.

Saredi laughed. "I'm happy to see you so concerned for the fate of the archives, Lady Dineri. Spoken like a true scholar. Do not worry, though. The glass doors on each shelf were crafted to seal water out in case of this very situation. I know some of the items may be beyond repair due to the fire, but we have additional copies of almost every tome here stored beneath the palace. We won't be able to replace these copies with new ones until after the war, I'm afraid."

"Do you believe any destroyed items were impossible to replace?"

The Lord Chamberlain stared hard at Fusette, who refused to meet the Vesikoi's eyes and whistled to herself. "I can think of several items that were one-of-a-kind and kept here for political reasons. Master Galen's journal, for one."

Lucretia looked ready to faint. "Truly? The Sage's journal is lost?"

"I watched Her Grace set fire to it, against my wishes, no less." Everyone turned to the woman in shock.

Fusette scanned the incredulous stares and bit her lip. Kai tilted his head, wondering how to approach the subject when the duchess exploded into laughter. The sudden mirth caused the group to share uneasy glances. Nobody seemed sure how to respond.

"Y-you all actually believed I destroyed it?" Fusette wheezed out.

Saredi blinked. "What do you mean, milady? I was standing there when you put it to the candle!"

"I shall have to thank Archbishop Jovanni when we return to Whistlevale. If there's one thing that man is good at, it's putting on a show." Kai watched as Fusette reached into her cloak and pulled out a pair of familiar books.

The apothecary sputtered. "Wait a tic, you kept both journals? How did you hide them?"

"It's a sleight of hand trick the Archbishop taught me from his days plying the bard's trade. While I was rummaging through the shelves, I made it look as though I was hiding Cacovis's journal in the shelf while burning Galen's in front of Duarte. What I really did was slip both into my sash, using other tomes of the same size as decoys. It's a common misdirection used by bards during a show. Having you all surround me made making the switch easy."

Saredi dropped to his knees, eyes staring at the ground without blinking. After a few moments of silence, he finally met Fusette's gaze. "Your Grace, please do not do that ever again. My poor heart might not be able to take it."

The duchess rolled her eyes and helped Saredi back up. "Oh hush, you old fish. You've still got another twenty good years in you."

With an indignant huff, Saredi straightened his robes and snapped a pivot on one foot with the execution of a sailor.

"If something like that happens again, milady, I may decide to retire before you cause my heart to fail. Now, I believe it's time we make our way back. Once the fire has subsided, we shall have men come down to determine the extent of the damage."

CHAPTER XXVIII

After the battle, Kai was exhausted. Rialta left once more to her quarters, this time with a signed note from the Grand Duchess and one of her personal apothecaries to tend her injuries. Saredi led the party to the duchess' lodgings near the Citadel. Despite everyone's steadfast intentions to return to their inn, Fusette refused to hear of it and ordered the party to step in line and follow. On the way back, she had Saredi tell the sailors to retrieve their belongings.

The building they arrived at was a small manor, triple the size of the inn. While the outside looked earthy and subdued for its size, the inside was lavish and decorative. Lush wool rugs lay across the floor. Cotton curtains dyed in violet and stitched with elaborate designs covered the windows. When Fusette brought them to her bedroom, they noticed the bed linens were made of silver silk. Everyone gaped at the extravagance and kept close with arms at their sides and eyes pointed downwards.

Kai stared at the luxurious bed and bit back an urge to crawl between the linens himself. His back was sore, and every muscle throbbed with pain. His ribs felt the worst, spasming at the slightest movement. The bed looked like Finyt brought to life. "Sweet Tapimor, I don't think I've hurt this much since the last time my old teacher decided to test my fighting skills," the apothecary sighed.

"Are you sure we're permitted to be here, Your Grace?" asked Ione. The tavern maid gripped the skirt of her dirndl with both hands, casting furtive glances at Fusette.

The royal smiled and threw herself backwards onto the bed, bringing a cheerful Tuvi with her. The girl squealed in joy as she snuggled into the blanket. "Of course. And for the last time, call me Fusette! If it wasn't for you all, I doubt Saredi and I would've escaped the Citadel alive tonight. Especially you, Ione. You saved my life, and I owe you a lot for that. I ask that you all make yourselves at home. If you don't, I'll simply make it an order."

"She sure likes bossing people around, doesn't she?" commented Morgan, earning Saredi's disapproving gaze.

"I don't take joy in it like you might think, Sir Morgan," replied Fusette, who sent the sellsword a confident smirk, "but sometimes being in charge does have its benefits."

Morgan guffawed, nearly toppling himself and Orelia over when he leaned back. "You sure don't mince words, do ya, Fusette?"

"Certainly not. I prefer to speak the truth rather than sweeten my words. If you want something layered with false sweetness, go eat a custard."

Everyone broke out into laughter, unable to hold back seeing the exaggerated haughty look on Fusette's face. Saredi shook his head and reminded the duchess to mind her decorum.

"Oh, posh to that, Saredi. We're among friends, aren't we? And not just friends, either," she said, giving Kai a sweet smile, "We're among family as well."

"Your Grace, we don't know for certain if that Duarte brute told the truth. For all we know, he was blowing airs about his master's search for Erklaus's family."

Cheeks puffed out, Fusette snatched Cacovis's journal from the side table where she placed the tomes, waggling it in the chamberlain's face. "What if it's true? We know from this that Erklaus existed. It's not a far reach to assume he refused the throne and went into hiding. The evidence is quite strong, given Kai's history. If that bastard *was* telling the truth, it means there is still life in the Cacovis line. It means I have true family, no matter how distant."

"Your Grace, you can't be considering endorsing Gravebane as a member of House Ardei. It was scandal enough when you made him an Exarch.

Parliament would call for your abdication, which they might do anyway! The palace floor would erupt into riots."

The more Kai thought about it, the more he wondered if Saredi was right. Even if it meant Fusette couldn't officially call him family, he didn't want anyone hurt because of him.

Fusette stared hard at the Vesikoi, meeting his eyes with a look of intense concentration. After a few minutes, she let out a small gasp. "Now I see what this is about." The party turned to see Fusette's cheeks flush with anger. "You don't want Kai to be considered a part of House Ardei because you think it interferes with the line of succession."

A hacking gasp came from the party, who watched as Lucretia jabbed a finger at Kai. "Wait a tic, she is right! If Lady Fusette performs the rite of acceptance, that would make Kai next in line for the throne!"

Silence reigned. Everyone turned to look at Kai, whose skin blanched to a shade appropriate for polished marble. "Oh no. I don't know the first thing about ruling a realm!"

"Damn right you don't," Saredi remarked. "I'll admit your battle prowess is exemplary, but you have neither the bearing nor training to be a true Grand Duke. Besides, acknowledging you would expose Her Grace's secret. We cannot allow that to be brought to light yet."

An unexpected knock on the door jarred everyone for a moment. Saredi ordered the visitor to enter. A sailor walked in and saluted, relaxing when Saredi requested his report.

"Lord Chamberlain, we've retrieved your guards' belongings and divided them into separate rooms. Also, a full search of the Royal Archives was performed as requested." Saredi waved for the man to continue. "There was significant damage to over half the materials, with less than a quarter of the shelves remaining undamaged. We also retrieved the body of the late Highmaster. However, there were no other bodies down there."

Kai's gaze snapped to the sailor. "What do you mean no other bodies?" he asked. "There should have been another one near Nerod's body: a Soltauri in Cadist monk attire."

The sailor shook his head. "There was nothing there when we searched. Perhaps the body was incinerated?"

"That's impossible. There wasn't enough time." Kai ran a finger through his mane and hissed. "Well damn, that means both those bastards might've escaped." Out of the corner of his eye, Kai watched Saredi dismiss the sailor and lock the door once more.

"You didn't think you could kill Duarte that easily, did you?" Lucretia asked, giving the apothecary an aloof glance. "I grew up knowing him, and even as a child, he had a stubborn streak wider than the sea. You may have knocked him out, but he's never been one to stay down long. Should we encounter him again, I'd prefer it if you let me handle it."

With a heavy sigh, Kai nodded his assent, "Very well, though he better hope his allies have a competent apothecary on hand or he won't last long. I'm quite certain I shattered his shoulder, and if not treated soon, an infection could kill him." Everyone gaped at Kai, stunned silent by the admission. "Something in my tails says he'll survive through pure willpower, regardless. I will say he seems devoted to this master of his. Even if you knew each other as children, it's possible he won't listen. There's no telling what happened in those Corlatian slave houses and how it affected him."

"I understand your concern but thank you for allowing me to handle this my way. And you are correct about his injury. Duarte is too bullheaded to let something so simple kill him. I am sure I can reach him."

Before Kai could respond, Maple cut in with a firm chirp, "Just cause we're letting you handle him if there's a next time, doesn't mean we plan on leaving you alone. If he does anything to threaten you, we're stepping in and helping. *All of us.* Are we clear?"

The rest of the party nodded and swore to have the scholar's back if Duarte showed his face again. Lucretia emitted a soft sniffle and wiped her face.

"This is all well and good," Saredi piped up, "but might we return our focus to the danger of revealing Her Grace's secret?"

"Regardless of what you think of his bearing, Saredi," Fusette countered. "Kai would be next in line, with or without your approval. Even if it is from a branch of the family that split off 300 years ago, he is my only living relation besides my mother and the only one with the blood of Cacovis running through his veins. Not only that, but he has also proven steadfast loyalty to Livoria on numerous occasions."

Orelia tapped her staff on the ground, drawing everyone's eyes to her. "We must also consider the strong possibility now that Duarte and Adalbard survived the fire. Either one of them could spread the information to the public, which would damage Fusette's reputation. Perhaps it is time she reveals the truth herself. It would hurt less if the news came from her directly rather than through rumors and heresy."

Inhaling deep, Fusette placed a hand over her breast. "You bring up a very valid point, Sister Orelia. However, I still need to assess our options before doing so. Thus, I cannot make it official in the eyes of the public as of now."

The duchess locked eyes with Kai. "Instead, I say this here and now with you as my witnesses: Kaigo Travaldi, the Exarch Gravebane, is from this moment forward my chosen representative in our civil war against the Liberation Army. The rest of you are to be considered sworn royal officers under my direct orders to assist. Your duties are as follows:

"First, you will help recruit additional manpower against our enemy, beginning with returning to Havenfall to rally the Hunter Corps. Second, you are to track down the Soltauri Duarte and his allies, so that we may identify this master of his, who seems to be chest deep in this entire mess. Finally, if given the chance you are to kill the beast known as Grimghast. I do understand this one may be difficult, so only attack if capable of doing so without taking unnecessary losses.

"Should anything happen to me before I bear a child of my own, I decree that Gravebane is to become the next Grand Duke, by virtue of his lineage."

Kai staggered a bit, collapsing into a plush chair. His legs shook throughout Fusette's declaration, and the shock of it all hit him with the force of a typhoon. He cupped his face in his hands and took short, quick breaths. "Fusette, I couldn't possibly accept such a tremendous duty," he managed to choke out.

Placing a gentle hand on his shoulder, Fusette shook her head and whispered that she trusted him. He looked into her eyes and felt warmth spread through his body.

Saredi scoffed and turned away in a slump. "I still question this decision, Your Grace. However, I shall endeavor to accept it and support you as I always have."

Maple strode forward and rested a wing on Kai's back. "I don't know about you being Grand Duke. Personally, I think you'd look silly dressed out in silk and fine leather." Kai couldn't hold back a light chuckle but stiffened when Maple leaned in and hugged him. "But Fusette is right about one thing, and that's putting her trust in you. I've had no reason to doubt you yet, so I'm behind you every step of the way." Kai met her stare, seeing a blend of emotions roiling in her violet eyes as her face leaned in close. The sound of Lucretia clearing her throat startled the merchant, causing her to pull away with rosy cheeks. Kai's gaze shifted aside to see Fusette regarding him with a curious expression.

"That goes for me as well!" Morgan declared, standing behind Kai and slapping a thick hand on the Norzen's other shoulder. "You saved my life when you had no bloody reason to. And you've been a fine leader and true friend through our travels, and to me that makes us as good as brothers. You'll have my blade for as long as ya need."

The next to approach was Orelia. "Teos and I haven't known you as long as everyone else, but I know a good man when I see one. Even with what happened at Faith Hollow, you've helped me cope with my loss despite your own suffering. For that, you have both my thanks and eternal support."

Teos followed and reached down, clasping Kai's hand in a firm handshake. "Orelia couldn't have said it any better. I figure I'm already neck deep in this thing. Besides, with the Libbies still around I can't procure another boat to start my business back up," said the smuggler with a wink. "So you're stuck with me as well."

Ione rushed forward and threw her arms around Kai in a crushing hug. "I know I'm only good for cooking and such, but I hope you'll let me keep traveling with you! You've been nothing but kind and compassionate since the first time we met, even with all the hardships you've faced. I'm proud to call you my friend."

Kai returned the hug with a blush splayed across his features and reminded the tavern maid that she was more useful than she thought. "You've always been our voice of reason, like a doting big sister. And you protected the Grand Duchess on your own, like a proper knight. Don't ever doubt yourself."

Everyone turned and locked eyes with Lucretia, who stared back unamused. "If you expect me to get sentimental over this fool, you are going to be disappointed. And I am still furious that the royal family has kept such a secret for so long."

Fusette groaned, pleading for the scholar to be more accepting. Lucretia hummed to herself, eyes closed as she pondered the idea. Her boot tapped in a steady beat. Eventually, she regarded Kai with an irritable frown. "Very well. Until this war is over, I will endeavor to fulfill Her Grace's wishes, but *only* because she is still our ruling monarch. Once the war ends, no matter which way the hammer falls, I will take my leave and return home. Is that sufficient?"

The party broke out into cheers and pulled the disgruntled scholar into a massive hug over her protests. Even Tuvi leapt from the bed and joined in, throwing her arm around Orelia's waist. Fusette laughed at the scene and marched forward, thrusting Cacovis's journal into Lucretia's hands.

"I have a special assignment for you, Archivist Dineri. I would like you to fully translate this journal, as a special favor to me and the Order of the Windbringers. Who knows what secrets it holds? Besides, this tome is one of the final physical links we have left of my family, if not *the* last. I'm trusting you to take care of it and write a detailed report once the translation is done."

Holding the journal in a loose grip, Lucretia sighed and gave a single nod. "I understand. I still feel nervous carrying this, but you are correct. There may be secrets inside that could change everything we know about the Desolation Wars and the Wind Saints' involvement. I am, at my core, a woman of knowledge, so I will accept this duty for the sake of that knowledge."

The Grand Duchess smiled and gave a short bow to the stunned scholar. "Thank you! In that case, I suggest you all rest well. Come morning, you will join me in returning to Whistlevale. We shall make sure you're fully equipped for the journey ahead. I'll leave those insufferable Liberators in Larimanz's capable hands."

Kai stiffened when he felt something tugging on his tunic. Looking down, he saw Tuvi staring at him with sad eyes. "Mister Kai, what's going to happen to me? Am I going to be sent back to the temple so you and Sister Orelia can leave?"

Giving the girl a smile, he shook his head and removed some cloth from his satchel. Removing the leather from her injured arm, a growl rumbled from Kai's chest seeing the raw stump. It looked as though they used a torch to cauterize the wound after amputating her hand. He patted Tuvi's head and took care to wrap the injury properly.

"I believe I may have a solution for our young friend," Fusette declared, drawing everyone's attention. "Saredi, I would like you to arrange a tutor for Miss Tuvi upon our return. She shall stay with me at the palace for the remainder of the war. While under my care, I'll ensure she receives proper schooling and training for whatever trade she may desire to pursue. It's the least I can do after her terrible ordeal with those brutes."

Tuvi's eyes shone with joy as she threw herself at Fusette in a powerful hug. "Oh thank you, Your Grace! Thank you so much! I promise I won't let you down."

"I'm sure you won't, Tuvi. And none of that 'Your Grace' silliness, understood? If you must be formal with me in front of others, I permit you to call me Lady Fusette. Now then, it's time for us to get some rest."

Clapping her hands together, Fusette dismissed the party and Saredi hurried the weary travelers into the hall before bidding the duchess good night and shutting the door. A small group of sailors stood waiting to lead them to their rooms. A kind-looking maid took Tuvi by the hand and offered to lead her to her own room, which brought a wide smile to the girl's face. The Lord Chamberlain gave a stiff nod and left for his own chambers at a brisk walk.

With little else to talk about, the party followed the sailors downstairs and split up, with the men following one hall and the ladies going the opposite way.

The sailor leading Kai opened a door and stood aside, gesturing for the apothecary to enter. "We shall wake you and your party for breakfast. Until then, pleasant evening, sir."

While the room was much smaller and less ornate than Fusette's, it was still grander than anything Kai was used to. The sheets were crafted of fine cotton and the pillow was as soft as he imagined a cloud to be. For a man used to resting his head on burlap sacks and anything else he could get his hands on, Kai wasn't sure if he would be able to wake up. A soft chuckle escaped him when an image passed his mind of a sailor coming in and throwing him out of bed by force.

Deciding to make the most of it, Kai shed his clothes and climbed into the luxurious bed, letting out a moan of joy at the sensation. "Now I know what Fusette meant when she said being in charge had benefits. Anyone could get addicted to this."

The throbbing in his limbs dimmed, and his back refreshed in mere minutes. As sleep overcame him, a rush of glee flooded Kai's mind, tempered by thoughts of the mission he'd found himself embroiled in and its magnitude.

Nothing is going to be the same, is it?

Kai already knew the answer to that question, but he felt so relieved at a chance to rest he refused to let it weigh him down. For now, he was content in his accomplishments that evening.

He'd kept his oath to protect those he cared about, and that was what truly mattered.

GLOSSARY

Aerivolk – A bird-like faumen tribe able to take running glides at high speeds. They have the strongest eyesight and are considered the most peaceful of the tribes.

Alezon (pronounced Al-a-zon) – The southern continent of Nixtral. Consists of five realms and is infamous as the origin point of the faumen tribes.

Ausrina the Wanderer – One of the Wind Saints. An Aerivolk traveler who joined the Wind Saints during the Desolation Wars. Not much is known about her.

Belomas Highlands – An ancient Alezonian realm known as the birthplace of the faumen. They are led by a Chiefs Council, currently headed by Chief Velibor.

Berelmir – A warlord that conquered several Galstein provinces until meeting his end at the hands of the Wind Saints.

Cacovis the Shadow – The Wind Saint of Pride. A Norzen who became infamous for bringing about the Desolation to free the lands that would become Livoria. Also known as the Fallen Saint.

Centric – The primary trading language of Nixtral.

The Citadel – Livoria's foremost learning academy. Located in Runegard, it was once the fortress of the warlord Berelmir and now consists of four scholar divisions that work together to accumulate and advance knowledge within Livoria.

Corlati Federation – The most technologically advanced of the five Alezonian realms. Human superiority is preached as gospel, faumen are often kept as slaves, and most inhabitants follow the teachings of the warrior monk Cadell. Led by President Gideon Harmod.

The Desolation – A massive explosion caused by Cacovis that wiped out a swath of land between Livoria, Galstein, and Corlati; no one knows how she accomplished this.

Dolmaru the Quillblade – One of the Wind Saints. A Wasini warrior scholar who joined the Wind Saints during the Desolation Wars. He was responsible for opening the Citadel.

Edeval the Bandit Lord – One of the Wind Saints. An Aerivolk thieving band leader who joined the Wind Saints during the Desolation Wars. Not much is known about him.

Exarch Knights – The most prestigious order of Livoria. Known as the duchy's most skilled protectors, they are a special class of noble given a unique epithet by the Grand Duchess called a Brand.

Faumen – Demi-humans with animal characteristics that originated from the Belomas Highlands. There are five known tribes with their own unique strengths.

Feswili (pronounced Fez-wi-lee) – The northern continent of Nixtral. Not much is known about this place other than that it is much colder than the other continents.

Finyt (pronounced Fe-neet) – The land of paradise, according to Windbringer doctrine. It is said to be full of gardens and rivers where no war or conflict exists.

Fullblood – A faumen of pure lineage with no intermixing among humans or other tribes.

Galen the Sage – The leader of the Wind Saints. A human warrior monk who led the fight against the warlord Berelmir. He was known for his wisdom and sense of justice.

Grand Duchy of Livoria – The youngest of the Alezonian realms. It was once a series of Galstan provinces conquered by Berelmir, but gained independence after the end of the Desolation Wars. Led by the Grand Duchess, Fusette Ardei.

Holy Queendom of Galstein – A peaceful realm located in southeastern Alezon. The historical ally of Livoria. Led by Queen Isolde Graffeld.

Luopari the Oracle – One of the Wind Saints. A Vesikoi soothsayer who joined the Wind Saints during the Desolation Wars. She is among the most popular of the Saints.

Mixblood – A faumen of mixed heritage, usually with one faumen and one human parent. Mixbloods of two tribes are possible, but exceedingly rare and considered taboo.

Nixtral – The planet upon which the story takes place. It encompasses four primary continents, one at each cardinal direction.

Norzen – A cat-like faumen tribe known for their two tails and sensitive ears. They are ostracized for their association with Cacovis, the one who caused the Desolation.

Nulyma (pronounced Nu-lee-ma) – According to Windbringer doctrine, a hellish void made of five levels where the damned go to suffer for their sins.

Order of the Windbringers – The primary church within Livoria and Galstein that reveres the Wind Saints as heroes and protectors.

Soltauri – A bovine-like faumen tribe that have hooves for feet and usually two horns atop their heads. The tallest and strongest of the tribes, they are commonly seen as guards and soldiers.

Tapimor the Lifeweaver – One of the Wind Saints. A human apothecary who joined the Wind Saints during the Desolation Wars. Now considered a patron of the healing arts and the harvest.

Vadako the Maiden – One of the Wind Saints. A Soltauri priestess who joined the Wind Saints during the Desolation Wars. A popular Saint among young women, she was known for her kindness and generosity.

Vesikoi – A fish-like faumen tribe noted for the pale skin on the front of their bodies with darker skin on the back. They are primarily water-based and famous for their craftsmanship.

Voidlands – The uninhabitable wasteland where the Desolation occurred. Once a thriving forest, it has been reduced to a barren desert where nothing can grow.

Wasini – A faumen tribe who have snake-like tails covered in armored scales for their lower bodies. They are the heaviest of the faumen and historically known as great warriors.

Wind Saints – A group of 8 heroes led by Galen the Sage who saved the lands that would become Livoria from the warlord Berelmir.

About the Author

Cyrus Whelchel grew up in Converse, Texas, where both his local and school libraries were his home away from home. His favorite book growing up was *The Thief Lord* by Cornelia Funke, followed closely by *Harry Potter*.

After hopping between various jobs in early adulthood, Cyrus re-discovered his love of books and dedicating himself to being a Children's Librarian, where he now shares a passion for stories with the next generation.

An avid reader of fantasy and mystery, Cyrus loves the challenge of anticipating the end of a good story. Inspired by the historical challenges faced by his father's Jewish ancestors, *The Faumen War Chronicles* shows the importance of accepting each other's differences, being true to oneself, and standing strong against discrimination, no matter where you may find it.

Oaths of Life and Death is Cyrus' first book.